A DEADLY SILVER SEA

Also by Bob Morris

Bermuda Schwartz
Jamaica Me Dead
Bahamarama

A DEADLY SILVER SEA

Bob Morris

St. Martin's Minotaur ❧ New York

This is a work of fiction. All of the characters, organizations, and events portrayed in this novel are either products of the author's imagination or are used fictitiously.

A DEADLY SILVER SEA. Copyright © 2008 by Bob Morris. All rights reserved. Printed in the United States of America. For information, address St. Martin's Press, 175 Fifth Avenue, New York, N.Y. 10010.

www.minotaurbooks.com

Library of Congress Cataloging-in-Publication Data

Morris, Bob, 1950–
   A deadly silver sea / Bob Morris.—1st ed.
     p. cm.
   ISBN-13: 978-0-312-37725-0
   ISBN-10: 0-312-37725-8
1. Chasteen, Zack (Fictitious character)—Fiction. 2. Hijacking of ships—Fiction. 3. Cruise ships—Fiction. I. Title.
   PS3613.Q75555D43 2008
   813'.6—dc22

2008034155

First Edition: December 2008

10 9 8 7 6 5 4 3 2 1

For the crew: Debbie,
Bo, and Dash

Acknowledgments

The research, that's the fun part. And in the case of this book, I am grateful to Trish Reynales and Marika McElroy, editors at *Virtuoso Life*, who offered me a couple of plum assignments to travel aboard small, luxury cruise ships and write about it for that fine magazine. First came the *Seabourn Spirit*, a three-week cruise from Hong Kong to Vietnam, Thailand, and Singapore. Next was a ten-day sojourn on the *Silver Whisper*, part of the Silversea fleet, through the eastern Caribbean. In both instances, the experience was nothing less than stellar and neither of those most excellent ships should be mistaken as a model for the *Royal Star* and the hell that ensues in these pages. Still, as anyone who has spent time on cruise ships might similarly testify, there were some passengers who deserved killing.

I am forever indebted to Fred Brock, of Fernandina Beach, a veteran of several cruise-ship lines and a man who possesses a seemingly endless knowledge of their inner workings. Not only did Fred create "A Cruise Ship Primer for Mystery Writers" just for me, he was on call during the months it took to write this book, always available to answer questions like "What kind of ceiling tiles are in the crew cabins?" and "How do you lower a lifeboat?" If I got anything wrong, and that's a distinct likelihood, then it is all my fault and not Fred's.

As always, I relied on the expert knowledge of several sources at the U.S. Department of Immigration and Customs Enforcement (ICE). As always, they asked not to be identified. Actually, demanded is more like it. Anyway, they know who they are and I thank them.

Marc Resnick, Sarah Lumnah, Harriet Seltzer, Andy Martin, Sally Richardson, Hector DeJean, and all the good people at St. Martin's Minotaur indulged me as this boat of a book took its own sweet time to reach home port. Ditto with Joe Veltre, of Artists Literary Group, who is too much of a gentleman to ever begin a conversation with "So when are you going to finish the damn thing?"

As for my wife, Debbie, she asked me that almost every morning. But she's my first reader, my sounding board, my compass. And she can get away with it.

Thanks all.

Ultra-Luxe Cruise Ship Launches with Glitter and Glamour

By Tom Wallace
Miami Herald Staff Writer

MIAMI—The 430-foot *Royal Star*, hailed as the most exclusive cruise ship in the world, sails today from the Port of Miami on its much-anticipated inaugural voyage. On board—250 cases of $100-a-bottle champagne, 100 pounds of beluga caviar, and a star-studded guest list.

"It will be a week-long floating party," said Heissam "Sam" Jebailey, the Florida entrepreneur who spent a reported $400 million building the *Royal Star*.

The ship's itinerary has been kept secret—not even its glitterati passengers know where the *Royal Star* is going.

"I call it Sam's mystery cruise," said interior designer and society maven Marie Lutey, one of just 100 invitees. "It's fine by me if we never set foot in port. The ship is fabulous, a waterborne Taj Mahal."

An exaggeration, perhaps, but only a slight one.

In addition to its plush suites, the *Royal Star* boasts a luxurious spa and four restaurants. For recreation and diversion, guests can shoot trap and skeet, exercise with personal trainers, gamble in the casino, or take out a Jet Ski, part of a fleet of 30 personal watercraft in the ship's onboard marina. Guests will be waited on by their own private butlers and can take advantage of 24-hour concierge service.

"With a 120-person crew, we have the highest crew-to-passenger ratio in the industry," says Captain Thorvald Falk. "This is far and away the finest ship I've ever had the pleasure to be at the helm of."

It's also a relatively green machine. Unlike standard cruise ships, which rely on diesel fuel, the *Royal Star* employs state-of-the-art turbine engines. And an onboard wastewater treatment facility purifies any discharges while the ship is at sea.

The *Royal Star* would seem to reverse a trend that has led the cruise industry to create larger and larger ships. At the top of the heap is *King of the Seas*, a 1,500-foot-long behemoth that can carry more than 5,200 passengers with a crew of almost 2,000. But exclusivity comes at a price. The average cost for a week aboard *King of the Seas* is about $2,200, while a week's passage on the *Royal Star* will run about $10,000.

"The *Royal Star* is for those who expect and deserve the best of the best," said Jebailey. "I guarantee our passengers will have the time of their lives."

BON VOYAGE

1

The topic of conversation was boob jobs. And Barbara Pickering thought the bejeweled matron sitting at a table next to ours was too old for one.

"I mean really, she must be every day of seventy," Barbara said. "It looks creepy."

"Like someone erected a pup tent on her chest," I said.

"Probably brand-new. Bought just for the cruise."

"Safety measure," I said. "The ship goes down, she can use them as flotation devices."

We were two hours out of port aboard the *Royal Star*, chugging across the Gulf Stream, Miami just an insolent glow on the pistol butt of Florida.

The bon voyage bash was in full swing. Much popping of champagne corks, much nibbling from long silver trays offered by tuxedoed waiters, much merry buzz from passengers gathered on the main deck.

All in all, a pretty swank crowd. Not that I was much good at recognizing A-list types. That was Barbara's job.

She pointed out an actor or two or three. A fashion model who had just married a tennis star. A film director chatting up a brand-name heiress. A famous lawyer, a famous artist, a famous somebody else. And a scattering of corporate tycoons who even though the suggested attire for the evening was something called "casual elegant," had shown up in suits anyway. Some guys are just like that.

A waiter moved in with a long silver tray. Barbara took a big dab of caviar. She scooped up some tempura prawns when they came around a few minutes later. An enthusiastic eater, Barbara. Just one of many things I love about her.

I was saving my gluttonous self for the tray of stone crab claws that was slowly heading in our direction. Much too slowly, in my opinion. We were two days into stone crab season, October 17 to be exact. You couldn't get claws much fresher than the ones on that tray. Not unless you pulled the pots yourself.

The waiter serving the stone crabs was a compact fellow of Asian extraction with shiny black hair and busy eyes. He stopped at Pup Tent's table. He saw me watching him and smiled, lips parting just enough to reveal a shiny gold tooth.

Pup Tent and her pals helped themselves to the claws. They spooned out pale yellow sauce from a bowl on the tray, the same mustard sauce they serve at Joe's in South Beach. Colman's dry mustard, Hellmann's mayo, A.1., Worcestershire, and just a bit of heavy cream. I had the recipe down cold, often used it with boiled shrimp. It is the kind of sauce you can dip your finger into and happily gnaw it to the bone.

I began making room on the table. I managed not to drool, but I did let out a few anticipatory grunts. I do love stone crabs.

But it was not to be. As the waiter started our way, he was intercepted by the maître d', a short, dark, heavyset man with a mustache and slicked-back hair. The two of them huddled for a moment, then the maître d' waved for the other four waiters and they all disappeared through a set of double doors.

I thought about chasing them down, but my focus was broken when Pup Tent stood up. She strolled past our table. Everything about her—eyes, cheekbones, boobs, butt—defied gravity. It was like staring at a car wreck. Couldn't help but.

"Really," Barbara said. "One shouldn't be terrified of a tiny bit of sag. It's only natural."

I looked at Barbara. More specifically, I looked at her breasts.

"I like natural," I said.

Barbara smiled. She sat up straight, all the better for me to admire her.

"And what is your position on sag?"

I observed her breasts some more. Lately, there had been an increasing amount of them to observe.

"With you, it is not a matter of sag."

"What would you call it then?"

"I would call it fullness. I would call it abundance. I would call it plentitude."

"And I would call you quite full of it." She stroked my cheek. "But in the best possible way."

The band was one of those cruise-ship ensembles that can play just about anything and, in the process, suck the soul right out of it. They started in on "What a Wonderful World." The lead singer was no Satchmo. Didn't really make any difference. It's one of those songs that no matter how badly the band plays it, you want to reach out and hold the one you love.

Barbara took my hand.

"Let's dance," she said.

We were the first couple on the floor. I held Barbara close. Well, as close as the situation would allow. Dancing cheek to cheek was out of the question. But belly to belly worked just fine.

Barbara flinched.

"Ooh," she said, "did you feel Critter kick?"

"I did," I said. "Must like the oldie-goldies."

Another kick. And then another.

"Critter's dancing," said Barbara.

"A regular Rockette's chorus line."

"Which would indicate a girl."

"Not necessarily so," I said. "Boys can grow up to dance in chorus lines."

"And that wouldn't bother you?"

"What?"

"To have a son who danced in a chorus line?"

"Not in the least," I said. "However Critter comes out is fine by me."

"Me, too."

The band kept playing songs we liked, and we kept dancing. I could waltz through hell with Barbara Pickering and it would be just fine with me.

Truth was, being on a cruise ship, even the world's most luxurious one, came pretty close to my personal vision of hell. For Barbara, it was just another day at work. She is owner/publisher of *Tropics*, the best travel magazine in the world. Not that I'm prejudiced in such matters. But such is her standing in the business that she was the only media type invited to join the *Royal Star* on its maiden voyage. Copies of the most recent issue of *Tropics* adorned all the tables, the *Royal Star* gracing its cover.

I'm Barbara's husband, her chattel and helpmate. I was along for the ride.

My name is Zack Chasteen. And my résumé would include abundant use of the word "former." I am a former football player (Florida Gators, Miami Dolphins, blew out a knee), a former inmate of federal prison (subsequently pardoned on all counts), and a former charter captain/fishing guide/dive-boat operator (gave it up when I decided that trying to make money on the water was ruining my love for it).

Nowadays, I am owner and head flunky of Chasteen's Palm Tree Nursery in LaDonna, Florida. I grow and sell rare specimen palms. It's a business I inherited from my grandfather, and it includes thirty-some-odd acres along Redfish Lagoon, just south of Minorca Beach, where I make my home.

Let me rephrase that. It's where Barbara and I make *our* home. I'm still enough of a newlywed that the whole collective pronoun thing throws me for a loop sometimes.

In any event, on the evening the *Royal Star* set out from Miami, bound for ports unknown, Barbara and I were celebrating our six-month anniversary. And she was roughly eight months pregnant. If that upsets your sensibilities, I have three words: Get a grip.

The band segued into "Slow Boat to China."

"I'm glad we came," Barbara said.

"Me, too."

"You're just saying that. You hate being on a cruise ship."

"I don't hate being on a cruise ship with you."

"Good save, Chasteen," Barbara said, settling back into my arms. "Just think, we're almost parents."

"Nervous?"

"More like anxious."

"Anxious in the sense of not wanting anything to go wrong? Or just wishing Critter would hurry up and get here?"

"Mostly hurry up and get here. But some of the other, too."

"You've just got the pregame jitters."

"Oh, do I now?"

"I used to throw up before every game. Just like being pregnant."

"Mmm, yes, just like it in every way."

"That's why I always asked to be on the kickoff team. Get in a good lick, lay somebody low, and it got rid of the jitters just like that."

Barbara looked up at me.

"Are you seriously trying to draw an analogy between your experiences playing football and mine of giving birth to our child?"

"In my own feeble way."

"You used to wear a helmet, right?"

"I did."

"So try passing that."

"You're not talking forward pass here, are you?"

"No, I'm talking push-push, squeeze-squeeze, out the bottom."

"Thanks for sharing that imagery."

"What's mine is thine," Barbara said.

2

THURSDAY, 7:48 P.M.

The killing started on Deck One, the lower level of the engine room, when the assistant motorman pulled the SAR-21 from its hiding place by the main turbine and opened fire on the chief engineer and the junior chief as they made their evening rounds.

The assistant motorman wore a blue jumpsuit, the gold crest of the *Royal Star* above his heart, the name "Glenroy" stitched in white below it. Glenroy Patterson. That was the name on his passport, the name everyone knew him by, although every now and then one of the crew, someone from Jamaica or Barbados, might call him Trini, in the easy, familiar way of the islands, because that was where he came from, Trinidad.

He was a big man. He had to stoop when going through hatchways, turn his thick shoulders to negotiate a tight squeeze, since the lower regions of the *Royal Star*, like all cruise ships, favored men with compact frames. But Glenroy's bulk belied his nimbleness and he moved with that economy of motion, a blend of grace and speed that gives advantage to gifted athletes. And warriors.

Like the rest of the engine crew, he wore earmuffs under his hard hat. Still, the rifle shots were louder, much louder, than he'd expected.

The first five shots hit their targets. The next five went high and wide. Then Glenroy took a breath, lowered the rifle, and triggered the last shots home.

The impact blew the chief engineer and the junior chief backward, over the catwalk rail and onto a boiler. Their bodies sizzled on the hot metal, sending up little puffs of steam before sliding to the slick gray floor. The floor had been mopped just an hour or so before, the job completed at 6:30 P.M. to be exact. Glenroy knew because he had done the mopping.

Three other crewmen were on the catwalk, near the control-room door, guys who worked side by side with Glenroy. They froze as Glenroy wheeled around on them. Nowhere they could go, nothing they could do.

One of them, Wendell, accent on the Dell, had grown up in Port-of-Spain, just like Glenroy. Hard worker, Wendell. Another veteran of the cruise lines. Put in his shift in the engine room, then played steel pan in ship bands when they wanted to give it an island flair, playing crap like "Hot, Hot, Hot" and "Day-O," not soca like Wendell preferred. Wendell, a good Christian man. Had just bought a house up in the hills by Tunapuna, down the road from the monastery where the monks kept bees and sold honey from a store by their chapel.

Glenroy shot Wendell first. Then he shot the other two, adrenaline pumping, pumping so hard that before Glenroy could back off he had emptied the thirty-shot clip.

And to think he had been skeptical about the SARs, had worried they might not work, had worried over so many things.

No time for that now.

Glenroy gave the bodies wide berth. Wendell looking straight at him it seemed, dead eyes that still could see.

Glenroy glanced into the engine control room. It was empty, the door secure. Plexiglas walls enclosed the room, and Glenroy could see the bank of monitors mounted near the ceiling, their screens blank.

One less thing to worry about.

Sonny had come through. Sonny, the Korean kid who was the ship's entire communications department. He had disabled the network of closed-circuit cameras placed throughout the ship, then phoned the bridge, telling the watch officers it was just a minor glitch, something he'd fix in a hurry. No reason they wouldn't buy it. They bought everything Sonny told them.

Now Sonny was on his way to Deck Eight where he would climb a ladder to the roof above the Observation Room and disconnect the two satellite dishes, along with the backup Inmarsat system. It would cut off all communication with the *Royal Star*. There were still a few VHF and short-wave radios scattered around the ship, but Sonny knew where they all were. He would take care of them.

Glenroy removed his hard hat and earmuffs, dropped them on the floor. He grabbed his backpack, pulled out a new clip. He slapped it into the rifle.

He moved out of the engine room, down the hallway, and up the stairs to Deck Four.

There had been no chance to test-fire the SARs. They had arrived only the night before, seven of them hidden in fifty-five-gallon containers of EZ laundry detergent and delivered to the provisions station on Deck Two by an official, Transportation Safety Administration–inspected Port of Miami supply truck loaded down with cases of liquor, dry-ice lockers filled with meat, and drums of canola oil.

Arranging the buy had proven easy enough. In the long-standing tradition of the cruise industry worldwide, the tight-knit Chinese cabal that ran the laundry on the *Royal Star* not only controlled the ship's loan-sharking enterprise but provided procurement services for everything from dope to fake passports and, in this case, assault rifles.

Yap-Yap, the laundry manager, hadn't asked any questions when Glenroy placed his order. He was a small man with tar-black eyes and skin so smooth and flawless it was impossible to tell his age. Maybe thirty, maybe sixty. All the Chinese were like that. Glenroy thought it must have something to do with working in the laundry. The heat, the steam. It dried them out, preserved them.

"What you want, it cost much money," Yap-Yap said.

"I've got money."

Yap-Yap studied him.

"It take long time," he said. "Weeks maybe, months."

"Bullshit, mon. This Miami. Everyone selling guns."

Yap-Yap narrowed his lips. If snakes could grin so could he.

"You come back two days," Yap-Yap said.

When Glenroy returned, he could tell Yap-Yap had found a source and was ready to dicker because right off he started talking about how tricky it would be getting the rifles on board and what would happen if they got caught, going on and on, working it, making it sound harder than it really was in order to jack up the price.

"Very dangerous, very dangerous. TSA, they watch everything. I no want go jail."

"How much?"

Yap-Yap told him. It was twice what the SARs cost on the open market, but about what Glenroy expected to pay. Still, they went round and round and finally settled on a number. Yap-Yap said he would need it all up front. Glenroy pulled out a roll of hundreds and paid him, making sure Yap-Yap saw the roll was still plenty thick when he returned it to his pocket.

On the night of the delivery, Yap-Yap was there waiting for the supply barge, along with the provisions master, a fat Belgian with big ears whose job it was to inventory everything that came aboard the *Royal Star* and let no opportunity for personal gain go unseized. The provisions master had been more intent upon requisitioning a case of single-malt scotch and a flat of beef tenderloins than paying attention to Yap-Yap and the three other Chinese as they loaded the detergent containers on handcarts and hauled them away.

Glenroy met Yap-Yap just after midnight in the laundry storeroom. He brought along Pango, the Indonesian maître d'. Pango had been Glenroy's original recruit, before Sonny even, the first person Glenroy had entrusted with his plan, or at least part of it, back when the crew of the *Royal Star* first signed on.

Yap-Yap eyed Pango with suspicion, uneasy that a third party was in on the deal.

Glenroy counted out another thousand dollars, handed it to Yap-Yap.

"That's for the guarantee," he said.

"What guarantee? I no guarantee nothing. You pay money, I find guns, I get them on ship. That that. No guarantee, no guarantee."

Glenroy let Yap-Yap finish talking. When the laundry manager got wound up he really did sound like a little dog barking.

When he was done, Glenroy looked at him and said, "It's my guarantee."

"You guarantee? You guarantee what?"

"Guarantee you say anything about this I'll kill you."

Yap-Yap was quiet after that. He took the money and pointed to a corner of the storeroom. Then he walked out, leaving Glenroy and Pango alone with the rifles.

The SARs came bagged in plastic. So did the ammo clips. Despite that, Glenroy and Pango had to use hair dryers to blow out little blue balls of detergent that had slipped past the wrapping and threatened to gum up the rifles.

Pango had some experience with assault rifles. He claimed to have been an officer in Tentara Nasional Indonesia, attached to an elite guard unit at the presidential palace in Jakarta. Claimed, too, that he would have been there still had not a past election brought in a new regime.

Glenroy figured it was a lot of talk. He couldn't see Pango as an officer in any country's army, not even some fucked-up one like Indonesia. Still, when it came to commanding the wait staff, Pango was Patton of the dining room. Strutted like him, too. All puffed-up and self-important. Wore a big diamond pinkie ring and liked to flash it. Glenroy had once caught him dabbing shoe polish on his mustache, making it look thicker than it really was.

But there was no denying that Pango enjoyed considerable influence aboard the *Royal Star.* At least half the waiters were related to him, one of them a nephew and several others cousins, loyal to the core. His sway extended to the galley crew and the room stewards, most of whom were Indonesians and owed their jobs to Pango putting in a favorable word with the recruiting agents. True, he extracted a little something from their pay on a monthly basis to insure continued goodwill. That was just the way it worked.

"Like union boss," Pango had explained to Glenroy. "Make sure all the wheels greased. More grease, more happy."

And there was no doubt Pango knew his way with the SARs. Once they had gotten the rifles cleaned up, Pango showed Glenroy how to insert the clip, how to switch from single shot to full automatic, how to give the clip a sharp slap on the butt end to make sure the ammo didn't jam.

Pango assured Glenroy that his money had bought the real deal, that Yap-Yap hadn't cheated him.

Pango held up one of the rifles.

"You watch out this. Get hot, get hot fast," he said, tapping the muzzle. "But SAR very good. Made in Singapore. You like very, very much."

Glenroy edged down the hallway on Deck Four, closing in on the security office. The door was closed. Glenroy heard men talking behind it. He knocked.

"Who is it, please?"

Glenroy recognized the voice of the chief security officer, a retired sergeant from Scotland Yard with the rheumy eyes and bulbous nose of a not-so-reformed drunk.

Glenroy said, "Delivery, sir."

The door swung open and Glenroy found himself face-to-face with one of the assistant security officers, a recent departee of the Royal Thai Army. His boss sat behind a desk.

This time Glenroy was much more efficient with the SAR. Two quick blasts and that was that.

Pango was right. Glenroy liked the SAR. He liked it very, very much.

He spent a few seconds poking around the bodies, not coming up with anything. Neither of the men had been armed.

That's what had amazed Glenroy about cruise ships, what had planted the seed of his plan. In eleven years of employment with various cruise lines, Glenroy had never once seen a gun on board a ship. They were kept stashed away in secret lockers with access given only to a select few.

No one—not the captain, not the officers, not even the chief security officer—ever carried a weapon in public.

It was all for the benefit of the passengers. A cruise was a chance for them to escape, leave all their cares and worries behind.

And seeing a gun, well, that might upset them.

3

We took a break after "My Girl" and headed back to our table. I looked around. Still no sign of the waiters.

"Don't just sit there and sulk," Barbara said.

"First stone crabs of the season. I didn't get any. That's worth sulking about."

"Bar's open. Get a drink."

"What goes with stone crabs?"

"Maybe if you stopped thinking about them . . ."

"I don't want to stop thinking about them. I am trying to visualize them. So they will appear. On a plate. In front of me. Pre-cracked but not brutalized, so that when you pick off the shell you are rewarded with a perfect and unblemished piece of meat, ideal for dipping into Joe's mustard sauce. I'm thinking rum goes with stone crabs. Goes with lack of stone crabs, too."

"A Pellegrino for me, please, while you're at it."

The bar boasted an impressive selection of rum. Made it tough to choose. I opted for the alphabetical approach. I would start with the Appleton Estate V/X Reserve, then should I feel the urge, move on to the Barbancourt Réserve Spéciale and the twelve-year-old Flor de Caña. I knew my urges. I was confident that I'd feel one.

By the time I got back to our table, the band was wrapping up a zippy rendition of "Moondance." Barbara pointed out a man who was approaching the stage, champagne flute in hand. He was small but walked big, more confidence than swagger. Dark features and large sad eyes, like

Omar Sharif, the way he looked in *Lawrence of Arabia*. He wore some kind of black silky outfit that could have passed for pajamas—oversized jacket with a sash at the waist and billowy pants. It was like something you'd see on the runway at New York Fashion Week and hope never to encounter in real life. This guy somehow managed to pull it off, but not so much that you wanted to empty your closet and start dressing up like him.

"Sam Jebailey," Barbara said.

"Pretty young to be so rich."

"They all are these days."

"So what's his story?"

Barbara shrugged.

"Has piles of money. Likes spending it."

"Piles of money are nice. Where'd they come from?"

"Don't know," said Barbara.

"Care to speculate?"

"He's a Miami guy. Leaves lots of room for speculation."

"I'm a Miami guy."

Barbara looked at me.

"You *played* for Miami, Zack. That does not make you a Miami guy." She laughed, shook her head, laughed some more. "You are so *not* a Miami guy. You lack the . . ."

"The flash?"

"Your words, not mine."

Barbara smiled. I smiled. She sipped Pellegrino. I sipped rum. Near the stage, Jebailey sipped his champagne and moved with the music. It wasn't quite dancing, but it was more than just tapping a foot. A Miami guy thing.

"You ever met him?"

"Only once," Barbara said. "In a receiving line."

"A party he threw?"

Barbara shook her head.

"No, a party I threw, actually," she said. "A little soiree at the Raleigh Hotel a few years back to unveil our special 'Winter Cruises' issue. All the industry hotshots were there—Royal Caribbean, Carnival, Seabourn, Windstar."

"A party to suck up to the advertisers?"

"I prefer to think of it as a party to honor our alliances with strategic partners."

"Spoken like a true publisher."

"Why, thank you," Barbara said. "I'd never even heard of Sam Jebailey until that evening. But he made an impression."

"What, he wore an outfit like he's got on tonight?"

Barbara laughed.

"I don't remember what he wore. Just what he told me. He introduced himself and said: 'I'm Sam Jebailey. I'm building the finest ship the world has ever seen. And one day it will be on the cover of your magazine.'" She nodded at the copy of *Tropics* sitting on our table. "Lo and behold."

"Cocky bastard."

"That's one way of looking at it."

"There's another?"

"A man of vision, a man who knows what he wants and won't stop until he gets it."

"Like me, in other words."

Barbara looked at me.

"You have a vision?"

"Most definitely."

"Care to share it?" Before I could answer she put up a hand. "If you say stone crabs, I'll smack you."

4

When the music ended, Jebailey took the stage and planted himself behind the microphone. I'd moved on to the Barbancourt by then.

"Good evening," Jebailey said. "Are we enjoying ourselves?"

Applause and cheers from the crowd. Jebailey held up his champagne
flute.

"Please join me in lifting your glasses," he said.

I hoisted my rum, Barbara her Pellegrino. Across the deck, other guests
joined in, too.

"My father, who was born in Lebanon and who moved to Miami when
he was a young man, had a favorite toast for special occasions such as this.
Sadly, he died some years ago, but I honor him tonight by sharing what
surely would have been his words had he been here with us."

Jebailey paused, milking the moment. He lifted his glass higher.

"Great are our blessings," he said. "Greater still the love of our family."

Glasses clinked. Voices called out "Hear, hear!" and "Salut!" I drank
some rum.

Jebailey let the commotion die down before continuing. Then he held
out his arms.

"I am truly blessed by your presence here tonight," he said. "And I welcome all of you to our *Royal Star* family."

I looked at Barbara.

"Makes me feel warm and tingly all over," I said.

She ignored me. She's smart like that.

Speakers blared a trumpet processional, the double doors at the end of the deck swung open and out streamed the ship's crew. Or the better part of it anyway.

Four of the ship's Norwegian officers led the way, resplendent in their dress whites. The captain looked like a captain should look, with a trim beard and fierce countenance, straight out of the Viking gene pool.

Others followed, some wearing snappy blue-and-maroon uniforms that were cut smart and didn't really look like uniforms—the hospitality staff heads, the food and beverage director, chefs of every sort, the chief purser and the front office staff, the casino crew and entertainers, right on down to room stewards and housekeepers, even the laundry workers.

It took a few minutes, and by the time the parade was complete nearly a hundred people were squeezed around the stage.

Jebailey said, "These are the people who will see to it that you enjoy the experience of a lifetime. And leading them, a man who brings more than twenty-five years of oceangoing experience to the helm of the *Royal Star*, Captain Thorvald Falk."

The captain stepped forward, acknowledged the applause with a curt nod, then rejoined his fellow officers as Jebailey introduced other key crew members—the hotel director, the cruise director, the executive chef.

Jebailey said, "Now, I know the one question on most of your minds: Where is this cruise taking us?" He grinned, enjoying himself. "For me, the true joy of travel is embracing the unknown, waking up each morning and not knowing what the day will bring. So, if you will indulge me . . . I'm not going to tell you where we're going. I want it to be a surprise."

A happy uproar from the crowd. Some called out, like fans shouting requests at a rock concert: "St. Bart's!" "St. Martin!" "Martinique!"

Jebailey quieted them down.

"I will tell you this," he said. "I want you to have every opportunity to experience the many delights this magnificent ship has to offer—from its exceptional cuisine to its spa and casino. I want you to relax in the most luxurious suites of any cruise ship in the world. I want to give you the chance to get to know the *Royal Star* and each other. So, to that end, our first two or three days will be spent at sea, just cruising, relaxing and enjoying ourselves. After that"—another grin—"we'll see what happens.

"Too often, cruise ships are criticized for taking advantage of the beautiful destinations they visit, of not showing a real commitment to the islands and their people," Jebailey said. "The *Royal Star* strives to partner with all Caribbean nations, working for our mutual benefit and fostering goodwill. As you already know, this is a green ship. We avoid polluting the sea with our state-of-the-art wastewater treatment facility. And we have reduced our carbon footprint by using turbine engines that do not require diesel fuel."

More applause from the crowd.

"Also this evening, I am proud to announce the creation of our Royal Star Foundation, which is dedicated to enriching the educations of the young people who are the future of this region."

Jebailey gave a nod to the cruise director, a tall blond woman with the smile of a perennial beauty queen. She rolled a cart to center stage. On it—a big box emblazoned with a computer company logo. Beside the box, a computer terminal and tower workstation.

"As part of its outreach program, the Royal Star Foundation will purchase computers like this one and donate them to schools on islands where the *Royal Star* drops anchor. On board for this week's itinerary, we have one hundred of these computers. And we will be delivering them to schoolchildren on the island of . . ."

Jebailey stopped, put hand to cheek, made an "Oh, how silly of me" face.

"Sorry, but I almost let the cat of the bag, didn't I? This is supposed to be a mystery cruise."

He smiled. The crowd ate it up.

"Don't worry," Jebailey said. "You'll soon see the happy faces of those children, lining the dock to greet us. And should you be moved to support the ongoing good deeds of the Royal Star Foundation with your generosity, you'll find donation forms with the guest packets in your suites."

Jebailey continued, introducing other members of the crew, and Barbara reached for her purse. She pulled out her cell phone. It was black and chrome and brand-new. It was, she kept telling me, much more than just a cell phone. It was an organizer and Web browser and GPS and who-knows-what-else all in one. She punched away on it.

"Who you calling?"

"No one. Just taking some notes."

"You can do that on one of those?"

She looked at me.

"Oh, Zack. Really." She patted my cheek. "You are so adorable sometimes."

"Just sometimes?"

"Especially when you display your innocence."

"Innocence? Or ignorance?"

"A bit of both, I suppose. You're the only person I know who doesn't have a cell phone. Or who refuses to e-mail."

"I prefer human contact."

Barbara stopped punching. She patted her stomach.

"To which I bear witness," she said.

She put her cell phone away.

"So what were you taking notes about?"

"About the Royal Star Foundation. Might make a nice little human-interest blurb in the magazine," she said. "And about naming opportunities."

"Naming opportunities?"

"Yes. If I'm going to write a check on behalf of *Tropics* to buy one of those computers for a school, which I fully intend to do, then I would like to know that the magazine gets some bang for its buck. Maybe a little metal plate affixed to the computer that says 'Donated by Globe Communications.' I want to ask Jebailey about that."

"Charity for charity's sake is not enough?"

Barbara gave me a smile. It was a practiced smile, an indulgent smile, a smile that might be given to a child who had just said something precious yet utterly inane.

"There you go again," she said. "Being adorable."

"Speaking of naming opportunities . . ."

I rested a hand on Barbara's stomach. I felt Critter squirm. I gave a little pat. Critter squirmed again. How very cool. Already the two of us had established a rapport.

Barbara said, "I thought we had agreed not to make any decisions about a name until our baby is born."

"Yeah, but it might help if we at least narrowed the list so we're ready with a name when it happens."

"So if it's a boy?"

"I'm thinking Shula," I said.

Barbara made a face I'd never seen her make before. Appalled did not even begin to describe it.

"You're not serious," she said. "Shula? As in Don?"

"A great man, a great coach, a great name."

"And if it's a girl?"

"Again, I'm thinking Shula. Like Sheila, you know, but coolah." I thought it was a pretty good line, but Barbara wasn't amused. "Plus, it will appease your aunt Trula in Bermuda. Shula. Rhymes with Trula. We can tell her it's an homage. Shula Chasteen. Of course, we still need to come up with a middle name, so I'm thinking . . ."

Barbara put up a hand.

"No more," she said. "This discussion is officially tabled."

As she spoke, the five waiters who had abandoned us earlier filed out of a passageway behind the bandstand and onto the deck.

The waiters moved with swift precision, encircling the crowd. They carried long trays draped with white towels. They took their stations and set the trays down on stands.

None of them headed our way bearing stone crab claws. They just stood there, waiting.

I finished off my rum.

5

The bridge of the *Royal Star* sat on Deck Seven, its three access points each controlled by separate keypads, the code known only by the captain and a handful of crew.

Two doors, one port and one starboard, opened from the bridge to the exterior of the ship, their top halves made of tinted glass, letting the watch crew see anyone who approached. These two doors led to the bridge wings, the open-air control stations that jutted out from each side of the *Royal Star*, giving unobstructed views along the full length of the ship. Typically, the bridge wings were only used when the ship was docking or approaching a harbor with pilot boats. Only ship's officers and select crew were allowed on them to oversee the tight maneuvers.

The third door to the bridge sat at the forward end of the hallway on Deck Seven. It was the main door, the one through which authorized personnel came and went. And it was this door that Glenroy now approached.

It was a serious door—burnished aluminum reinforced with solid steel. The keypad that controlled it was mounted on the portside wall.

Glenroy kept his eyes on the door, heart pounding as if it would burst from his chest, partly from running up the three flights of stairs from the security office—passing no one, no one at all—but mostly from the thrill of it all. The blood, the spectacle. His plan. Going down.

Nothing marred the main door's cold gray finish, not even a peephole.

No need for one. All the watch crew had to do was check a monitor on the bridge and the closed-circuit camera would show them who was outside in the hallway.

Except Sonny had fixed that. Just as he was now fixing the satellite dishes and the Inmarsat system and everything else that linked the *Royal Star* with the rest of the world. The hallway monitor was useless.

The captain's private office sat next to the bridge, its door set in a shallow alcove. All the doors along the main hallways, from the top deck down to the crew quarters, were set in similar alcoves, just big enough to hold one or two people. A bit of smart planning by the ship's designer, who didn't want passengers or crew stepping out of their cabins only to be blindsided by a steward rolling a cart down the hallway. The alcove provided a buffer zone.

Glenroy slid into the alcove outside the captain's office, caught his breath, calmed his mind.

He peeked out of the alcove and looked down the hall. Empty. He checked his watch. He had arrived on schedule. Where was Pango?

Glenroy leveled the SAR at the bridge door. If it should open, he'd be ready. In fact, he was hoping the door would just go ahead and open. It would be better that way. Simpler. Glenroy could start shooting and get it all over with.

But it wasn't as if he could stand there waiting for someone to exit the bridge. There wasn't time. That was why they needed the bridge access code. To get this thing done. Now. While the passengers and crew were gathered on the main deck.

Glenroy tried to visualize the bridge. He'd never been inside. It wasn't as if the captain and officers would ever invite a lowly assistant motorman to join them there.

Glenroy figured there would be four officers on duty, maybe five, depending on how many had participated in the dog-and-pony show on the main deck. He and Pango would have to get the jump on them.

Footfalls in the hallway . . .

Glenroy peered out, surprised by what he saw—three people heading his way. He was expecting only two.

First came Pango, SAR cradled against his chest, strutting like the grand marshal leading a parade.

Then came Swenson, first officer of the *Royal Star*. Swenson was naked, face bruised, an eye swollen shut. He wobbled as he walked, hands cupped over his privates.

Pango and Swenson, they were the two Glenroy had been expecting.

The third person, the one behind Swenson, the one clutching a shock of Swenson's hair with one hand, holding a pistol to his head with the other . . . she was the surprise.

Todora, one of the housekeepers. Bulgarian. Dark hair pulled back in a severe bun under her lacy white maid's hat. Eyes as dark as her hair. A gaunt, angular face that seemed in conflict with her full body. Tall, taller than Pango, almost as tall as Glenroy.

Todora had been the last recruit. Pango's idea. And the key to gaining access to the bridge.

While most of the *Royal Star*'s officers were married and had families back in Norway, a good many of them also kept "ship wives." The arrangement was commonplace throughout the cruise industry, not endorsed by official ship policy, but not actively discouraged.

Pango had worked with Todora on other ships, knew she liked the perks that came from bunking down with an officer—the gifts, the juice it gave her over the other housekeepers, the extra cash that came her way from time to time.

Pango had worked with First Officer Swenson, too, knew his tastes in women, had helped him with certain arrangements in the past.

Pango had put the proposition to Todora. And she had taken care of the rest.

As they drew closer, Glenroy saw that Swenson had been gagged, something silky and black jammed in his mouth. Woman's panties.

Todora's work, thought Glenroy. Nice touch.

The plan had been for Todora to keep Swenson occupied in his cabin until all the other pieces fell into place. Then Pango would come to collect Swenson, force him to open the door to the bridge. And Todora, her work done, would step aside and let everything play out.

Now here she was, Todora in her housekeeper's uniform. Baby-blue cotton dress falling below her knees. White smock cinched tight at the waist. Little white lace cap atop her hair. A vision of purity and servitude.

Except for that pistol.

Glenroy shot a look at Pango. The maître d' shrugged.

"I tell her she no come, but . . ."

Glenroy waved him quiet.

Swenson strained against the gag. He coughed, slumped forward. Todora kneed him in the back, pulled him upright, jammed the pistol against his head.

She looked at Glenroy. Her thin lips curled into a smirk.

"So," she said. "We do this? Or not?"

As if they could turn back now. Glenroy nodded her toward the keypad on the wall.

The steel door would open from left to right. Glenroy fell into position on the left, flat against the wall. Pango took the other side.

Todora shoved Swenson into the wall by the keypad. She let go of his hair. Swenson twisted around, gave her a pleading look.

Todora jammed the pistol into the base of his skull.

"Open," she said.

Swenson reached for the keypad. And in the instant before he touched it, Todora grabbed his hand. She leaned in, inches from his face, her voice a raspy whisper.

"You want to die?"

Swenson shook his head.

"Do not press alarm code," Todora said.

Swenson blinked, looked away.

"You think I don't know? You press certain numbers, alarm goes off. You do that, I shoot you right here. You understand?"

Swenson nodded.

"Now open, you fucking pig."

Swenson turned to the keypad and Todora turned with him, watching as the first officer tapped the numbers.

Glenroy heard a beep. A pause. Then another beep.

And the door slid open.

Glenroy swept into the bridge, firing even as he crossed the threshold.

The watch crew—three officers and a helmsman—stood shoulder to shoulder at the conning station. The helmsman managed a half turn, lunging for the red Mayday button, falling short as the bullets struck.

It was easy pickings. Three sweeps with the SAR and all four of them lay dead on the floor. It was over before Pango even made it into the bridge.

Then from the hallway, a shot. A moment later, Todora stepped into the bridge, pistol at her side.

Glenroy moved to the console, scanned the controls, found a big black button in the center—the ship's horn. He pressed it and kept pressing, sounding it loud and long.

6

The ship's horn bellowed against the night, a blaring invasion that shook the very deck. And it didn't let up. A sound so loud it was painful.

"My God," Barbara said, huddling close to me.

A blast from a ship's horn is no random event. It means something. And it had clearly caught the crew by surprise.

I saw Captain Falk shouting orders to his three officers, pointing them to the stairs that led to the bridge. They set off in a run.

And then I noticed the waiters. They yanked off the white towels on their trays and came up holding automatic rifles, wicked black things with crescent-moon stocks and stubby barrels.

The waiter nearest the stairs took aim at the three officers. As the ship's horn finally relented, it was replaced by the sick rat-a-tat-tat of shots fired.

The officers tumbled, their white uniforms ripped by red blotches.

The waiters turned on the crowd, and I wrapped myself around Barbara, cushioning her as we hit the deck, covering her body with mine.

I braced for more shots, but they didn't come. I heard passengers screaming, tables toppling, glasses breaking. Chaos all around.

Then above it all, the waiters shouting: "Down! All down! Down now!"

Barbara groaned.

"You OK?" I asked her.

She nodded, then squirmed, uncomfortable under 220 pounds of me. I rolled off her just enough to get a look at what was going on.

I saw the three officers, by the staircase, bloodied and unmoving. It was pretty clear they wouldn't be moving again.

Jebailey and the ship's crew lay sprawled around the bandstand. One of the waiters had seized Captain Falk. As he struggled to break free, a second waiter slammed a rifle butt into his stomach, doubling him over, then slammed it hard into Falk's face.

Blood gushed from the captain's mouth as he folded to his knees. Still, he managed to flail at his captors, and they began beating him even harder until he collapsed on the deck.

One of the waiters pulled a roll of duct tape from a pocket, taped the captain's hands behind his back. The second waiter pointed his rifle at the captain's head and shouted so everyone could hear: "No move, you listen me? You move, he die!"

Other waiters moved through the crowd, rifles at the ready, yelling: "Down! Down! Everybody down!"

Most of the passengers were already huddled under tables and alongside toppled chairs. Those few who were still standing, frozen by the spectacle they had witnessed, were shoved down by the waiters as they commandeered the deck.

I looked at Barbara.

"You sure you're OK?"

"I'm fine," she said. "Just . . ."

Her purse still hung from the back of the chair. She grabbed it and rummaged inside. She pulled out her cell phone. She flipped it open, punched numbers.

And immediately one of the waiters was upon her. He reached for the phone.

"Give here!" he shouted.

Barbara jerked away. The waiter grabbed her by the hair, yanked her head. She let out a cry, and I leaped at the waiter, driving a shoulder hard into his midsection, knocking him down.

No sooner had we hit the deck than a blow hammered the back of my head. Then another.

Pain, awful pain. Things went black. I fought it off, felt sharp kicks to my shoulders, my sides. Tried to block them . . .

And then I was on my back, gasping for air. I grabbed at my throat, felt a shoe. I opened my eyes. Points of light scattered, images fractured, only slowly came together.

I was looking up at another waiter, the one with the gold tooth, the one who had been serving stone crabs. He had a foot planted firmly against my neck, his rifle pointed down at me.

I twisted my head, found Barbara. The waiter I knocked down had succeeded in wresting the phone away from her. He held it up, studied it, a grin creeping onto his face.

"Ha!" he said. "No good."

Then he held up the phone for all the passengers to see, shouting: "See? No good. We fix. No cell phone work. Cell phone no good."

He slung the cell phone aside, then reached down to grab Barbara.

I tried to flip out from under Gold Tooth's foot, but that only made him press down harder. He jabbed his rifle in my face.

"You want to die, Mr. Big Man? You want to be hero?"

"Tell him to get his hands off my wife."

Gold Tooth looked at Barbara.

"She your wife?"

I nodded.

Gold Tooth pointed his rifle at Barbara.

"You," he said. "Stand up."

Barbara didn't move.

"Stand up, now!"

Again, I tried to break free, but Gold Tooth pressed down harder with his foot. It blocked my windpipe. I couldn't breathe.

Gold Tooth put his rifle to my forehead.

"No!" Barbara shouted.

She pulled herself to her feet. The waiter eased off on my throat. I sucked in air.

Now Gold Tooth pointed his rifle at Barbara.

A hush fell across the deck. A hush of sorts, anyway. No more moans or cries from passengers, just the sound of a ship moving through the night—the whistle of the wind, the dull drone of the engine, the slap of the hull against the sea.

Gold Tooth waved his rifle toward the starboard rail.

"Over there!" he told Barbara. "You go. Now!"

Barbara gave me a long last look and then started making her way toward the rail. She kept a hand low on her stomach, easing her load.

Gold Tooth barked out something in a language I didn't recognize. And the other waiters began dragging women passengers to their feet and herding them to the starboard rail.

"All women! Now! Go, go . . ." Gold Tooth shouted.

Some of the women had to be pried away from their husbands and companions. Others clung to one another, crying as they stepped in line.

Gold Tooth yelled out something else and the waiter with the duct tape headed our way. The two of them flipped me over and as Gold Tooth kept the barrel of his rifle pressed into the back of my head, the other waiter taped my hands together. Then he started in on my mouth and eyes.

The last thing I saw was the long line of women being led away by two of the waiters, Barbara at the head of the line, craning her head to see me. Then the tape turned everything black.

Gold Tooth leaned close, his breath sour and bitter as he spoke.

"Your wife gone now, Mr. Big Man. Say good-bye."

7

THURSDAY, 8:21 P.M.

They heard the gunfire coming from the main deck.

"Get down there," Glenroy told Pango. "Now!"

Pango hesitated. And Glenroy could tell it rankled him, Glenroy giving him orders, this black man from the engine room telling the high-and-mighty maître d' what to do. But this was the way it had to be. Glenroy's plan, he called the shots. Now was the time to make that clear. If Pango didn't like it . . .

A flash of venom in Pango's eyes, but he didn't argue. He turned to go, stopped short at the steel door. It had shut automatically after Todora stepped inside.

The bridge was dark, as it always was at night, to aid with navigation. The only illumination came from the control panels and a soft fluorescent glow from under the console that cast an eerie amber light across the floor. Just enough so they could see to walk.

"The door," Pango said. "How do . . . ?"

Todora stepped from the shadows. Three buttons—green, red, and yellow—glowed on the wall next to the door. She tapped her pistol on the green button. The door slid open.

"Just like elevator," she said.

As if she were talking to an idiot.

Pango disappeared through the door. And Todora punched the yellow button, which held the door open. Light streamed into the bridge from the hallway, across the bodies of the watch crew.

Killing people, that didn't bother Glenroy. But once they were dead . . . that was another matter. He could not bear the sight of them. He had long since denounced the misguided beliefs of his forebears, they who worshipped the white man's god along with the dark deities of their tribal heritage. Ignorant people, blind to the real ways of the world. Still, he could not quite rid himself of their notion that the dead never truly departed. And the recent dead, they walked among the living, mourning their loss and fully capable of revenge.

He turned from the bodies, looked out to the hallway, Todora watching him. She had made a mess of shooting Swenson, left little of his skull. Nasty bits everywhere, on the floor, the walls, the keypad by the door.

Todora dropped the pistol into the front pocket of her blood-dabbled smock. She brushed past Glenroy toward the console. A pack of Camel Lights sat near the handset for the ship's PA system, a slim silver lighter beside it. Todora picked up the cigarettes, shook one loose.

Officially, the *Royal Star* was a "smoke-free" ship, meaning no smoking in the guest suites, the crew quarters, or any common area, except for a cramped, sequestered zone on a fourth-level aft deck. But those rules didn't apply to the bridge where cigarettes helped break the tedium of long watches. New as the *Royal Star* was, its bridge already reeked of nicotine.

Todora lit up, drew deep. She started to put the Camels and the lighter back on the console, then reconsidered. She examined the lighter.

"An S. T. Dupont. Very nice." She dropped the lighter and the Camels into the pocket of her smock, blew smoke toward the bodies at her feet. "You guys got problem with that?"

She laughed.

She nudged one of the bodies with a foot, then knelt beside it, going through pockets. She pulled out a wallet, took the cash, snorting at how little of it there was. She moved quickly to the others, ransacking them, too. Taking a gold watch from the wrist of one of the officers. Removing a gold chain from the neck of the helmsman, a young Filipino.

Glenroy fingered the SAR. Shoot her now, he thought. Save doing it later. This woman, she was trouble. He didn't need her anymore.

When Todora was done, she leaned against the console, smoking, studying Glenroy.

"So," she said. "What about the real money?"

"Not yet," Glenroy said. "The bodies, we must get them off the bridge."

He could feel their eyes upon him, knew their spirits were afoot.

He rested the SAR against the console. Todora helped him drag the bodies of the three officers out the door. They were coming back into the bridge for the helmsman when Todora said, "This boat you have arranged, when does it meet us?"

"You don't worry about the boat, OK? I take care of the boat. I take care of everything. You just do as I say and . . ."

Behind them, a voice from the hallway: "Oh, Jesus . . . no."

Sonny . . .

And then the young Korean was at the door, reeling from the sight of the bodies, horror gripping his fat face as he surveyed the scene on the bridge. He dropped to his knees, knocking off his black glasses, gagging, then spewing onto the floor.

Glenroy walked over to him, put a hand on his shoulder.

"Easy, mon, easy. You did good."

Sonny looked up.

"You killed them," Sonny said.

"There was no other way."

"But you said . . ." Sonny covered his face. He was crying now. He stood, heading out the door, but Glenroy pulled him back. And Sonny collapsed against Glenroy, clutching his arms around him, burying his head in Glenroy's chest, sobbing.

Todora stubbed out her cigarette on the seat of the helmsman's pants.

"Cute couple," she said. "I wondered how you got the little chink faggot to help you out."

Glenroy ignored her. He put both hands on Sonny's shoulders, gently broke his embrace.

"Look at me," he said.

Sonny blinked back tears, wiped a chunky hand across his nose. Everything about him disgusted Glenroy. The way he acted. The way he looked. Especially the way he smelled. That kimchi shit he ate, sour cabbage and garlic seeping from his pores. But Glenroy had to put all that out of mind. He had worked hard, coaxing Sonny along, convincing him to be a part of their plan. Glenroy couldn't afford for Sonny to wig out on him now.

"It's going to be OK, you hear me?"

Sonny nodded.

Glenroy picked up Sonny's glasses from the floor, wiped them clean, put them back on him.

"Now, you listen to me, Sonny. I need you to do one more thing. Can you help me out?"

Sonny nodded.

"Yeah, I guess so."

"That's good. That's real good. Because I need you to turn the monitors back on. Can you do that for me, Sonny?"

Sonny looked around the bridge. A computer station sat at one end of the console. The sight of it seemed to comfort him.

"Yeah, I can do that."

Sonny walked to the computer, hunched over it, began punching at its keyboard.

"Piece of cake," he said, turning to grin at Glenroy.

A bank of monitors hung from the ceiling. They lit up. Five screens flashing a feed from dozens of cameras placed throughout the ship, quadrants of four images appearing on each screen and changing in ten-second intervals. Shots of the main deck—two waiters leading a long line of women away, Pango directing two more waiters as they began rounding up the crew, another waiter with his rifle trained on a tall man who had been bound and gagged with duct tape, the man struggling to get loose but not having any luck at it. Elsewhere—shots of empty hallways, empty decks, an empty engine room. Everything under control.

Glenroy turned from the monitors.

"You," he said.

Meaning Todora . . .

"Get those bodies out of the hallway," he said, wanting them as far away from him as possible. "Down to the main deck."

Glenroy told her about the five who were dead in the engine room, the two in the security office. One of the monitors now showing the three officers who had been shot on the main deck. Fourteen dead in all. Glenroy knew there would be more.

"Where to put?" Todora asked him.

He started to tell Todora to toss the bodies overboard, then reconsidered. The bodies would float. Another ship might come along and find them. They could weight them down, but even then . . .

Glenroy wasn't worried about the smell. Less than two days and this would all be over.

"Just put them away somewhere," he said. "Somewhere we don't have to look at them."

It would keep her busy, out of his way.

Todora retrieved another Camel, stuck it between her lips.

"Maybe you ask your boyfriend to help me," she said.

And this time Glenroy hit her, a backhand across the face. He seized her by the throat, rammed her into a wall, blood dribbling from her mouth as she tried to kick him away. He'd kill her with his bare hands. Why waste good bullets?

He didn't see her reaching for her smock, but felt the pistol when she jabbed it in his stomach. He tensed. Nothing happened. He let her go, backed off.

Sonny, his back to them, still hunched over the computer, oblivious. Not that he would do anything anyway.

Glenroy said, "You shoot me, what does it get you?"

"Pleasure," Todora said.

"But no money."

Todora snorted.

"This money, I have yet to see it. Maybe it is just talk."

"There's money."

"How much?"

"Enough."

Todora backed toward Sonny now, keeping her eyes on Glenroy as she aimed the pistol at the back of Sonny's head.

Sonny tapped away, not noticing a thing.

"Bang, bang," Todora said.

She dropped the pistol into her smock, gave Sonny's shoulder a shove.

"Come on, fat boy," she said.

Sonny turned, looked at her, then at Glenroy.

"Do what she says," Glenroy told him.

Sonny got up, followed Todora into the hallway.

Glenroy pushed the red button on the wall. And the steel door slid shut.

8

THURSDAY, 8:41 P.M.

The Galaxy Lounge was at the aft end of Deck Five and that was where the two waiters took the forty-eight female passengers.

A nightclub setup, like something out of Vegas, way-way overdone. Silk brocaded walls in gold and burgundy. Black lacquered walnut floor. Plush divans, settees and armchairs fanning out stadium-style to face the stage.

It was a place that looked best when the lights were dim, but the chandeliers—authentic Baccarat, no less—were still turned up bright from when all the passengers had gathered there a few hours earlier for a briefing that preceded the lifeboat drill. Exclusive as the *Royal Star* was it still had to abide by certain annoying maritime regulations and the lifeboat drill was one of them.

Barbara thought about Zack, about how the two of them had struggled to fasten the life preserver around her belly. They'd given up, laughing, Zack kidding her that even if the ship sank she would survive.

"And how's that?" she'd asked.

"Whales can swim."

Well, it had seemed funny at the time.

Barbara was at the head of the procession, and now the waiter walking beside her pointed his rifle toward the steps that led to the stage.

"Up," he said. "Up there."

Barbara took the first step. And immediately she felt it—a twinge from deep within.

The second step. And now she really felt it. Yes, that was pain, real pain, shooting up inside her, the pressure against her lower back. She doubled over, grabbed the handrail. A collision of women behind her.

The waiter, shouting: "No stop! You go! Up, up . . ."

"Leave her alone!" The woman behind Barbara, yelling at the waiter. "Can't you see, she's . . . just leave her alone."

And now the woman had Barbara by the arm, helping her up the steps, onto the stage.

"Are you alright, dear?"

The older woman who'd been sitting at the table next to Barbara and Zack, the one with the boob job. Her hair looked as if it had been spun out of a cotton-candy machine, colored a sort of orangey-pink not otherwise found in nature. Her eyes were bright, maybe too bright, a shade of blue that perfectly matched the Pashmina shawl draped over her shoulders. And her skin, it was perfect. Which made it all the more eerie. Still, she had a nice smile.

"I'm OK, just need to get my breath," said Barbara. "It surprised me. A contraction, I think."

"Believe me, when it's a contraction you don't think. You know."

"Well, that's what it was then. A contraction. Lovely. Just lovely."

The woman patted Barbara's hand, walking with her to the middle of the stage, the other women filling in around them, huddling close.

The two waiters who had led them into the lounge spoke low among themselves. They still wore their tuxedos, brass nameplates on their jackets. Tony and Felix.

Now Felix, a little taller and a little older, stepped away, hurrying out of the lounge. Tony approached the edge of the stage. He was a moon-faced young man, nervous, jittery with his rifle.

"Sit," he told the women. "All down."

Most of the women did as told, but Barbara hesitated. She just wanted to stand there. She didn't want to move. She felt that if she moved it would stir things up, bring on another contraction. And she didn't want that.

She breathed in, breathed out, slowly, trying to calm herself. The woman still patting her hand.

"Can you make it, dear?"

"I . . . I don't know. Just give me a moment."

Tony was impatient. He pointed his rifle at Barbara.

"Down! You down!"

And the woman turned on him.

"Back off, you little prick!" The force of her words stopped the waiter cold. "This woman cannot possibly sit on the hard floor. She's getting ready to have a baby. Those chairs out there. Let her sit in one of those."

Tony looked at the chairs, then back at Barbara and the woman. He reached up, pulled off his black bow tie, unfastened the top buttons on his shirt. He took off his coat, dropped it on the floor.

Then he eased himself down on a front row couch, stretched out, made himself comfortable.

He pointed his rifle at them.

"Sit," he said. "All sit."

The woman started to say something else, but Barbara stopped her.

"It's OK, really. I'll manage."

The woman took off her blue shawl and spread it out on the floor.

"It's not much, dear, but . . ."

"Here, you can use this, too."

Another woman, taking off her sweater, handing it to Barbara. And then another, offering her jacket.

Until there was a bed of sorts, and with gentle hands all about to offer comfort, Barbara lay down.

9

THURSDAY, 8:55 P.M.

Glenroy stood at the conning station, studying the bridge controls. They were familiar to him, almost identical to the ones in the engine room. The ship could be steered from down there, too.

Gauges and indicators, their red and green dials glowing, showing the rudder angle, rate of turn, lateral thrust, propeller revolution. Digital charts and positioning readouts.

To his left, a telephone built into the console and the handset for the ship's PA system. To his right, the helm. No big impressive wheel like the ships of yore. Just a black joystick, only slightly more substantial than you'd find on a video game.

Glenroy checked the heading. The ship was on autopilot, routing south-southeast. He found the steering control override, pressed it. Immediately, a shrill ring broke the silence in the bridge. It sounded every time the autopilot was switched off, demanding that an actual human being verify the action. Glenroy pressed another button—the watch alarm acknowledgment. The ringing stopped.

He put his hand on the joystick, gave it a slight nudge to the east. He watched the new coordinates flash before him and, ever so slowly, felt the ship respond to the change.

The *Royal Star* was at his command.

———

Glenroy marveled at how easy it was. A ship this size and all it took was one man to control it, a man who knew where he wanted to go, a man with a plan.

He spent a few minutes acquainting himself with electronic charts and the GPS. He was merely a motorman, barely above the maintenance crew, but he had made the most of his engine room experience. The chief engineers he'd worked with had been generous with their knowledge, not minding when Glenroy spent his off hours down in the engine control room. He had watched and he had learned. And over the years he came to know everything he needed to know.

In recent weeks, as his plan had taken shape and gained momentum, he had plotted and calculated routes and positions, working it out on paper, over and over again, then keeping it in his head.

Nothing complicated about it. The *Royal Star* needed only to be at a certain place at a certain time.

The final destination wasn't that far away—Glenroy, punching coordinates into the GPS, watched as it instantly told him the distance from here to there—just 274 nautical miles. A straight run, top end, ten hours, maybe twelve.

But it wasn't as if Glenroy could just take the ship to the appointed place, then sit and wait. No, that wouldn't work. The *Royal Star* had to keep moving, destination in mind but pointed elsewhere, not attracting attention, slowly closing in and in and in. Until the time was right.

Barracuda, thought Glenroy. Just like a barracuda.

He'd been fascinated by them ever since he was a boy, swimming along the little patch reefs off Maracas Beach. Solitary creatures, they hung in the water, silver torpedoes, mindful of everything around them, but wholly unto their own. They moved slowly, effortlessly, as if going nowhere really. They would ignore one school of fish after another and then, when they struck, it would seem almost at random.

But, Glenroy knew, there was nothing random about a creature so deadly. Its every move was calculated. When it killed, it killed according to plan.

Yes, Glenroy thought, just like a barracuda.

He came up with a course, a series of concentric circles, and punched it into the GPS. Instantly, the screen flashed line after line of coordinates, vectoring in on the destination. A bar at the bottom flashed the time—twenty-four hours, eleven minutes. Call it just after nine o'clock on Saturday night.

Glenroy reset the autopilot with the new course, then moved away from the conning station, turning his attention to the bank of monitors.

Cameras on the main deck showed that all the passengers and crew had been led away. All except for one—the tall man who had fought with the waiters. He was still being difficult, struggling with Pango and one of the waiters, giving them a time of it, even though he was bound and gagged.

Glenroy picked up the PA handset, spoke into it.

"Yo, Pango," Glenroy said.

The tall man was a nuisance. Best to get rid of him.

Glenroy spoke into the handset again. Pango showed no sign of hearing him.

Glenroy looked at the console, saw at least a dozen PA switches, different zones throughout the ship. He flipped one, tried again.

"Yo, Pango. You hear me?"

And now the monitor was showing the deck from a new angle, Pango and the waiter finally getting the upper hand, forcing the man across the deck and disappearing through a passageway.

Glenroy put the handset back in its cradle.

They'd have to keep an eye on the tall man. Any more problems and he'd get a bullet, too. Another body on the pile.

FIRST WATCH

10

Two waiters led me away, one at each arm, rifles against my ribs. They didn't do any talking.

As we walked, I could feel a slight shift in the ship's direction. A more easterly bearing. You spend time on boats, you notice even the subtlest change of course. It's something that becomes ingrained.

We got to the stairs and went down. Eight flights altogether, with seven landings between them, four decks' worth.

We left the stairs and they walked me down a hall, counter to the ship's forward motion, walking toward the aft.

I'd briefly seen a diagram of the ship. And now I tried to repicture it in my head, along with a little red dot that said: "You are here."

But I wasn't having much luck. I'd only been on the ship for—how long now? Maybe five hours. It wasn't as if I'd had a chance to do much exploring. I didn't know ship from shinola.

Barbara and I had gotten a late start from Minorca Beach earlier in the day. Months before I had agreed to give a tour of the nursery to some nice ladies from the local garden club. Some of them had been friends of my mother, so it wasn't like I could cancel on them.

What I thought would take an hour or so had stretched into the afternoon, with the garden club ladies bringing picnic lunches and turning it into a real gabfest. They'd been genuinely interested in the history of Chasteen's Palm Tree Nursery and wanted to know all about my grandfather and his exploits in amassing a collection of specimen palms from all over the world. My grandfather had been a remarkable guy, the Indiana

Jones of horticulture. And ordinarily I would have charmed the ladies with all kinds of fascinating stories. As it was I had to run them off. Ever so politely, of course.

Traffic southbound on I-95 had been a bitch. Plus, Barbara needed to make numerous pit stops along the way. We'd made jokes about her Incredible Shrinking Bladder.

By the time we reached the Port of Miami, the *Royal Star* was almost ready to set sail. We'd gone straight to our cabin to get ready for the party. I'd hoped to roam around the ship, find out where everything was, get the lay of the land. But there hadn't been time for that.

Our suite was fairly dazzling, in a totally ostentatious kind of way. Lots of shiny finishes, no surface left unadorned. It was spacious, gigantic as cruise ship suites go, with a broad balcony big enough for several deck chairs and a hot tub. But it felt a little fussy. Too much stuff in too small a space. Stuff just for the sake of having stuff.

"Splendidly tacky" was how Barbara had described it.

I had stretched out on the big bed while Barbara finished primping in front of the vanity mirror. I studied the ship's diagram while simultaneously studying Barbara. I took much more pleasure in the latter. She was a beauty to behold. Especially now that there was so much more of her.

All that stuff they say about pregnant women and how they've got a special glow about them? In Barbara's case it was dead on the mark. She positively sparkled.

In the last day or two, Critter had dropped. And when I say dropped, I mean Critter's next move would definitely be out the escape hatch.

Our obstetrician had given Barbara the thumbs-up to go on the cruise. And just to cover all the bases, Barbara and I had checked in with the *Royal Star*'s physician, Dr. Louttit, when we boarded.

"Have a ball," Dr. Louttit had told her. "It'll be the last chance in the foreseeable future for the two of you to enjoy some one-on-one time."

Truth was, our one-on-one time had been remarkably rich of late. Before Critter came along, I had never considered the erotic potential of a pregnant woman. But the evolution of Barbara's body presented new discoveries every day. Our lovemaking, never pedestrian to begin with, had enjoyed its own evolution. And as Barbara's belly bulged, creating an obstacle to our preferred approaches, we had seized upon numerous innovations. Necessity may well be the mother of invention, but when necessary, mothers-to-be can prove wonderfully inventive.

Barbara's eyes had met mine in the vanity mirror. She'd given me that look.

"Don't even think about it, buster."

"Too late."

"Yes, I can see. Perhaps I should ring our butler, ask for a bucket of ice to stop the swelling."

"Perhaps you should join me on this bed and attend to it yourself."

"Later," she'd said, turning to face me, putting a hand on her hip. "I'll make it worth your wait, big boy."

So, no, I hadn't given that ship's diagram my full and undivided attention. I knew that our suite was on Deck Six, the same level as the main deck and the bon voyage party. Beyond that, about the only thing I had noted from the ship's diagram was that the main dining room was on Deck Four. I am not one to miss a meal.

At any rate, the two waiters were leading me down a hall on what I was guessing was Deck Two. As for what might be on that deck, I had no idea. There were no sounds aside from our footsteps and the underlying drone of the ship.

I've never been bothered by claustrophobia. But now it began to seep in. It came not so much from being in a confined space as from being in a space that was unknown. That it was on a ship made it all the worse. And that my mouth and eyes were covered with duct tape and my hands tied behind me made it even worse than that.

I tried to take in a deep breath, but the tape on my mouth tightened, like a vacuum lid on a Mason jar. I gagged and stumbled. The waiters dragged me forward. I breathed in through my nose, tried to calm myself, tried to visualize the sea, the broad expanse of water, the sky, the sun.

It wasn't working. There was just darkness.

Then we stopped.

The guy on my right let go of my arm. I heard him fumbling around, then the click of a card key entering a lock, the creak and whoosh of a door opening.

The two guys pushed me forward.

And behind me the door slammed shut.

11

The air in wherever it was they had shoved me was close and damp. It smelled more than slightly septic, the innards of a ship. If human fear has an aroma then, yes, it stunk of that, too.

A cough, bodies shuffling. Then movement beside me. A man's voice: "You alright?"

I grunted something.

"What say we get you undone here, buddy."

A twang, Southern. Panhandle Florida, maybe, or Alabama. He began working at the tape that sealed my mouth.

Another man said, "Leave him like he is."

The man beside me stopped working the tape.

"What do you mean, leave him like he is?"

The other man said, "That's how they want him, OK? If we undo him it's only going to make them mad."

"Screw them, Diamond. The guy's gotta breathe."

The man beside me gave the tape on my mouth a yank. I gulped air as he started in on the tape around my eyes. Another yank. I flinched against the sting.

"Sorry about the eyebrows," the man said. "They'll grow back."

He grinned, a fortyish guy in a white shirt and dark tie, the tie still snugged tight at the collar. Good hair, well cut, blond going gray. Lean and angular. Sun wrinkles and laugh lines framing his eyes. Knowing the breed, I pegged him for a former athlete, still in passable good shape.

As he undid the tape around my wrists I checked out my surroundings. A small cabin, about a quarter the size of the suite that Barbara and I shared. No balcony. Not even a window. Drab green walls. Yellow light from a bulb stuck in the middle of a low ceiling, just barely enough clearance for me to stand up straight. A pair of narrow twin beds, bare metal frames with skinny mattresses, not even a yard between them. Crew quarters.

On one of the beds sat a guy in a navy-blue pin-striped suit. Early fifties, jowly, his thin hair worn too long. Barbara had pointed him out to me when we'd been dancing, but I would have recognized him anyway. A brand-name face—Ron Diamond, an L.A. real estate baron turned media entity. And the guy who had wanted to leave me bound and gagged.

I looked at him. And kept looking at him until he looked away.

A few years earlier Diamond had published a book, *Diamond in the Rough*, a memoir of sorts, telling how he had started off buying cheap properties and flipping them for profit until he had amassed a sizable fortune. His book had sold millions of copies and Ron Diamond had parlayed that into a multitude of high-profile pursuits—Diamond Casinos, Diamond Hotels, even his own line of Diamond Cologne.

On the bed opposite Diamond sat two others guys. I recognized one of them, but couldn't quite summon his name. Twenty-something, an actor, famous for his roles in several high-grossing movies I'd never seen. More famous for his offscreen pursuits. Scuffles with paparazzi. A couple of short-lived marriages, career boost kinda things. Trips in and out of rehab. The typical tabloid résumé. I'll admit to having scanned some of the headlines while in the checkout line at Publix.

And then it clicked—Kane Kinsey. Something told me his momma and daddy hadn't been quite that alliterative on his birth certificate.

Kinsey wore a week-old beard on a face that didn't wear a beard well. At least not in his current condition. Hollow cheeks, sallow complexion, droopy eyes. A poster child for the dissolute lifestyle. Then again, maybe this was just Kane Kinsey, dedicated young method actor, getting into character for his next role. Yeah, maybe.

As for the guy next to Kinsey, I couldn't make out much about him. He sat hunched over, head in his hands, face hidden, as if trying to block out the cabin and everyone in it, as if trying to imagine that none of this was happening. Which seemed like a reasonable enough reaction.

The man looked old. Frail and shriveled. Silver-gray hair and lots of it, but without much sheen or gloss.

"Sons a bitches sure wrapped you up tight, buddy."

The man beside me, finishing with the duct tape. He stuck out a hand. I shook it, told him thanks.

"Carl Parks," he said.

"Zack Chasteen."

"Yeah, I know," Parks said. "You used to play for the Dolphins. Now you grow plants or something, right?"

"Palm trees," I said.

Diamond looked at me.

"You do what?" he said.

"I grow palm trees. Rare specimens. From all over the world."

"You make money doing that?"

"Naw, it's charity work," I said. "Just doing my bit to make the world a better place."

Diamond couldn't tell if I was messing with him. Guys like him, they usually can't. Guys like him, it's all about the money. And guys like him, they think they know all the ways there are to make it. Guys like me, we don't play well with guys like him.

My head hurt. I rubbed the back of it, where the waiter had pounded me with the rifle butt. There was a pretty good-sized knot. My hand came away with a gob of blood and hair and assorted Zack matter. I wiped it on my pants.

Parks said, "Let me get you something for that."

He stepped into the tiny bathroom. A toilet and sink on one wall, a showerhead on the wall opposite. Drain in the middle of the floor. You wanted to bathe, you closed the door, the whole thing became a shower stall. Cramped, yes. But then again, you could take a shower while sitting on the john. Highly efficient. Perhaps even pleasurable.

Parks came back with a towel, dabbed the back of my head.

"Quite a wallop, buddy, but I think the bleeding's almost stopped."

I told him thanks.

He said, "Hell of a thing, huh?"

"Yeah, you could say that."

"What do you make of it?"

I shrugged.

"What's there to make?"

"Terrorists?"

"Be my first guess."

"What do you think they want?"

I let out some air, shook my head. It passed for the answer I didn't have. Or didn't want to think about.

"Here's what I don't understand . . ." Diamond was talking now. "That captain, the officers. They couldn't do anything? You're telling me there's no armed security on this ship? A bunch of Filipino waiters, whatever they are, they pull out assault rifles and there's no one to stop them? No one even puts up a fight?"

Parks put a hand on my shoulder.

"Chasteen here, he put up a fight."

Diamond rolled his eyes.

"Some fight."

"So where the hell were you?" Parks said, glaring at Diamond. "I'll tell you where you were, curled up under a table hiding your ass, that's where. I know, because I was curled up right beside you." Parks turned to the other two. "Where the hell were any of us, huh?"

Kane Kinsey was in deep thought.

"I was with this chick, Penelope. She was freaking. Crying and everything," he said. "It was fucking insane, man."

The old man was silent, still hunched over, head in his hands.

"That was our only chance," Parks said. "What were there, a couple of hundred of us up there? And six or seven of them?"

"Had to be more of them than that," Diamond said. "No way was it just six or seven of them."

"That's all I saw," Parks said. "All I'm saying is, that was our chance. We had them outnumbered. We could have rushed them, could have done something. That was our chance."

"Let's roll," said Kane Kinsey.

We looked at him.

"You know? Like on that plane, the one on 9/11. The terrorists and everything."

"Flight 93," said Parks.

"Yeah, the movie. I was up for the lead. You know, the guy who said it, 'Let's roll.' Only they gave it to this other guy. And my agent was like, 'OK, we can't have the lead, we're out of here.' Because, you know, 'Let's roll,' that's what it was all about. And then everyone dies."

The silence that followed was welcome.

12

Parks took another look at my head, applied the towel, examined it for more blood—there wasn't much—then tossed it into the bathroom.

"You need to lie down, Chasteen? Those bastards worked you over pretty good. Diamond there can move off the bed, let you stretch out."

Diamond obviously didn't embrace the idea. He didn't move.

"I'll be alright," I said. "But tell me something."

"Yeah?" Parks said.

I pointed at the cabin door.

"What's out there?"

"What do you mean?"

"I mean, when they were bringing you down here what did you see?"

"Oh, that. I don't know." He thought about it. "A long hall, cabin doors lining it, maybe ten or twelve on each side."

"And what was at the end of the hall?"

Parks shook his head.

"I don't remember," he said. "Tell you the truth, I wasn't paying that close attention to what was out there, just what was going to happen next. I thought they were bringing us down here to shoot us."

I looked at the others.

"That's about all I remember," Diamond said. "The guys with the guns, they'd unlock a door, tell some of us to go inside. Then they'd close the door and move down the hall with the rest of us."

Kane Kinsey had drifted off, as removed from our conversation as the old man sitting next to him.

I looked at Parks.

"Where along the hall is this cabin?"

"I don't know, maybe a third of the way down it. As I remember, they split off five or six groups into cabins before they got to us." Parks looked at Diamond. "That the way you remember it?"

"Something like that," Diamond said. "We came down the stairs, entered the hallway, and then they started splitting us off. Yeah, maybe a third of the way down. Maybe a little more."

I squared myself to the cabin door. Then I closed my eyes, tried to picture it.

"So that way . . ." I pointed right, toward the ship's bow. "That way are four or five cabins and then the stairs. And that way . . ." Pointing now to the ship's stern. "That way are more cabins and we don't know what at the end."

"Sounds about right," Parks said.

I looked at the cabin door. A peephole in the middle of it. A dead bolt above the lever handle. I remembered the sound of the card key from when the waiters pushed me inside the cabin. Still, these were crew quarters, not storerooms. No way could we be locked inside.

I stuck an eye to the peephole. Not much to see. No waiters with guns. No movement of any kind. A door directly across the hall. And walls angling out from our cabin door. I tried to remember the way it was in the suite I shared with Barbara. Seemed there was an alcove just outside the door. Maybe that explained why I was seeing the walls jut out like they did.

I gripped the door handle, gave it a turn.

Diamond said, "What the hell are you doing?"

"Just gonna take a look around," I told him.

"You can't go out there. You'll get us all killed." Diamond stood up and headed for me. "I won't have this."

Parks said, "Sit down and shut up."

And he pushed Diamond back onto the bed.

The cabin fell quiet. I gave it a few seconds, looked out the peephole again. Same scene as before.

I pushed down on the handle, the door cracked open. I counted to ten. Then I cracked it open some more. Another ten count. And I slipped outside.

13

I stood in the alcove, letting the door close without locking, weighing what to do next. One of the waiters might be patrolling the hall, might soon walk by. What then?

"Why, hello there, perhaps you could help me. See, I ordered room service at least an hour ago and was just checking to see if . . ."

I edged along the wall to my right, peeked out. No guard. Parks and Diamond had been fairly accurate. I counted four doors and then the stairwell maybe twenty yards away.

I fell back inside the alcove. I could hear myself breathing, tried to notch it down. Then I edged along the left wall, peeked out the other way.

A waiter, twenty yards in that direction. Sitting in a chair, fiddling with his rifle. I slid back into the alcove before he noticed me.

Then I tried to recapture what I had just seen. The end of the hall looked to be another twenty–thirty yards beyond where the waiter was sitting. And while I couldn't be sure, it appeared the waiter had placed his chair at a spot where side corridors met the main hallway. I had no idea where they led.

I stepped back inside the cabin, closed the door.

Parks and Diamond looked at me.

"So here's the good news," I said. "Only one waiter in the hall. And five of us."

Kane Kinsey was still off in the ozone somewhere. And the old guy still sat with his head in his hands.

"Make that three of us," I said.

Parks said, "And the bad news?"

"Bad news is there's a lot of hallway beween him and us and even if Marlon Fucking Brando and The Thinker were coherent, which they aren't, then the waiter can probably get off enough shots to kill all five of us. Just three of us, we're ducks on the pond."

Diamond got up from the bed, pacing the cabin. Which meant two paces in one direction and then back the other.

"Goddammit, how could Jebailey and his people let this happen? Here he's got one hundred invited guests on board—people of means, mind you, very affluent people, people with exceptionally high net worth, people who are obvious targets for terrorism or piracy or whatever this is—and there is nothing on board to protect them?"

That's when the old man raised his head.

"Be quiet," he said. "You have absolutely no idea what you are talking about."

Diamond stopped pacing. The sound of the old man's voice even brought Kane Kinsey back from la-la land.

Now that I could see his face, the old man didn't really seem all that old. At least not when you saw his eyes. The rest of him might have appeared decrepit, but there was plenty of life in those eyes. They were bright and piercing eyes. Eyes that absorbed each of us as he looked around the room.

"For the record," the man said, "the *Royal Star* carries a full complement of weaponry, certainly in line with other vessels of her size and comportment. By established cruise industry protocol and primarily to avoid undo stress to passengers, ship's officers do not carry sidearms. And only a very few officers—in the case of the *Royal Star*, just one, the first officer—are permitted to keep weapons in their quarters. The rest, six pistols, I believe, perhaps that many rifles, are kept in a small armory located in the office of the chief security officer. And that explains, Mr. Diamond, why Captain Falk and his officers could not respond with any degree of force."

The man rubbed his forehead. He looked tired, very tired.

"The prevailing wisdom regarding cruise ship security, such as it is, holds that any threat will most likely come from exterior sources, i.e., hostile agents attempting to board the ship while it is at sea. Case in point—the fifth of November 2005, approximately 5:30 A.M., the *Seabourn Spirit*, cruising a hundred fifteen kilometers off the coast of Somalia and carrying a hundred fifty-one passengers, was attacked by two speedboats launched from a nearby mother ship. The pirates—and that's what they were, pirates—first strafed the ship with machine-gun fire then followed with rocket-propelled grenades, one of which lodged itself, unexploded, in a cabin. Fortunately, the *Spirit* was equipped with LRAD and crew members used it to successfully repel the pirates. As for the *Royal Star*, it, too, is equipped with LRAD . . ."

"Hold on," Parks said. "What's this el-rad?"

"Long-range acoustical device. A sonic cannon. Essentially, it emits a high-frequency sound wave that can hit ninty decibels even at a range of three hundred meters, enough to give someone second thoughts about coming any closer, like a smoke alarm going off in your ear. For the average person, the threshold of pain is about a hundred thirty decibels and at a range of a hundred meters and less the LRAD can shoot a burst of a hundred fifty decibels. Enough to bring someone to their knees. Closer than that, well, let's just say anyone who gets too close can expect permanent bodily harm."

None of us said anything. We just sat there listening. Some guys, they talk like they've swallowed an encyclopedia. He was one of them. He spoke with just the hint of an accent, so slight it was hard to identify.

He cast his gaze upon Diamond.

"As for your presumption that it would be difficult for six or seven hostiles to seize a ship with a crew that numbers in the hundreds, well, I'm afraid that history proves you wrong. Are you familiar with the *Achille Lauro?*"

Diamond shook his head, but the name registered with me.

"That cruise ship the Palestinian terrorists took over," I said. "Somewhere in the Mediterranean. Years ago, I don't remember when."

The man nodded.

"October 1985," he said. "The *Achille Lauro* was in Egyptian waters, sailing from Alexandria to Port Said. The hostiles, members of the Palestinian Liberation Front, had booked passage and were accidently discovered by a crew member while assembling weapons in their cabin. They seized him and took over the entire ship—four hundred passengers and a hundred fifty crew. Just four of them. Guns and leverage, that's all it takes. The numbers are really insignificant."

I said, "They killed passengers, didn't they?"

"Just one. A man named Leon Klinghoffer. When Israel refused to release a group of Palestinian prisoners, the terrorists shot Klinghoffer. He was in a wheelchair . . . a wheelchair! They shot him because he was Jewish and dumped his body overboard."

No one spoke for a few moments.

And then the man looked at me.

"I can assure you that I am totally coherent . . . Mr. Chasteen, is it?"

"It is," I said. "And I'm sorry if I suggested otherwise."

He nodded, accepting the apology.

"I agree with you that we must act. We must do something to stop these . . . these people, whoever they are. God only knows what they have in mind and they have already demonstrated that they will not balk at taking human life." He trembled as he spoke, those eyes filled with rage. "But you are right, Mr. Chasteen. The idea of such a small group of people trying to overpower one of the gunmen, it is foolhardy at best. There is, however, another option."

The man looked up at the ceiling, then back at us.

"Seven feet," he said. "Quite a low ceiling, have you noticed that?"

"Matter of fact, yes," I said.

I reached up and touched it, hardly a stretch.

"Eight feet, four inches," the man said. "That's the standard ceiling height, the one you'll find in the upper deck suites. But down here, well, there was need for a crawl space. Granted, it is a very tight crawl space, not even sixteen inches. Still, if need be, someone can get at the guts of the fiber optics, all the other wiring running around between decks. And someone, if he's clever about it, can travel almost the entire length of this deck and no one will know he's up there."

We all stared at the ceiling.

It was Parks who spoke first.

"Listen, mister, what you say is all very interesting. And I'm ready to hear more. But, before we go any farther, you mind telling me exactly how it is you know all this?"

The man smiled.

"No, not at all. Forgive me. It is quite rude not to introduce myself." With no small effort he stood, offered us a small, courtly bow. "I am Hurku Linblom. And I designed this ship."

14

THURSDAY, 10:15 P.M.
Aboard the *King of the Seas*

Captain Luca Palmano sipped grappa from his perch on the starboard bridge wing. A nightly ritual, just a little something to help him unwind at the end of the day.

He had been in command of the *King of the Seas* for almost a year, ever since its inaugural launch. Still, the ship never ceased to thrill and amaze him. What a truly stupendous vessel it was, 16 passenger decks, 165,000 gross tons, the length of 5 football fields (almost 600 feet longer than the *Titanic*), and the bridge wings extending outward nearly 240 feet above the water.

My God, the view was dizzying. The lights of Ocho Rios well behind them now, the moon lighting up the water, the surge of the mighty ship sending its towering wake across a frothy sea.

A precious few minutes of peace, away from the relentless activity aboard this floating city. As usual, the ship was at full capacity—5,218 passengers, 1,942 crew. And there was always something going on. Palmano could hear the music coming from two decks below—a sixteen-piece Latin jazz ensemble no less. Waiters and chefs bustling on an aft deck, setting up for the Midnight Pizza Party. Passengers in tank tops and shorts, heading to the casino. Others in formal attire spilling out onto the breezeways, signaling the end of a performance in the nine-hundred-seat cabaret. There would be another show at 1:00 A.M. And dancing in the disco until dawn.

Palmano took another sip of grappa, enjoyed the burn.

True, he had been at the helm of far more elegant ships, ships with graceful lines, beauties to behold. There was nothing particularly graceful or beautiful about the *King of the Seas*. It was a brick in the water, a giant brick, a Miami Beach high-rise condo turned on its side with six V-12 diesels powering three Azipod electric propulsion units and eight bow thrusters, all of it consuming, at a cruising speed of twenty-two knots, some twenty-eight thousand pounds of fuel per hour.

It was what it was—the world's largest cruise ship. The top of the heap, a marvel of modern transportation. And Palmano was proud to be its captain.

He knew the cruise line had chosen him not so much for his nautical skills, which were far more than adequate, as for his social graces, which were impeccable. He could host night after endless night of dinners for VIPs at his table in the main dining room—on an elevated, halogen-drenched platform in the middle of everything—enchanting them with the same old stories, answering the same old questions, always performing with an enthusiasm, not altogether disingenuous, that made the passengers feel as if they were the most fascinating people with whom the captain had ever dined.

It was a talent, it really was. The same talent he applied during the countless interviews with media types—there was always a group of them on board, representing outlets from all over the world—who delighted in his sharing various bits of minutiae about the ship. The eighty-six thousand lightbulbs on board, the thirty-two thousand eggs consumed in a week.

It was a talent well applied to his administrative duties, too. He ran the ship with a fair hand, didn't waste time on posturing or politics, and kept an open door to anyone who bore a grievance, be it the purser or the poor bastard who had spent the day repainting the starboard rails. With few exceptions, universal popularity being unattainable, the officers and crew liked him and were loyal to the core.

Plus, it didn't hurt that he looked really good in uniform. He had a tailor in Milan to thank for that. It cost Palmano a fair bundle and he absorbed the expense himself. The cruise line paid him well and he could afford it.

Palmano buttoned his coat, shot the pleat of his pants, made sure a half inch of shirtsleeve was showing, all the better for highlighting the monogrammed gold cuff links (a jeweler in Florence). He finished off the grappa, turned his gaze to the north.

Next stop: Isla Paradiso, Hispaniola. The "private island" leased by the cruise line to give its passengers the sense of exclusivity that can only come from being with 5,217 other passengers.

Technically, Isla Paradiso was a peninsula, not an island. And technically, it was part of Haiti, Hispaniola being a name originally bestowed by Columbus on the dual-nation island occupied in the east by the Dominican Republic.

But Isla Paradiso, Haiti? That just didn't work. Haiti conjured such unparadisical images—the poverty, the politics, the pestilence. Isla Paradiso, Hispaniola—much more romantic. And that's the way it was referred to by the cruise line in its brochures, itineraries, and daily in-room newsletters. No mention of Haiti anywhere.

Not that it mattered to the passengers. They were Americans, mostly, and their ignorance of the Caribbean was truly staggering.

Palmano remembered the woman who had dined at his table after a day spent at Isla Paradiso.

"I loved Hispaniola, just loved it," she said. "I always thought Puerto Rico would be so ugly, but . . ."

Others assumed it was part of the Bahamas, which in the mind of the typical passenger also included Jamaica, Grand Cayman, Aruba, and all points in between, the Bahamas being interchangeable with the Caribbean, all of it under governance of the United States because, you know, it was so close.

Ah, well, Palmano thought as he left the bridge wing and headed for his quarters, they were the passengers and they did not pay good money to confront the realities of the world.

Reality would return soon enough. A day after leaving Isla Paradiso, the *King of Seas* would be back in Miami. Then it would turn right around and do it all over again.

15

Glenroy checked the ship's clock, saw it was closing in on midnight. There was something he must do. True, he had until dawn to get it done, but he preferred to complete the ritual before another day began. He had let nearly six hours pass since the last one and he knew that was too long. He knew, too, that in a circumstance such as this, with its glorious goal so close at hand, he would be forgiven if he missed a time or two.

But the ship was on autopilot and it would be a simple matter of going down to his cabin and spreading out his *sajjada* on the floor, the floor he kept so clean and spotless, in accordance with the words of the Prophet. The fifth and final *salat* of the day, a quick one. Ten minutes, that's all it would take.

He turned to the door. And only then did it hit him: How would he get back in?

You fool, thought Glenroy.

In the rush of seizing the bridge, the confusion brought on by Todora's presence, he had neglected to notice the security code that Swenson punched into the keypad. Something so crucial, how could he have let that happen?

He stood there, studying the door.

Yes, he could press the yellow button and it would remain open. But for how long? What if there was a security override that automatically shut the door after a prescribed amount of time? What then? He did not know if such an override existed. But it seemed plausible. After all, he had not even considered that there would be an alarm code, what Swenson might have pushed to alert the bridge crew. But Todora had interceded. How had she known about that?

Could he risk leaving the door open? What if there were crew members still unaccounted for? What if one of them was to reach the bridge, find it empty and unguarded? Glenroy's plan could unravel in an instant.

No, Glenroy told himself, he must stay there. At least for now. There were other things, critical things that would eventually require him to leave the bridge. But there was still plenty of time left before he had to attend to those matters. Besides, Captain Falk was still alive. He knew the security code. Glenroy could get it out of him. Until then . . .

He would pray.

A small bathroom sat tucked away on the port side of the bridge. Glenroy stepped inside. He removed his shoes, stood there in his bare feet, cleansing himself at the sink. First his hands and arms. Then his mouth and nostrils. Finally, using a washcloth now, his legs and feet.

He pulled a terry-cloth towel from the rack. It would have to take the place of his *sajjada*, his treasured *sajjada*, the prayer rug personally bestowed upon him by Imam Ben-Yafati. He kept it in his cabin, hidden beneath his mattress.

It angered him that he had been forced to conceal his faith, to make his prayers in private. But to do otherwise might have raised suspicion.

It angered him, too, that he had been forced to conceal his real name, the name that spoke to his true calling, not this false name, Glenroy, emblazoned on his uniform, like a brand upon his skin.

Glenroy stepped out of the bathroom and scanned the bridge. It was an abomination to offer prayer here, amid such filth and gore. But again, he knew he would be forgiven.

He found a spot far removed from the conning station, near the door to the starboard bridge wing. The ship's compass pointed him to the Quibla, at this latitude almost due east.

He spread out the towel on the floor. He raised his hands to his ears, pronounced the takbir: *"Allahu Akbar."*

Then he followed with the al-Fatiha, intoning it in Arabic, by rote, the English resonating within:

Praise belongs to God, the Lord of all Being, the All-Merciful, the All-Compassionate, the Master of the Day of Doom.

He recited another *takbir,* followed by a bow. Then he prostrated himself, touching his forehead to the floor.

And in that moment of submission and humility, he heard the door to the bridge as it slid open behind him.

16

Glenroy raised up and saw Todora and Pango looking down on him, uncertain what to make of him kneeling on the towel.

"What, you drop something?" Todora asked.

Glenroy ignored the question. He held Todora's gaze, saw the sneer forming on her lips. She was enjoying the moment. She knew the security code. And she knew it gave her leverage. Glenroy would deal with her later. When Pango wasn't around.

Glenroy picked up the towel and walked to the conning station. He began wiping the console, cleaning off the blood that still remained. It seemed like a reasonable explanation for why he would have the towel in the first place.

"You finish everything like I told you?" he asked Todora, making sure she remembered her place in all this.

"Yes, the bodies they are put away. Now, for the money, it is time—"

"Where is Sonny?"

A smirk from Todora.

"Like you, on hands and knees. Only he is in front of toilet." She blew out air. "He does not have stomach for this. I worry about him, no? He keep telling me how you promise him that no one will be killed. It upset him, make him cry. Such stupid boy. What else did you promise him?"

Glenroy ignored her, looked at Pango.

"Everything under control? The crew, the passengers?"

Pango nodded.

"Yes, women in the lounge, on the stage. Tony, he watches them. We put some crew in casino. Some in library. Two of my men watching all of them from the atrium outside the purser's office. Casino doors and library doors they lock from outside. That's good, very good. Crew, they no get out."

"The captain. And Jebailey?"

"Each in a cabin by himself. Deck Two with all the rich men. One of my men in hall. They try something, he shoot. Just like you say."

Glenroy did the math. Altogether, four waiters standing watch. That left one.

"Your other man, what's he doing?"

Pango shrugged.

"Sleeping. Two hours. Then he relieve one of the others."

"Sleeping?" Todora turning on Pango. "There is no time for sleep! Whose idea was that? Please tell me it was not yours, Pango, eh?"

Pango opened his mouth, then shut it. Glenroy had to agree with Todora on this one. None of them had yet earned the right to sleep.

Todora reached into her smock. Glenroy shot a quick look at his SAR, on the other side of the bridge. Todora caught him at it, looked amused.

"What, you think I shoot Pango for that? No, no, no. Pango, he is my friend." She leaned over, put an arm around Pango, kissed the top of his head, a hand still in the pocket of her smock. "You are sweet man, Pango."

Pango, anxious, squirmed out of her embrace.

Todora pulled her hand from the smock, held out a plastic pill bottle. She opened it, shook out a dozen or so tiny yellow pills.

"Here," she said, holding out her hand to Pango. "You wake up your man, give him one of these. Give them to all your men. For you, too. For all of us. There is no time for sleep."

Pango looked at Glenroy, then at the pills. He took the pills, put them in a pocket.

Todora shook loose another one.

"The helmsman, these were in his pocket," she said. "Swenson, he told me the watch crew has plenty amphetamines. Watch candy, they call it. Funny name, eh? Watch candy."

She popped the pill into her mouth. A water bottle rested in a holder on the console, its cap off. She grabbed it.

"Salut," she said, then took a swig.

She shook loose another pill, offered it to Glenroy. He shook his head, no. Todora shrugged, put the pill back into the bottle, and tucked it away.

Pango headed for the door.

"OK, I go now."

"No," Glenroy said. "Not yet."

Pango stopped.

Glenroy said, "Have you accounted for all the crew?"

"Why yes, I think so."

"You *think* so?"

Pango looked away, on shaky ground.

Glenroy keeping after him, said, "A head count. Did you do a head count? One hundred and twenty officers and crew. Including us. Minus fourteen. Did you count one hundred and six heads? Tell me."

"No, I did not, but . . ."

"But what?"

"But I did not see anyone else, down below, anywhere. I am certain that—"

"How can you be certain? How? Unless you count the heads. Just one person . . . he, she, they can bring us down. You want that?"

"No, Glenroy. I do not want that."

"Then go. Count heads. And then you come back here and tell me everyone is accounted for."

Pango turned to go without a word. He punched the green button and left the bridge, the door shutting behind him.

Todora had moved to the conning station. She bent down to look at the dials and gauges, touching them, her hands finally coming to rest on the helm. They lingered on the joystick, rubbing it, getting its feel.

"So this is it, eh? This tiny little black thing. It takes us where we go?" She looked at Glenroy, pouting. "I am disappointed. Such a fine, handsome ship, such a tiny little thing. You think it would be bigger, no?"

"Get away from there," Glenroy said, moving toward the helm, picking up the SAR from where he had rested it by the wall.

Todora let go of the joystick. She made room as Glenroy brushed past her and stood at the helm. She rested against the console, eyes never leaving Glenroy.

Glenroy spent a few moments checking the ship's course, examining blips on a screen that showed the whereabouts of other vessels, none of them nearby. He looked out through the broad bridge windows, making a visual check of the waters.

Todora moved closer to him, cast her gaze in the same direction as his.

"Which way is it?" Her voice almost soft now.

"Which way is what?"

"Cuba," she said. "Which way?"

"It is that way," Glenroy said, pointing starboard. "Still to the south."

"And the boat, when it comes, it will take us there?"

She moved closer, her hip against his thigh.

Glenroy didn't answer. He kept staring ahead, looking for lights on the water. But there was nothing but dark and more dark on all sides.

Finally, he turned to Todora.

"The security code," he said. "What is it?"

She clicked her tongue, raising a hand now to his cheek, touching it.

"Oh, it is just some numbers. Some silly numbers."

"Tell me."

"You fine, handsome man . . . you have so many things to think about. I will remember the silly numbers for you."

Glenroy swatted her hand away, raised the SAR between them. He jabbed its barrel into the soft spot beneath her chin.

Todora did not flinch. She was smiling, the SAR's barrel poking against her skin.

"Tell me," Glenroy said.

Todora reached up, grabbed the barrel of the rifle with both hands, held it there, seemed almost to caress it.

"You will shoot me?"

Glenroy, clinching his jaw, gripped the SAR tighter.

Todora, lifting her chin, let go of the rifle, and backed away.

"We get money," she said. "Then I tell you."

17

I don't know about this, dude. What if one of those guys finds me up there?"

Kane Kinsey sat on a bed, huddled against the wall, arms around his skinny legs.

"The chance you have to take," I said. "It works, you'll be a hero. It doesn't . . ."

"A dead hero," Kinsey said.

I stood on the bed. Just behind me and next to the back wall was a small rectangular hole from where I had pushed up one of the ceiling tiles and slid it aside.

Standing on the bed, I could stick my head in the hole and look around. Dim light shone up from our cabin and from cracks and crevices in the ceiling tiles in other cabins along the hall.

It was a rat's nest up there, crammed with AC ducts, cables, and bundled wires. I could see the crawl space that Hurku Linblom had told us about. It ran above the aluminum wall braces and looked even tighter than sixteen inches.

No way I could squeeze up there. Neither could Parks or Diamond. As for Linblom, he was small enough, but not physically up to it.

That left Kane Kinsey.

"Tell me again what it is you want me to do," he said.

I looked at Parks and Diamond, sitting on the other bed. Linblom was in the bathroom, had been for several minutes, ever since he'd finished describing what was above the ceiling and we'd all conspired on a way we might turn it to our advantage.

Parks and Diamond appeared as dubious about the plan as I was. But it wasn't like we had much in the way of options. And we had to convince Kane Kinsey it was worth putting his life on the line for. Not an easy sell.

"Once you're up there, you'll crawl to the other cabins, see what you can see, try to make contact with whoever's in there."

"And tell them what?"

That's where the plan fell apart. We had this vague notion that we could somehow marshal our forces and somehow time it so we could all storm out of our cabins at once and somehow overcome the guard without all of us getting shot and somehow . . .

A whole lotta somehows. And somehow it all depended on Kane Kinsey, strung-out boy actor, to jump-start everything.

"Just tell them that we're working on a way to get us all out of here. Tell them you'll come back with details. Tell them to hang tight," I said. "It will give them hope. And that counts for a lot."

Pretty stirring words, I thought. Almost had me believing them.

Kane Kinsey thought about it. He seemed to slip away, deep within himself. When he came back, something about his eyes, his bearing, it was like looking at another person.

"OK," he said. "I'm your man."

A few moments later, Linblom stepped out of the bathroom. He looked a little better than he had going in. Still, he wobbled as he crossed the cabin.

Kane Kinsey got up and took Lindblom by the arm. He walked him to the bed, helped him sit.

He gripped Linblom by the shoulders, looked him in the eyes.

"I'm going up, sir," he said, his voice heavy with portent. "Keep faith. And wish me godspeed."

All Linblom could muster was a puzzled nod.

Kinsey turned to Parks and Diamond. He shook Diamond's hand with both of his. Did the same with Parks.

"Hang tight, men," he said. "When this is done the Dom is on me."

Then he hopped up on the bed beside me. I clasped my hands together, ready to give him a boost. He put a hand on my shoulder, looked at me for a long and deeply meaningful beat.

"Let's get this party started," he said.

"Good line," I said.

"Yeah," he said. "I thought so, too."

18

FRIDAY, 12:50 A.M.

"We counted, again and again," Pango said. "And each time it was the same. Maybe . . ."

"Maybe what?" Glenroy, slamming a hand on the console. "Maybe you stick your head up your ass and count there, too?"

Pango looked away, thinking: I should have just lied to him. Told him, yes, Glenroy, everything is good. All one hundred and six crew members have been accounted for. Every single one of them. But no, they had come up one person short. And Pango had duly reported back to Glenroy, told him the truth.

"Maybe there were not one hundred twenty to begin with," Pango said. "Maybe someone, a cook, a dishwasher, I don't know, maybe they got sick and stayed in Miami."

"But you can't be sure?"

Pango shook his head.

"No," he said. "I cannot be sure."

Glenroy paced the deck. He really wasn't so concerned about this one person who might have managed to escape the crew roundup and might now be hiding somewhere. Not as long as Glenroy was in command of the bridge. One person, how could one person possibly regain control of the ship? Glenroy tried to picture it, this one person, somehow finding a weapon, getting the upper hand on Pango, the waiters, or Todora, using them to force his way onto the bridge. It was something that Glenroy enjoyed picturing, actually, this person holding a pistol to Todora's head and saying he would shoot her unless Glenroy opened the bridge door. Not a hard choice there. Or with Pango. Or with anyone for that matter. It would soon come to the point when Glenroy would need none of them.

No, Glenroy was not worried about this missing person. He thought Pango might even be right. Maybe one of the crew had taken ill at the last moment, had an accident, a death in the family, and been forced to stay behind.

Still, Glenroy thought, it was good for Pango to squirm. It would make Pango much more attentive to his duties, anxious to redeem himself for the blame that had been heaped upon his head.

Glenroy looked at him.

"So how are you going to make the problem go away?"

For this, Pango was glad he had a ready answer.

"Already, I have asked one of my men, the one who was sleeping, to go through the ship and find this person."

"Do you know who it is you're looking for?"

Pango shook his head.

"No," he said. "We do not have the crew list so we cannot go down it name by name, checking off to find who is missing. But we will take care of this problem. It will be OK. Do not trouble yourself. We will not stop until this person is found."

Glenroy studied the maître d', certain that he had taken one of the pills Todora had given him. His eyes were wide. He was jumpier than usual, more talkative. Before this was over, Glenroy, too, might need a pill. But he had not wanted to show weakness in front of Pango and Todora.

"OK, then. Make sure it is taken care of," Glenroy said, dismissing Pango.

"There is one other thing," Pango said.

"Yes?"

"It is the woman, the housekeeper."

"What about her?"

"She took the purser and made him open the ship's safe. Then she made him take the money from the casino, too."

"What of it? We had planned to do that sooner or later. So what if it has already been done? Where is she now?"

"In the purser's office, counting the money." Pango paused, measuring his words. "There is not so much of it."

"What do you mean, not so much of it?"

"Not so much as . . ." Pango almost said it was not as much as Glenroy had promised would be in the ship's safe and the casino. "Not so much as we had thought. She is still counting it, but she is not pleased with what was there."

Glenroy didn't say anything.

"She wants next to take jewelry from the women. Then she wants to take the men from down below, in small groups, and make them empty the safes in their suites."

"That is as we planned, too," Glenroy said.

"Yes, but . . ."

"But what, Pango?"

Pango shrugged.

"That one, she scares me. She has the ice inside. She would not stop at killing me, at killing you."

"And why would she do that, Pango?" Glenroy clapped a hand on Pango's shoulder, reassured him. "Without you, without me, none of this works. That woman, she cannot steer the ship. She does not know where to meet the boat."

The words seemed to brighten Pango.

"When does the boat come?"

"Soon, my friend, soon. But don't you worry about the boat. First, the money, eh? That is what this is all about."

"Is there more of it, you think?"

"Why, yes, certainly. It is just a matter of finding it. Tear the ship apart looking for it. Meanwhile, let me take care of things up here, eh?"

"What about the housekeeper?"

Shoot the bitch, Glenroy wanted to tell him, anything, just keep her away from the bridge. All the pieces of the plan were coming together. And Glenroy needed time alone to focus on them. If he wanted to know what was happening throughout the ship, the monitors would tell him. He didn't need interruptions from Todora. Or Pango. Let them find all the money they could find. Let the waiters keep the passengers and crew under control. And let them all keep believing a boat would soon arrive to take them away.

Glenroy put a hand on Pango's shoulder.

"You and her, the two of you escort the male passengers to their cabins," Glenroy said. "Small groups, just two or three people at a time. Do not rush. Be thorough. Make them give you everything, look everywhere for more. Take your time. And do not let the woman out of your sight."

19

FRIDAY, 1:05 A.M.

These were the real-deal contractions, no doubt about it. Barbara had been timing them—about twenty minutes apart, each lasting maybe thirty seconds. Painful, yes, but really not as bad as she'd been expecting. The worst part was after they were over, anticipating when they would start again, worrying that the intervals would grow shorter and shorter, meaning the next stage of labor was on its way.

Just relax, Barbara kept telling herself. Just relax, slow things down.

Her water hadn't broken yet. A good thing. Contractions like this can start three or four days before a baby is born. By then this whole hostage thing would be over. She refused to have her baby on this ship. And she refused to have it without Zack right there beside her.

But right now she had to pee.

Barbara rose to her knees, got ready to stand.

"Let me give you a hand, dear."

It was the woman who had helped Barbara to the stage and since then assumed the role of her guardian angel, doing whatever she could to make a bad situation a little less bad.

Barbara had learned her name—Marie Lutey—and volumes of other information to go along with it. Where she lived—Fort Lauderdale, a condo on the Intracoastal Waterway. What she did—owned an interior design firm, the one that had decorated the suites on the *Royal Star;* hence her invitation to the inaugural cruise. Her marital status—once divorced, once widowed, now happily unattached and "trolling for something younger, maybe a Brazilian boy toy." Her political leanings: "You ask me, this country won't be right until we elect a big black woman president. Yeah, I'm thinking Oprah." The name of her plastic surgeon—"Dr. Eshbaugh out of Boca, a wonderful, wonderful man. If you like, I can make a referral, not that I'm saying you need work done or anything." Even how much she had spent on her recent boob job: "Fifteen thousand for the platinum model. But hey, I don't have kids or pets. Instead, I've got these puppies."

A real piece of work, Marie Lutey. Despite the grim circumstances she made everyone laugh. And in the process she had drawn them out, gotten them talking, helped them understand they were all in this together—forty-eight women, held at gunpoint, facing the unknown.

Barbara had chatted with some of them. Leslie Dillon, the twentyish actress who was being talked up as a surefire Oscar nominee for her latest role. Attavia Linblom, the wife of the ship's Finnish designer, who worried about the condition of her husband following his recent heart surgery. And Ron Diamond's latest girlfriend, a very blond former model who said she was now "into charity work, helping poor little African babies" and whose name, for the life of her, Barbara couldn't remember. Mandy. Brandy. Something like that.

Marie Lutey asking Barbara now, "You have to go again?"

"Afraid so," Barbara said.

"Think I'll start calling you TM."

"TM?"

"Tinkle Machine," Marie said.

Marie helped Barbara to her feet. The waiter, Tony, eyed them from his chair. He sat up, leveled his rifle at them.

"Down boy," Marie told him. "We're just making another trip to the bucket."

There was a restroom in the lounge, but Tony wouldn't let the women use it. He found some ice buckets and stuck them at one end of the stage, refusing even to put the buckets behind the curtains so the women could have some privacy. No, they had to go right out in the open, Tony watching them the whole time.

Already, in the four hours they had been held captive in the lounge, Barbara had gone to the bucket three times. Now Marie helped her to the end of the stage again.

Barbara pulled up her skirt and eased down over the bucket while Marie stationed herself between Barbara and the waiter, arms crossed over her chest, glaring at him, blocking his view, allowing Barbara at least one small shred of dignity.

Barbara was still doing her business when the doors of the lounge burst open and Todora strode in, walking down the main aisle toward the stage, Pango close behind her.

Todora carried a laundry bag and she shook it open as she mounted the steps to the stage. Some of the women were lying down, exhausted by the ordeal. Others sat in small groups, talking.

A young woman lay curled up near the steps. Barbara remembered seeing her on the main deck, at the party, dancing with Kane Kinsey, feeling no pain. She had taken off her jacket and offered it to Barbara to help make a bed on the hard stage floor. Penelope, that was her name. And she was one of the few women who had actually been able to fall asleep, thanks no doubt to all the champagne she and Kane Kinsey had been guzzling.

Todora kicked her in the ribs and Penelope jolted awake.

"Get up! Everyone up!" Todora shouted. "Make a line. Now!"

Penelope moaned, holding her side, groggy, still trying to figure out what was going on. Todora grabbed her by the hair, pulled her up. And Pango moved in, poking his rifle at other women, urging them to their feet.

Todora held the laundry bag open, shook it.

"Your purses, empty them," she said. "Jewelry, too. Everything. In here."

Penelope reached for her diamond necklace, covering it. Todora grabbed her arm, twisting her down to the floor. She yanked off the necklace and dropped it in the bag.

"The earrings, too," Todora said. "In here. Now!"

As Penelope removed her earrings and the other women lined up, Todora spotted Barbara and Marie at the far end of the stage.

"You two, get over here with the rest. Now!"

"Cool your jets, sister," Marie said. "She's not done yet."

Todora started for them, but stopped, distracted by Leslie Dillon who was removing a glittery necklace. She held out the laundry bag and Dillon dropped the necklace into it.

Barbara rubbed her ring, the one Zack had given her just months before, during their wedding in Bermuda. Compared to the rocks some of the other women were wearing, her diamond was a small fry. But it had belonged to Zack's mother, who had died when he was just a boy, she and Zack's father, killed by lightning while in their boat on Redfish Lagoon.

Barbara took off the ring. And making sure Todora and Pango were occupied with the other women, she lifted her skirt and dropped the ring into the bucket.

She looked up at Marie, who immediately began unclasping the gold pendant she wore, its cluster of emeralds dangling between her recently enhanced cleavage. She slipped off a big diamond ring and a diamond bracelet. She handed everything to Barbara. It went into the bucket, too.

By the time the two of them made it back across the stage, Todora and Pango had reached the end of the line. Todora shook the laundry bag at Marie.

"Give to me," she said.

"Sorry, sweetie," Marie said. "Been a tough year. I had to hock everything."

"You have nothing?"

"Zilch. Nada. Bupkus."

Todora turned to Barbara now. "And you. What about you?"

Barbara shook her head.

"No. Nothing."

Todora looked Barbara up and down. Then she grabbed Barbara's left hand, saw the pale circle on her ring finger.

"Your ring. Where is?"

"My hands are too swollen. I left it at home."

Todora wasn't buying it. She glanced at the far end of the stage. And she was starting toward the buckets when Barbara moaned, clutching her stomach, doubling over.

Marie stepped in to help her.

"Hey, you!" Marie shouted.

Todora stopped.

"This woman is getting ready to have a baby," Marie said. "The ship's doctor. We need the doctor."

Todora studied Marie for a long moment, chewing her lip.

"Yes, no problem," she said. "I will get doctor, bring him to you. Maybe, too, I will get masseuse from the spa, get her to come give you massage. Or maybe from the salon, someone to fix your hair, give you nice manicure. Would you like that, eh?"

She slung the laundry bag over a shoulder and stalked off the stage.

20

So who are these guys? What do they want?"

Carl Parks was asking everyone, but looking in my direction.

"Beats hell out of me," I said. "Best we can hope—they're just after money."

"Because if it's a hostage thing . . ."

Parks let it hang.

"Complicates matters," I said.

"No shit it does," said Parks.

Kane Kinsey was still on his recon mission in the crawl space. He had returned once to report making contact with the cabins on either side of ours. But we hadn't heard from him in almost an hour.

"I will tell you what concerns me," said Hurku Linblom. "Separating the men and the women."

Since Linblom revealed his background, we'd learned a little bit more about him. A third-generation ship designer. Born in Helsinki, now splitting his time between Finland and the States. Linblom specialized in cruise ships, but had designed his share of freighters along with a few private yachts. He seemed to know everything about anything that could float. Along with every possible problem that might befall a ship at sea, from outbreaks of Norwalk virus to security issues.

Linblom said, "What has happened, it is something terrorists would do, not pirates. Keep the men and women apart—it is a psychological advantage. We worry that our women are being harmed. It makes us crazy with worry. And it makes us do whatever we are told in order to save our women. All of us, we have women here, no?"

Diamond and I nodded.

Parks said, "Not me. I came alone. But you're right. Splitting us up, that's not really something that someone would go to all the trouble of doing if they were just after money."

"No, it makes no sense that they would do this for the money," Linblom said. "The risk, it is just too great. After all, how much money could there possibly be on this ship?"

Parks shot a look at Diamond. Neither of them spoke.

"We only know one thing," I said. "Whoever they are, they aren't scared of killing people. And there's no reason to believe they've lost their taste for it."

Parks looked at me.

"So what are you saying, Chasteen?"

"I'm saying we have to assume the absolute worst—that they intend to kill all of us. We can't just sit here waiting for them to do it. We have to stir the pot, take things into our own hands. And the sooner we do that, the better for all of us."

Diamond said, "You're out of your mind, Chasteen."

I didn't say anything.

"Who gave you the authority to make decisions for the rest of us? This isn't some football game. You don't just charge out that door and start something that might get us all killed."

Parks said, "So how would you play it, Diamond?"

"You ask me, they just want money. That's all anyone wants," Diamond said. "I say give them what they want and let them get out of here."

Parks said, "And if you're wrong?"

Diamond shrugged.

"If they're terrorists, then anything we do is only going to set them off. Who knows? They might have the whole ship rigged, ready to blow it up. We start acting like a bunch of cowboys and, boom, it's all over. Did you ever consider that, Chasteen?"

I didn't say anything.

"But let's pretend they really are terrorists. Say they've already notified the rest of the world and broadcast their demands. What does that mean, huh?"

We waited for Diamond to answer his own question.

"It means we just sit tight," he said. "Because at this very moment the U.S. government is doing everything it can to get us out of here. Why, if we could take a look outside, I'd bet we'd see helicopters and planes circling overhead, attack boats closing in. Uncle Sam won't stand for this. No way. I guarantee you, if these are terrorists, then a team of Navy SEALS is already in the water, getting ready to storm on board and . . ."

It was a perfect time to cue up "God Bless America." Instead, what we heard were voices in the hall.

I got up, went to the peephole. I saw two people—a man and a woman, their backs to me, standing outside the cabin across the hall. The man was short and stocky and wore a tuxedo shirt, tie off, black pants. I remembered seeing him on deck, giving orders to the waiters. The maître d'. He carried a rifle. The woman wore a blue housekeeper's uniform. She used a card key to open the cabin door across the hall.

I saw them enter the cabin. A few seconds later, they left the cabin with two men I'd seen at the party on the main deck. Then the hallway was empty again.

I stepped away from the peephole, told the others what I'd just seen.

Diamond said, "There's a woman in on this?"

"Appears that way," I said.

Parks said, "Think there could be more of them than we figured?"

A few minutes later, we were still trying to sort out what it all meant when we heard: "Yo, somebody help me get down from here."

And Kane Kinsey popped his head through the hole in the ceiling.

21

Kinsey gave us a quick rundown on what he'd found out. Besides our cabin, there were eleven others where male passengers were being held. Sam Jebailey and Captain Falk were in separate cabins at the end of the hall.

"How're they all doing?" I asked him.

"The captain, he's pretty beat-up. But he's walking around."

"Everyone else?"

"Kinda shook up, I guess. And it really freaked them out when I started talking to them through the ceiling. Like, you know, the voice of God coming down at them or something. It was wild, man."

"What did you tell them?"

"Just what you said: Hang tight. We'd get back with them."

"You see anything else?"

Kinsey shook his head.

"Not much. I mean, it's not like I went exploring or anything. Plus, I kept worrying that the guard was going to hear me up there, start shooting into the ceiling. That woulda sucked, man."

He fell back onto one of the beds, drained by the ordeal.

"You did good," I told him. "Real good."

He nodded.

"So what next?"

"Don't know. Still trying to figure it out."

I heard something in the hall, went to the peephole. I saw the head-waiter and the housekeeper leading the two men back to the cabin. They had been gone about twenty minutes. They let the two men back inside, then escorted three other men away.

I told the others what I'd seen.

"Well, at least they didn't take them out and shoot them," Parks said. "That's a good sign."

I sat on the floor, my back against the door. I closed my eyes, tried again to picture the hallway and how it might all play out. I wasn't coming up with anything. At least not anything that didn't wind up ugly.

So I thought about Barbara instead. Where on this ship could she be? And how could I get to her? And how could I get both of us—make that three of us—off this goddam thing?

Barbara's due date was still several weeks away. Otherwise we wouldn't have chanced going on the cruise. But any number of things could upset the timetable. Like stress, for instance. Which was in no short supply.

Stress, hell. It was terror. The terror of not knowing where my wife was, of not knowing if she was OK, of not knowing if our child would enter this world free of harm.

Yes, it was making me crazy.

So I tried to think calm thoughts and focus on getting us out of there. Every now and then I'd tune into the conversation around me, Diamond asking Hurku Linblom if he knew a nautical designer by the name of Lootenhall, based in Amsterdam.

"Yes, I am familiar with him," said Linblom. "Designs mega-yachts mostly."

"Yeah, that's him," said Diamond. "He designed mine for me. A hundred-sixty-five-footer—the *Ace of Diamonds*."

Diamond talking about his yacht. About its helipad and its swank staterooms and how he employed a full-time crew of twenty even when he wasn't able to use it.

"Got it in the Bahamas right now," said Diamond. "Getting some work done. Then it's down to St. Bart's for the winter."

I tuned him out, tuned into the drone of the ship, the dull rumble of its engines. I thought I sensed another slight shift in course, to the south now. Tried to piece it all together, chart the course in my head.

Where were we?

Eight or nine hours out of Miami. Cruising at twenty-five to thirty knots. Moving past the Cay Sal Banks and the southernmost islands of the Bahamas. Between them and Cuba. Beyond that Haiti and the D.R. A whole lot of open water.

I conjured a nautical map, the *Royal Star* plodding across it. We'd been heading southeast, now more to the south. Envisioned an arc, a half circle . . .

Where were we going?

Diamond saying, "Another reason I don't think they're terrorists. We're in the Caribbean, for chrissake. No terrorists here."

Then Linblom said, "No, that is where you are wrong again. There is Trinidad. And Guyana."

I opened my eyes, looked at him.

I said, "What do you mean?"

"JFK Airport. June 2007. Do you recall what happened then?"

I tried to dial it up.

"Some kind of plot to blow up something. Beyond that, I'm a little foggy."

"Three men, one from Trinidad, two from Guyana, arrested for conspiring to sabotage fuel lines serving the airport. They never came close to succeeding, never even secured the explosives. But they had been planning it for a long time and were doubtlessly committed to their mission. One of them had even worked as a fuel supervisor at the airport for a number of years. They talked about creating a catastrophe far worse than 9/11. And they all had ties to Jamaat al Muslimeen."

Parks said, "Come again?"

"Jamaat al Muslimeen. One of at least three or four radical Islamic groups based in Trinidad and drawing an increasing number of supporters from throughout the region. They practice an Afro-Caribbean form of Islam, not particularly aligned with Sunni or Shia traditions. And violently opposed to the Indian majority, primarily Hindu, that runs things in Trinidad.

"All these groups began as glorified street gangs, really, working the drug trade, intermediaries in the narcotics traffic from Colombia and Venezuela, moving dope up through the Caribbean archipelago. Then they made the shift to Islam, began building mosques and schools and community centers, recruiting followers from the slums and tenement yards. They rage against all manner of things. The Indian aristrocracy. The exploitation of the Caribbean Basin by U.S. and European interests, whether it be sugar companies or big resorts or cruise ships. Jamaat al Muslimeen itself has since spawned several splinter groups, all bickering with one another to get the upper hand in the drug trade and all with known connections to Al Qaeda."

Then Parks said, "For a ship designer from Finland you seem pretty savvy about Caribbean politics."

Linblom shrugged.

"The nature of my business," he said. "There are oil refineries in Trinidad. And freighters transporting that oil to the U.S. I am a consultant to the shipping companies. If there are terrorists who pose a threat—from Trinidad, from anywhere—then I must know about them and use that to determine how best to build ships that are impervious to attack."

Diamond said, "Didn't work out so well with this ship, did it?"

Linblom ignored him.

And then, behind me, the click of a card key, someone shoving the door against my back.

I got up. The door swung open. There stood the housekeeper and the headwaiter, their eyes wide and wild, like they were on something.

"You. And you." The housekeeper pointing at Parks and me. "Come with us. Now!"

SECOND WATCH

22

Glenroy liked the swivel chair that sat beside the helm. It was made for a big man like him—wide enough that it didn't squeeze him and raised high enough that his feet barely touched the floor.

It made him feel like a little child, really, like on that first day he arrived at the madrasa, the school run by Islaam Karibe, and the teachers welcomed him by letting him sit in the big chair at the head of the long dinner table, the chair typically reserved for Imam Ben-Yafati when he visited the school. That golden day, almost twenty-two years ago, when he was rescued from the streets of Port-of-Spain, when he learned of the work of Islaam Karibe and was told that his life would have purpose.

Glenroy leaned back in the swivel chair. Yes, it was a fine, fine thing. Some kind of Scandinavian design with soft leather and a gentle contour. Glenroy could relax in the swivel chair. Or he could spin around and look at whatever he wanted to look at.

Like the monitors. There wasn't much else to look at on the bridge. The dark night. The empty sea. The dials and gauges with their needles and numbers. Truth was, Glenroy was antsy, ready to leave the bridge. It was just so confining. Plus, he still needed to do a few things—very important things—elsewhere in the ship. But he couldn't risk leaving, not before he had forced Todora or the captain to give him the code. Until then he was stuck there.

The monitors made the bridge seem less confined—a multitude of windows onto the outside world, changing with rapid regularity, twenty images flashing at a time. Empty decks and hallways mostly. But every now and then a glimpse of people. The waiters, Felix and Marcos, stationed in the atrium. Shots of the casino, shots of the library. The crew, docile, some of them stretched out on blackjack tables, others sitting on the floor. And now a shot of the main dining room, a waiter moving across it—the one who had been sleeping, Benny—looking for the missing crew member.

At first, Glenroy had kept an almost constant eye on the monitors. But now he found that he could only watch them for a few seconds at a time. All those images coming at him. It just became too much. More than he could process.

He spun away, eased back in the chair, let his mind wander . . .

"Are you hungry, child?"

The woman had awakened him with a touch to his cheek. He sat up on the flattened boxes and grimy rags that had been his bed for weeks. A hidey-hole behind a pan yard off The Lady Young Road. He had picked the place because the men who played music there built big fires at night and sometimes roasted chickens or goats, eating while they drank overproof rum and banged their steel pans and prepared for Carnival. The two seasons of Trinidad—Carnival and getting ready for Carnival. After the men had gone home, he would pick through the bones they tossed into the fire, suck them dry. Sometimes he would find burnt pieces of bread, charred corncobs, maybe the husk of a mango that had escaped the flames, some sweets bits of flesh still clinging to it.

But the men had not gathered to play their music for several nights now. And yes, he was hungry.

The woman smiled at him. He had seen her a time or two before, walking through the neighborhood, sometimes alone, sometimes with other women dressed just like her. Long white robes with golden hems, white scarves wrapped tight around their heads. He had heard of angels. Surely, that is what they must be.

"What is your name, child?"

"Glenroy," he said.

"Do you have a surname?"

He thought about it. At one time, yes, there was another name. But he had a hard time recalling it. Just as he had a hard time recalling the tin shanty where he once lived, the other children, the women who lived there, too. His mother, one of them. He was unsure which one. It was so long ago. He was almost seven now.

"Glenroy Patterson," he said.

"A white man's name, a slave name," the woman said. "Did you know that?"

He shook his head, no.

The woman touched his cheek again.

"It is not the name for a proud young black man."

The woman took his hand, helped him to his feet.

"Come, child," she said. "We will feed you."

And so his new life began.

The madrasa was part of a twenty-acre compound owned by Islaam Karibe. A mosque, a dining hall, and two large dormitories, the dormitories strictly segregated, one for males, one for females.

Nearly a hundred people lived inside the compound and dozens of other followers came there throughout the day to answer the calls to prayer and to put in their hours of service, as prescribed by Imam Ben-Yafati. Some worked in the fields and groves surrounding the compound, harvesting yams and dasheen, citrus and mangoes. Others tended livestock, helped out in the laundry, or took part in the constant maintenance necessary to meet Imam Ben-Yafati's rigid standards. The men whitewashing the compound walls or painting and repainting the mosque's shiny golden dome. The women forever raking and sweeping, making sure the broad courtyard was without litter or blemish.

Shortly after Glenroy arrived at the compound, he began hearing talk that Imam Ben-Yafati would soon be coming there. The imam, Glenroy was told, lived on a grand estate in Port-of-Spain, overlooking Queen's Park Savannah, a place where he could properly receive the many dignitaries who came from all over the world to see him.

On the day of the imam's visit, there was a special ceremony in the compound. Imam Ben-Yafati stood alone on a small stage, a most imposing figure. Not an old man as Glenroy imagined he would be, but young, scarcely in his thirties, tall and strong, his shaved skull gleaming in the sun. He wore a white satin robe cinched at the waist by a gold sash, gold chains around his neck. Just before the ceremony began, one of the elders of the compound, a man with a long white beard, approached the stage carrying a pillow with a hat on it, a tall hat, shaped like a thick piece of bamboo, with gold embroidery. The imam placed it atop his head, raised his hands to the crowd. His deep voice boomed out over the courtyard. Glenroy didn't recognize the words the imam spoke, nor was he familiar with what the men and women chanted in response. It didn't matter. Glenroy was swept up by the moment, felt at one with the people around him, transfixed by this powerful man on the stage.

The ceremony continued for nearly an hour and as it neared its conclusion, Glenroy saw people turning and looking at him, felt hands gently urging him toward the stage. Two men lifted him up and placed him on the stage in front of Imam Ben-Yafati. The imam looked down at Glenroy and smiled. He put a hand atop Glenroy's head and told him to kneel.

"Today we welcome unto us this boy, a child once lost in the world. By Allah's will he came to us. Therefore we will raise him as one of our very own sons and he will become the man he was meant to be," the imam said. "Now, look at me, child."

Glenroy looked up at the imam. The sun was high overhead and the imam seemed to radiate in its glow.

"Today you are born anew. And we gather here not only to witness your birth, but to give you your one true name. Henceforth, my son, you will be called Inshallah Shaheed," the imam said. "It is a very powerful name, with a very powerful meaning. Inshallah Shaheed—Martyr by Will of God. Now speak your name, Inshallah Shaheed."

"Inshallah Shaheed," Glenroy said.

"Speak it loud, child, so everyone can hear."

"Inshallah Shaheed."

"Louder!"

"Inshallah Shaheed!" Glenroy shouted.

And then the crowd began shouting his name, too.

Inshallah Shaheed. Martyr by Will of God.

Glenroy had no idea what a martyr was. But he liked the sound of the name. It was a much better name than Glenroy Patterson, a name that meant nothing.

And as Imam Ben-Yafati took his hand and helped him to his feet, Glenroy faced the crowd and joined in shouting his name, shouting and shouting until it burned itself into his soul.

After that day, Glenroy enjoyed a special status within the compound. Along with a dozen or so other boys, some of them older, some of them younger, all of them orphans or children of the street, Glenroy was spared duty on the work details. For them, the days were wholly devoted to study—learning Arabic, memorizing the Qur'an, or, Glenroy's fondest pastime, reading tales of those who had died for their faith. Martyrs. Just like him.

He learned of Sumayyah bint Khabbab, the old woman of Mecca, the very first martyr, who was slain in the street by invaders when she refused to renounce her allegiance to Muhammad. And he reveled in the story of Husayn bin Ali, grandson of the prophet Muhammad, who was killed when his army of two hundred men went up against four thousand infidels at the Battle of Karbala.

Later he learned of modern-day martyrs—Ramzi Yousef, serving a life term in the U.S. for plotting the 1993 bombing in the parking garage of the World Trade Center; the proud warriors who gave their lives in a 1995 car bombing at a U.S. military housing complex in Dhahran, Saudi Arabia.

On his frequent visits to the madrasa, Imam Ben-Yafati would take Glenroy and the other privileged boys aside and tell them how Allah had entrusted them to Imam Ben-Yafati for equally high callings. He called them "my soldiers," and they alone out of all the followers of Islaam Karibe were permitted to sit side by side with Imam Ben-Yafati, as equals, and call him "Father."

"With his own hand, Allah has chosen you to do his will. Each of you has his own glorious destiny," he told them. "And when the day comes, I will reveal that destiny to you."

As some of the young men completed their studies and left the madrasa, stories of their exploits would make it back to the compound. Some had been sent to join various jihads, in Africa and the Middle East. Others were undergoing special military training at camps in Afghanistan and Sudan. Glenroy knew that some had died in these pursuits. While the exact details of their deaths were never discussed within the compound, photographs of these young men were enshrined in a small alcove outside the mosque.

Glenroy paused often there to honor them. He longed for the day when he, too, would go out into the world to meet his destiny.

23

We weren't gone from the cabin long, just fifteen or twenty minutes. First thing, they took our wallets. Then they herded us up to my suite on Deck Six, Parks and the maître d' standing in the hall, watching through the doorway, as the housekeeper followed me to the room safe.

I opened the safe. A couple thousand dollars in cash. An old Rolex Oyster that I had inherited from my grandfather. And one of Barbara's necklaces, a big black pearl on a braided gold pendant, a little something I'd given her for a birthday.

"Where is my wife?"

The housekeeper ignored me. She scooped everything out of the safe and dropped it into a laundry bag already bulging with cash and jewelry. She wore a brass nameplate on her uniform. "Todora," it read. And under her name: "Bulgaria." A nice little touch, letting you know where people come from. Just like they do at Disney World. Really makes you feel connected on a deep human level.

Todora turned to leave. I stood in the doorway, blocking her.

"Where is my wife?"

She pulled a pistol from an apron pocket, pointed it at me.

"Move," she said.

I backed out of the doorway and they marched us down the hall.

The same drill at Parks's cabin. I stood in the hallway with the maître d' while Parks and the housekeeper stepped inside.

From behind me, the maître d' whispered, "Your wife, she is with the others."

"Where?"

"It does not matter. She is fine."

"She's getting ready to have a baby."

The maître d' didn't say anything. The nameplate on his jacket read: "Pango. Indonesia."

"I need to see my wife," I told him. "I need to know she's alright."

"She is fine, I promise you . . ."

Inside Parks's suite, Todora slammed the safe shut.

"Quiet, Pango!" she shouted. "You fool. You tell them nothing. Do you understand? Nothing."

She nodded Parks out of the cabin and they escorted us away. We followed a different route this time, coming to a stairwell located more amidships. A diagram of the *Royal Star* was posted on a wall, but they hurried us along before I could make much out of it.

Passing Deck Five, I glanced down a corridor and caught a quick glimpse of two waiters, armed and standing in an atrium. I vaguely recalled walking through it when Barbara and I boarded the *Royal Star*. I couldn't remember what lay beyond it, but the fact that two waiters were stationed there had to mean something.

I stopped on the landing, turned to Todora.

"That where you're keeping them?"

She gave me a shove.

"Go," she said.

I've got a pretty good set of lungs on me. I can make a racket when I want to. I let it rip.

"Barbara! I'm here! Barbara . . . !"

I was still yelling when the maître d' jabbed his rifle in my gut and pushed me backward down the stairs, colliding with Parks, both of us tumbling onto the landing below. Parks got the worst of it, me falling on top of him.

And then the housekeeper was upon us, her pistol against the side of my head.

"Do that again and I shoot. Both of you. You hear me?"

I took her at her word. I helped Parks to his feet.

"Keep a lid on it, Chasteen," he growled. "I don't need this shit."

Todora kept her pistol drawn as she and Pango followed us down the stairs and back to Deck Two.

I slowed the pace when we entered the hallway, tried to take it all in. Counted cabin doors as we passed them—one on the left, one on the right, two, three, four. Saw a sign pointing to the laundry. Saw a red fire extinguisher clamped to a wall. Saw the waiter sitting in his chair, just like before.

The waiter stood as we approached, rifle leveled. There wasn't much to him. Scrawny guy with a pissant mustache. Just a kid.

We stopped at the door to our cabin. Todora opened it with her card key.

Kane Kinsey and Hurku Linblom sat on one of the beds, Ron Diamond opposite them. Parks and I filed into the cabin.

Todora said, "Now, the rest of you, come with us."

The others filed out. The door closed.

Carl Parks stretched out on one of the beds. He put his hands behind his head, made himself comfortable.

I didn't feel like stretching out. Barbara was somewhere three decks above me. I had to figure out a way to get to her.

I went into the bathroom. A cup sat on the edge of the sink. I filled it with water and drank some. Tasted like old eggs and ashes. I splashed the rest of it on my face, dried off with a sleeve.

I looked at myself in the mirror. My left ear was still caked with blood from the beating the waiters had given me on the main deck. A cut on my lip. Another cut under my right eye, the bruise blossoming out across the cheek.

I'd looked worse. But never had I felt worse. Not physical pain, but the hurt that comes from helplessness. I was captive in a tiny cabin on a ship bound for who knows where. My wife and child-to-be were in peril. And I had no clue what to do about it. I hurt bad.

I stepped out of the bathroom, looked up at the ceiling. I stood on the bed, pushed back the ceiling tile, stuck my head through the hole, and looked around. The crawlspace hadn't gotten any bigger since the last time I looked. No way my large self could maneuver up there.

I replaced the ceiling tile, stepped off the bed. Carl Parks was watching me. I still hadn't figured him out. Didn't know who he was or why he was here. One of those guys who didn't make an immediate first impression but after a while you got the idea there might be more to him than you originally thought.

I moved to the door, looked out the peephole. An empty hallway.

I calculated the odds of me being able to rush out the door, jump the waiter, beat hell out of him, get his gun, and then use it on Pango and Todora when they returned to Deck Two. Call it a million-to-one shot. And that was if I could figure out the goddam gun. I don't much like guns.

Don't own one. And any experience I've ever had with one has always ended, shall we say, ignominiously. No, I couldn't count on doing much with the gun.

I could always use the old Naked Man ploy. I had seen it work, oh, twenty years earlier when I was in college up at Gainesville. The season was over—we'd beaten Syracuse in the Gator Bowl—and three of us, Mac Steen, Larry-Bud Meyer, and me, decided we needed a road trip. Wound up at a joint in the Panhandle where we proceeded to behave in a way that only college jocks can behave when massive amounts of beer are involved and good-looking women are present. Actually, they might not have been all that good looking. Doesn't matter. We did not endear ourselves to the local populace, which included a sizable contingent of fighter pilots-in-training from the Naval Air Station in Pensacola.

When it comes to unseemly displays in public, fighter pilots can out-asshole college jocks most any day. Still, we were giving them a good run. And the shoving had already begun when Mac Steen suddenly decided he needed to use the men's room.

"Where you going, college boy?" one of the pilots hollered after him. "Home to momma?"

"Taking a leak," Mac said. "Then I'm gonna whip some Navy ass."

He walked off, leaving me and Larry-Bud to contend with the six of them. They had us backed up in a corner when I heard a loud whoop, the bar crowd parted, and there was Mac Steen, naked as a newborn, barreling toward us.

There is something about a naked man—a naked man running at you from out of nowhere, all floppity-flop and howling—that can give one pause. And that little bit of pause is all a naked man needs.

Mac took down three of the pilots. Larry-Bud and I held our own with the other three. And by the time the cops got there we were all of us fought out and ready to be friendly again.

Yeah, I could try that on the waiter in the hall.

I recalculated the odds. Call it nine hundred thousand to one. And not only would I be dead, I'd be butt-naked dead. Not my idea of going out in a blaze of glory.

That's when Parks said, "I could use your help, Chasteen."

"We all could use some help right now."

"The help I need, it's special."

"Yeah?"

"Yeah," Parks said. "Twenty million dollars special."

It got my attention.

Parks said, "What if I were to tell you there was twenty million dollars on this ship. Twenty million dollars. Cash."

I looked at him. Then I looked at him some more.

"Talk to me," I said.

24

Parks said he had to explain fast, before Ron Diamond returned to the cabin.

"Because a big chunk of that twenty million, it's his," Parks said.

"And the rest of it?"

Parks shrugged.

"Some of it belongs to our gracious host, Sam Jebailey. Some to parties who are known to us, but who are not on this ship. And the rest, about two million, belongs to us."

"Us?"

"I'm with ice," Parks said.

It took a moment for it to sink in. ICE. Immigration and Customs Enforcement. Part of the behemoth federal agency that was now Homeland Security.

Parks read my skepticism. He patted his back pocket, where his wallet used to be.

"It's not like I've got ID, Chasteen."

"Talk some more," I said.

The way Parks told it, he was part of an investigation that had been in the works for nearly four years, getting the goods on various enterprises that moved huge sums of cash out of the U.S., narco-profit mostly. His word, "narco-profit." It included money that had been laundered in all kinds of creative ways, from casinos and car dealerships to real estate. Which was where Ron Diamond entered the picture.

"Money launderer to the stars," said Parks. "The stars being some very bad people who call Colombia home."

I sat down on the bed across from him.

"So why is the twenty million on this ship?"

"Because these days, it's getting to be a giant pain in the ass to move large amounts of cash out of the country. I'd like to think that ICE is largely responsible for that. The human courier business just ain't what it used to be," Parks said. "You know how much a million dollars weighs, don't you, Chasteen?"

I had a pretty good idea, my past experience being what it was, but I shook my head no.

Parks shrugged.

"OK, play it your way, I don't care. Twenty-two pounds, that's what it weighs. Hell, my aunt Bessie could carry that. And she's dead." Parks grinned. "Trouble is, it's goddam bulky. About four shoe boxes' worth. Still, you could cram it in a good-size suitcase. Or tape it on your body, wear a baggy coat, take your chances. But more and more, we're making it not worth taking chances. So far this year, at the Bogota airport alone, working with Colombian authorities, we've confiscated more than twenty-seven million dollars from individual couriers. Just a trickle from an ever-rising river, but it's having an effect. Until the goddam euro does us in, that is."

"What's the euro have to do with it?"

"You living in the twenty-first century, Chasteen? You follow the news?"

"As much as I have to."

"Well, then you know that thanks to this fucked-up economy of ours the euro is worth a helluva lot more than the dollar. Be that as it may, the hundred-dollar bill remains the preferred medium for smuggling cash. It's got a lot of tradition going for it, beloved the wide world over. But it's not like the creeps are a sentimental bunch. That's why the five-hundred-euro bill is starting to come into play, especially through the cartels working out of Spain, where more and more of them are opening shop. Five hundred euros, current market, is worth better than seven hundred fifty dollars. Hell, using euros you can carry a quarter million dollars in your fucking pants pockets. The five-hundred-euro bill, I'm telling you, it's a goddam nightmare. Which is why our government has been lobbying those pointy-head bastards who run the EU to limit its circulation. Don't know that we'll win that one. It's a dicks-on-the-table kind of thing. And right now, they've got the biggest dicks."

Parks got up from the bed, went to the door, looked out the peephole. He turned around, leaned back against the door.

"But it's not my job to worry about the euro. My guys, we're chasing dollars. And we're busting hump," he said. "We've pretty much shut down the goddam wire transfers. Used to be, it was a fairly easy thing for someone to make a deposit in a U.S. bank, less than ten thousand dollars, it went under the federal radar, and then go to the Western Union or wherever and wire that money to a foreign country, to family members."

Parks wiggling his fingers, making quote marks when he said family members.

"Even the laziest creep, working a few hours a day, driving around a big city, wiring from a different place each time, used to be he could move half a million dollars in a week. We did a little snooping around—thank you, Patriot Act—and found out that more than four billion dollars left the U.S. in wire transfers to Colombia in 2001. Ain't no way all that was just paying the electric bills for the mamacitas back home. Bottom line: Thanks to new laws, wire transfers are restricted to three thousand dollars or less and all the details of who sends what to whom goes into a central data system. You got people crying about how it's an invasion of privacy. Fuck 'em. It's working. We're putting creeps in jail."

"So how does Sam Jebailey figure into it?"

"Bright boy, Jebailey. He sees the future—bulk cash smuggling. And by bulk, I'm talking tens of millions at a time. We've had some success at stopping it. Couple months back, at Mexico City International, we found seven-point-eight million dollars stuffed into the hydraulic cylinders of an AeroMexico jet bound for Cartagena."

"Jebailey was involved with that?"

Parks shook his head.

"No, Jebailey has even bigger ideas."

"Like what?"

"Like I told you," he said. "We're sitting on it."

"He's using the *Royal Star* to smuggle cash out of the U.S.?"

Parks nodded.

"That's his business plan. And, I gotta hand it to him, it's a brilliant one, really. Get the bad guys to foot the bill for building a ritzy-titsy ship, then charge rich people twenty thousand dollars a week to go cruising on it. All the while it's just a scumbag transport operation, moving dirty money, lots and lots of it, from lots of different clients like Ron Diamond and a few others, moving it from one place to another. The brilliant part being that it's high profile as hell and cloaked with the respectability that comes from having the crème de la crème on board. I mean, who would ever suspect it?"

I sat there thinking about it. Parks looked out the peephole again.

I said, "But whoever these people are, the ones who've taken over the ship, they don't know about the twenty million dollars."

"No," said Parks. "I don't think so."

"Because why would they waste time taking our wallets and emptying room safes?"

"Exactly."

"And if they were terrorists . . ."

"Same thing. Terrorists wouldn't bother with the chump change either. They'd be making demands or blowing up things."

"So who are they?"

Parks shrugged.

"Bunch of pissed-off crew members trying to make a quick haul? I don't know. And I don't really care as long as they don't unravel everything I've worked four years putting together."

Parks studied me for a moment. I studied him back. I had a pretty good idea what was coming next.

"I know things about you, Chasteen."

I didn't say anything.

The previous few years had been good ones. I'd met a smart, gorgeous woman and somehow convinced her that her life would be more meaningful if I were a permanent part of it. We had a baby on the way. The glory days stretched out ahead of us. What was there to kick about?

Sure, that one year, nine months, and twenty-three days that I spent at Baypoint Federal Prison Camp, I'd like to have them back. But the people who set me up, I'd gotten even with them. My good name had been restored. Well, as much as it ever will be. And the whole experience, while nothing I'd recommend to anyone seeking self-improvement, had served to put my worldview into sharp, clear focus.

I did plenty of reading while I was in prison. Worked my way through stacks of books, including most everything by Shakespeare. I had latched on to that famous line from Hamlet, the one where Polonius bids his son farewell and tells him "to thine own self be true." That's the line that gets all the attention, anyway. And it would seem to suggest that we all do as we damn well please and to hell with everyone else.

But it's the next line that spins the real meaning, Polonious saying: "And it must then follow, as the night the day, thou canst not then be false to any man."

You can't be true to yourself if you don't play honest with others.

Which is not to say that my life post-prison had been a model of righteous living. Circumstances had from time to time forced me to affiliate myself with certain people who made a living outside the law. Way outside the law. And I had profited from those affiliations.

The money I got, I never worried where it came from. I just knew that I had worked hard for it. The people who paid me, I played them honest. Any mirror I passed, I could look myself straight in the eye.

And so here we were, Parks saying he knew things about me.

"You've got a friend in Jamaica by the name of Freddie Arzghanian . . ."

"Not exactly a friend."

"A business associate then."

"Not even that. I helped him out once."

"And he helped you. Made a couple of million dollars suddenly appear in a correspondent account bearing your name at the National Bank of Bermuda."

I didn't say anything.

Parks said, "That money disappeared a few months back. We're not quite sure where it went . . ."

"That's because someone stole it from me."

"But you got it back."

"I got it back."

"And now you'd like to keep it, right?"

Nut-cutting time.

"Is this the part where you ask for my help but it's not like I really have a choice?"

"Yeah," Parks said. "Something like that."

25

They had left Kane Kinsey's suite on Deck Six and moved to Hurku Linblom's room. Todora was ransacking its safe when Linblom collapsed on the floor beside her.

Todora glanced down at Linblom, saw him gasping for air, his face gray.

"Please," Linblom said.

Todora ignored him, finishing with the safe, removing a small amount of cash and a gold bracelet. It went into a second laundry bag, the first one already filled and sitting now in the purser's office along with the cash taken from the casino and the *Royal Star*'s main safe.

Linblom tried to pull himself up, fell back to the floor.

"Please, my medicine."

Pango was just outside the open door, keeping an eye on Kane Kinsey and Ron Diamond. Kinsey darted into the room and knelt beside Linblom.

"You OK, man?"

"My medicine," Linblom said, reaching an arm toward the bathroom. Kinsey got up and headed in that direction.

"Stop!" Todora shouted. "What are you doing?"

Kinsey turned to her. "Look, the guy's in bad shape. All he needs is his medication. Just let me get it and everything's cool. OK?"

Todora thought about it. She looked at Pango.

"You," she said. "Stay here with the two of them. I will go with the other one."

Pango didn't like it. Glenroy had made it clear that Pango was not to let Todora out of his sight. But she was already moving past him, pointing Diamond down the hallway.

Pango stepped into Linblom's room. The old man did not look good.

Pango pulled a pillow from the couch and placed it under the old man's head.

"Just breathe," Pango said. "I'll get you some water."

"So you are famous rich man, huh?"

Todora watched Ron Diamond as he stepped to his room safe.

"Yeah," Diamond said. "That's what they tell me."

"Queen Latifah, you know her?"

"Not personally, no."

"So you cannot be that famous, eh?"

"I know some of her people, OK? I don't know her. I know lots of people who are bigger, way bigger, than Queen Latifah. Trust me."

"Queen Latifah, she is very good. *Set It Off*? Did you see it?"

Diamond shook his head, no, as he punched the safe's code.

"She play bank robber. And car thief. Very good. The money, all she wants it for is to fix up her car. And to spend on her girlfriend. She play lesbian. Very good."

Diamond opened the safe and stepped aside as Todora swooped in. She reached into the safe and came out with a two-inch stack of hundred-dollar bills, a paper wrapper holding them together. She flipped through them, impressed.

"Twenty-five thousand," Diamond said.

"Nice," Todora said. "Now, we go."

She nodded Diamond toward the door. When they got there, Diamond turned around to face her, easing the door shut behind him.

He said, "Maybe you and me, we could work something out."

Todora studied him, not saying anything.

"There's more money," Diamond said. "Much more."

Todora's eyes darted around the room.

Diamond said, "It's not in here."

"Where is it then?"

"Well," Diamond said, "that's the problem."

26

I've got to hand it to Jebailey. Guy does things first class," Parks said. "I drive into Miami the night before the ship is set to cruise, he puts me up in a suite at the Mandarin Oriental on Brickell Key. Got a view of Biscayne Bay that will break your heart and a brand-new Halliburton sitting on the master bed, waiting for me to fill it up."

"Halliburton," I said. "Those big ugly aluminum suitcases."

"Best big ugly aluminum suitcases that money can buy. After Erle Halliburton, that's Erle without the 'A,' same Halliburton that sucks up all the government contracts, the one Cheney worked for. Anyway, the new twenty-six-inch Zero Halliburton Carry-On, you can get it in chocolate or silver, goes for about twelve hundred a pop. You put something in it, buddy, it's locked up tight."

"And so you put two million dollars in the Halliburton?"

"Yeah, and Jebailey sends a driver around to pick it up. Old Cuban guy in a chauffeur's uniform. Speaks exactly no English. He takes the money and he hands me my boarding pass for getting on the ship the next day."

"A little perk for doing business with Jebailey."

"Yeah, like I say, the guy does things right. I mean, he's getting six percent for moving the money, so figure I'm paying him, what's that, a hundred twenty grand for a boat ride."

Parks gave the peephole another look.

I said, "What about Diamond? How much is he in for?"

"I'm thinking four million or so. Don't know exactly."

"And the rest of it?"

"Like I said, some of it is Jebailey's, the people he moves money for. The rest it's split between two guys—Andrew Beeker, out of San Diego, and Charles Hoffmeister, lives in Miami. Both of them attorneys. Both very, very slick. Neither one of them is on the ship."

"Why's that?"

Parks shrugged.

"Who needs the aggravation? That's the beauty of this boat. You can put your money on it and let Jebailey take care of the rest."

"So why's Diamond on board? Seems like he wouldn't want to risk getting caught if something went wrong."

"Because he's Ronald Big-Deal Diamond, that's why. Loves the glitz, loves the glamour, all the pretty people. Wanted to show off that new girlfriend of his. Gets off on the thrill of being closely connected to bad guys and no one knowing for the better. Besides, it's not like he can personally be tied to anything. It's not like he gives four million to Jebailey, gets a receipt, and we can use that against him in court. Doesn't work like that."

"So how does it work?"

"How it works, we're after people bigger than Diamond, bigger than Jebailey even. We want Jebailey to make a few successful runs so we can get a better handle on how all the money spreads out. Like after it gets deposited in St. Kitts . . ."

"Is that where we're headed, St. Kitts?"

"Where we *were* headed. Until the shitstorm hit," Parks said. "But yeah, St. Kitts. All those smiling schoolkids Jebailey was talking about, lining the dock to greet us and get their hands on those computers? A sweet piece of PR on his part. A nifty bit of distraction. Meanwhile, all those Halliburtons, I'm guessing ten of them, are rolling into the offices of Sovereign Bank, Ltd., in downtown Basseterre. Which is owned and operated by guess who?"

"That would be ICE?"

"Bingo," Parks said. "Biggest sting operation in agency history. We set up an offshore bank, take in the money, watch where it goes. Then we lower the fucking boom."

"That's all real nice," I said. "What I'm not clear on—how am I supposed to help you?"

"By making sure these assholes don't find the twenty million dollars."

"Where is it?"

Parks looked away.

"Don't know."

"You don't know?"

Parks shook his head.

I said, "So let me get this straight. You don't want someone to find something, only you don't know where that something is. So you want to find it before they find it and then keep on making sure they don't find it."

"You make it sound more complicated than it really is, Chasteen."

"Maybe you could explain what's simple about it."

"The simple part is, I get Jebailey to tell me where the money is."

"Why would he do that?"

"Because part of it is my money."

"It's ICE's money, Parks."

Parks waved me off.

"You're missing the point, Chasteen. The point is, these guys find that twenty million dollars, there goes four years of work down the drain."

"And there goes a big promotion for you."

Parks looked at me, didn't say anything.

I said, "Don't see why I should risk my ass just so you can get bumped up a pay grade."

Parks started to say something, stopped.

Finally, he said, "Look, there's a lot at stake here. I just wanted you to see the big picture, understand my motivation." He looked at me. "Plus, there could be something in it for you."

I waited.

Parks said, "Think of it as a fee for services rendered, a very handsome fee. All on the down-low, of course. The way you like it."

I didn't say anything.

Parks said, "Don't tell me it doesn't interest you, Chasteen."

"It doesn't interest me," I said.

"Oh, really? That surprises me."

"Well, maybe that's because you're the one needs to see the big picture, Parks, understand my motivation."

"What, you think our plan strikes a little too close to home? Afraid that by setting up a fake bank to launder money through St. Kitts we might lower the boom on someone who is near and dear to you, one of your business associates?"

"That's not it at all."

"Well, then," he said, "please illuminate me."

"It's like this—one way or another, I'm getting out of here. And when I do there'll be nothing I'm interested in except finding my wife, making sure she's OK, and settling the hash of anyone who would have it otherwise. That twenty million dollars? It isn't even a blip on my radar. You got that?"

Parks smiled.

"Very nobly spoken," he said. "Far be it from me to force money on you for being a good citizen and helping out your government."

"Like I said, helping out my government is not my top priority here."

"Duly noted," Parks said.

He looked through the peephole, said, "Here they come."

He stepped away from the door and looked at me.

"Just help get us out of here, Chasteen, and that's all the help I need. Do that and I'll do whatever I can to help you. And your wife. We good on that?"

I nodded. Parks stuck out his hand. I was shaking it when we heard the click of the card key in the door.

27

Pango held the door open while Kane Kinsey and Hurku Linblom filed past him, Kinsey walking Linblom to one of the beds, helping him lie down.

The door closed shut.

Parks said, "Where's Diamond?"

Kinsey shook his head.

"Last I saw, that woman was taking him to his room. Then she came back and told that maître d' guy to bring us back down here. I never saw her or Diamond after that." Kinsey turned his attention back to Hurku Linblom. "You doing alright?"

Linblom nodded.

"Much better, thank you. It is my heart. They say I need one more surgery. Until then, I cannot miss my medication."

I went to the door and looked out the peephole.

Instead of going to the next cabin and escorting its occupants away, Pango was exiting the hallway alone. Not what I'd hoped. I'd been timing the comings and goings and figured we had a fifteen-to-twenty-minute window of opportunity when Pango and Todora would be occupied elsewhere, taking valuables from the room safes. Now it was anyone's guess when they might turn up down here again.

I sat down on the bed across from Linblom.

"You feeling up to a few questions?"

"Of course," he said. "What do you wish to know?"

"Say we get lucky and take out the guy in the hall. Maybe it buys us a little time before the others get wind of what we're up to. What's our best plan of attack? Where should we head, what should we do?"

"The lifeboats," Linblom said. "On the main deck."

"Lower them?"

Linblom shook his head.

"No, there will not be time for that. There are cameras throughout the ship and you must presume that someone is watching the monitors from the bridge. From the time you set foot in the hallway, you may have no more than a minute or two before the rest of them are alerted that something is wrong," he said. "But if you can make it to the main deck, each of the lifeboats is equipped with an emergency signaling device. It's in an orange bag under the bow. Just pull the cord. It sends out a universal distress call, monitored by satellite. Any ship within range must respond. This close still to U.S. waters, the Coast Guard will also get the call. Plus, the lifeboats have flares. You can use them to signal another ship, show your location."

"OK," I said. "Say we manage to do that. What then?"

Linblom thought about it.

"The ship's marina," he said. "Like I tell you, it will be impossible to lower the lifeboats. They are out in the open. You will be seen. But the ship's marina. There are boats there, too. Two skiffs with outboard motors. Several Jet Skis. The ship's tender. Maybe you can reach them. Maybe someone can get away, get help."

"Where's the marina?"

"Deck Three, at the stern. It shares a space with the main provisions storage area. A rear hatchway opens to launch boats."

"But there are cameras watching it, too, right?"

Linblom nodded.

"Cameras everywhere," he said.

"Any way to disable them?"

"Short of destroying them one by one, the only way is by tapping into the ship's internal security system. And that requires at least three levels of access codes. None of which I know."

"Who knows them?"

"Well, the captain, of course. Other ship's officers. But . . ."

He stopped. We had seen what happened to three of the officers on the main deck and had no reason to believe any others were still alive.

"On most ships there is a communications officer whose job would entail such matters," Linblom said. "But Mr. Jebailey was adamant that the *Royal Star* have the latest technology and, frankly, few officers of the line were up to his standards. He chose to outsource the position with a private contractor that supplied a network technician."

"An IT guy," Parks said.

"Yes, I suppose," Linblom said. "I met the young man briefly. A Korean fellow, don't remember his name."

"So unless we find him," I said, "we don't stand much chance of either disabling the cameras or getting the ship's communications back online?"

"Sadly, yes," Linblom said.

I got up from the bed. There was a small closet along one wall. I slid open its door, looked around. Black shoes and sneakers on the floor. Towels, T-shirts, and underwear folded and stacked on shelves. White shirts and blue plants on plastic hangers hooked over a plastic rod. Nothing that would do us any good.

I went into the bathroom, grabbed hold of the shower curtain rod, shook it. Hollow aluminum. Worthless.

I opened the cabinet under the sink, got down on my hands and knees, and looked inside. PVC pipe. Better. But too many bends and elbows to serve our purposes.

I went back to the bed I'd been sitting on. I pulled off its blanket and sheet. I removed the flimsy mattress and propped it in a corner.

"Dude, what are you doing?" Kane Kinsey said.

The bed's frame was welded to the floor, five metal crossbars attached to it to support the mattress. I knelt and examined the crossbars—about four inches wide and fastened to the frame with tiny knobs in narrow slots. Thank you, Sam Jebailey, for cheaping out on the crew quarters.

I grabbed one of the crossbars and, after a few violent wrenches, succeeded in prying it loose. It was about three feet long with an L-shaped shaft configuration that was hardly ideal for getting a good grip. But it was all we had.

I slapped it against the palm of my hand. Yeah, it would work.

"Gentlemen," I said, "meet your weapons."

CALL TO ARMS

28

They stopped outside a door at the end of the hallway on Deck Six, the forward end, directly below the bridge. A plaque on the door read: "The Sultan's Suite."

Todora said, "Jebailey, he stay here."

She stuck her card key into the lock, opened the door, motioned Ron Diamond inside. She stepped in behind him and closed the door.

Diamond stood there, taking in the main salon: Gauzy damask sheets billowing from the ceiling all the way down to the floor. Overstuffed sitting pillows atop oriental carpets. Settees with elaborate silk embroidery. Tapestries on the walls. Shiny brass tables with shiny brass urns. The whole thing looking like a movie version of *A Thousand and One Arabian Nights* that had run way, way over budget.

"Is beautiful, no?"

"It's something alright," Diamond said.

Todora moved beside him, said, "The money, you are certain it is in here?"

"No, I'm not. But if I were Sam Jebailey, this is where I would keep it."

"OK, then," Todora said, stepping into the salon. "We find it."

"Not so fast," Diamond said.

Todora stopped.

Diamond said, "Before we go any farther, we need to agree on something, you and me."

"What is to agree? We find the money. I take it. That is that."

"Then what?"

"And then . . ." Todora stopped. "Then it is not your business."

"Do you even have a plan?"

"Why, yes, of course we have plan."

"Let me hear it."

Todora thought about it.

She said, "There is a boat. It will meet us."

Diamond laughed.

"That's your plan? Seriously?"

"It is Glenroy's plan."

"Glenroy? Who's he?"

"The one who is in charge. The one who bought the guns. The one who makes all this happen."

"And so this Glenroy guy, he has arranged a boat to pick you up. Any idea where this boat of his is going to take you?"

Todora looked at him.

"That I will not tell you."

"OK, then, let me guess," Diamond said. "Cuba."

Todora didn't say anything.

"That's it, isn't it? Cuba."

Todora didn't say anything.

"Of course, it's Cuba," Diamond said. "Cuba, the place everyone thinks they can just run off to and disappear, avoid the law."

"It is enemy of America. We will be safe there."

"Safe?" Diamond laughed. "Oh, yeah, you'll be safe alright. Safe in a Cuban prison. Then maybe, depending on what kind of mood the Cuban government is in, maybe they'll ship you back to the U.S. to stand trial. They would do that, you know. They've done it before, several times actually, when some fool has hijacked a plane and sought asylum there. They've shipped them straight back to the U.S. It's a political thing. Makes Cuba look good. They can say 'We don't harbor terrorists' and crap like that."

"We are not terrorists," Todora said.

"Sorry, lady. You hijack a cruise ship, you're a terrorist. And you get on this boat of yours and go sailing up to Cuba and one of their gunboats stops you—because that's what they do, they stop everyone—you're terrorists with bagfuls of money and jewelry. Which they will confiscate from you before they throw you in prison and no one will ever see it again." Diamond shook his head. "Oh, yeah, this is some brilliant plan you've got, you and this Glenroy guy and your . . ."

"No more!" Todora said.

She stormed off, moving through the salon, into the master suite. Diamond heard her tearing through things, slamming drawers.

By the time he got there, she was standing at the entrance to the closet staring at something. Diamond stepped beside her, saw the Halliburton sitting upright against a closet wall.

Todora said, "The money, it is in there?"

Diamond looked at the Halliburton, trying to decide if it was one of the two suitcases that he had filled, that Jebailey had sent to his hotel. He couldn't tell. The Halliburtons all looked alike. Diamond thought: *This is one of them, so where are all the rest?* Thought: *It's OK, don't worry, she doesn't know how many of them there really are.* Diamond didn't know either, but he knew it was more than just this one.

Diamond said, "Yes, that's the money."

"How much?"

"Two million," he said.

Todora stepped to the suitcase. She turned it on its side, fiddled with the latches.

"Forget it," Diamond said. "You don't have the key you're not opening that without a jackhammer."

Todora stepped back from the suitcase. She stood there looking at it. Diamond, looked at it, too, thinking: *Why would Jebailey do this? Why leave one of them here and not the others?*

Diamond said, "How many of you are there?"

Todora looked at him. She didn't say anything.

Diamond said, "What, seven or eight of you? This Glenroy guy, you, the waiters, whoever else you've got. How many?"

"There are nine," Todora said.

"Nine."

"Yes, nine."

"That's a lot of people."

Todora shrugged.

Diamond said, "Do you really want to split all this money with the rest of them?"

Todora didn't say anything.

Diamond said, "I've got a boat. A big boat. In the Bahamas. This boat, it has a helicopter."

Todora looked at him, interested now.

Diamond smiled.

"Now, you want to hear a real plan?"

29

This time it took Kane Kinsey less than forty minutes to negotiate the crawl space, reach the other cabins, and let everyone know how it would go down.

"They buy into it?" I asked him after he returned.

"Yeah, mostly. A few of them, they didn't want any part of it. Said they thought it was crazy."

"That's because it is crazy," I said. "But unless someone has a better idea . . ."

I looked at the others. Parks and Kinsey held their metal crossbars, anxious, jittery. Hurku Linblom was still lying down. He was in no condition to join us. Still, he'd insisted upon a crossbar of his own. It rested beside him on the bed.

I checked the time—3:56 A.M. Kinsey had taken my watch with him, synchronizing with the other cabins. We still had a few minutes.

"We all clear on what we're doing?"

Parks and Kinsey nodded.

"I go with you," Parks said.

"And I go for the camera," Kinsey said.

I looked at my watch again—3:57. This was the worst part, the waiting.

I visualized the hall outside, the waiter sitting halfway down it. And again, I sensed another subtle shift in the ship's course, farther still to the south, maybe arcing slightly to the west now. Then again, my inner compass might have been totally out of whack.

Parks said, " 'Half a league, half a league/Half a league onward.' "

I looked at him.

"Tennyson, *Charge of the Light Brigade*," he said. "English lit, eleventh grade. We had to memorize it."

"Thought it rang a bell."

Parks said, " 'Into the jaws of death/Into the mouth of hell/Rode the six hundred.' "

"Not quite that many of us."

"No," Parks said. "But riding into a world of hurt, all that, it's the same."

"I forget how it ended," I said. "Those six hundred, they make it out alive?"

"Some of 'em did, some of 'em didn't. But their courage made them immortal."

"Gee," I said. "I'm feeling better about this already."

I looked at my watch—3:58.

I moved to the door, Parks and Kinsey behind me.

I eased the door open, slid into the alcove. Parks and Kinsey squeezed in beside me.

I looked left, down the hall, to where the waiter was sitting, rifle across his lap. He sat sideways to us, gazing straight ahead, down one of the corridors that intersected the main hallway. I still had no idea where those corridors led, what might be down them. I should have asked Linblom, but it was too late for that now.

Across the hall, the cabin opposite ours, the door cracked open. A face peered out. The door opened wider. Out stepped a middle-aged man, close-cropped gray hair, glasses, pudgy around the middle. I vaguely recalled seeing him at the bon voyage party, a few tables away from Barbara and me. He held a crossbar at his side.

The man looked scared. Which, given what we were about to attempt, is how any sane person should have looked. Behind him, I could make out two other people in the doorway, couldn't really tell much about them.

I gave the man a thumbs-up. He gave me one back. He didn't look any less scared when he did it.

I looked right, down the hall, toward the stairwell. I couldn't see anyone, but shifting light on the alcove walls told me doors were opening.

I looked back at the waiter. No change. But just beyond him, from one of the alcoves, I saw a face quickly peek out and then pull back.

I looked at my watch—3:59.

30

Glenroy had just finished readjusting the *Royal Star*'s course—plotting the coordinates yet again, making sure the ship was slowly zeroing in on its destination—when there came a pounding on the bridge door. He let Pango in and listened as the maître d' said what he had to say.

"What do you mean, you don't know where she is?"

"She tell me she take the man, Diamond, to another cabin," Pango said.

"Which cabin?"

Pango shook his head. "She not say where. She tell me stay with the other two."

"And you just let her go? I put you in charge and you let her tell you what to do?"

Glenroy fuming now, glaring down at Pango.

"I will find her," Pango said.

"Just like you have found the missing crew member?"

Pango hung his head. He didn't say anything.

Glenroy stepped to the bank of monitors, studied them for a moment. No sign of Todora and Diamond in any of the hallways. Everything under control in the lounge, the atrium, the casino, the library.

Glenroy turned from the monitors, brought his full rage to bear once again on Pango.

He said, "When the boat comes to take us to Cuba, do you want to be on it?"

"Why yes, of course."

"Then you will find her."

Pango nodded.

Glenroy said, "And when you find her, you will bring her to me. Do you understand?"

Pango nodded again.

And Glenroy envisioned how he would do it, binding Todora to a chair, then starting in on her with a knife, the first cuts to her forehead, blood streaming down her face, stinging her eyes, staining her lips, letting her taste her life seeping out. Then he would remove things—fingers, toes, the tip of her nose. Until she gave up the security code to the bridge. And then he would be done with her.

Pango's eyes going wide now as he looked past Glenroy to the monitors, his mouth opening, but no words coming out.

Glenroy turned to see a flash of images—men, lots of men, racing down a hallway, their backs to the camera. And now the face of one man, a young man with a wispy beard, looking up at the camera before swinging something, a metal bar, and the monitor suddenly going blank.

Pango shouted, "Deck Two!"

Glenroy grabbed his rifle. He lurched for the bridge door, punched the green button, and, after the door opened, hit the yellow button to keep it from closing again.

He shot a final look at the monitors, saw men converging in a hallway, a pack of them, swinging wildly at something on the floor.

And then he and Pango were gone.

31

It was over in seconds . . .

Parks and me, leading the charge, yelling and hollering, alerting the others—game on . . .

The waiter, spotting us, leaping to his feet, fumbling to get a grip on his rifle . . .

Behind the waiter, from the alcove nearest him, two men wielding crossbars, one of them striking a blow against the back of the waiter's head, the other his neck.

The waiter dropping to his knees, falling forward . . .

Then all of us were upon the waiter, kicking and swinging, crossbars crashing down, until he lay still on the floor.

More men rushing out of cabins, gathering in the hall. I saw Captain Falk staggering toward us, a hand on the wall for support. Sam Jebailey appeared behind him, holding back, stopping to take it all in.

Kane Kinsey ran up to join us, breathing hard.

"I got the camera down at that end," he said. And then he was off, to the other end of the hall, past Falk and Jebailey. He found a second camera mounted against the ceiling and knocked it out of commission, too.

Men peered over the backs of other men, looking down at the bloodied waiter.

"Holy shit," someone said.

Someone else said, "Is he dead?"

It was Parks who reached down and pulled the rifle from under the waiter. He put a finger to the side of the waiter's neck.

"He's still alive," Parks said.

"Tie him up," I told no one in particular. "Use bedsheets or something."

Men grabbed the waiter by the legs and hauled him away.

Parks was turning the rifle over, tapping its ammo clip, checking it out.

"You know how to use that thing?" I asked him.

"Think I can figure it out," he said.

The way we planned it, Parks and I would beat a path up to Deck Six and the lifeboats, set off a distress signal. After that, we'd race down to Deck Three and the marina. If we could manage to somehow launch one of the boats or a Jet Ski, then Parks would head off on that. And I'd go looking for Barbara.

After that . . . well, after that we'd be playing it as it lay.

All eyes were on Parks and me, waiting to hear what came next.

"Good job," I told them. "Now, just hang down here until you get the all clear."

"What if you don't make it?" someone asked.

"Then keep trying," I said. "Just remember, there's more of us than them."

For rallying the troops, it wasn't much. But it was all I had.

Parks and I turned to go, heading for the stairwell at the end of the hall.

"I'm going with you."

It was Captain Falk. He made his way through the other men and hobbled toward us, using a metal crossbar for a cane. His white uniform was covered in blood, an eye swollen shut.

I said, "You sure about that?"

He nodded.

"This is my ship. Those were my men they killed."

We hadn't factored Falk into the plan, didn't know that he would be up to it. But there was no doubting his determination. And with him knowing the ship's layout, its systems and security codes, it was one much-needed advantage against a whole lot of firepower.

I told him we planned to head straight for the lifeboats.

"Yes, good, that first," he agreed. "And then to the bridge."

32

I set out for the stairs, Parks following me, Captain Falk bringing up the rear as best he could. The stairwell was enclosed on the lower two decks, but became an open spiral as it reached the Deck Three landing.

From somewhere—footsteps pounding. I looked up and saw Pango and another man three flights above and heading our way. I'd never seen the other man before. Not one of the waiters. A big man, a black man in a blue jumpsuit. But before I could warn Parks and Captain Falk, a flurry of gunshots peppered the banister and I dove into the Deck Three hallway.

Parks and Captain Falk froze on the landing between the decks as more gunshots tore into the steps that separated us. Parks got off a couple of wild shots in a general upward direction, effective only in that they succeeded in putting a momentary stop to Pango and the other guy. I couldn't see them, but no longer heard them running, imagined them angling for position so they could get a better shot at us.

The hallway gave me some protection, but Parks and Falk were exposed with a dozen stairs between us. I motioned them to drop back down to Deck Two.

"Don't risk it," I said. "Protect the other guys."

Parks said, "What about you?"

No way were we getting up to the lifeboats. Not right now anyway. I pointed down the Deck Three hallway. The marina was at the end of it somewhere.

"Going that way," I said.

As I started off, Captain Falk moved past Parks to join me. Shots showered down, tearing into the landing, hitting Falk as he fell in my direction. I dragged him off the landing and into the cover of the hallway.

He was hit in half a dozen places, maybe more. Too much blood to tell for sure. Spilling out of him, onto me, onto the floor.

I looked across the landing at Parks. He was coiled, ready to make a dash to join us. I waved him back. And as more shots struck the landing, he beat a retreat to Deck Two.

Captain Falk stared up at me, chest heaving, struggling for air. There was nothing I could do for him, nothing.

"Go," he said.

"I'll get to the lifeboats," I said.

He closed his eyes, nodded.

"And the bridge," he said.

"Yes, the bridge. Get to the bridge. And . . ."

He began to tremble, convulsing. He looked at me, his eyes wide now, as if he were seeing not me, but beyond me, at whatever lay next for him.

He struggled to speak.

"Oslo," he said.

"Oslo?"

He nodded, clutched my shoulder, pulled himself closer.

"Oslo," he said.

And then he was gone.

I eased his body onto the floor, folded his arms across his chest.

I ran down the hall, away from the stairs toward the aft of the ship.

I passed a couple of cameras and bashed them with the crossbar, dislodging them from their mounts. Just call me Zack-a-Whack, a one-man wrecking crew.

More shots rang out in the stairwell behind me. I didn't turn to look, just kept running.

I reached a bulkhead that split the hallway—a sign on the wall pointed left to the marina. I went that way, reached a set of double doors, a camera whirring on the ceiling above it.

I smashed the camera and pushed open the doors.

33

Twelve minutes apart and getting closer . . .

Barbara watched the clock on a wall of the lounge, the contractions coming in painful waves now, each new one more urgent than the last.

She focused on her breathing, like they had taught her in Lamaze class, the one she and Zack had attended together. Zack saying: "Just mind over matter, baby. And if you don't mind and it doesn't matter, then I think I'll smuggle a little Mount Gay into the hospital, help with my end of the ordeal. And some Schramsberg Brut for you when it's over."

Oh, how she missed him, needed him here beside her.

And now, more gunfire echoing from outside the lounge, coming from somewhere distant. It had first erupted a few minutes earlier and continued off and on.

Marie Lutey patting Barbara, giving her a hug. The other women on the stage huddling closer together. No one speaking, waiting, imagining the worst.

The gunfire stopped.

Tony, the waiter who had been guarding them, ran toward the lounge door to see what was going on.

Voices of other waiters, shouting from the rotunda. Tony, turning to the women on the stage . . .

"Stay here!" he said. "No move!"

And then Tony ran out of the lounge.

No sooner was he gone than Marie Lutey got to her feet and told Barbara: "I'll be right back, honey."

"Where are you going?"

"Don't know for sure," Marie said. "But there has to be another way out of here."

Another woman said, "He told us not to move."

Marie gave her a wilting look.

"Yeah, and he's been telling us to piss in a pot, too. Screw him."

Marie headed to the rear of the stage. She parted the curtains, stepped behind them. She reappeared a few seconds later.

"There's a door back here," she said. "It opens onto a stairwell. I'm going to see where it leads."

Penelope, the young woman who Todora had kicked and grabbed by the hair, got up.

"I'm coming with you," she said.

And as more gunfire rang out, the two women disappeared behind the curtain.

34

After the low ceilings and cramped confines of the lower deck cabins and hallways, the space I entered seemed positively voluminous—a wide-open area, like a warehouse, with a slick concrete floor and the mingling aromas of brine and disinfectant. It was loud here, not just from the ship's engines but from the surge of the sea against the hull.

The light was dim, just enough to let me take in the layout. The area was divided into two spaces. On one side, stack after stack of boxes on pallets, piled almost to the ceiling and held in place with braided straps and tie-downs so they wouldn't topple over. All kinds of things from cleaning supplies to barrels of paint and engine lubricants. A small forklift sat parked near an open-air office with a desk and file cabinets and a couple of chairs.

To the other side, the boat bay—a giant cage, heavy gauge wire mesh from ceiling to floor. Inside it, various watercraft—kayaks and sailboards, twenty or so Jet Ski's with sparkle paint finishes and two Boston Whalers, twenty-one-foot Montauks with 150 hp Evinrudes. On rolling skids—a midsized tender, painted orange and black, fully enclosed and capable of ferrying sixty or seventy passengers from ship to shore.

The aft wall was rigged with metal tracking, pulleys and chains like a giant garage door—the marina hatchway. I headed for it, searching the wall for a control box, some way to open the hatch. Couldn't find anything.

Maybe by the office. I headed there, glimpsed motion—something, someone—to my right. I stopped. From behind a pallet stacked with cardboard boxes—a pair of feet sticking out.

I gripped the crossbar, crept closer. The feet edged behind the pallet, I couldn't see them now.

I reached the pallet. Waited. Nothing. I slapped the crossbar against a box. Nothing. I slapped the box again, harder, this time moving behind the pallet, crossbar raised and ready.

A man on the floor, hunched up against the boxes, hands out to protect himself, scared.

"Please, no," he said.

He was fortyish, thick, with a head that looked too small for his body. Maybe it was the ears. They seemed hugely out of proportion to the rest of his head. Dog ears, they'd work on a basset hound.

I lowered the crossbar.

"I'm not going to hurt you," I said.

He put down his hands, studied me. He wore a nameplate. "Thom," it said. "Belgium."

"What are you doing here?" I asked him.

"I am the provisions master," he said. "A man, one of the waiters, came in here with a gun, took away my assistant. I . . . I hid from him."

I helped him to his feet. He looked at me, said, "What is happening?"

"They killed the officers, took everyone hostage." No time for details. I pointed at the hatchway. "You know how to open that thing?"

"Yes, but . . ."

"But what?"

"It is supposed to remain closed while the ship is moving."

"Open it," I said.

He hesitated, then moved to the open-air office and a control panel on a wall beside the desk. He punched a button. Pulleys and chains began to clank, wheels moved on tracking—the hatchway yawned slowly open.

And as it did it became immediately obvious why it was supposed to stay shut while the ship was moving. Seawater rushed in, a torrent that swept over the concrete floor, covering my feet, up past my ankles, spreading to all corners of the large room.

The provisions master sensed my alarm.

"It is OK," he said. "It will reach a certain level, a few inches, and then it will stay there."

I sloshed through the water to the boat bay, its broad gate fastened with a padlock. I waved the provisions master over.

"Open it," I said.

He shook his head.

"That is for the dockmaster," he said. "I don't have a key."

"You know where to find one?"

"No, I would have to search for it. Maybe somewhere in the dockmaster's desk. But it is locked, too."

I looked at the padlock on the wire cage. It was a case-hardened Kryptonite U-lock. I used one just like it on my boathouse back home in LaDonna. No way I was going to bust it open.

I stepped to the hatchway, looked out. Sea foam churned in the ship's wake, the sky black with a blanket of clouds. I could make out a few lights on the horizon—other ships. We had to do something to draw their attention.

"Got anything that will start a fire?"

The provisions master looked startled.

"Why do you wish to do that?"

"So someone will see us."

I began rummaging through the stacks of stuff, trying to find anything that might create a big flame.

"But we cannot start a fire onboard ship," the provisions master said. "It is too dangerous. It will . . ."

"Yeah, but maybe we could find something that will burn, put it on one of these pallets, send it out the back . . ."

I found some barrels of lube oil. We could maybe pry one open, smear oil on boxes, put them on a pallet, maybe set them on fire, lower them off the back. Maybe, maybe, maybe. And who knew if we could even get the damn stuff lit. Or if shlossing around on the water wouldn't immediately douse it.

The clock was ticking. I had to go for the sure thing. I had to get up to the lifeboats, set off a distress signal. Then, if possible, I would get back to the marina and figure out a way to open the cage, free the boats.

Still, it seemed like a missed opportunity. This big gaping hole to the rest of the world. And us, not doing anything with it.

"You got any Magic Markers?"

"Magic what?"

"You know, felt tip pens, something to write with, make a sign."

The provisions master went to his desk, opened a drawer, pulled out a black Marks-A-Lot.

"That'll do," I said.

I stepped to the pallet nearest the hatchway. It was piled high with white boxes. Computer boxes. Like the one Sam Jebailey had showed us during his speech. The boxes were strapped together with plastic web tape, too tough to just rip apart.

"Knife?"

The provisions master produced a box cutter from a pocket. I used it to cut the tape. I grabbed one of the computer boxes, walked to the hatch, and slung it overboard. The box disappeared below the churning water, then bobbed to the surface. Lots of protective plastic foam inside, helped it float.

"Give me the marker," I said.

I grabbed another one of the computer boxes.

"OK," I said. "Here's what you're going to do."

I uncapped the marker and scrawled on the side of the box:

SOS
ROYAL STAR
SOS

Then I tossed the box overboard and watched as it bobbed up. I handed the marker to the provisions master.

"All these boxes. Write that on them. Then toss them off. You got that?"

He nodded.

I looked at the double doors, the ones I'd just come in through. I didn't really want to go back the way I just came.

"Is there another way out of here?"

The provisions master pointed to a far corner of the room.

"An elevator. There," he said. "It goes up to the galley."

I looked at the double doors.

"Can you secure those? Make sure no one gets in here?"

"They do not lock from the inside," he said.

"Can you put something in front of them, anything?"

"The forklift," he said. "I could move a pallet, park the forklift behind the door."

"Good. Do it," I said. "And then start throwing off boxes."

I grabbed my crossbar, headed for the elevator. On the way, I found two more cameras and decommissioned them.

I stepped inside the elevator, pressed the up button. As the doors creaked shut, I saw two things:

The provisions master driving the forklift, picking up one of the loaded pallets, moving it to block the big double doors.

And, along a rear wall, pretty as you please, some ugly aluminum suitcases. Halliburtons. I counted nine of them.

35

It was just a service elevator and it only traveled between Deck Three and Deck Four, from the provisions area to the galley.

The door opened and I stepped out. I stood at the rear of the galley, by a conveyor belt used to carry dirty pots and pans to the dishwasher. Ahead of me—long metal prep tables filled with food for a dinner that would never take place, banks of gas stoves upon which stock pots steamed and bubbled, some overflowing into the flames. Smoke curled out of ovens— the smell of burnt bread and charred meat.

I moved through the galley, hungry despite the circumstances, wolfing down stuff as I went—a hunk of blue cheese, some nuts, some grapes, a slice of salami from an antipasto tray.

A meat cleaver lay atop a cutting board. I grabbed it. Then I continued through the galley, through swinging doors that opened to the main dining room. It was all done up for the bon voyage banquet—fine linens, huge bouquets on the tables, wine buckets ready and waiting.

The dining-room doors were open. Beyond them a hallway led to a stairwell.

Was it the same stairwell I'd been heading up when Pango and the guy in the blue jumpsuit spotted us?

I thought so, but couldn't be sure. The ship was a confounding warren of hallways and cabins, staircases and corridors. I couldn't get its layout straight in my head.

I moved out of the dining room into the hallway. From the stairwell ahead—gunshots.

I flattened against a wall. The shots stopped. It sounded as if they had come from below. I pictured the men on Deck Two, hunkered down with their crossbars. Parks with a single rifle, trying to ward off the waiters and all their weapons.

I had to get to the lifeboats. But I couldn't risk taking the stairwell.

I edged along the wall, to the end of the hallway. I looked around the corner, saw a set of doors that opened to the outside, a promenade deck.

I was getting ready to make a run for the doors when, from the dining room, I heard a clatter of dishes. Something breaking, falling to the floor.

I pulled back, found a door—the men's room—stepped inside.

I cracked open the door, peeked out, saw two women leaving the dining room, heading into the hall. I recognized one of them, the old gal with the notable boob job, the one who'd hogged all the stone crabs before they made it to me. The other one was much younger, barely out of her teens, pretty, with long blond hair.

The blond girl clutched the older woman's arm as they crept down the hall. As they neared, I leaped out of the men's room and pushed them back inside it.

Shrieks and gasps, they started to scream. After all, I was holding a meat cleaver.

"It's OK," I told them. "Quiet."

"You scared the bejesus out of us," the older one said.

I said, "Where did you come from? How did you get here?"

The blond one pointed up. The older one said, "From the lounge. That's where they've been keeping us. We got out."

"My wife. Barbara Pickering. She's . . ."

The older one smiled.

"You're Zack."

I nodded.

The woman said, "She told me all about you."

"She's OK?"

"She's fine, really, just fine. The contractions have started. A bit more urgent than she wants to believe, I think. But, yes, she's alright."

"How did you get here?"

The woman pointed back to the dining room.

"Stairs in the kitchen," she said. "They lead up to the lounge, behind the stage."

I told them what had happened on Deck Two. Then I told them to go back to the lounge, round up the other women, and lead them down to the marina, using the elevator in the kitchen.

"There's a guy down there, the provisions master. He's blocking off the main doors to the marina."

The older woman said, "What about you?"

I told them about the lifeboats, how each of them had a distress signal.

"Soon as I set it off, I'll head back down to the marina," I said. "Think you can handle that?"

They both nodded.

I cracked open the men's room door, checked the hallway. Coast clear.

I waved them out, back toward the dining room.

"Tell Barbara I'm coming for her," I said. "No matter what, I'll be there."

36

I gave it a moment, making sure the two of them had made it safely into the dining room.

No more gunshots from the stairwell. I stepped out of the men's room, rounded the corner of the hallway, and ran for the doors leading to the promenade deck. They parted automatically.

And then I was outside. A choice to make: Which way?

I looked right—a long stretch of deck lined with lounge chairs. To my left—a set of steps leading up.

I bounded up the steps, energized by the fresh night air, the rush of wind above the sea.

Deck Five. Another long stretch toward the bow, more lounge chairs. Toward the stern—more steps leading up. I took them.

And then I was on Deck Six looking at the lifeboats strapped in their cradles. Three of them, a matching set on the other side of the ship.

I headed for the closest one, envisioning what I would be looking for—an orange bag stuffed under the bow. The lifeboat rested in a cradle, which put its gunwale a couple of feet above my head. I'd have to pull myself up. But unlike the other lifeboats, the blue tarp covering this one had been removed. One less thing between me and the distress signal.

I put down the cleaver and the crossbar. I gripped the gunwale, caught a foothold on the cradle, gave it all I had.

Up and over the gunwale. And onto something—not the fiberglass floor I'd expected, but something odd, something vaguely human.

The face stared up at me, dead eyes, a bloody brow. One of the ship's officers who'd been gunned down on the main deck.

I rolled off and onto another body. Beside it, another. And another. A dozen of them easy.

I couldn't help it. I screamed. I defy anyone to suddenly find themselves in a boat full of dead bodies and not scream. You could have heard me all the way to Havana.

I tumbled over the gunwale, thudded onto the deck. And as I regained my feet, if not my wits, doors a few yards forward slid open. Out rushed one of the waiters.

He spotted me, leveled his rifle. A burst of shots spackled the deck between us, splinters of teak exploding.

I grabbed the cleaver, hurled it at him. The waiter fell to the deck, dodging it.

And then I was running, running for the stern, running for I didn't know where, just running along the port rail, the sea roaring far below.

More shots from behind me. And then, ahead, a second waiter appearing from another set of doors. He wheeled around, took aim.

My reaction was instant and unthinking.

I grabbed hold of the rail. And I vaulted over it—free-falling into the night.

MAN OVERBOARD

37

I did not fall with grace or good form. No knifelike, splashless dive. I tumbled ass over elbows. The judges did not award style points.

I must have blacked out, either from the certainty that I was about to die, or from the sheer force of crashing into the water.

I don't remember the instant of impact. But I do remember looking up and seeing a monstrous cloud, like a roiling thunderhead just before the storm. How cool, I thought, how beautiful.

And then: I can't breathe.

And then: I can't breathe because I'm underwater.

No one ever accused me of being quick to connect the dots.

And then the water was tugging at me, trying to pull me somewhere I instinctively knew I did not want to go. I fought against the pull, flailing against a monstrous undertow, losing to it, then struggling from its grip until I was swept away by an opposing current and rode it upward.

I don't know how long I was underwater. Maybe ten seconds, maybe a minute. All I know is that when I finally surfaced, the *Royal Star* had moved past me and I was staring at its transom.

I didn't have time to panic. Riding the ship's wake was like body surfing a Class IV whitewater river. I went up, down, all around. Peaks and valleys, one wicked roller coaster.

I'd lose sight of the ship for a moment, then I would crest atop a wave and see a sliver of light at the base of the ship's transom—the marina—and the dark form of the provisions master moving busily about, tossing off boxes, just like I'd told him.

I yelled. But the rush of the waves, the churn of the sea, the massive backwash of the ship, drowned out my voice even unto my own ears.

For one brief, insane moment I thought I might actually catch the ship. I paddled and kicked with a fury. I got nowhere. The ship kept surging onward, sending out a wall of water that knocked me back.

I rode wave after wave, yelling and waving, trying to get the provisions master's attention.

Then a commotion in the marina—the provisions master twisting, falling to the floor. Another man, one of the waiters, straddling him, holding a rifle. The waiter stepped away. The marina hatchway closed tight, the sliver of light went dark.

And the *Royal Star* kept on its course, moving ever farther away.

38

FRIDAY, 4:45 A.M.

"You saw Zack?" Barbara said. "He's OK?"

"Yes, dear. I'll tell you all about it. But later. Now we must hurry."

Marie Lutey and Penelope had been delayed returning to the lounge. Coming back through the dining room, they just missed being spotted by one of the waiters as he made a sweep through the galley. They hid under a table, heard the gunfire from outside on the deck, stayed hidden until things quieted down.

Even after they got back to the lounge it had taken time to convince the other women that they should chance making their way down to the ship's marina. Several of them were dead set against it.

"Listen," Marie told them, "there are men out there risking their lives so we can escape. You mean to tell me that counts for nothing?"

They had argued back and forth, but finally Marie had prevailed.

And now all the women were gathering their things, Marie telling Barbara about Zack's plan to set off the distress signal in the lifeboat, then join them in the marina.

"Quite a guy," Marie said. "The kind of guy who won't let anything stand between him and what he wants."

"That's Zack alright," Barbara said. "Hardheaded as they come."

"Don't let that one get away, honey. Definitely a keeper."

They made their way to the rear of the stage, through the curtains, to the door.

And then they heard the waiter shouting: "Stop! You stop now!"

Tony, the one who had been guarding them when the commotion broke out. Running toward the stage, rifle at the ready.

And behind Tony—two other waiters entering the lounge, guarding the men they had rounded up from down below, almost all the male passengers it looked like. Some of them calling out to their wives, breaking past the two waiters, heading for the stage. Women rushing to join them.

Barbara spotted Sam Jebailey, others she recognized. But no sign of Zack.

A few women ran for the steps, trying to get off the stage. Tony pointed his rifle, stopped them.

"You stay here," he said. "No go down there."

The other two waiters were trying to corral all the men, keep them away from the stage. But they weren't having much luck. Men swarmed forward, reached out for their wives. Tearful reunions and embraces.

Barbara saw Kane Kinsey working his way to the edge of the stage. Penelope squeezed past Barbara. She knelt, hugged him.

"We tried," Kinsey said. "But they had us pinned down, we couldn't get out of there. And we couldn't get back into the cabins. The doors locked behind us. There was nowhere to go."

"But you're OK," Penelope said. "You're here."

"Yeah, I'm OK." Kinsey looked around, made sure the waiters were out of earshot. He spoke low. "They didn't get all of us. The old guy, Mr. Linblom, he designed the ship. He's still down there in the cabin. They didn't find him. And this one other guy, he got away. He's still out there somewhere."

"You mean Zack?" Barbara said. "Zack Chasteen?"

"No, this guy named Parks. He had a gun. I don't know where he went," he said. "You're Zack's wife?"

She nodded. Kinsey looked away.

"What?" Barbara said. "Where's Zack?"

Kinsey shook his head.

"I don't know, I . . ."

"Tell me," Barbara said.

"The waiters were talking when they brought us up here, saying things, that's all."

"Saying what things?"

Kinsey looked at her.

"They said they shot him. They said he went overboard." Kinsey reached for Barbara's hand, took it in both of his. "I'm sorry. I'm so, so sorry."

39

It was the pills, Glenroy thought as he headed up the stairs and back to the bridge. The waiters had taken them and now they were wired and it was making them do stupid things.

Like using up all the ammo.

Glenroy should have told them to switch the rifles off automatic, put them on single shot. But too late for that now.

Pango especially should have known better. But no, Pango and Glenroy heading down to Deck Two, spotting the captain and the two men coming up the stairwell. Pango opening fire with the SAR, not backing off, emptying the whole clip, thirty shots gone just like that.

Then Pango turning to Glenroy, looking at him, as if to say: "What now?"

The extra ammo was in Glenroy's backpack and he had left the backpack on the bridge. There weren't that many clips left, just one or two. Yap-Yap had been unable to provide more when he sold the guns to Glenroy and, besides, it wasn't as if Glenroy thought they would need a lot of ammunition. Just enough to seize control of the ship.

Fortunately, it hadn't taken much to subdue the male passengers. Glenroy fired a couple of shots down the hallway and that was that. By then, the waiters had shown up to help, coming in through the laundry and one of the side corridors. The men on Deck Two had nowhere to go. They couldn't get back into their cabins. They were locked out, didn't have card keys. When Glenroy and the others stormed the hallway, the men were on the floor, hands over their heads, scared out of their minds. Just a simple matter of rounding them up. The waiter they had beaten up, Benny, he was in bad shape, still unconscious.

The passenger with the gun had abandoned the others and slipped away, probably after emptying his clip, Glenroy thought. Or even if he had any shots left, there couldn't be that many of them. Glenroy had gotten a glimpse of him in the stairwell, a tall guy with sandy blond hair. Glenroy had dispatched Pango and one of the waiters, Jati, to find him.

And then the two fool waiters, Felix and Marcos, out on Deck Six, unloading on the man who jumped overboard. Idiots. Firing into the water, wasting ammunition on a man who was no longer a threat to them. Between that and the shots they fired at the bon voyage party, killing the three officers, they had used up all their ammo, too.

But the passengers didn't have to know that. As far as the passengers were concerned, the rifles were fully loaded, and the waiters were ready to cut them down should they get any more bright ideas about trying to escape.

As for the ammo in his backpack, Glenroy would keep that all for himself. Just in case.

He was anxious to get back to the bridge. He'd been gone almost an hour. He wasn't overly concerned that the *Royal Star* was in danger of colliding with another ship. Sea traffic was light. And the course he had programmed—a lazy, ever-eastward oval—kept the *Royal Star* well offshore, its southernmost point some twenty miles from the Cuban coast, far enough removed to avoid the suspicion of patrol boats.

Still, before rushing off with Pango he should have powered down the engines, let the ship idle. It would have been easy enough to recalculate the course, make up for any lost time.

As he hurried up the stairs from Deck Six to Deck Seven, Glenroy thought about what still remained for him to do. Sometime within the next twelve to fourteen hours, he would have to leave the bridge at least twice to put the final part of the plan in motion. In each case, he would need to be gone at least an hour, maybe longer. He would have to take his time. He could not rush. If he rushed he could too easily make a mistake. And if he made a mistake, well, there simply was no room for mistakes.

Glenroy could not risk distraction. He could not focus on these two final things while part of his mind was worrying about the bridge, about someone seizing the helm of the ship.

If only there was another person he could trust. Yes, that would be most helpful, especially now. Someone to watch his back, someone to whom he could give an order and know with confidence it would be carried out. But from the beginning he had acted alone, a cell of one. That was the way it had to be. If a chain has no links, then its strength is not determined by the weakest one.

"Go, my strong one . . ."

The words of Imam Ben-Yafati, a final blessing before he set out.

"Go, my strong one and make us proud."

Not even Imam Ben-Yafati or others within Islaam Karib knew the exact details of the plan. They had simply provided the necessary training. And the money. Lots of money. But the plan? That was all Glenroy's.

He kept reviewing the final pieces as he rushed up the stairs, reached Deck Seven, and hurried across the landing. But what he saw at the end of the hallway stopped him in his tracks.

The door to the bridge was closed.

40

Glenroy crept along the hallway, rifle at the ready.

How could this have happened? How?

Was the bridge door on some sort of timer? Had it shut automatically? He should have thought to jam something in the doorway to prevent it from closing—a chair, anything. But no, he had been in too much of a hurry.

Glenroy tried to calm himself, tried to think this through.

If he was locked out of the bridge, it presented a problem, yes, but one for which he had already planned. He would go down to the engine control room. Its door, too, was operated by a security code, but all it would take was a sledgehammer and he could probably smash the room's Plexiglas windows. If that didn't work then an acetylene torch would do the job. Yes, he could get into the engine control room. Once inside, Glenroy could steer the ship from down there. And while he wouldn't have the benefit of the view from up top, cameras mounted on the bridge fed monitors in the control room and would let him see all he needed to see.

But what if someone had entered the bridge and shut the door? If so, who could it be?

Glenroy's first thought—Todora. Now that the captain was dead, she and she alone knew the security code. Glenroy hadn't seen her for hours, not since she had split off from Pango when they were taking money from the passengers' safes. But what could Todora gain by seizing the bridge? Yes, she might be able to figure out how to steer the ship, but where would she go? It wasn't as if she could do anything to alert the authorities. At this point, she was just as involved with hijacking the ship as the rest of them. She, too, had killed someone. Maybe Todora had gone to the bridge and shut the door just to show Glenroy that she still had leverage over him . . . for whatever good that might do her.

Or, what if it was the man with the gun, the tall man with the blond hair who had escaped during the skirmish on Deck Two? A real possibility, thought Glenroy as he stepped ever closer to the door. And a real wrench in the works, if that was the case. Chances were the man, whoever he was, could buy enough time on the bridge to draw the notice of other ships. The communications system was still disconnected, but the man could sound the ship's horn and keep sounding it until another vessel heard it and drew close to investigate. Then everything would unravel.

If it was the man with the gun, Glenroy knew what he would do. He would bring the passengers onto the bow of the main deck, where the man could see them. And Glenroy would shoot the passengers, one by one, until the man had no choice but to give up control of the bridge. Kill them now, kill them later. It made little difference to Glenroy.

He crept along the hall. Twenty feet from the door, now ten feet.

Glenroy squared off. As he did, the door slid open.

Glenroy braced to fire . . .

And saw Sonny in the doorway.

The words spilled out of Sonny, "Omigod, Glenroy, I'm so glad to see you. I was worried. I heard the gunshots and I came up here, but you were gone and I didn't know what to think, I thought you were dead. Are you OK?"

Sonny reached out for him, but Glenroy stormed through the doorway and headed for the helm.

"What's happening, Glenroy? Is everything alright? Where have you been? I was going crazy. I thought you had been hurt. And then I came up here. I didn't know what else to do. I came up here and I shut the door because I knew I would be safe. And I waited and waited. I kept watching the monitors, looking for you. And then I saw you coming down the hall and I opened the door and . . ."

Sonny chattering away as Glenroy scanned the horizon and saw ship lights ahead. A freighter, it looked like. Far enough away that it wasn't a problem. Still, no sense taking chances. He punched the steering control override and immediately the warning alarm sounded.

Sonny let out a cry, covered his ears. He lurched forward, wrapped his arms around Glenroy, and pulled him close.

"What's that noise, Glenroy? What is that? Is something wrong?"

Glenroy elbowed him away. Then he slammed a fist under Sonny's chin, snapping his head back. Sonny crumpled onto the floor.

Glenroy pressed the watch alarm acknowledgment button. The ringing stopped. He reached for the joystick and turned the ship slightly southward, away from the freighter.

He looked down at Sonny, who was moaning now, trying to sit up, a string of drool bubbling from his pouty lips.

Recruiting Sonny had been tricky business. The success of Glenroy's plan rested on cutting off the ship's communications. But it wasn't just a matter of holding a gun to Sonny and forcing him to shut down the In-marsat system, the satellite links, the radios. No, the communications were far too complex. Sonny was the only one who fully understood the setup. He might secretly leave something on, send out a signal, make a Mayday call, and no one would be the wiser.

Unlike Pango and the waiters, Sonny was not someone who could easily be bought. Glenroy had made some casual forays on that front during the weeks of training that led up to the *Royal Star*'s inaugural voyage, striking up conversations with Sonny in the crew dining room, turning talk to the crew's low wages, saying that on a ship which would carry some of the world's richest people there ought to be a way for hardworking people like themselves to share in the wealth. The same kind of talk he had used on Pango. All it got from Sonny was a chilly rebuff.

So Glenroy had taken a different tack. He set out to befriend Sonny.

It had proven easy enough, thanks to Sonny's unique position on the *Royal Star*. An outside contractor, hired for a specific job, the young Korean didn't fit in with the ship's officers or upper management. And he wasn't part of the general crew, the rank and file who had worked together on other ships.

He was all by himself, really. And Glenroy had latched on to this, exploited it.

During the weeks of training, the crew was given plenty of shore time. And one evening Glenroy invited Sonny to join him for a night out. He picked a bar in Fort Lauderdale, a place on Dixie Highway that Glenroy had found once before by accident. A dark place. Not a particularly romantic place. But a private place, ideal for such purposes, a place where men often met other men. Because it was plainly obvious to Glenroy that Sonny was not interested in women. A batty boy, they called them in the islands, a chi-chi man.

By the second margarita, Sonny was nudging Glenroy's leg under the table. After the third one, he was snuggled beside Glenroy, a hand in his lap.

Cute couple . . . I wondered how you got the little chink faggot to help you out.
Todora's words from a few hours earlier.

No, it wasn't so much that Glenroy had befriended Sonny as he had seduced him. Glenroy had only let it go so far in the weeks that followed—tender private embraces, a great deal of touching on Sonny's part, just enough to string him along. Glenroy enduring his revulsion for a greater glory, slowly reeling Sonny in, sharing his confidence, revealing his plan, or at least that part of it that he could reveal. Telling Sonny that when it was all over, when they had all that money, they could live the life they wanted to live. Just the two of them.

It had worked. Had it ever worked. Sonny was in love with Glenroy. He'd do anything for him. And there were still some things, some very important things, that Glenroy needed Sonny to do. As much as Glenroy was sickened by the very thought of Sonny, he couldn't risk losing his allegiance now.

Glenroy reached down and helped Sonny to his feet.

"Sorry," Glenroy said. "I didn't mean to hit you. I just . . ."

"No, no, that's OK. You're under a lot of pressure. I understand. I'm just so glad that you're safe."

Again, Sonny reached for Glenroy. And this time, Glenroy pulled him close, wrapped an arm around him, patted his back.

"Sonny," he said. "I'm going to need your help."

"Yeah, sure. I'll do anything. You know I will."

"I need you to go back to your cabin and get some sleep."

"But I want to stay here. With you."

"No, not right now. It is more important that you get some sleep. Because for what you must do, you'll need to be rested, wide awake."

Sonny unwrapped himself from Glenroy's embrace.

"OK, whatever you say."

Glenroy checked the ship's clock. Five A.M.

"I need you back here in six hours," he said. "OK?"

Sonny brightened.

"Is that when the boat is coming to pick us up?"

"Just go get some sleep," Glenroy said.

After Sonny was gone, Glenroy stood at the helm, looking east. Sunrise was fast approaching. Time for Fajr, the dawn prayer, the most important prayer of the day, the one most favored by Allah.

Glenroy stepped to the bathroom and cleansed himself. He took a fresh towel, spread it on the floor by the door to the starboard bridge wing.

This time he was not interrupted. He completed the *salat* from start to finish. And when that was done he added an additional prayer, one for courage.

Then he stepped back to the helm. He ran the coordinates again, reset the course. He saw the numbers flash on the screen of the GPS. The *Royal Star* would reach its destination in sixteen hours, thirty-seven minutes.

41

I've always considered myself a waterman. Boats of every sort, scuba, surfing. There was even a time when, trying to strengthen a rotator cuff I'd torn playing raquetball, I would walk the few hundred yards to the ocean every morning from my house in LaDonna and get in a mile or so of open-water swimming.

But no amount of training can prepare you for bobbing along all alone in a big empty sea.

Because you know you aren't really all alone. And the other things that are out there with you, well, you're better off not thinking about them.

Only it was impossible not to. It was fall, the time of year when those microscopic critters that create bioluminescence come out to party. As I treaded water, every sweep of my hands left a green and sparkly trail.

It's a wondrous phenomenon, really. The marine version of a free fireworks show, the kind of thing that should rightly elicit oohs and ahhs.

But as the *Royal Star* chugged into the distance and its wake subsided, I became aware of other green and sparkly trails all around me. Fish. Some of them pretty big fish. And some of them fish so big that I had a sudden and humbling awareness of what it meant to be bait.

I kept turning in the water, looking in all directions. If something toothy was planning to swim up and swallow me, then I preferred to meet it head-on.

I was working far too furiously, wasting energy. Already I was winded, a dull ache growing in my arms and legs. At this rate, I gave myself a couple of hours, maybe less.

I slowed my breathing, tried to paddle with more efficiency. I thought back to the years I'd spent in Boy Scouts—yes, I was at one time an upstanding lad—and how Mr. Worley, our scoutmaster, had taught us drown-proofing. He made us jump, fully clothed, into the deep end of the Minorca Beach public swimming pool and wouldn't let us come out for an hour, adding extra minutes to our drill if we so much as laid a hand on the wall of the pool.

It was all great fun and adventure back then. But now it was the real deal. And I tried to dredge up what we young Tenderfeet had learned.

There were all sorts of ways to increase the odds against drowning. For one, if the water was warm, which it was, you could remove your shirt and pants, then tie off the arms and legs to create a makeshift life preserver.

So I did that. I remembered the how-to diagrams in the old Boy Scout Handbook showing an enterprising young scout floating merrily atop clothes inflated like giant sausages. Yeah, right. My silk shirt and linen pants didn't hold much air. Still, they gave me a little something to hold on to. And clad only in my underwear, without the wet clothes to drag me down, I was slightly more buoyant.

It bought me another couple hours before I did the Big Sink.

And then I remembered the dead man's float. If you kept treading water, sooner or later you'd wear out. The dead man's float conserved energy. Instead of fighting to keep your head above water, you took a big gulp of air and floated, face down, arms outstretched. Like a corpse.

So I did that, too, resting my arms on my not-so-inflated shirt and pants. I'd take a deep breath, hold it for half a minute or so, and then lift my head for more air, trying to move as little as possible, trying to relax, keep calm.

Ten minutes passed, twenty. The first pale fingers of dawn palmed out across the eastern sky.

Each time I came up for air, I looked for the *Royal Star*. Its lights kept getting dimmer and dimmer. The current might have been turning me, throwing my bearings off, but I was certain the ship was traveling in a big circle, moving first to the west and then edging northward.

And then something bumped me, square against my back, the way sharks do it, tapping first to see if you're edible and then circling back for the kill.

I whipped around and found myself face-to-face with . . . a cardboard box. One of the computer boxes tossed off the ship, the SOS message scrawled on its side. It was well sealed and floating upright, pretty as you please. Trailing behind it—a long piece of the webbed strap that had held the boxes together on the pallet.

I spotted another box floating just a few yards away. Beyond it another. The more I looked, the more boxes I saw. A dozen or so of them. The provisions master had done one heck of a job tossing them out the marina hatchway.

For a fleeting moment I entertained the fanciful notion that I could round up all the boxes, lash them together, and build myself a raft. Do a Huck Finn thing on the high seas.

But that's all it was, just a fanciful notion. In the end, before current and waves sent them far out of reach, I was able to gather up just three more boxes.

I tied two of them together with my pants, the other two with my shirt. Between the pairs of boxes, I tied the webbed strap.

I couldn't lie across the boxes. They weren't nearly buoyant enough to support all my weight. But I could hold on to the strap and hang in the water between them.

Things were looking up. Oh, yeah, way up. If I was lucky, I figured I might survive an entire day.

42

They were in the salon of Sam Jebailey's suite, Ron Diamond on a couch, Todora pacing the room and smoking a cigarette.

They had heard the gunfire when it first erupted, Todora rushing off to see what it was all about, leaving Diamond alone for nearly two hours, warning that she would shoot him if he tried to sneak out. Todora had hung back, away from the action. And when the time was right, when Glenroy had returned to the bridge, when Pango and the waiters were busy escorting the male passengers to the Galaxy Lounge, she had slipped into the purser's office and retrieved the two laundry bags filled with cash and jewelry. They now sat on the floor by the couch, right next to the Halliburton.

Todora said, "So this helicopter of yours. It is where?"

"George Town, Exuma. With my yacht," Diamond said. "I spoke with the pilot right before we left Miami. He was getting ready for a checkout flight. It's fueled up and ready to go."

"And it would take how long for him to get here?"

"I'm thinking two hours, tops."

"But he cannot land on the ship. Glenroy will see him and . . ."

"No, we'll have to figure out a way to get off the ship. Take one of the lifeboats or something. You know how to lower them?"

Todora nodded.

"Yes, of course. We are all trained to know. For emergency." She thought about it. "It could work. It only takes a moment to prepare the lifeboat."

"Good," Diamond said. "Then they would pick us up from the lifeboat."

"They?"

"The pilot and whoever he brings with him, someone to lower the sling."

"Sling? What is this sling?"

"What they pull us up with." Todora looked at Diamond, not understanding. "The helicopter can't land in the water, see? They lower a sling—it's a harness, you just strap yourself in—and they pull us up one at a time."

"Over the water?"

"Yes, over the water. I mean, where else . . ." Diamond stopped, seeing the look on her face. "What is it?"

Todora shook her head.

"Is nothing."

Diamond studied her.

"You can't swim," he said.

She didn't say anything. She snubbed out her cigarette on a brass table.

"This sling," she said, "it will take the money, too?"

"Yes, of course, the money, too. Just strap everything in the sling and pull it up." Diamond pointed at the laundry bags. "You might want to find something a little sturdier than those things, duffel bags or something."

Todora lit another cigarette, thinking about it.

"OK, then," she said. "First they pull up me. Then money. Then you."

Diamond shrugged.

"However you want it. Makes no difference."

"And then to Cuba."

Diamond shook his head.

"Not in the helicopter, no way. The Cubans aren't real big on unannounced flights into their airspace."

"What then?"

"Back to the Bahamas. I'll hire a boat that will take you to Cuba, if that's where you really want to go. Bahamian boats go back and forth to Cuba all the time."

"Yes, Cuba," Todora said. "But a question."

"What's that?"

"How will you explain it? How will you say you escaped this ship, how you got away?"

"I'll tell the truth."

"Truth?"

"You stuck a gun to my head and forced me to do as you said. And as soon as you were gone, I immediately contacted the authorities, told them the ship had been hijacked, and let them come to the rescue."

"And what will you tell them about me?"

"I will tell them that you disappeared, that you forced me and my people to drop you off somewhere, on some island in the Bahamas or someplace, and I don't know where you went from there," said Diamond. "Don't worry, whatever I say they'll believe it."

"So, you will be hero, the famous man who helped rescue the people on the ship."

Diamond smiled.

"Yeah. And you will be two million dollars richer," Diamond said. "Plus whatever's in those laundry bags."

Todora took the pill bottle from her smock, shook out one, and swallowed it. She offered the bottle to Diamond.

"What is it?" he asked.

"For staying awake."

Diamond shook out a pill, examined it.

"What the hell," he said and swallowed it.

Diamond sat back on the couch. Todora sat down on the divan across from him. She lit another cigarette.

"Just one thing, one big thing," Diamond said. "How do we get a call through to my pilot?"

"I will take care of that," Todora said. "There is a bigger thing."

"What's that?"

"I've been thinking," Todora said.

Diamond waited.

Todora nudged the Halliburton with a foot.

"This fancy suitcase," she said. "I've been thinking that maybe there are more than just one of them."

Diamond didn't say anything.

Todora said, "I am right, aren't I? There is more than just one suitcase."

Diamond shrugged.

"Maybe you should ask Sam Jebailey about that," he said.

"Yes," Todora said. "Maybe I should."

43

I kept cussing the night, anxious for the sun to break through. Come daylight, I told myself, this would all be over. Someone, somehow, would find me.

I could see ship lights, specks on the horizon. Once, just before dawn, I caught a glimpse of what I felt for sure was the *Royal Star* as it looped back on its curious circular route. It came within a mile or so before turning north and then east again.

I took encouragement from the fact that I was bobbing along in one of the most frequently traveled and watched-over stretches of ocean in the world. A major thoroughfare for cruise ships and island-hopping sailors. Florida and the Bahamas to the north. To the south—Cuba and Hispaniola, separated by the Windward Passage, the most direct route between the Panama Canal and ports of the Eastern Seaboard. And, given the twitchy state of affairs between the U.S. and Cuba, along with the ongoing gambits of drug smugglers and refugees, a place where lots of eyes were always watching.

There was no shortage of military traffic in these parts. Constant vigilance by U.S. Coast Guard cutters and Cuban gunboats. Regular flyovers by fighter jets out of Key West Naval Air Station and the base at Guantanamo Bay. Plus, all kinds of light aircraft doing the puddle-jumping thing.

Yes, if you had to leap off a ship and get stranded in wide-open water, then this was definitely the place to be. It was just a matter of time. Sooner or later, someone would come along and fish me out.

But daytime didn't bring relief. Ship lights that offered hope during the night dimmed with the advance of the sun. As the sky brightened, the world became a vast and empty place. And with that emptiness, fear surfaced to fill the void: *No one knows I'm out here. No one is looking for me. Absolutely no one.*

The wind died, waves flattened. Harsh light strafed the water, created a surface almost metallic, a blinding glare.

I looked and looked, saw nothing and more nothing. No fish swirled the water, no birds soared the sky.

Just me, alone, on a deadly silver sea.

I don't know how I managed to doze off. The lull of Mother Ocean, I suppose. That, coupled with total exhaustion.

I woke up gagging. I'd lost my grip on the strap, become briefly submerged. The boxes had drifted a few yards beyond me.

And in my wild paddle to reclaim them, I spotted the cargo ship.

Far to the south, three or four miles, but plowing northward on a course that would take it just to the west of me.

It was my best shot. Maybe my only shot. I didn't know how much longer I could stay afloat. The computer boxes weren't holding up well. They were getting soggy, riding lower in the water.

I wasn't holding up well either. Arms and legs cramping. Mouth dry. Head pounding. Dehydrated. Water, water, everywhere, nor any drop to drink. "The Rime of the Ancient Mariner." Only, this particular mariner might never make it to ancient.

I had to get to that cargo ship, had to figure out a way for someone on that ship to see me.

I tried lying across the strap and swimming between the boxes, using them like water wings. But my weight pulled the boxes down and threatened to sink them altogether. So I flipped over, hooked my feet behind the strap, and started backpaddling, using just my arms, windmilling them to power forward. It seemed to work.

I had one thing going for me—the current. The Atlantic North Equatorial Current, to be exact, the southern terminus of the subtropical gyre, the huge wheel of water that's on a perpetual spin cycle from the Equator up to the Arctic Circle. Fueled by the prevailing trade winds, the current here bore westward before melding forces with the Yucatan Current in the Straits of Florida to form the Gulf Stream. If I was a man of leisure, maybe kicking back in a floating lounge chair, beverage in hand, I could let the current carry me all the way to Ireland.

But right now I would settle for it helping me trudge a half mile or so to the west, where I projected the cargo ship would pass.

I briefly considered abandoning the boxes and going it on my own. I could make better time. But the bulk of the boxes created a profile on the water, provided the crew on the bridge of the cargo ship with something they might see. Plus, I didn't want to let go of the boxes. They were all I had. Without them it was just me and the sea.

So I paddled. And paddled. And paddled some more. The cargo ship loomed larger and larger. I was making definite headway. Our paths drawing closer and closer.

Twenty minutes and I was worn out. I took a break. The ship was at least a mile away. I wasn't anywhere near where I needed to be, but I could see that the cargo ship was actually two vessels—a long storage barge towed by another barge with a towering wheelhouse.

I started paddling again. My shoulders ached, my back ached, everything ached. I began counting strokes. After a hundred I would stop, stretch, catch my breath. Then I would start all over again. Hard, hard going.

But it was paying off.

Three-quarters of a mile from the ship, and I could see orange, white, and green containers stacked on its decks. Cargo ships don't carry a lot of crew. Maybe no more than a dozen on one this size with at least a third of them sleeping or off-duty at any one time. But there had to be someone out and about. Had to be.

Another hundred strokes. Then two hundred, three hundred.

And now there was a distinct hum in the water, the cargo ship's engines. I caught a whiff of diesel fumes in the air.

I stopped swimming, checked my position.

On our present paths, the ship would pass about a hundred yards away. Close, but not close enough.

Another hundred strokes. The ship was closing in, less than a quarter mile, with me about fifty yards abeam.

I stopped.

I was at a disadvantage with the sun. Anyone on the ship would have to stare straight into the glare to see me. Far better if I was on the ship's portside. But there was no chance of that now.

I waved my arms. I hollered.

I wanted only to hear the ship's horn, signaling that it had seen me, calling the crew to action.

But nothing.

The ship's bow drew even with me.

I waved my arms. I yelled. I slapped the boxes. I thrust myself down, then surged up, waist-high out of the water, splashing, creating a commotion.

Nothing.

Spooked by the ship, a school of flying fish skittered across the water, parting as they passed me with balletlike precision.

Still no signal, no sign that I'd been seen.

Just behind the wheelhouse, gantries extended to either side of the ship. Between them hung a pair of hammocks, a man resting in each, gently swaying from port to starboard.

I hollered. I waved. I splashed.

Nothing.

And now the first barge was past and I was abeam the second. No sign of anyone on its deck. Just stacks of containers.

The sea rose up—the ship's wake. It carried me forward, then sent me down its backside. Another wave followed. And another.

Then I was staring at the ship's transom, at its name and registry: "*Titan IV*, Panama."

Bound for wherever it was going. Leaving me behind.

44

FRIDAY, 9:00 A.M.

Just try not to think about it, dear."

Marie Lutey was doing her best to comfort Barbara, the two of them still on the stage of the Galaxy Lounge with the other women, Barbara resting with her head in Marie's lap.

"It's impossible not to think about it," Barbara said. "The waiters said they shot him, that he fell overboard."

"Do you want to believe that?"

"Of course I don't want to believe that."

"Then don't believe it, dammit. You don't have to believe anything you don't want to believe."

"But . . ."

Marie put up a hand.

"Not another word," Marie said. "Just visualize."

"Visualize?"

Marie nodded.

"Yes, I do it all the time. Like whenever I get on an airplane and I am convinced the plane is going to crash and burn and we're all going to die. Which is each and every time I get on an airplane. So I visualize. I visualize the airplane's wings and how they are strong and perfect and how they are going to get us where we need to go and nothing bad is going to happen. And then I visualize a zillion tiny angels under those wings, holding them up, their tiny angel wings just beating like crazy, like they were hummingbirds or something. I am proud to report that no airplane I've been on has ever crashed," Marie said. "Of course, a couple or three martinis along the way helps, too, but that is neither here nor there."

Barbara smiled.

"Zack always downs a martini when we fly somewhere," she said.

"Gin? Or vodka?"

"Gin," Barbara said. "He maintains there's no such thing as a vodka martini."

"The more I know about that man, the more I like him," Marie said. She patted Barbara's cheek. "Just close your eyes, dear, relax."

Barbara closed her eyes.

"Now visualize your husband drinking a martini and smiling at you over the rim of the glass with those gorgeous big brown eyes of his."

"He does have gorgeous eyes, doesn't he?"

"Yes, he does. And the rest of him is pretty gorgeous, too. So you might as well go ahead and visualize every delicious inch of him," Marie said. "And feel free to share all the details because I am old and horny and enjoy such things."

Barbara laughed.

"You're terrible."

"Beyond your wildest imagination," Marie said. "Now shut up and visualize."

Barbara lay quiet. Marie stroked her hair and looked around the Galaxy Lounge.

Two waiters, Tony and Marcos, were still keeping the passengers separated—women on the stage, men in the seating area. After the initial commotion when the men had been led into the lounge, the waiters had allowed no talking back and forth between the two groups. A couple of men had tried to speak with their wives and been rewarded with jabs from rifle butts and sent sprawling on the floor.

Nearby, Attavia Linblom let out an occasional sob. Her husband hadn't been among the male passengers brought up from Deck Two and Attavia feared the worst.

Barbara said, "We're sitting in a restaurant."

"What's that, dear?"

"Zack and I. I'm visualizing us sitting in a restaurant, both of us with martinis and toasting each other. I'm holding the baby."

"Oh, my, that's wonderful. A boy or a girl?"

"I can't tell. It's all bundled up and I can't really see it," Barbara said.

"But we're happy. All three of us. Zack is smiling. He has a big plate of stone crabs sitting in front of him."

"That's it, bring him to life," Marie said. "But don't just picture him, smell him, too. He's got a good smell, doesn't he?"

"Uh-huh. He uses bay rum like it was bathwater. Smells like clove and cardamon."

"And the way he sounds."

"He's got a nice voice. Comforting. Just a touch of a Southern accent. Not too twangy or anything."

"Taste him, too. How's he taste?"

"Mmm," Barbara said. "Salty."

"That's the way all men taste. And I'm not just talking about their man juice either."

They both started laughing. Then Barbara bolted up. She grabbed her stomach, let out a moan.

"Another one?" Marie asked.

Barbara grimaced, managed a nod. Marie checked a clock on the lounge wall.

"Eight minutes apart," she said. "Getting closer."

As Barbara focused on her breathing, trying to get her mind off the pain, Todora appeared in the doorway of the lounge. She stood there, looking around, surveying the male passengers. Spotting Sam Jebailey, she headed for him. Todora grabbed Jebailey by the arm, pulled him to his feet.

"Come with me," she said.

Marie yelled at her: "Hey, you!"

Todora stopped.

"How about you go get the ship's doctor and bring him here to see this woman? She's about to have a baby. She needs help."

"Her problem," Todora said.

Todora pushed Jebailey toward the doorway and followed him out of the lounge.

45

For five hours Pango had been searching the ship, looking for the passenger who had gotten away, the man with the gun. No telling where he might be, no telling if he was even still alive.

Pango thought there was a good chance the man might have been wounded when they'd fired at each other, first in the stairwell and then in the hallway on Deck Two. Maybe the man had crawled off somewhere and died.

Pango had first gone to the ship's marina, taking the elevator down from the galley with Jati, his nephew, one of the waiters. That's where they had encountered the provisions master tossing boxes out the hatchway, Jati opening fire and killing him before Pango could intervene.

A foolish waste of ammunition. The provisions master hadn't been armed. They could have just led him off and locked him away with the rest of the crew in the casino or the library. Maybe he'd even seen the passenger with the gun, could tell them where they might find him.

But no, Jati had shot the provisions master, had fired off most of his clip. Pango had taken the rifle from Jati and sent him back up to Deck Five to help the other waiters keep an eye on the passengers and crew. And Pango had set out, with four maybe five shots left, trying to find the missing passenger. Going through storerooms, the galley, the engine room.

Dead or alive, Pango had to find him. No way was he going to face Glenroy again without having something good to report.

Pango was having his doubts about Glenroy. Nothing was working out the way Glenroy had told them it would.

There had been only a few thousand dollars in the ship's coffers, not the hundreds of thousands, even the millions that Glenroy had promised. Even with the cash and jewelry taken from the passengers, it still wasn't adding up to nearly as much as they had expected. But Glenroy, he didn't seem particularly concerned about that.

And where was the boat that was supposed to take them away?

From the beginning, Glenroy had been vague about the boat. He had offered few details about who would be driving it, when it would arrive. Glenroy telling Pango, "You do your job, I do mine."

Pango hadn't pressed him on it. Mainly because Glenroy had paid him some meaningful up-front money—twenty thousand dollars. A recruiting bonus, as it were. Pango keeping ten thousand dollars for himself and divvying the rest among the five waiters to get them on board with the plan.

Yes, the money had gotten Pango's attention. Glenroy was a serious man. And he had serious money. He shelled out a lot for the SARs. And there was plenty more where that came. Pango couldn't help but notice the thick roll of bills that Glenroy had produced when he paid off Yap-Yap that night in the laundry.

Where had all that money come from? It was unlikely that Glenroy could save that much. Pango knew what an assistant motorman got paid. Almost nothing, with no opportunity for tips or for earning a little on the sly. And the boat that was supposed to meet them and take them away? Pango couldn't even begin to imagine how much that would cost.

All along, Pango had assumed the boat would come within a few hours after they seized the *Royal Star*, allowing them to escape in the dead of night. Now here it was, well into the next day, and Glenroy was holed up on the bridge, no mention of the boat, Glenroy not even seeming to care about the shortfall in money, interested only in keeping the ship on course. On course to where?

Pango didn't like it. The longer they stayed on the *Royal Star*, the greater the chance that something would go wrong. Another ship might try to hail them and, getting no reply, alert the authorities. No, Pango didn't like it at all.

He felt responsibility for the waiters, for getting them into this. They were loyal to Pango. They did what he told them to do, trusting in promises that they would soon be richer than their wildest dreams.

Maybe Glenroy was up to something. Maybe he was just using them.

Maybe it was time, Pango thought, for him to come up with a plan of his own.

46

Pango took the service elevator from the galley down to the marina. Yes, if he was going to devise an exit strategy for himself and the waiters, then it would have to be here.

They could forget using the lifeboats on Deck Six. Glenroy would spot them. Things would get ugly.

But there were several boats in the marina. All Pango had to do was figure out a way to get to them. And to do it without Glenroy's knowledge. That meant disabling the closed-circuit cameras before doing anything else.

Pango stepped off the elevator, aware that Glenroy could be watching him on the bridge monitors. He would have to be careful about this. He could justify what he was doing in the marina—looking for the missing passenger, of course—but he would have a hard time explaining why he was messing with the cameras.

He moved slowly, cradling his rifle, eyeing the wall above him. His shoes crunched against broken glass at the same time he spotted a camera dangling from its bracket overhead, wires going every which way. Someone had already destroyed it.

Pango remembered standing on the bridge when the skirmish on Deck Three had broken out, watching the monitors, the face of the young man with the wispy beard as he swung a metal bar, followed by static on the screen. That had been part of their plan, to take out as many cameras as they could. Obviously, one of the passengers had made it down here. And as Pango moved around the perimeter of the marina, weaving past towering stacks of boxes, he found two other cameras, each of them de-commissioned, too.

A lucky break, Pango thought, a sign that this plan of his was a good plan. And he relaxed a bit with the knowledge that Glenroy was not watching his every move.

He moved across the storeroom to the boat bay. He found the gate and the big lock that held it closed. He leaned his rifle against the wire enclosure and gripped the lock with both hands, gave it a tug. Then he looked around, saw the provisions master's cubicle office, and headed for it.

After the earlier incident in the marina, when Jati shot the provisions master, he and Pango had dragged the body into the cubicle. And now Pango stepped over it to get to the desk. He riffled through drawers, looking for a key that might unlock the boat bay. Nothing.

He knelt by the provisions master's body, went through his pockets. Nothing there either. Pango thought about it. Who else might have a key or know where the key might be? The dockmaster. A young Australian guy with sun-bleached hair, a surfer type. Pango remembered seeing him among the crew members who were being held in the casino. He would go up there, get the key from the dockmaster.

But as Pango moved out of the cubicle he heard a creaking noise from the far side of the cavernous storeroom. The service elevator. He ducked back behind the provisions master's desk, heard the elevator doors slide open. Then a voice.

"Get out, both of you."

Todora.

What was she doing down here?

Pango edged out from the cubicle, then darted toward a long row of pallets, stacked high with boxes. He crept along behind the boxes, making his way closer to the elevator, trying to get a glimpse of what was going on.

And then he spotted them—Todora, Ron Diamond, and Sam Jebailey. Todora had her pistol pointed at the men and all three of them were looking at something that Pango couldn't see. He moved to get a better angle, saw nine aluminum suitcases lined up side by side along a wall. Pango had noticed the suitcases when he stepped off the elevator. But he had been more concerned with the cameras and hadn't paid them close attention.

Todora turned to Jebailey, said, "That is all of them? There are no more?"

"That is everything," Jebailey said. "I promise."

"How much?" Todora asked.

"Altogether—twenty million dollars," Jebailey said.

Todora said something to Diamond. Pango couldn't make out the words. And then Jebailey's voice rose above theirs, saying: "I'm coming with you."

Todora turned on him, "No! There is not room on the helicopter. Not with the two of us and all these suitcases."

Diamond, getting in on it, told Jebailey: "That's the way it is, Sam. This is something she and I worked out. You're late to the dance."

With a wave of her pistol, Todora pointed Jebailey and Diamond back to the elevator. The doors closed and Pango listened as it creaked up to the galley.

He gave it a few moments, then walked over to the suitcases. He reached down and lifted one of them. It wasn't as heavy as he might have expected, still it had a good weight. He went down the line, lifting each of the suitcases, each of them weighing about the same.

Pango had a corkscrew in his pocket—after all, he was the maître' d'—and now he pulled it out and opened it, tried to jiggle a lock on one of the suitcases. No luck. But he took comfort in that. If he had twenty million dollars then he would keep it in suitcases that were not so easily opened.

Then he thought: I *do* have twenty million dollars. And it's sitting right here in front of me. In these fine suitcases that I will eventually figure out a way to open. Now it's just a matter of getting a boat and getting away with them.

But what was that about a helicopter? What did Todora and Diamond have up their sleeves? Whatever it was, Pango couldn't afford to wait around and find out. He had everything he needed right here.

All he needed to do was grab his rifle, then head up to the casino, find the dockmaster, unlock the boat bay. After everything was in place, he'd tell the waiters what was going on and they'd all make their escape. No need to let them know the details until everything was in place. Simpler that way, less room for something to go wrong.

Pango hurried across the storeroom. He reached the boat bay, stopped by the gate. He looked at the spot where he had leaned his rifle against the wire enclosure. He kept looking. It didn't change what he saw.

The rifle was gone.

47

Glenroy kept fighting it. He didn't want to sleep. Sonny would soon be coming to the bridge. Still, Glenroy needed to be well rested for what lay ahead. His mind would have to be clear and focused. A short nap couldn't hurt.

And as he allowed himself to drift off, sitting in the swivel chair at the helm, he dreamed about the madrasa, the school in the hills above Port-of-Spain. His home for nearly eleven years, the happiest days of his life.

Shortly after Glenroy turned eighteen, the imam summoned him for a private audience. They sat on embroidered rugs in the shade of a tamarind tree in a corner of the compound. Young women in long white robes served a feast for just the two of them—cashew nuts and sweet currants, stewed chickpeas with cornmeal dumplings, curried lamb and honey cakes.

And after the women had been dismissed, the imam said, "You will leave tomorrow, my soldier."

Imam Ben-Yafati presented him with a newly minted passport, one that bore his birth name, Glenroy Patterson.

"To me and before Allah and all the faithful, you will always be Inshallah Shaheed," the imam said. "But for what you must do, this other name will be of service. It is a white man's name. It will help you avoid suspicion."

Glenroy nodded and waited, expecting that the imam would follow by giving him an airplane ticket to London or Tehran or any number of other places, faraway places, where the young men who went before him had been sent.

Instead, the imam handed him a manila folder.

"Your work papers and permits," the imam said. "They have been filled out and are in order. All you must do is take a bus into Port-of-Spain and get off at the main cruise terminal. I am told you should be there by 7:00 A.M. The ship is named the *Caribbean Queen*."

"The ship?"

"Yes, a cruise ship. Some of its crew, Jamaicans mostly, quit after a dispute over wages while the ship was in Barbados. You know Jamaicans, always stirring up trouble. I was able to secure a job for you in the engine room."

Glenroy hung his head, not wanting the imam to read his hurt, to see the tears that stung his eyes.

"What is it, my son?"

Glenroy's shame was so great he could not bear to look at the imam.

"I am sorry to have disappointed you, Father," he said.

The imam reached out, touched Glenroy's face.

"Look at me," he said. "You have not disappointed me. No, you among all my sons, I trust to find a path of his own. You are a warrior above all warriors, a general, a mighty army unto yourself."

"Thank you, Father. But I had prepared myself to leave here, to travel far away. And now you are telling me that I must go to work in the engine room of a ship? I don't understand . . ."

The imam raised a hand to silence him.

"Please, my son. For too long I have sent your brothers off to join the battle in distant places. No more. The time has come for us to do battle closer to home."

"What sort of battle, Father?"

"The war of Islaam Karibe. A jihad in the Caribbean. A war against those who would poison these islands with the ways of the unfaithful. You will join the war, Inshallah Shaheed."

"This war, when will it take place?"

"It has already begun, my son."

"Then I am ready."

The imam smiled.

"In such a war as ours, victory belongs to the patient," he said. "The battle you must fight, it might not come for years, many years. When the time is right, you will know."

"But what am I to do?"

"Just go, my son. It is my duty to point you in the proper direction. The hand of Allah will lead you the rest of the way. From time to time, others may contact you. They will greet you by your true name and you will do as they say." The imam drew Glenroy close, kissed his forehead. "From this day forward, you will not return here to Trinidad. We will not see each other again, not until that glorious day when we are united in Firdaws, the highest level of Paradise, with Allah and all the prophets."

Eleven years ago . . .

Over those years, Glenroy had worked and watched and waited. His job aboard the *Caribbean Star* had led him to positions on other cruise ships, always in the engine rooms. And while his skills could easily have earned him advancement, he remained a motorman, responsible for the grunt work, the maintenance and cleaning of the engines.

He kept the words of the imam close to his heart: "The humble and the lowly serve Allah in the highest."

Still, they were lonely years for Glenroy. He made few friends. He kept his head down. He practiced his faith and performed the daily *salats*, but always alone and away from the eyes of others.

Twice he received packets in the mail. They bore no return address, but Glenroy had little doubt they came from the imam. The first contained a copy of the *Trinidad Guardian*, dated Oct. 13, 2000, the headline blaring: "Terrorist Bomb Boat Cripples U.S. Battleship in Yemen—17 Dead." A photo showed the USS *Cole*, a gaping hole amidship, the work of suicide bombers thought to be affiliated with Al Qaeda.

Something for Glenroy to think about.

The second packet contained another copy of the *Guardian*, from the Sept. 28, 2004, edition. Under the headline, "Philippines Ferry Disaster Thought to Be Work of Terrorists," the article told of an explosion aboard the nine-hundred-passenger *SuperFerry 14* sailing out of Manila. While investigators originally blamed it on an accident in the engine room, they later concluded that terrorists had placed eight pounds of TNT inside a television set stored in the cargo hold. According to the story, the 116 resulting deaths made it the world's deadliest terrorist attack at sea.

Something else for Glenroy to think about.

Not long afterward, the cruise line Glenroy was working for at the time transferred him to its newest vessel, its pride and joy, the 5,200-passenger *King of the Seas*. And it was here, in the vast underbelly of this giant ship, that Glenroy's plan began to take form. He would destroy this ship. He would take it down. Hundreds and hundreds would die. Thousands even. Glenroy had the access. He knew where the ship was the most vulnerable, where a well-placed bomb could do the most damage. It was just a simple matter of putting together the right materials, waiting for the appropriate time.

Then an unforeseen setback. The cruise line merged with a competitor. Several older ships were put out of service. And the new chief engineer of the *King of the Seas* replaced most of the engine-room crew, including Glenroy, with men he had worked with in the past.

Glenroy had saved plenty of money. He could get by easily enough until he found work on another ship. He went back to the cheap apartment he kept in Miami, in a neighborhood populated by all kinds of folks from the greater Caribbean diaspora. And one evening, when he was sitting in a roti shop off Unity Boulevard, eating dhalpuri ripe with cumin and garlic, a man sat down across from him.

"Good evening, Inshallah Shaheed," the man said. "The women in the kitchen here, dey have a sweet hand, yeah?"

The man was older than Glenroy and he spoke in an accent Glenroy recognized. Sweet hand, that was a Trinidad thing. A man always wanted a woman with a sweet hand.

The man said, "I will give you an address. Do not write it down, you understand?"

Glenroy nodded. The man told him the address, a house in Hialeah.

"Go there tomorrow," the man said. "They will be expecting you. They will teach you what you need to know."

The man stood to go.

"You will need money," the man said. "Come here. I will find you."

And with that the man was gone. Glenroy never learned his name.

He went to the house in Hialeah. Over the course of a week he learned what he needed to know. The materials were easy to come by. Alone they were not dangerous, but when combined they were deadly beyond belief.

It did not escape Glenroy's notice that several of the men in the house in Hialeah were missing fingers, one of them his entire right hand. They were young men, younger than Glenroy. Few bomb makers lived to be very old.

Not long afterward, Glenroy landed a position on another ship. It was there he met Pango. And two years later, both were recruited to work aboard the *Royal Star.*

In Glenroy's dream, he had returned to the compound in the hills above Port-of-Spain. He wore a long white robe with golden trim. And he seemed to float across the courtyard, past men, women, and children who had lined up to greet him.

They chanted his one true name: "Inshallah Shaheed! Inshallah Shaheed!"

Some reached out to touch the hem of his robe. Others knelt before him.

From somewhere a bell began to ring, and as it grew louder, Glenroy floated past the crowd and made his way toward Imam Ben-Yafati, who was standing outside the mosque. The imam embraced Glenroy, kissed his forehead.

The bell continued to ring as the imam pointed toward the alcove and the shrine to the young men who had left the madrasa to fulfill their missions, the young men who had never returned.

There on the wall, beside the other photos, Glenroy saw a photo of himself, with bouquets of flowers piled high on the floor below.

And the bell rang even louder . . .

48

Glenroy jolted awake.

He shot a look at the clock. He'd been asleep for almost half an hour. And the ringing was coming from an alarm on the primary radar panel. Glenroy had programmed it to go off if another vessel came within a one-mile radius of the *Royal Star.*

He jumped up from the chair and studied the waters ahead. No sign of another ship. To starboard he could make out the faint silhouette of a coastline—the eastern tip of Cuba, where it met the Windward Passage. Beyond it, another fifty miles, lay Haiti.

The alarm kept ringing. Glenroy flipped it off. He hurried from one side of the bridge to the other, looking out the tall bridge windows, using the binoculars now. Still no sign of another ship.

He looked at the bank of monitors. Some of the screens showed only static—cameras destroyed by the male passengers. Several of the exterior cameras were mounted to scan the waters aft and abeam of the *Royal Star,* but the images were jumpy and Glenroy couldn't make out much from them.

What had caused the alarm to sound?

Glenroy didn't think the ship was in any immediate danger. But he had to be certain.

That meant leaving the bridge, going out on one of the bridge wings to get a better look.

A plastic crate sat under the console, filled with papers and folders. Glenroy dumped it out. He headed to the door leading to the starboard bridge wing, punched the green button to open it, then the yellow one to keep it open. He stuck the crate in the doorway to make sure the door didn't close behind him.

Ahead of him, the starboard bridge wing jutted out ten yards from the side of the ship. He walked out along the narrow catwalk, gripping the rails until he reached the platform at the end. He looked out on the water.

A hundred feet below, a small fishing boat bobbed atop the waves, its hull patched and unpainted, the trim in need of repair, a plume of black smoke tailing off its transom.

A man worked a makeshift tiller, fashioned from a broomstick, fighting to keep the boat from capsizing as it ran parallel to the ship. A boy stood on the bow and when he spotted Glenroy he waved and held up a stringer of fish—some tiny snapper, a bonito or two.

The boy was smiling now and shouting something. Glenroy couldn't hear his words above the roar of the ship. Just a Cuban fisherman and his son, hoping to make a little money unloading their meager catch.

Glenroy looked right then left. No other boats to be seen. Just this poor excuse for a fishing boat. Still, he was pleased that the alarm had worked.

The boy on the boat reached into a big bucket and pulled out a long silver fish, a king mackerel it looked like. He held it up with both hands. Their prize catch, no doubt.

"Go!" Glenroy shouted. "Go away!"

He waved the boat off and left the bridge wing, kicked the crate out of the doorway and shut the door behind him. He stepped to the helm and nudged the throttle forward, moved the joystick to take the ship farther offshore. He didn't want to be bothered by any more fishermen.

Then came a knock on the main bridge door.

Glenroy glanced at the monitors. One of the screens showed Sonny outside in the hallway. Right on time, just like he'd promised.

49

The passengers were getting restless. The *King of the Seas* had been sched-
uled to dock at Isla Paradiso by 9:00 A.M., but the engine had conked
out on one of the pilot boats and by the time repairs were finished the ship
was running two hours late.

Now the decks were jam-packed with people, impatient, ready to go
ashore. This was the last stop on the itinerary, the last chance for them to
buy souvenirs, to hit the beach, to get hammered on the local rum. Many
of them had signed up for special excursions or activities. Scuba diving.
Parasailing. A booze cruise on a "pirate" ship. They were champing at the
bit.

Captain Luca Palmano had made an announcement over the ship's PA
system, explaining the glitch and assuring the passengers they wouldn't
miss out on anything. They would have more than enough time to see and
do everything that Isla Paradiso had to offer. The final boarding call
wouldn't come until 8:00 P.M. An hour later, the *King of the Seas* would be
on its way to Miami.

If necessary, the ship could have docked without the aid of the second
pilot boat. But regulations stipulated a pair of them, the cruise line paying
a twenty-five-hundred-dollar fee per boat, plus an extra five hundred dollars for the pilot who boarded the *King of the Seas* and stayed on the bridge
until docking was complete. Remove one boat from the equation and it

not only took income from the pilot and his crew, but robbed local officials of the kickbacks they extracted each time a ship came to visit. The money got sliced a lot of ways.

Besides, requiring two pilot boats was prudent maritime procedure. Docking at Isla Paradiso could be tricky.

The private port had been created by the cruise line twenty years earlier, when the largest ships weren't even half the size of the *King of the Seas*. The mouth of the harbor was narrow and plagued by crosscurrents colliding at the tip of the island. Approaching it without incident meant navigating waters that were in constant flux due to extreme tides and shifting sandbars. Conditions could change on a daily basis.

To make matters worse, a misguided dredging operation the year before had resulted in several hundred tons of limestone being deposited on both sides of the slender channel. The idea had been to build a breakwater that would protect the harbor entrance from violent surges and make passage into Isla Paradiso less tumultuous. But Hurricane Naomi tore through with plans of her own. The storm demolished the breakwater and left behind a treacherous, rocky gauntlet. The local knowledge provided by the pilots was essential.

As the *King of the Seas* completed its docking maneuvers, Captain Palmano left the bridge and headed down to Deck Five and the main gangway. He wanted to be there when it opened, wanted to make an appearance, to personally thank the passengers for their patience as they exited the ship for a day of sun and fun at Isla Paradiso.

People were stacked deep around the gangway, all the way up the staircase to Deck Six. The crowd parted as Palmano descended, looking upon him with awe and respect.

A couple of the men gave him grinning salutes, which Palmano returned in sharp, serious fashion. Several of the passengers, women mostly, prevailed upon him for a quick photograph. He happily obliged them. He never turned anyone down.

It was good PR. The cruise line was big on brand loyalty. It paid close attention to its percentage of repeat passengers and handed out bonuses accordingly.

Palmano took up position just past the security checkpoint, by the gangway steps, so he could help any older passengers who might need a hand.

Outside of the ship's temperature-controlled bowels, the sun was unrelenting, the air hot and sticky. Wooden huts lined the beach and vendors displayed their wares—hand-dyed fabrics, wood carvings, crude jewelry.

Others were frying fish, grilling pork, stirring big pots with peppery stews—aromas mingling on the light breeze.

Palmano had been greeting disembarking passengers for about ten minutes when a phone rang at the security checkpoint. A junior officer answered, handed the receiver to Palmano.

"The bridge calling for you, sir," the junior officer said.

The watch commander was on the other end of the line. He told Palmano the pilot was getting ready to leave the ship and wanted to confirm when he should return for the ship's departure.

"He is asking me if we would consider delaying departure by a few hours," the watch commander said. "Leave at midnight instead of 9:00 P.M. He says the tide might be more favorable then."

Palmano knew what the pilot was up to. It had nothing to do with the tide. The pilot had no doubt been pressured by the vendors on the beach at Isla Paradiso. An extra few hours would give them a chance to recoup losses caused by the ship's late arrival.

Palmano was sympathetic. But he didn't have a few hours to spare. The ship couldn't risk being even a little bit late returning to Miami. The turnaround time was that tight. The *King of the Seas* had to dock by 6:00 A.M. on Sunday. All passengers had to be off by 8:00 A.M. Then the ship had to be cleaned, provisioned, and ready to greet the incoming hordes by 3:00 P.M.

"No, tell him we'll stick to the schedule," Palmano told the watch commander. "Depart as planned—9:00 P.M."

50

I had never given much consideration to how I would play it when my number was finally called. I flattered myself to think I would take my cue from Dylan Thomas. Come the fading light, I would rage and struggle. No way would I go gentle into the good night.

But my futile pursuit of the cargo ship had left me exhausted in body and spirit. With midday approaching, sun-addled and bone-weary, I wanted nothing more than to slip away and let the sea embrace me.

Let go. Just end it. Let go. Down, down, down—the deep drop. Of all the ways there are to die, it's surely not the worst.

I released my grip on the web strap between the boxes. I felt the gentle tug of the ocean, let myself be pulled away.

And in that instant, I conjured Barbara's face, her smile, her love. I thought about our child, the child I might never know. So much to lose.

I kicked my way back to the boxes, grabbed the strap. I hung on.

I faded in and faded out. Real became unreal. I could not separate what was from what was not. Or from what used to be.

No longer was I a grown man lost at sea, clinging to waterlogged boxes, just barely afloat. I was a boy, no more than three or four, splashing around in the wading pool that had been a present for my birthday.

The wading pool sat in the backyard of our home on Redfish Lagoon, the house I grew up in, the same one Barbara and I shared. Living on the water as we did, my parents made sure I could swim before I could walk. By the time I was two, I was jumping off our dock into the arms of my grandfather. He first taught me to dog-paddle, later helped me perfect the Australian crawl.

"Fishboy," he called me. "If you don't watch out you're gonna sprout gills."

I believed him, used to study my neck in the mirror to see if it were true.

My mother didn't like me swimming in the lagoon. Stingrays schooled in the shallows and she was afraid I might get barbed. It had happened to my dad when he was a boy. Almost severed his Achilles tendon. Left him with an ugly scar and a limp.

So my mother bought the wading pool and put it between the back porch and the clothesline, the better for keeping an eye on me.

That was my first real memory, in that wading pool. My first understanding that I was of this world, yet apart from it. My first sense of being me.

The water in the wading pool was only a few inches deep. I could rest on my back, completely submerged but for the tip of my nose, just enough to breathe. I would lay there, motionless, imagining things that only a child can imagine when watching fluffy clouds course across an endless sky.

The most distinct memory of all—hearing my mother sing as she hung out laundry to dry.

The shrimp boats are a-coming, they're coming, they're coming
The shrimp boats are a-coming, there's dancing tonight . . .

The clothesline only a few feet from the wading pool. Sheets billowing above me, rustling in the breeze.

Why don't-cha hurry, hurry, hurry home
Why don't-cha hurry, hurry, hurry home . . .

I could hear her voice. Her sweet, sweet voice.

Just slip away. So easy to let go. Hurry, hurry home . . .

I opened my eyes, sought a final glimpse of sky. Saw something white arcing above me. A sheet on the clothesline. Could hear it flap-flap-flapping.

So real, so real.

A giant sheet. Only, with numbers on it. And an insignia of some sort—a cross.

Flap-flap-flapping.

Not a sheet. A sail.

A man's voice: "Allo! Allo you!"

And then something thrust my way, something long and aluminum. A boat hook. I looked at it, not comprehending.

A woman's voice: "Take, take!"

I grabbed the boat hook, felt myself pulled through the water, my head hitting something hard—a fiberglass hull.

Then arms reaching down, pulling me from the sea.

THIRD WATCH

51

When Pango returned to Deck Five, he was relieved to find that the waiters had everything under control. Tony and Marcos were in the Galaxy Lounge with the passengers. Felix and Jati were still stationed in the atrium. It was the most strategic position for keeping an eye on the crew, which was split between the casino and the library.

The fifth waiter, Benny, the one beaten by the male passengers, was lying on a blanket in the atrium, outside the purser's office. Benny's face was horrible to behold—a mass of bruises, his lips split and pulpy, eyes swollen shut. Most of the blood had been wiped away, but more of it oozed from the stitches across his cheekbones and along his forehead.

An owlish man with a gray beard and wire-rim glasses sat next to Benny, dabbing at the wounds with a washcloth—the ship's doctor, Dr. Louttit. A semiretired physician from Orlando, he had signed on for a three-month stint aboard the *Royal Star* with hopes that the easy duty would give him time to work on his memoirs. He'd have plenty to write about now.

"How is he?" Pango asked the doctor.

"A concussion, but he's conscious. A half-dozen broken ribs, a broken collarbone. I was just getting ready to give him something more for the pain," Louttit said, reaching for the black leather bag beside him. After quelling the skirmish with the male passengers and moving Benny up to Deck Five, Pango had escorted the doctor to the ship's clinic to retrieve the bag. Now he watched as the doctor filled a hypodermic needle with some sort of clear liquid and injected it in Benny's arm.

"Is it OK to move him?" Pango didn't want to leave Benny behind when he and the other waiters made their escape.

"Move him where?" the doctor asked.

"A cabin maybe, where he can be more comfortable."

"Should be alright to do that," the doctor said. "It looks worse than it is."

"Thank you, Doctor, for taking care of him. Under the circumstances . . ."

Dr. Louttit looked at him.

"How much longer is this going to last?" he asked. "Can't you just give us an idea, please, of where we are going, what is happening . . ."

"Soon," Pango said. "It will be over soon. I promise."

Pango stepped away to join Felix and Jati in the middle of the atrium. From the casino and the library, crew members looked out and, seeing Pango, a few of them began to pound on the windows. He could hear their muffled shouts.

He spotted Yap-Yap and his gang from the laundry by one of the casino windows. Yap-Yap giving Pango the death stare, the cold, hard glare of a man betrayed. Behind Yap-Yap, Pango thought he saw the dockmaster, standing on one of the blackjack tables, trying to get a better look outside. Pango would have to go in there to get the dockmaster.

Just one problem . . .

"Where is your rifle?" Jati asked him.

"It jammed," Pango lied. "I could not fix it."

Pango had convinced himself that he had simply misplaced the rifle, that the heaving of the ship had caused it to slide on the slick marina floor, away from the spot where he had left it. It was probably under one of the pallets, somewhere Pango could not easily find it. The other explanation—someone had taken the rifle, the missing passenger maybe—was something Pango didn't want to think about.

Jati cradled a SAR in his arms. The same rifle Pango had emptied on the stairwell, when he shot the captain. Pango looked at Felix, then turned so the doctor could not overhear him.

"Your rifle, Felix," he said. "How many rounds in the clip?"

"Just one," Felix said.

More crew members had come to the windows in the casino and the racket from inside was increasing. They couldn't get out—the doors to both the casino and the library were locked from the atrium side. The only thing that prevented the crew from breaking out the windows was the two waiters standing watch with their rifles. Their empty, worthless rifles.

Still, there was no getting around it. Pango would have to go into the casino. Yes, he could bluff it. Felix and Jati could put up a menacing front, maybe keep the rest of the crew at bay for the short time it would take Pango to remove the dockmaster from the casino and find out where he kept the keys to the boat bay.

But what if someone decided to be a hero? That's all it would take, just one person, rushing them. And when there was no burst of gunfire to stop that person, then others would follow. Forget how badly Benny had been beaten. If the crew got their hands on Pango and the waiters they wouldn't stop until they had ripped them from limb to limb. Yap-Yap and his men would take particular pleasure in it.

Pango stepped to the doorway of the Galaxy Lounge. He saw Tony sitting in a chair near the stage, his rifle on his lap. The other waiter, Marcos, stood just inside the door. Pango got his attention, drew him aside.

"Your rifle," Pango said.

He took it from Marcos, checked the clip. A half-dozen rounds.

"What about Tony, his rifle?"

Marcos shrugged.

"Two shots, maybe three," Marcos said.

Pango looked around the lounge. The passengers were watching him, wondering what was up. He was surprised to see Sam Jebailey, sitting by himself, off to one side of the room. So Todora and the other man who was with her, Diamond, they were cutting Jebailey out of whatever it was they were planning. Interesting.

Pango heard someone moan, saw the pregnant woman on the stage. She was in pain, struggling. Her time was drawing near.

Pango needed Marcos's rifle. But he didn't want to take it with all the passengers watching, didn't want them to suspect anything. He handed the rifle back to Marcos.

"Two minutes," he told Marcos. "You join me outside."

Pango stepped back to the atrium. He walked over to where Dr. Louttit sat by Benny.

"When I return we will take Benny away, to somewhere else," Pango said. "What medicines will he need?"

The doctor rummaged around in his bag, pulled out two vials of pills, a handful of small aluminum packets.

"For pain and the swelling," the doctor said. "And antiseptic to keep the wounds clean."

Pango stuck everything in one of his pockets. He nodded to the Galaxy Lounge.

"There is a woman in there who is about to have a baby," Pango said.

"Yes, Ms. Pickering," the doctor said. "I met her and her husband earlier. Is she OK?"

"Go," Pango said. "Take care of her."

Dr. Louttit grabbed his bag and hurried away as Marcos stepped into the atrium.

Pango waved for Felix and Jati to join them. He explained that he needed to open the door of the casino and get the dockmaster. He told Marcos to stick by his side.

"Shoot anyone who makes a move," Pango said. "Jati, you and Felix, I want you to keep your rifles on Yap-Yap and his men. I am worried most about them. Make them think that you will kill them if they try anything. It should only take a moment. All we have to do is get the dockmaster."

"Why?" Jati asked.

"I will explain everything later," Pango said. "You will see."

52

Mixing the last ingredient, creating the compound, that was the tricky part.

Glenroy had been at it for more than an hour now, down on Deck One, working at a bench outside the engine control room, not far from the turbines and the fuel supply lines.

Just three ingredients. The first two came in five-gallon jugs and Glenroy had poured them into the big container on top of the bench. No problem with the first two ingredients. They formed a stable solution. You could slosh it around all you wanted to and nothing would happen.

But the last ingredient, that was the bitch. If Glenroy made a mistake with it—and a mistake would almost certainly result in an explosion—then at least it would ignite the supply lines and turn the *Royal Star* into a giant ball of fire. Glenroy had guaranteed that by cutting one of the auxilliary supply lines. Fuel had spread across the floor and puddled around his feet.

He worked slowly, taking his time, confident that Sonny could handle everything on the bridge. There was little that Sonny needed to do, really. Just make sure the bridge remained secure, keep an eye out for other ships, listen for the alarm on the primary radar panel.

Glenroy had considered leaving his SAR with Sonny, just in case. But he knew it would be useless in Sonny's hands. So Glenroy had put a fresh clip in the rifle, his last one, and brought it with him. It was leaning against the door of the engine control room, just a step away if he needed it.

Glenroy had a walkie-talkie, too. If anything happened, all Sonny had to do was call him.

Sonny had checked in once already, before Glenroy had even started mixing the ingredients, wanting to know when Glenroy would return.

"Soon," Glenroy told him. "Just sit tight."

"What are you doing down there?"

"I told you. I'm getting the money."

"How much?"

"Lots of it," Glenroy said. "Bags and bags of money."

"And then the boat will come to take us away?"

"Yes, then the boat will come."

"What does the boat look like, Glenroy? What if I see it, how am I supposed to know?"

"It will not come until after dark. Don't worry."

"Yes, but what if it comes early? I don't want for us to miss it. What does it look like?"

"It is a red boat," Glenroy told him. "A big red boat."

Because he had to tell Sonny something, get rid of him, focus on the work at hand.

Now Glenroy concentrated on releasing hydrochloric acid drop by drop into the big container on the workbench. Inside the container was a mixture of acetone and hydrogen peroxide. Not the everyday hydrogen peroxide found in medicine cabinets. That was a weak, three percent solution. This was industrial hydrogen peroxide, the thirty-five percent stuff, hard to come by without proper permits.

How fortunate that Sam Jebailey had decided to build a "green" ship. The *Royal Star*'s wastewater system, praised for its eco-friendliness, required industrial hydrogen peroxide by the vatful. As for the acetone and hydrochloric acid, they were common cleaning compounds, used throughout the ship. It had been a simple matter for Glenroy to get all he needed without drawing suspicion.

How fortunate, too, that Jebailey had chosen to shrink his ship's carbon footprint by forgoing the diesel engines used on most cruise ships in favor of turbines that ran on jet fuel. Much cleaner, jet fuel. Much more flammable, too.

Yes, everything Glenroy needed to make a bomb, a giant bomb, right here on the *Royal Star*. Including the turkey baster that Glenroy had stolen from the galley and now used ever so carefully, squeezing its bulb to dribble the hydrochloric acid, watching as the acid mingled with the solution, sparkling, creating little white flakes that were already collecting at the bottom of the container.

A pint of hydrochloric acid to ten gallons of solution. Enough to produce nearly five pounds of deadly explosive.

The Mother of Satan.

That's what the men at the house in Hialeah had called it when Glenroy had visited them. They had told him its real name, too. Some chemical name. But he had long since forgotten it. The Mother of Satan. That said it all.

The same substance that Richard Reid, the infamous shoe bomber, had tried to use to detonate plastic explosives in his boots aboard a flight from Paris to Miami. The same substance used with success on the Madrid trains in 2004 and the next year on the London subway.

The men at the house in Hialeah had shown Glenroy what just a small amount of the white flakes could do. In the garage of the house, there was a freezer and that was where they kept a jar of the deadly compound.

"After it is made, it must be stored at ten degrees Celsius or below," one of them men told Glenroy. "Otherwise—kaboom!"

The men had laughed. Glenroy didn't know who they were or where they came from. Colombians, he suspected. He didn't ask and they didn't tell.

The men had measured out less than a teaspoon of the compound and put it on a metal table in the garage. One of them hoisted a concrete block on a pulley above the table.

"Stand back," the man said.

He released the pulley's rope. The concrete block slammed down on the compound. And the explosion rocked the garage, sent Glenroy reeling against the wall, covering his head from the flying debris.

Just that little bit, and it had ripped the metal table apart.

"No fuse, no detonator," said one of the men. "A beautiful thing, yes?"

Yes, Glenroy agreed, a most beautiful thing.

"Twenty-five thousand," the man told Glenroy. "And we will show you how to make this Mother of Satan, all that you want."

Glenroy returned to the roti shop off Unity Boulevard. His contact, the man from Trinidad, gave him the money. And later, when Glenroy needed more money, money to buy the SARs, money to pay off Pango and the waiters, the man never asked questions. He just gave Glenroy all that he asked for.

Glenroy finished squeezing out the last of the hydrochloric acid. He studied the container, marveled at how the solution inside had taken on a life of its own, a terrible beast about to be unleashed.

He checked his watch. It would take about six hours to complete the process, for all the white flakes to settle to the bottom. Then Glenroy would pour off as much liquid as possible and use a small gas stove to boil away the rest until he was left with about five pounds of powder.

Then came the truly dangerous part. Even at ten degrees Celsius, the compound was volatile, particularly if something slammed hard against it. But at room temperature, the least little thing could set it off.

That's why Glenroy had waited until now to make it. He didn't want to risk an explosion until the last possible moment.

In six hours, he would separate the powder into five portions, which he would put in plastic bags and place around the ship. Three bags distributed around the forward end of the ship—at the bowsprit, in the anchor well, deep in the bow storage hold. They would explode upon impact. The other two bags would remain in the engine room, placed under the turbines and the fuel supply.

Then Glenroy would guide the ship to its final destination.

And ka-boom.

Glenroy had practiced making the compound several times at his apartment in Miami. It could be finicky. The proportions had to be just right. It had always worked in the past, but he had never made such a large quantity as this. He was confident of the measurements, and looking now at the container, he could see the white particulates drifting down through the solution, just like they had on smaller batches.

But just in case this big batch didn't turn out, Glenroy had some insurance. He left the engine control room to check on it now, taking the stairs three flights up to the galley.

He headed straight to the big walk-in freezer, opened the door. A beaded chain dangled in front of him and Glenroy pulled it, turning on the freezer lights. He stepped to the back of the storage area, making his way past big tubs of ice cream, crates of frozen chickens, sides of beef. The condensing unit, an aluminum box about three feet tall, sat against the rear wall of the freezer, chugging away. Glenroy knelt down and reached behind the condenser, finding what he had hidden there three nights earlier, hanging from a hook on the wall.

What an ordeal that had been, Glenroy wrapping it so carefully in his apartment, taping it to his chest under his uniform, and then sneaking it on board the *Royal Star*, fearing all the while that it would explode and him with it. Then waiting with it in his cabin, waiting until he was sure all the galley crew were gone. The freezer was the only place where he knew it might be safe.

And now he gently removed it from behind the condenser—a heavy-duty freezer bag containing half a pound of white powder, the most he'd ever made before now. If the batch in the engine room didn't turn out, then this could do plenty of damage on its own. Placed next to the fuel supply it could easily cause an explosion that would destroy the *Royal Star*.

Glenroy wanted to leave the bag in the freezer, but he needed it to be easily accessible. He didn't want to just sit it on one of the shelves. The seas would be picking up as the ship approached the Windward Passage. Something might slide around and smack it.

The light chain.

Glenroy gathered the top of the plastic bag together and tied the beaded chain around it. Perfect. The bag could swing freely, safe no matter how turbulent the seas became. And if he needed it, all he had to do was reach inside the freezer.

He shut the door and left the galley, heading for the bridge.

53

FRIDAY, 12:25 P.M.

Y our water still hasn't broken," Dr. Louttit said. "That's a good sign."

"What's so good about it?" Barbara said. "I feel like I'm ready to burst."

Dr. Louttit opened his bag.

"Would you like something to ease the pain?"

Barbara shook her head.

"No, I'm going to try and hold off as long as I can."

"Oh, honey, please. Don't be such a brave soldier. No one is handing out purple hearts here. Take what the nice man is offering," Marie Lutey said. "What you got in there anyway, Doc? A little Valium? Some Vicodin maybe? Enough to go around?"

"Sorry," the doctor said. "I need to keep what I have for extreme emergencies."

"Can't blame a girl for asking," Marie said. She sized him up. "You married?"

"A widower," Dr. Louttit said. "Two years now."

"Me, too," Marie said. "A widow, I mean. Almost three years. Bernie was the dearest, dearest man. Then his heart conked out. Just like that. Went to sleep right beside me one night and when I woke up he was dead. Never made a sound. But that was Bernie. Dear, dear Bernie. What was your wife's name, Doctor?"

"Ruth."

"Ruth, such a nice, sweet name. Like in the Bible."

"Why, yes, I suppose so," the doctor said.

"I'm Marie." Marie stuck out her hand. The doctor shook it. "And I can assure you, Doctor, there's absolutely nothing biblical about me."

"Excuse me," Barbara said. "But maybe the doctor can give me an idea exactly how long we're looking at here?"

Dr. Louttit asked Barbara to bend her legs. He draped a shawl over them, began probing around underneath.

Barbara tried to focus on something else. She looked around the lounge. The men were politely averting their eyes, trying as best they could not to intrude on her privacy.

One of the waiters who had been guarding them had stepped out of the lounge a few moments earlier. The other waiter, Tony, had moved away from the stage and was watching over them from the doorway. He was jittery and kept glancing out to the atrium, as if something was going on out there.

Dr. Louttit finished his inspection down below.

"You're about five centimeters dilated," he said. "Some discharge. How far apart did you say the contractions were?"

Marie answered before Barbara could.

"About six minutes," she said, giving the doctor a big smile and adjusting her chest just so.

"Well, then, I'd say you are definitely into second-stage labor."

"But I'm only at about thirty-one weeks," Barbara said. "I thought I'd have at least another month or so."

"These things happen when they happen, Ms. Pickering, the calendar notwithstanding," the doctor said. "And right now, I'd guess that you are anywhere from six to fifteen hours away from having yourself a baby."

54

Pango lucked out. The bluff worked. At the sight of the three waiters marching into the casino with their rifles, the crew members had fallen back. No one had offered the least bit of resistance when Pango grabbed the dockmaster and hauled him out to the atrium.

The dockmaster was no pushover. Pango asked him where to find the keys to the boat bay.

"Go fuck yourself, mate," the dockmaster said.

Jati slammed a rifle butt against the side of his head, dropped him to his knees. That had gotten his mind right. He didn't put up a fight when Pango went through his pockets and found a key chain. The dockmaster even showed him which key was for the boat bay and told him where to find the controls to open the marina hatch.

Now Pango was in the marina, unfastening the U-lock, rolling back the gate to the boat bay. A pair of skiffs, seventeen-footers with twin 150 hp engines, sat near the gate. They would take one of them. Pango wouldn't be able to roll it out by himself. He would need help from the waiters for that. But at least he could load the suitcases now and be ready to go. He wanted their exit to be a quick one. Tell the waiters to follow him, then get on the boat and go.

Pango moved down an aisle lined high with boxes, occasionally stopping to look under pallets for the missing rifle. Not that he really needed it now. He had taken Felix's rifle. Still, it would be nice to know what happened to it.

He reached the end of the aisle and looked along the wall near the elevator, looked at the exact spot where, not an hour earlier, Todora and Diamond and Jebailey had stood inspecting the nine suitcases.

Now the suitcases were gone. Not a sign of them anywhere.

It was too much for Pango, too much. He gripped his rifle, spun around, and looked down the aisle from where he'd just come. Nothing there.

What was going on? First the rifle, now the suitcases. Just what the hell was going on?

He backed toward the elevator. The sooner he gathered up the waiters and got off the ship the better. But all that money. He hated the idea of losing it. Once the waiters were down here, maybe they could all fan out and help him look for the suitcases. They had to be somewhere. They couldn't have just disappeared.

Pango pushed the elevator button. The doors opened and he backed his way on.

No sooner had Pango stepped off the elevator and into the galley than he spotted Glenroy standing in the door of the freezer.

Pango crouched behind a prep table. The last thing he wanted now was to cross paths with Glenroy. Glenroy would want to know if he had found the missing passenger and Pango would have to tell him no. Or Glenroy would ask him about Todora, where she was, what she was doing. Pango would have to tell him that he didn't know. And that would just set Glenroy off again.

No, better to keep hidden and out of Glenroy's way. But what was he doing in the freezer?

Pango watched as Glenroy fiddled with the light chain. But he couldn't make out exactly what Glenroy was doing.

Then Glenroy stepped out of the freezer and closed the door. Pango watched as he left the galley, saw him exit through the double doors that led to the main dining room.

Pango gave it a couple of minutes. And when he was fairly certain that Glenroy wasn't returning, he continued on his way through the galley.

He moved past the freezer. Then stopped.

What had Glenroy been doing in there? Maybe Pango should take a look.

He opened the freezer door. He saw the light chain, saw something hanging from it. He pulled on the chain and the lights came on.

A plastic bag. And in it some kind of white powder. A cup of it maybe.

Cocaine? Was that Glenroy's game? In addition to whatever else he was up to, was he moving dope?

Not much of it in the bag. But even a little bit of cocaine could bring a lot of money. Might come in handy. Especially if Pango and the waiters couldn't locate those missing suitcases.

Pango grabbed the plastic bag. He yanked it loose from the light chain.

Just a little taste, he thought. The pills he'd taken earlier had long since worn off. The buzz would do him good.

He opened the bag. He licked the tip of his finger. He dabbed it against the powder, then touched it to his tongue.

And it was like napalm, burning him, a fire erupting on his tongue. He spat. He cussed. He spat again. The burning only got worse, spreading now to the back of his throat. He coughed, gagged.

He threw the bag down on the floor. And in his rage, in his pain, he raised a foot and stomped it.

55

Glenroy was on the landing between Decks Six and Seven when he felt the rumbling from deep within the ship.

He knew instantly what it was. Nothing else it could be. But how had it happened? Had the bag slipped from the light chain and fallen to the floor? That alone shouldn't have caused an explosion. What then?

Didn't matter. It was done. Now Glenroy had to get back to the galley to find out how bad this was.

The explosion could have blown out the hull all the way down to the waterline. The *Royal Star* could be in danger of sinking.

Or the explosion might have started a fire. Glenroy would have to put it out or, short of that, come up with a way to contain it. The *Royal Star* was designed with a series of fire locks, making it possible to compartmentalize a blaze, seal it off before it could spread to other parts of the ship. And since the engine-room crew also served as the ship's fire department, Glenroy had some experience on that front.

As Glenroy hit the stairwell to head back down, his walkie-talkie crackled—Sonny.

"Glenroy? Are you there? Are you alright?"

"Yeah, OK," Glenroy told him.

"What happened? The last I saw you were down in the engine room . . ."

Glenroy thought: *The last he saw?* He'd forgotten about the cameras, forgotten that Sonny could track his whereabouts on the bridge monitors.

"I'm going to the galley," Glenroy said. "Can you see anything there?"

A pause on Sonny's end, then . . .

"No, nothing from the galley. All those cameras are out."

"What about the rest of the ship? Any sign of trouble, fire?"

Another pause.

"No, nothing that I can see," Sonny said.

"Any alarms going off on the bridge? Gauges all in the safe zone?"

"No alarms. Let me check the other," Sonny said. "No, everything looks OK."

"Alright, just stay there."

"But, Glenroy," Sonny said. "The engine room. What were you doing down there? I saw . . ."

Glenroy clicked off the walkie-talkie.

He smelled smoke by the time he hit Deck Five and spotted two of the waiters running from the atrium to the stairwell. He waved them back.

"Stay here!" Glenroy shouted. "I'll handle it."

He grabbed a fire extinguisher from the wall as he reached Deck Four and headed toward the dining room. Tables were toppled and the double doors leading to the galley had been blown off their hinges.

A few tablecloths near the door were aflame. Glenroy quickly doused them before heading into the galley. The smoke was thick but not so bad that he couldn't take in the extent of the explosion. The freezer's thick walls had contained much of the blast. Still, the entire middle section of the galley—prep tables, stovetops, racks of pots and pans—had been peeled up and plastered against the portside wall. Splitting the wall from ceiling to floor, a four-foot-wide gash, likely made by a dual-door oven that had been catapulted across the galley. Glenroy watched as the oven teetered on the precipice and then toppled over, disappearing outside.

Small fires burned throughout the galley, but nothing the fire extinguisher couldn't handle. Glenroy made quick work of them before stepping over to examine the gash in the wall. If nothing else, it was airing out the galley, sucking out what was left of the smoke.

Glenroy stuck his head through the hole, looked up and down. The damage had been confined to the galley deck. The ship didn't appear to be taking on water.

Glenroy made his way toward the freezer. Where the door once stood was now a jagged maw of metal. Inside, the smoke had not fully cleared, but Glenroy could tell that the explosion had obliterated everything, vaporizing entire sides of beef, knocking out the back wall to reveal the starboard side of the galley where the dishwashing station was located.

Outside the freezer, twenty feet in every direction, it was a burn zone. Anything once there no longer remained.

Glenroy took it all in, trying to figure out how it might have happened.

A hole in the floor near the freezer, three feet across. Glenroy stepped to its edge. The blast had blown down all the way to Deck Three and Glenroy could see the hallway below, its carpet blackened, but no sign of a fire.

He looked up. A hole in the ceiling, this one considerably smaller than the hole in the floor. Ceiling tiles smoldered, the light fixtures were mangled. But the hole did not extend all the way through to Deck Five, to the Galaxy Lounge, which sat directly above the galley.

Glenroy spotted something dangling from the hole in the ceiling. The twisted barrel of a SAR-21. He reached up and pulled it down.

A hand, severed at the wrist, still gripped the rifle's stock. Glenroy recognized the diamond pinkie ring.

So much for Pango.

56

Barbara was resting, making the most of a lull between contractions, when she heard the thunderous roar and felt the stage shaking beneath her.

She bolted up. Marie hugged her close.

"My God!" said Marie. "We must have hit something."

Cries of panic as men and women braced against the tumult, fearing what might come next.

But it was over in an instant. And then silence.

There was still only one waiter watching them. Tony. He was stationed by the door, looking as if he was ready to bolt and run.

Tony turned and shouted something to the waiters in the atrium. And in that moment of his distraction, Barbara saw Kane Kinsey and two other men charging up the main aisle toward the door. A few others swarmed in behind them.

And then Tony swung around.

Barbara heard the sharp pop-popping as the waiter got off two quick shots, hitting Kinsey, spinning him backward, knocking down one of the men behind him. The others froze.

Penelope leaped off the stage, running for the aisle.

"Kane! Omigod no, Kane!"

A man grabbed Penelope and stopped her as Tony leveled his rifle.

"Back!" Tony shouted. "All back! Now!"

The men moved away from the door and Barbara could see Kane Kinsey, trying to sit up now, clutching a shoulder, blood seeping through his fingers.

Dr. Louttit grabbed his bag and rushed off the stage. He moved past Penelope, through the crowd of men, up the aisle.

Tony pointed his rifle.

"Stop you! Go back!"

The doctor raised a hand.

"Easy now," he said. "I'm just trying to help that man. He'll bleed to death."

The doctor took one step, then another.

Waiters shouted from the atrium. Tony shot a quick glance in that direction, then backed off, waving the doctor forward. He knelt beside Kinsey.

It was only then that Barbara noticed that the floor at her feet was wet.

Marie Lutey saw it, too. She smiled.

"Ladies and gentlemen," she said. "It's showtime."

57

Sonny!" Glenroy shouted. "Open up! It's me!"

Glenroy had been standing outside the main bridge door for at least three minutes, pounding on it, yelling for Sonny to let him in.

He had even tried calling Sonny on the walkie-talkie. No response.

Glenroy kicked the door, started pounding again.

"Goddammit, Sonny. Open up!"

A sound from the other side of the door. It slid open.

Ron Diamond stood to one side of the doorway, by its control panel. Behind him, near the helm—Todora, her pistol jammed against the side of Sonny's head. Sonny sat at the computer station, its screen lit up.

"I didn't let them in, Glenroy. I promise," Sonny whimpered. "I just turned around and they were there."

"Shut up, faggot," Todora said.

She craned her neck to look past Glenroy, into the hall. She smiled.

"What, no rifle? No gun, no nothing?" She looked at the walkie-talkie in Glenroy's hand. "You think maybe you shoot me with that?"

Glenroy didn't say anything. He had been so caught up in the process of mixing the compound and the aftermath of the galley explosion that he had forgotten all about his SAR. It was still down in the engine room.

"You make this too easy," Todora said. "But please, come in and join us."

Glenroy stepped inside the doorway. Todora gave Diamond a nod and he punched the button to close the door.

"Your boyfriend here, he was arranging our departure," Todora said.

"They want me to turn on the Inmarsat system, Glenroy, help them patch through a phone call," Sonny said.

Glenroy didn't say anything. He was trying to get a handle on the situation. He didn't care if Todora shot Sonny. Glenroy didn't really need him anymore.

But Glenroy was at one end of the bridge and Todora was at the other. Could he get the jump on her before she got off a shot at him?

"You've been busy down in the engine room," Todora said.

Glenroy looked at Sonny.

"I didn't tell them anything, I promise," Sonny said. "I don't know what you were doing down there. I don't want to know."

"No, your boyfriend didn't tell us anything. We can see for ourselves."

Todora nodded at the bank of monitors. Images of the engine room flicked across a screen. The bench outside the control room, a big container on top, empty jugs beside it.

"I wonder what it is you make down there," Todora said. "I hear that big explosion and I wonder even more."

Glenroy edged forward. Todora pulled the pistol away from Sonny, aimed it at Glenroy. Behind her—two laundry bags, filled with loot she had collected from the passengers and the ship's safe.

"No, no, no," she said. "That's far enough."

"Look here," Diamond said. Glenroy turned so he could see him better. "All I'm asking for is one phone call. We get through to my people, I'm out of your hair. We'll get on one of the lifeboats, they'll pick us up. Whatever you do after that it's up to you. You want money? I've got money. I can make it worth your while."

"Quiet you," Todora said. "You talk too much."

Glenroy saw now how it might work, him grabbing Diamond, using the fool as a shield, something between him and Todora, just enough to get her off balance, just enough to buy him a second or two.

Glenroy slung the walkie-talkie at Todora. He saw her dodge it as he grabbed Diamond by the shirtfront and moved behind him.

Now Todora, both hands on the pistol, firing once, missing.

And then Sonny, leaping up from the chair, throwing himself in front of Todora as she squeezed off a second shot, the back of Sonny's head a burst of red as he fell to the floor.

And Glenroy, shoving Diamond forward, charged Todora before she could fire again, knocking her pistol away, the three of them tumbling in a heap, knocking over the laundry bags, cash and jewelry spilling out across the floor. Glenroy came out on top, Todora trying to slither out the bottom.

An elbow cracked hard against Glenroy's mouth. Then another. Diamond was actually putting up a fight. And before Glenroy could react, an elbow pounded his windpipe. He rolled off Diamond, gulping for air, and saw Todora scrambling across the floor. She got to her feet, lunging for the control panel by the door that led to the starboard bridge wing. The door opened. Todora stumbled out.

Glenroy slammed a fist into Diamond's face, felt the crack of teeth and bone. And then he was up, after Todora, punching the yellow button before he dashed out the starboard door.

Todora had reached a gate by the stairs that led aft from the bridge. Locked. She tried to hoist herself over it, but fell short. And as she turned, desperate for another escape route, she saw Glenroy heading for her.

Nowhere else to go. She stepped onto the bridge wing, backing out as Glenroy closed in.

He stopped.

"What, no gun, no nothing?" he said.

Todora didn't say anything. She was winded, struggling for air. She glanced over the catwalk rail, at the water far below.

"I will give you a choice," Glenroy said. "You can jump. Or I will kill you. With my bare hands."

A wild howl from Todora as she charged, clawing at Glenroy, kicking him, trying to bite his face, his nose.

His hands found her throat. He squeezed. She tried to break free. He squeezed harder. Still she kicked and clawed, but the fight was leaving her.

Glenroy lifted her by the throat now, moving out on the bridge wing. Squeezing harder and harder, feeling meaty parts of her yield to his hands. He looked in her eyes, saw the life ebbing away.

In the instant before Todora breathed a final breath, Glenroy lifted her up and heaved her over the catwalk rail. He watched as her body hit the water, face down. Watched as it floated back to the surface. Watched as it rolled over a bow wave, sucked in by the churning torrent, disappearing below the ship's hull.

Glenroy stood for a moment on the bridge wing, studying the water. The ship was drawing nearer to the Windward Passage and the sea swell was picking up. It wouldn't be long now. Just eight or nine hours. His glorious mission. Everything was almost in place.

As he turned to leave the bridge wing, he spotted Ron Diamond by the starboard door, saw Diamond punching at the control panel.

Glenroy made a run for it, leaping off the end of the catwalk, not bothering with the steps. An ankle turned as he hit the deck, but he caught himself before he went all the way down.

The door closing . . .

And Glenroy dove for it, one hand catching a lower edge as it slid shut, a vise against his fingers. But he held on. He pulled. The door gave just a bit, enough to squeeze his other hand in. He pulled harder. The door gave some more.

Lying on his side, Glenroy could see through the crack in the door, could see Diamond not three feet away, aiming Todora's pistol.

Two shots . . .

Shards of metal stung Glenroy's face. And the pain, awful pain, in one hand. He lost his grip, rolled away from the door, and watched it close.

58

When I finally came around, I was wrapped in a blanket, hunched up in the cockpit of a sailboat.

Opposite me, a man sat cross-legged on the cockpit bench. Fortyish. Tight-cropped hair, a scraggly beard. Baggy khaki shorts, shirtless. A white shell dangling from a leather cord around his neck.

A woman stood at the wheel. Pretty, despite a face worn by sun, wind, and salt. A headful of curly black hair streaked with gray, held back by a red bandanna. White shorts with a faded blue chambray shirt.

Lean, the both of them, skin burnished brown. Every bit the vagabond sailors.

A five-gallon jug of water sat on the bench next to the man. He held a coffee cup under its spigot, filled the cup, handed it to me. I drained it. The man took the cup and refilled it.

"Thanks," I said.

The man nodded. He looked at the woman. Neither one of them spoke.

There was something in their eyes. Not fear. More like apprehension.

Can't say that I blamed them. They had fished me out of the water and now they were wondering just what they had gotten themselves into. I could have been anyone. A murderer, a saint, an alien fallen from the sky. Now here I was, sitting on their boat, clad only in underwear and wrapped in a blanket.

I peeked under the blanket. Scratch the underwear. Somewhere along the way I'd managed to lose it.

My shirt and pants, what I'd used to lash together the boxes, were clothespinned to the lifelines, drying out. The man and woman had pulled the boxes aboard, too, and lined them up on the deck, what was left of them anyway, the cardboard falling apart, revealing the computers inside. Ruined. Pity the poor schoolchildren of St. Kitts.

I looked at the man, then at the woman.

"Thank you," I told them. "Don't know how much longer I would have lasted out there."

Again, the man just nodded. The woman smiled. A guarded smile.

The woman spoke to the man. French, it sounded like. Then she peered forward, keeping the boat on its course. She wasn't very tall. She had to stand tiptoe on a wooden box behind the wheel to see over the bow to the waters ahead.

I scoped out the boat. A trimaran. I pegged it at better than fifty feet long. Beamy as could be, nearly thirty feet across. The main hatch to the center hull was closed but I'd been on similar boats and knew what was down there. The galley, salon, and master stateroom. The port and starboard hulls each held a couple of cabins and a head.

A lot of boat for two people. It was in good shape. The deck well scrubbed, the teakwork oiled, the sails fairly new. Not enough accumulated clutter to be a full-time live-aboard. A charterboat, perhaps. Or maybe the boat was owned by someone else and these two were just hired to transport it down to the Caribbean for the winter. That happens a lot.

Except we weren't heading toward the Caribbean. Our course was west and north, toward Florida.

Away from the *Royal Star.*

I stood up. My legs buckled. I grabbed the back of the bench for support.

The man stepped across the cockpit. He took hold of my arm.

"Just give me a minute," I said. "I'll be alright."

The man kept holding my arm as I got my sea legs. I was dizzy, but I wasn't dead. That counted for something.

The woman reached into a console by the wheel, fumbled around. She pulled out a granola bar, unwrapped it, handed it to me.

"Eat," she said.

I finished off the granola bar in two bites. Amazing how a little sustenance can lift the spirits. I was alive, goddammit. Alive.

"I'm OK," I told the man.

He let go of my arm. I made my way to the stern, planted both hands on the rail.

We were on a broad reach. A good wind out of the south-southeast.

The jib and the mainsheet full. The boat felt a little sluggish, like it was nosing down instead of heeling up. Still, we were moving along at a decent clip.

I scanned the water behind us. Saw a boat or two, none of them big. The *Royal Star* was back there somewhere.

I looked at the man.

"How long ago did you pick me up?"

He shook his head.

"My English," he said. "No good."

"One hour," the woman said. "No more than that."

There was a radio in the console, its handset in a clip near the wheel. I pointed at it.

"We need to call someone right now," I said. "Get help."

The man and woman spoke back and forth. I couldn't make out a word of it.

The woman looked at me. She shook her head.

"The radio," she said, "it does not work."

I moved past her, toward the console. She stuck out a hand to stop me. I brushed her away, grabbed the handset, spoke into it.

"Mayday, Mayday. The cruise ship *Royal Star*. Mayday. The ship has been hijacked. Mayday. Does anyone copy?"

Nothing. Not even static.

I bent down and looked at the radio transmitter. No lights on. I flipped switches. Still no lights. The damn thing really was dead.

When I stood up I saw that the man had moved back to the cockpit. He opened one of the bench lockers. He pulled out a shotgun. He pointed it at me. Then he pointed it at the cockpit bench.

"Please," the woman said. "Sit."

I sat.

"We do not want trouble," the woman said, "but as I tell you, the radio, it does not work. It has not worked for two days now. Since we left. Finished. All the electronics. Kaput. Just like I told you."

"Sorry, but we have to get help."

"Help for what?" she said. "How did you come to be here?"

So I told her, told her everything. How the *Royal Star* had been hijacked, passengers and crew taken hostage. How I'd managed to escape. How we had to somehow alert the authorities.

It took a few minutes. The woman didn't respond, she just listened. Every now and then she would stop me and speak to the man, translating what I'd told her.

When I was done, the man lowered the shotgun. He sat down to face me across the cockpit, shotgun on his lap, but still wary.

"My wife is on that ship," I said. "She's getting ready to have a baby."

The woman put a hand to her face.

"Oh," she said. "I am sorry."

She said something to the man. He shook his head and looked at me, his eyes filled with sympathy.

The woman said, "I am Celeste. This is Girard, my husband."

"Zack," I said. "Zack Chasteen."

"We would like to help you," Celeste said. "But . . ."

"Please," I said. "We have to find the nearest ship, another boat. Use their radio. Do something."

The two of them spoke back and forth for a couple of minutes. It got heated. They argued. I couldn't tell what they were saying, but I got the idea that Celeste was prevailing.

Finally, Girard gave a shrug, apparently throwing in the towel. He gave me a long look. He opened the bench locker, put the shotgun back inside.

Then he stepped to the main hatch and opened it.

I wasn't prepared for what I saw—fifteen or twenty people in the galley and the main salon. Men and women. Young and old. Some sitting on the couch. Others stretched out, resting on the floor. Black faces looked out at me, faces that had seen more than their share of misery.

A woman stood in the galley, stirring a pot of something on the stove. A big woman, with thick shoulders, strong arms, and hands the size of fielder's mitts. When she turned to look at me, her bulk filled the hatchway. Her eyes were fierce, penetrating.

A little girl, no more than two or three, squirmed past the big woman and crawled up the hatchway steps, tilting her head, studying me.

Celeste gave me a sad smile.

"We would like to help you," she said. "But, you see, it is not so easy."

59

There were more people in the side hulls. Lots more people. The hatches were open now, the occupants looking out at me.

Girard spoke to the big woman in the galley. She replied with a flurry of words, not French but Creole. Then she turned her attention to me. She looked me up and down, kept watching me as Girard stepped across the cockpit and took over for Celeste at the wheel.

The big woman said something and other people crowded around her in the galley, jockeying to get a better look at me, chattering among themselves. I was causing quite a ruckus. Celeste said something to them and they quieted down, but they kept watching me, whispering to one another.

Celeste sat down across from me in the cockpit.

"How many?" I asked her.

"Forty-two."

"Haitian?"

She nodded.

"From Saint-Isidore. A farming village. Up in the hills."

"Where are you taking them?"

Girard interrupted, barking out something in French. Celeste looked at me.

"Girard, he thinks I am talking too much. He thinks we cannot trust you."

"And you think you can?"

She shrugged.

"I think we have no choice."

"Other than tossing me back into the ocean."

A faint smile from Celeste.

"Yes," she said.

"Where are you taking them?" I asked her again.

"To Florida."

"You've done this before?"

"Yes," she said. "Many times."

A lucrative business, smuggling illegal immigrants. And it attracts the sort of people who don't put much premium on the sanctity of individual lives. To them, men, women, and children are just flesh-and-bone freight. Get the money up front, the most the market will bear. And if things crap out along the way, cut your losses however you can.

There were countless stories of Haitian refugees who had mortgaged their lives to make the crossing to Florida. They crammed aboard leaky boats without enough food or water, only to have their transporters force them overboard while they were still miles offshore rather than risk interdiction by the Coast Guard. Some made it. Most didn't.

Forty-two people.

Who knew how much each of them had paid? Several thousand dollars apiece perhaps. I'd read about Haitian villages that had scraped together the necessary funds to buy passage for several of their residents, in hopes they would make it to the States, find work, send money home, make it possible for others to follow after them.

There was no shortage of opportunists ready to prey on such dreams. For them, it was a far less risky proposition than hauling dope. Those who got caught smuggling human cargo seldom served much jail time. Sure, their boats might get confiscated, but such was the price of doing business.

Celeste read my face.

"It is not what you think," she said.

"So what is it then?"

"We are helping these people," she said. "Helping them find a better life."

"And what do you get out of the deal? A nice bundle of money paid in advance?"

She shook her head.

"No," she said. "We get nothing."

"You smuggle Haitians to Florida. For free. Out of the goodness of your heart."

"We are part of an organization."

"So was Don Corleone."

"Excuse me?"

"Never mind," I said. "What kind of organization?"

"It is more a network, really. Haiti Liberte Internacional. People of a like mind. People who believe in justice, in freedom," she said. "So many Haitians die trying to reach America. Hundreds of them at a time on tiny, tiny boats. Boats that are not seaworthy. Plus, these boats, with so many people everywhere, filling the deck, they are easy to spot. Your Coast Guard, it knows a boat like that can only be doing one thing. But this boat of ours . . ."

"Nice boat," I said.

"Yes, very nice boat. We raise the money to buy it. A boat like this, it does not raise suspicion. Another boat comes along, they wave, we wave back, just a man and a woman on a nice sailboat." She nodded toward the cabins. "During the day, the people stay below where they cannot be seen. There is enough room. They are comfortable. There is plenty to eat and drink. During the night, they come up top, taking turns in small groups. We make two, maybe three such trips a year. We deliver them safely. We give them a future."

"So you and Girard, how long have you been doing this?"

"Since we left the church," Celeste said.

I waited.

Celeste said, "Girard, he was a priest."

"Hmmm," I said.

Celeste smiled.

"I was a nun."

"Double hmmm," I said.

60

I sat back and listened while Celeste told the story.

She and Girard had both been born in Paris, attended the same university a few years apart, and then, after taking their holy vows, met in the slums of Port-au-Prince—Girard, a member of the Salesians of Don Bosco, and Celeste a Salesian sister. It was the mid-1980s. As if squalor and hunger were not problems enough, HIV had arrived on the scene. They worked side by side with another Salesian priest—Jean-Bertrand Aristide.

"Aristide," I said. "Like the president of Haiti?"

"Former president," said Celeste. "But yes, the same. Back then, we knew him as *Pe Titid*, the little priest. The people loved him, the church did not."

"Why's that?"

"A radical, like Jesus," she said. "Aristide said Jesus would not tolerate a world where even one person went hungry and neither should the church. He said it was the responsibility of the church to help the poor even if it meant standing up against the rich."

"Not the kind of talk that encourages rich folks to drop big bucks in the collection plate."

"No, not at all," Celeste said. "He was expelled from the Salesians in 1988. For preaching too much politics. It only made him more loved by the people. Three years later, he was elected president. Still, for Girard, for me, for many others, what happened to Aristide, it was a mighty blow. There is a word, *désenchantement* . . . "

"Disenchantment," I said. "Same in English."

"Yes, that was us. Girard and me, we talked. We talked a lot. And then we . . ."

She shrugged.

"Love is a beautiful thing," I said.

She smiled.

"And a complicated thing," she said.

"You had to leave the church?"

"Yes and no," she said. "Girard, he could no longer be a priest. I had to quit the order. But there are other ways to serve the Lord."

"By smuggling Haitians to Florida?"

It stung her.

"You do not approve?"

"It's not for me to approve or disapprove," I said. "I just never considered it the Lord's work, that's all."

"Because it is illegal?"

"Plenty of illegal things have been done in the name of the Lord," I said. "Some of them noble, some of them not."

"But the laws of America are unjust," she said.

"We've got good laws, we've got bad laws. All in all, I like to think it balances out on the side of the good."

The whole time we'd been talking, people had been watching us from the hatchways. A woman cradling a baby. A teenage boy in an old Lakers T-shirt. A young man with an arm around a young womn.

Celeste nodded their way.

"For these people, your laws are bad laws."

I couldn't really argue with her on that one.

U.S. immigration policy is a snake pit of double standards, especially as it plays out on the shores of Florida. One set of rules applies to Cubans, who are considered political refugees. If they make it to the U.S. mainland in a boat, they are given safe haven. If they are intercepted at sea, they are sent back to Cuba. The wet foot, dry foot policy, it's called.

It's a whole different set of rules for those trying to flee Haiti. Despite a government in shambles and a political system as violent and corrupt as any in the world, Haitians are considered economic refugees. Even if they make it to dry land, they face deportation. As for the fact that many Cubans are light-skinned and most Haitians are dark . . .

"Black foot, white foot," I said.

Celeste nodded.

"Exactly," she said. "Racist laws. It is wrong."

"Look, I sympathize with what you're doing. Really. But I'm not here to argue immigration law. I need to get back to my wife. I need to get help for the people on that cruise ship. And right now, you're my only hope."

"What would you have us do?"

"That radio of yours, what happened to it?"

"A storm came upon us, the night we left. A very bad storm. Much, much wind. The mast, it break. Girard and some of the men, they were able finally to fix it. But we used up much fuel. And the electronics, the radio, all the wiring—no good."

"Then you've got to get me to another ship, another boat, anything that might have a radio. That's all I'm asking. Just do that and you can be on your way."

Celeste said something to Girard. They spoke back and forth for several moments. I could tell Girard didn't like the idea.

"Another boat, they might become suspicious about us, about what we are doing," Celeste said. "They might alert the authorities."

"So what are you telling me? The lives of the forty-two people on this boat are more valuable than the lives of two hundred people on the *Royal Star*? You get caught, all they'll do is turn you around and send you back to Haiti."

"But they could seize our boat, take it away."

"So you and this network of yours, you buy another boat. You try again," I said. "But the people on that cruise ship, they won't get another chance. If we don't do something, then there's a good chance they're going to die."

"But . . ."

"No buts, lady. That's the way it is."

I stood up, wrapped the blanket around me. I walked over to the lifelines, felt my shirt and pants. Still wet.

Screw it.

I turned my back on everyone, dropped the blanket and let them get a good long look at my bare white ass.

I could hear the commotion from the cabins behind me. Laughs and titters.

I stepped into my pants and, what the hell, wiggled my ass for the crowd. They loved it.

As I finished getting dressed, I scanned the water in all directions. No signs of other boats. To the south, no visible shoreline, but a bank of towering cumulus clouds, the kind of clouds that might hover over a landmass. Cuba probably.

I stepped back to the cockpit. All eyes from the cabins were on me.

Celeste had moved alongside her husband, sitting on the captain's bench behind the helm. Girard steered with one hand on the stainless-steel wheel, the other resting on his wife's knee. He shot a look toward the cockpit locker, where he'd stashed the shotgun. Then back at me. Two steps and I could grab the gun before he could do anything about it. Not that it hadn't crossed my mind. Get the gun, take the helm, turn the boat around. Easy-peasy.

I said, "Got any idea where we are?"

Celeste nodded.

"Yes, Girard, he learned to sail the old way. He does not need the electronics." She opened a hatch under the helm console, pointed at a sextant. It was an Astra III Professional, top of the line. It rested atop the current edition of Reed's Astro Navigation Tables. "Girard took his readings shortly before we found you."

She pulled a chart book from the console, folded out one of its laminated pages, and conferred with Girard for a few moments before sitting down beside me in the cockpit.

"Right here," she said. "More or less."

She pointed at a spot where Girard had written down the coordinates with a wipe-off marker: 20.7 S, 74.2 W. Call it thirty miles northeast of Baracoa, Cuba, maybe seventy miles south of Matthew Town, on Great Inagua, the southernmost point of the Bahamas.

And somewhere back to the east of us, toward Haiti, that's where we'd find what I was looking for.

I said, "You remember passing a ship that might have been the *Royal Star*?"

Celeste shook her head.

"I don't remember such a ship. In the hours before we found you, it was not my watch. I was sleeping. Perhaps Girard . . ."

She spoke with him.

She said, "Girard says yes, maybe he saw it. But that was many hours ago. And the ship was at some distance. He cannot be sure. We do not sail close to ships."

I studied the chart. Cuba was nearby. Maybe I could talk Celeste and Girard into making a run south, dropping me off, letting me fend for myself. Still, that would be a total crapshoot. I had no passport, no money, no nothing. Even if I convinced the Cuban authorities that I was who I said I was, no telling how long it would take to get the wheels moving. Scratch Cuba.

If the wind held, we could make it to Mathew Town in six or seven hours. But I knew what would be waiting there—the Bahamian Navy. In recent years, as more and more Haitian refugees have been left stranded in the Bahamas by scurrilous transporters, the Bahamian Navy, with full support from the U.S., has become increasingly vigilant about stopping the traffic in human cargo. Celeste's fears were well founded. The Bahamians would board the boat, conduct a thorough search, and that would be that. And even if I succeeded in convincing them that the *Royal Star* was in peril, the layers of bureaucracy in the Bahamas run so deep that time would run out on us. Scratch Mathew Town.

I kept looking at the chart. Where, oh where, could the *Royal Star* be?

Think, Zack, think. How far had I drifted in the ten hours or so I'd been in the water? Fifteen miles, twenty? And that curious circular route of the *Royal Star*—looping east and then back to the west—how did that factor into it?

I tried plugging everything into my internal honing device. But acute as it is, I couldn't get a peg on things. The *Royal Star* could be ten miles away. But it could just as easily be a hundred.

So much open water, so many variables . . .

"*Ka ma ou rele?*"

It was the big woman in the galley. Her arms were folded across her chest and she was speaking to me. Celeste said something to her. The big woman said something else. Celeste turned to me.

"Mommie Leena wants to know, what is your name," Celeste said. "I told her it is Zack. But she . . . she wants for you to say it to her."

I looked at the woman. I thumped my chest.

"My name is Zack," I said. "Zachary."

Mommie Leena narrowed her eyes, considered me with skepticism.

"Azacka?" she asked.

"Close enough."

"Azacka?"

"Sure, Azacka. Whatever you want."

Mommie Leena stared at me, stared at me hard. I stared back.

Then a broad smile lit her face. She turned to the other people in the main cabin.

"Azacka!" she said. "Azacka!"

Mommie Leena disappeared from the hatchway and began rummaging around in the galley. Other faces appeared from below, wanting to get a look at me.

"What's that all about?" I asked Celeste.

"I am not sure. After all these years, there is still much I do not understand about Sèvis Lwa."

"Sèvis what?"

"Sèvis Lwa. It is Creole. It means 'Service to the Spirits.' Voudon it is also called."

"Voodoo?" I said.

Celeste nodded.

"Yes, the same. Mommie Leena, she is very powerful in the Voudon. She is a mambo, a priestess, one who is said to speak with the spirits."

A defrocked priest. A former nun. A boatload of Haitian refugees. And now a voodoo priestess.

"Oh, boy," I said. "This just keeps getting better and better."

61

Mommie Leena reappeared in the hatchway. In one hand she held a bottle half filled with some kind of clear liquid. In the other hand, two glasses. She poured healthy portions into each glass. She handed one of the glasses to me.

"Room!" she said.

I sniffed the stuff.

"Rum," I said.

"Yes, room!" said Mommie Leena.

She held up her glass. I held up mine. She was waiting on me.

I slugged back the rum. It burnt the moment it hit my mouth, kept burning all the way down, burnt parts of me I didn't even know I had.

I let out a yowl. It was that kind of rum. Unadulterated cane juice. Damn close to pure alcohol.

Mommie Leena knocked back her rum. She let out a yowl, too, one that perfectly mimicked mine.

I yowled again. Mommie Leena yowled, too. Then others joined in, yowling up a storm and laughing.

Celeste said something to Mommie Leena. And as the two of them spoke among themselves an old man in a straw hat stepped to the hatchway. He took off the straw hat and handed it to me, insisting that I put it on. So I did. The old man clapped his hands, delighted.

"Azacka!" he said. "Azacka!"

A pretty young woman appeared in the hatchway. She held a wooden tray. She handed it to me. The tray contained an assortment of things—a banana, half an ear of roasted corn, a small piece of smoked fish, a packet of sugar, and a hand-rolled cigarette.

The pretty young woman urged me to help myself. So I ate the banana. I ate the fish. I ate the corn. I opened the packet and poured sugar into my mouth. I smacked my lips and rubbed my stomach.

"Mmmm, good," I said.

People laughed and clapped.

I picked up the cigarette and looked at it. Except for an every-now-and-then cigar, I haven't smoked since I was in high school, back when I was eager to experiment with most anything.

The young woman handed me a butane lighter. I didn't want to be rude. So I fired up. I took a drag. Even worse than I remembered.

"Mmmm, good," I said, picking flecks of tobacco from my lips. "Thanks."

Everyone was watching me, as if I were the most fascinating person they had ever met and they were anxious to see what I might do next.

Celeste and Mommie Leena continued to talk back and forth. Mommie Leena did most of the talking. Every now and then, she looked my way and smiled. I smiled back.

"Question," I said. Celeste looked at me. "What the hell is going on?"

Celeste shook her head and sighed one of those sighs that only the French can sigh, a sigh that somehow managed to convey exasperation, confusion, and profundity in equal measure. She spoke with Girard. He sighed, too, and shook his head, but not without amusement.

Finally, Celeste said, "Mommie Leena, the others, they think you are Azacka."

"Azacka?"

"Yes, Azacka. He is a *loa*."

"A what-a?"

"A *loa*," she said. "Do you know anything of Vodoun?"

"Practically nothing," I said. "Except for the part where they cut off the heads of chickens and that sort of thing."

"Yes, a sacrifice," Celeste said. "To please the *loa*."

"A *loa*, that's some kind of voodoo god?"

"No, no," Celeste said. "You see, in Vodoun the faithful worship one god, the good creator, Bondye. But Bondye is very distant from the human world, not particularly interested in the people he created."

"The Church of God the Utterly Indifferent," I said.

Celeste gave me blank look.

"Kurt Vonnegut. *The Sirens of Titan*," I said. "But never mind."

Celeste said, "The only way to get Bondye's attention, to ask him for favors, is through his intermediaries, the *loa*. There are dozens of different *loa*. Some male, some female. They are the spirits who walk among us and occasionally take human form."

"So that's what they think I am? Some kind of spirit. Like a ghost?"

"More than just a ghost. A ghost who has the ear of God."

I leaned back on the cockpit bench, trying to take it all in.

Celeste said, "There are many similarities between the church and Vodoun. Think of a *loa* as like a saint. A Vodoun saint. You know how Catholics pray to different saints for different things? St. Bernadette if they are sick? St. Jude if they are in desperation?"

I said, "This guy I know in Florida, he was having a hard time selling his house, so he buried a plastic statue of St. Joseph in his front yard. I told him he was nuts. But the house sold the next week. I think mostly it was because he cut the price by fifty thousand bucks. But this guy, he's convinced it was all because of St. Joseph."

"Yes, whatever, Vodoun it is like that," Celeste said. "Except the *loa*, they expect favors and gifts before they speak to Bondye on behalf of the people. That is why they give you food and drink."

"Nice work, being a *loa*."

Celeste smiled. She was quite pretty when she smiled. Her eyes sparkled and everything about her became much softer. I couldn't picture her as a nun. Not that nuns can't be pretty. I'm not saying that. I'm just saying she was pretty. I liked her face.

"The *loa*, when they take human form, they often do not—how do you say?—they do not act like saints. They misbehave. Especially Azacka."

"The one they think I am?"

"Yes. Azacka is known as a prankster. When he appears he often is not wearing any clothes. It makes the people laugh, just as you . . ."

"Just as I stood there buck naked on the deck and shook my backside."

Celeste smiled.

"Yes," she said. "And then there is your name. Zack. Azacka."

"Just a coincidence," I said.

Celeste shrugged.

"If you say."

"Hold on," I said. "Don't tell me that you, a former nun, married to a former priest, don't tell me that you buy into all this voodoo stuff."

"No, not all of it," she said. "Still, I take it seriously. I know what a powerful thing such belief can be for these people. And they are good people. Good Catholic people."

"Catholic *and* voodoo worshippers?"

"Oh, yes. The two exist side by side. The slaves who first came to Haiti, the Church forbid them to practice their African religions and so they became Christians. But in their own way. They went to church. They kept shrines to Jesus and the Virgin Mary. They became believers. But, in secret, they also held fast to Vodoun. They mixed the religions together," she said. "There is a saying: In Haiti, the people are seventy percent Roman Catholic, thirty percent Protestant, and one hundred percent Vodoun."

In the hatchway of the main cabin, the young woman had refilled her tray and was offering me more food. I took a piece of smoked fish, another banana.

"Azacka's favorite foods," Celeste said. "Simple food, but always on hand in case he shows up. Same with the rum. Azacka likes strong drink."

"So does Zack," I said.

"And the hat, the one the old man gave you. Azacka likes to wear a straw hat but he always shows up hatless . . ."

"Because he's naked."

"Yes. And so someone must give him a hat. It is how they welcome Azacka. All part of the ritual, all in hopes that Azacka will intercede with Bondye on their behalf."

"So they keep things on hand to give all the loa—special food, special drink, special hats? Seems like a lot of stuff to haul around, especially on a boat."

"No, these special things, they are just for Azacka. He is the *loa* who looks after those who are traveling," Celeste said. "Azacka, he is much beloved by the people. Especially these people. They are farmers. And Azacka, he is also the *loa* of agriculture, a man of the soil."

"Hmmm," I said. "How 'bout that."

Celeste studied me.

"What is it?" she said.

"Oh, nothing."

"No, it is something. Tell me."

Celeste might have been a good-looking former nun, but she still had that nun way about her. If she asked you to tell her something, you told her.

"I'm a farmer," I said. "Well, kind of a farmer."

"Oh, really. What do you grow?"

"Palm trees," I said. "Not that it makes me a man of the soil or anything. Not that I . . ."

But Celeste was already passing this information along to the people watching from the cabins.

"Just a coincidence," I said. "No big deal."

But apparently it was a big deal to Mommie Leena and the others. Big smiles, nods of approval.

"*Se bon enfòmasyon!*" Mommie Leena said. "*Te vu Azacka mas definiqe.*"

Celeste said, "She says this is good news, very good news. There is no doubt that you are Azacka."

What's a loa to do?

I turned to Mommie Leena. I tipped my straw hat. I handed her the empty glass.

"More room," I said.

62

Glenroy stood by the bench in the engine room, studying the solution in the big glass container. White powder was steadily accumulating at the bottom. Another three hours and the process would be complete. Then Glenroy could collect the powder and distribute his lethal packages throughout the ship.

Just one hitch, one big hitch—he would have to do it with only one hand.

The pistol shots by Diamond had mangled two of Glenroy's fingers. After the bridge's starboard door closed, locking him out, Glenroy had ripped off his T-shirt, wrapped it around the wound, and managed to stop most of the bleeding. But his left hand was useless. And it hurt, it hurt like hell.

The bridge windows were tinted, almost opaque from the outside. Still, Glenroy was able to look through them and see all he needed to see: Sonny lay dead on the floor. No sign of Diamond. And the main bridge door was closed.

That was that. There'd be no getting back on the bridge now.

Good thing Glenroy had a fallback plan. He scaled the security gate, ran along the Deck Six promenade, and reentered the ship near the main stairwell.

His chief concern was that Diamond might go cowboy on him, might use what few shots remained in the pistol to try and free the passengers and crew. Glenroy knew the waiters couldn't offer much in the way of resistance. Only a couple of them had ammunition left. But Diamond didn't know that.

Glenroy figured Diamond was out to save his own ass and to hell with everyone else. Still, he couldn't risk letting Diamond escape. He couldn't risk letting anyone escape, not the waiters, not the passengers, not the crew. If just one person managed to get off the ship, find help and alert the authorities, Glenroy's mission would fail.

A few more hours, that's all he needed.

He went down to Deck One, retrieved his rifle from the engine room, and checked on the progress of the compound in the big glass container. He wasn't worried about getting into the engine control room. He knew where to find an acetylene torch. It would take out one of the control-room windows, no problem.

Glenroy could steer the ship from down there. Not an ideal situation, but the engine control room existed just for such emergencies. The autopilot would take the ship to the destination. And when they were within close range, the ship's cameras would pick up the target. It was a big target. Hard to miss.

First though, Glenroy had to check on the waiters, make sure Diamond wasn't creating a problem.

Diamond was nowhere to be found on Deck Five. But things were unraveling anyway. There was a racket coming from the casino and the library. Crew members pounded on windows and yelled at the waiters.

The passengers in the Galaxy Lounge were more subdued. Glenroy saw the ship's doctor removing a bloodied bandage from the shoulder of one of the men, cleaning the wound.

"What happened to him?" Glenroy asked the waiters.

"Some of the men, they try to get past Tony," said the waiter with the gold tooth, Felix. "So he shoot that one."

Behind the doctor, other men had huddled together and Glenroy sensed they were already plotting something, trying to figure a way out of there. Nearly fifty of them, only four waiters, with the fifth one, Benny, stretched out on the floor of the atrium, barely conscious. Just a matter of time and the whole thing was going to blow.

The waiters were jumpy, beginning to lose it—the ragged downside of the pills Todora had given them to stay awake. They didn't know that Pango was now just mincemeat on the galley ceiling. And they were freaking out because they hadn't seen him in the nearly three hours since the explosion.

"Where Pango?" Felix demanded of Glenroy. "He say he come right back. But he no come back, long time. Where is he?"

"Don't worry," Glenroy said. "He's alright."

"No, you tell me. Where is he? You tell me now."

"He's on the bridge," Glenroy said. "I left him up there to steer the ship. He'll be back down here soon. Everything's fine."

"What about boat?"

"It's on its way," Glenroy said. "Pango has been in contact with the boat. It will be here to pick us up shortly after dark."

The waiters seemed to buy it. But in an hour or so, when Pango still hadn't shown up, they would grow more suspicious. They'd want to see Pango for themselves. And when Glenroy couldn't produce him, the waiters would cash in their chips and get off the ship any way they could.

Glenroy couldn't let that happen. Plus, he had to do something right away to stop another insurrection from the passengers, let them know that if they tried anything they'd face dire consequences.

"I'll be right back," Glenroy told the waiters. "Pango told me to give you something."

Glenroy was carrying a duffel bag when he returned to the atrium a half hour later. He set it down on the counter outside the purser's office. He waved Felix over.

Glenroy reached in the duffel bag and pulled out five banded stacks of hundred-dollar bills. It got Felix's attention. The last of the money given to Glenroy by his contact in the roti shop. Might as well put it to work.

"Fifty thousand dollars," Glenroy said. "Pango told me to give it to you, let you divide it up. He said to tell you there will be plenty more coming your way when we get off the ship."

Felix grinned. He liked the sound of that. He took the money.

Then Glenroy grabbed the duffel bag and headed for the Galaxy Lounge. Just one more thing to do and then, finally, he could focus on completing his mission.

63

The contractions were still six minutes apart, but the pain had gotten worse, much worse.

"Just breathe, honey," Marie Lutey told Barbara.

"I *am* breathing. Can't you see that? Breathe, breathe, breathe. That's all I'm doing."

Marie smiled.

"A bit testy, are we?"

"Sorry," Barbara said. "I didn't mean to snap."

"That's OK, honey. Snap all you want. That's part of it. Just do what you have to do."

"I wish Zack were here. I just can't . . ."

Barbara moaned.

"Don't think about that," Marie told her. "Just think good things. Think about this baby of yours. You're heading down the homestretch. Hang in there."

Dr. Louttit joined them on the stage. He gave Barbara another inspection. Then he helped her to her feet.

"I want you to walk around for a while, up here on the stage," he said. "You'll feel a little better. Plus, it might help speed things along."

"I don't want to speed things along," Barbara said. "I don't want to have my baby on this ship. I don't want my baby to be any part of this."

Marie took her by the arm.

"It's alright, dear. It will all work out. Really it will. Now let's do what the doctor says. You and me. Let's take ourselves a little stroll. You'll feel better."

They were walking around the stage when they saw the big man in the blue jumpsuit enter the lounge, a rifle slung over one shoulder.

"Who the hell is that?" Marie said. "Haven't seen him before."

They watched as Glenroy crossed the lounge, heading for the group of men gathered near the main aisle. Behind him, Tony kept his rifle trained on the men.

"Break it up. Everyone find a chair and sit down. Now!"

The men did as they were told. Glenroy waited until all of them were seated. Then he walked over to Sam Jebailey.

"You," he said. "Up on the stage. With the women."

Jebailey stood and walked to the steps, Glenroy following him. Glenroy pointed to a spot in the middle of the stage.

"There," he said. "Sit."

Jebailey sat. The women who were sitting nearby moved away, giving him plenty of room.

All eyes were on Glenroy as he opened the duffel bag and pulled out a red cylindrical object about a foot long, two inches in diameter. Duct tape had been wrapped around the middle of the cylinder. Glenroy placed it carefully on the stage beside Jebailey. Then, one by one, he pulled out eleven more cylinders, just like the first one.

"Is that what I think it is?" Marie whispered to Barbara.

"Dynamite?"

A gasp from a woman standing nearby as she overheard them.

"It's dynamite," she said to the woman next to her. Within seconds the entire lounge was abuzz. Some women headed for the steps, trying to get off the stage.

"Nobody move!" Glenroy shouted. "Sit down, all of you, or I blow up the whole place right now!"

Sam Jebailey wore a look of undistilled horror.

"Both arms above your head," Glenroy told him.

Glenroy went to work. Even with only one good hand he was quick and proficient. When he was done, six red cylinders were attached to each side of Jebailey's chest with several wraps of duct tape.

Glenroy pulled a walkie-talkie from the duffel bug. He unscrewed its back plate and pulled out three wires—one red, one white, one black. Using more duct tape he attached the walkie-talkie to the middle of Jebailey's chest, at his sternum, in between the red cylinders, leaving the wires hanging out.

He went back to his duffel and produced more electrical wire, some metal contact plates with brass switching devices. He attached wires to the contact plates, attached a contact plate to each of the cylinders, and connected the whole set up to the three wires running out of the walkie-talkie.

Just a little something he had learned from the men at the house in Hialeah, a little something extra they threw in as part of the twenty-five-thousand-dollar package. Suicide Bomber 101, they called it.

Jebailey sat frozen throughout the ordeal, scarcely breathing it seemed. Sweat rolled down his forehead, stinging his eyes.

When Glenroy finished rigging up Jebailey, he pulled out a second walkie-talkie, held it for everyone to see.

"I press the green button on this walkie-talkie, it signals the other walkie-talkie, sets off an electrical current," he said. "Jebailey goes boom. This whole room goes boom."

He pointed to the closed-circuit cameras mounted throughout the lounge.

"I'll be watching," Glenroy said, grabbing the duffel and moving off the stage. "Don't make me press the button."

64

This time around I sipped at the rum. It still burned like hell. But there was something elemental about it, something earthy and smoky and utterly soothing. It seemed to connect directly to my frontal lobe, to clear my thoughts. Maybe I was acquiring a taste for it. Then again, maybe I was just getting a buzz on.

The wind was picking up, shifting more from the east. Girard eased out the mainsail and the jib. We were clipping right along. Farther and farther from where I needed to be.

A sip of rum. I thought about the shotgun in the cockpit locker. It was looking more and more like I would have to make a move. Time was ticking away.

Another sip of rum. I tried to picture how it would play out. Grab the gun, force Girard to give up the helm. Make Girard and Celeste go below with the Haitians. Shut the hatches, keep everyone down there.

I could handle the boat, no problem. It was rigged for single-handed sailing, all the sheets and halyards within easy reach.

But if I turned the boat around, we'd be heading into the wind. I could sail close-hauled, tacking back and forth. That would eat up too much time. I'd have to crank the engine. Celeste had mentioned something about using a lot of fuel the night the mast broke. How much was left? I'd worry about that part when I got to it.

Were there more weapons down below? Doubtful. Keeping one gun on board was prudent for anyone sailing open waters. No reason why they should have an arsenal. Still, there were forty-two of them—make that forty-four with Celeste and Girard—and one of me. About the same odds as when we rushed the waiter on Deck Two. Things could get gnarly. I didn't want to shoot anyone. These were good people, people who had come to my rescue when I was ready to kiss the world good-bye. I wanted them to get where they were going.

But I wanted what I wanted, too. And, selfish bastard that I am, I would do whatever it took to get it.

Another sip of rum.

Mommie Leena sat in the hatchway, her feet in the cockpit. She sipped rum, too, the bottle resting beside her. Apparently sipping rum with Azacka was a privilege reserved for a mambo. None of the other Haitians joined us. Most of them had stepped away from the hatches, gone back to doing whatever they'd been doing before I arrived on the scene. Taking care of children. Resting in the cabins. Passing time the best they could, dreaming dreams of better days.

The mood had shifted, turned more somber. A reflection of my own black thoughts perhaps.

Celeste and Mommie Leena had been chatting among themselves. And now Celeste looked at me, said, "Mommie Leena thanks you. She says she called for Azacka to come to them two nights ago, during the storm, when they were afraid."

"Gee, never got the message," I said. "Else I would have been here sooner."

"She says your presence here is a good omen. It means this voyage will be successful and they will arrive safely in Florida."

"How nice for them," I said. "Makes me feel good all over."

Peevishness does not become me. But push was approaching shove. Something had to give.

I finished off the rum. I stood. I walked to the stern and looked east. Nothing back that way but open water. Nothing to the south, nothing to the north.

"Zack?"

I turned around.

Celeste said, "Mommie Leena wants to know, what is it you look for?"

"You know damn well what I'm looking for," I said. "I'm looking for a ship, a ship that has my wife on it, a ship where people have already died, where even more may die. Especially if we don't do anything about it."

Celeste was quiet.

"Go ahead, tell her what I just told you," I said. "And while you're at it, tell her I've had enough of this Azacka bullshit. Thanks for the food, thanks for the rum. Thanks for the freaking straw hat. But it's time to turn this goddam boat around."

At the wheel, Girard tensed. He didn't have to understand English to know what was going on. He barked out something to Celeste. She looked at me. Then she got up and went to the other side of the cockpit. She sat down on the locker that held the shotgun.

OK. If that's how they wanted to play it.

I turned my back on them, looked out over the transom. I could hear Celeste speaking with Mommie Leena, speaking soft and low.

From where I stood, it was about five giant strides to the cockpit locker. I'm nimble of foot when I need to be. I had no doubt that I could make it there and knock Celeste out of the way before she could do anything about it. But between me and the cockpit stood Girard at the helm. If he tried to stop me, I'd have no trouble bulling my way past him. Still, it might give Celeste enough time to grab the shotgun.

This is what it had come to: Taking down a former priest and bashing a former nun, people who were doing the Lord's work. Zack, old pal, you are bound for hell.

That's when I felt a hand on my shoulder.

I'd been so consumed with my shotgun strategy that I hadn't heard Mommie Leena move across the cockpit. She stood beside me. Her face shone, an obsidian gleam. She looked into my eyes. But it was a look that went deeper, way deeper, than that. I held her gaze. Indeed, something told me I couldn't look away even if I wanted to.

She put a hand on my chest, above my heart. Then she took my hand, put it on her chest. We stood like that for a moment. She was warm. Her heart beat strong.

Far be it from me to get all hippy-dippy about it, but something happened. I don't know what exactly. But something. Again, maybe it was the rum. I don't think so. Something else.

Mommie Leena took her hand away and for several minutes the two of us stood there at the stern, looking east. No words. Just the whoosh of the wind and the sea, the slap of the hull, the creak of the rigging.

Then she turned and stepped away. She went to the helm and faced off with Girard. She said something to him. I saw him shake his head, no. She kept at him. Then Celeste got in on it, the three of them talking back and forth. Loud words, not so much harsh as imploring. The words of people for whom there is much at stake.

I didn't understand what they were saying. But I knew. In my heart, I knew.

A few minutes later, they stopped talking. Girard gave the wheel a mighty turn. The boat's bow crossed the wind. We headed east.

BATTLE STATIONS

65

Somewhere along the line I stretched out in the cockpit and grabbed some sleep.

Napping has always come easy to me, even in situations that are not the least bit restful. Barbara maintains it is purely an atavistic trait, that I am a throwback to those ancient hunters who slept on their feet, ever ready to pursue the wooly mammoth, escape the saber-toothed tiger.

Whatever.

I like to think my predilection to doze is simply the sign of a clear conscience. Demons? Sure, I have my share. I allow them free ramble, but I do not let them haunt me.

Back in the 1990 season, when we were facing the Chiefs in the AFC Wild Card Playoff, I nodded off while Coach Shula gave his halftime harangue. I got fined for it—a thousand bucks on the spot. But in the third quarter, on Kansas City's second play from scrimmage, I snagged an under-thrown pass to set up what became the game-winning field goal. So, yeah, I believe in the restorative power of a well-taken nap. That thousand-dollar snooze gave me the extra oomph I needed.

When I awoke on the boat it was almost dark and twilight was playing its tricks. Sunset was behind us, yet the sky ahead was a romp of fiery streaks—the fleeting, prismatic afterglow of a long, long day.

I heard the cooing of young voices, saw children playing on the foredeck. A half dozen or so men and women had come up from the cabins to enjoy the fresh evening air and keep an eye on the kids.

Beyond the children, at the bowsprit, stood Mommie Leena. She surveyed our course, one hand on the stay of the now-furled jib. As ship figureheads go, a most daunting one.

Celeste was standing her watch at the wheel. The mainsail was up, but the engine was doing all the work, a low drone that provided a bass line to the higher registers of the whipping wind.

Girard sat in the cockpit across from me. He held a wooden bowl with both hands, taking an occasional slurp from it.

He looked at me.

"You want?"

"Sure," I said.

Girard said something to a man in the galley. Seconds later, another wooden bowl was passed out and made its way to me.

I examined the steaming contents. Saw a greasy, gray broth, bits of what looked to be green bananas and white yams. Some onions, a piece of carrot. And floating in the middle—an eyeball. Dolphin maybe, or a tuna by the size of it.

Fish water, they call it in the islands, a variation on the ubiquitous "boil-down" stew found throughout the Caribbean archipelago. Take the carcass and the head and cook it nearly forever, tossing in whatever else avails itself. Ground provisions. Plenty of pepper. It'll cure what ails you, put lead in your pencil.

I drained the broth, saved the eyeball for last. Supposed to be good luck. Popped it in my mouth, enjoyed the gummy sweetness. Like a boiled peanut. Not that I could polish off a bagful of them.

After Mommie Leena had intervened on my behalf, convincing Celeste and Girard to turn around, it had been agreed that we would run east. If we spotted another boat, we would approach it. Best-case scenario—this other boat would have a radio that worked. I'd hop aboard and my rescuers would sail happily away.

Worst-case scenario? There were a couple of them, actually. For one, said boat might not wish to be approached. While the law of the sea holds that all mariners have a duty to assist those in peril, our boat—fully afloat and under power—was in no apparent danger. And another boat, or a big ship, seeing us coming at them in open water, might alter its course to maintain plenty of leeway. We might not be able to run them down. We could signal with flares or our lights, but they could ignore it. Not honorable, but it happens.

Or this other vessel might be on patrol for boats such as ours, boats smuggling dope or hiding human cargo. While such a vessel would surely serve my cause, it would just as surely spell doom for the others on board. My shipmates—men, women, children—were risking every-thing for me.

But so far none of these scenarios had presented themselves. Four hours, and we had not spotted another boat beyond a few distant specks on the horizon, ships far removed from our reach.

The choppy waters of the Windward Passage were almost behind us and, off starboard, I could just begin to make out the looming silhouette of a headland—Haiti's eastern coast. The men and women on deck saw it, too. And while they put no words to it, their dejection was palpable. Three days earlier they had put this place behind them, entertaining visions of a grand new day. Now here they were, back where they started, hopes and dreams on hold.

I got up and stretched my legs. I was still wrung out from my time in the water. But a little sleep, a little food, and a little rum? It had done a lot of good.

I stepped to the stern and watched the frothy wash of our wake. Even with the full load, we were hitting every bit of twenty knots, the trimaran's twin 220 hp Cummins diesels doing their job.

There was black lettering across the transom, but from my angle I couldn't make it out.

"What do you call this boat anyway?" I asked Celeste.

"*Boukman*," she said.

"*Boukman?*"

"Yes, after Dutty Boukman. You know him?"

I shook my head, no.

"Dutty Boukman, he was a houngan, a Vodoun priest. Back in 1791, it was Dutty Boukman who held a Vodoun ceremony near Port-au-Prince. He told the people to cast off the chains of slavery and rise against their masters. It was the start of the Haitian Revolution."

"Boukman," I said. "Like 'book man.'"

"Yes, like that exactly. That is how he got his name. He was a book man. He could read. A slave who could read. A dangerous thing," Celeste said. "But it did not end well for Dutty Boukman."

"How's that?"

"The French, they cut off his head and put it on a stake in the middle of the city."

"Goddam French," I said.

Celeste laughed.

"You should not take the Lord's name in vain," she said.

"What about the French?"

"Fuck the French."

"No way for an ex-nun to talk, a French ex-nun at that."

"Fuck that, too," she said. "Fuck, fuck, fuck."

"Feels good sometimes just to get it all out."

"Yes," she said. "It does."

The four computer boxes that had helped keep me afloat were still sitting on the deck. Two of the men were now stripping off the cardboard and Styrofoam, revealing the monitors and desktop workstations.

"I'm afraid those things are shot," I said.

"Maybe, maybe not," Celeste said.

"Soaked with salt water? They're no good."

"These people are very resourceful," Celeste said. "You might be surprised."

It was then that the engines sputtered. Then sputtered again.

Girard sprung out of the cockpit and headed below. Celeste looked at me, grim. We were running out of fuel.

Celeste throttled back. The *Boukman* idled along for a few moments and then Girard returned to the deck. He spoke to Celeste.

She turned to me and said, "Girard, he switch to the auxiliary tank."

"How much in it?"

"Enough for an hour," she said. "Maybe less."

"Fuck, fuck, fuck," I said.

66

The stragglers—a gaggle of fraternity boys from Georgia Tech—were heading up the concrete pier toward the gangway, two of them so drunk they were legless, their buddies having to drag them along.

They had probably indulged in some of the local ganja, too, Captain Palmano figured as he watched their weaving progress from high above on the bridge wing. He didn't care what passengers did while they were on shore as long as they made it back to the ship on time. And the frat boys were pushing the limit.

Palmano had no qualms about pulling out of port and leaving tardy passengers behind. It happened on a fairly regular basis, actually. Those who missed the boat often expressed outrage. Some of them had even sued, unsuccessfully, to recoup the expense of hiring transport to catch up with the ship. But rules were rules, especially when they applied to the *King of the Seas* maintaining its schedule.

The final boarding call had sounded half an hour earlier. Most of the passengers had long since returned, not wanting to miss their dinner seatings. It was the last formal meal of the cruise, the big to-do where the wait staff paraded about and put on a show with flaming desserts, hoping to amp up their tips.

The two pilot boats were idling, one off the stern and one off the bow, and as soon as the chief security officer signaled that boarding was complete and the gangway had been raised, the *King of the Seas* could start to pull away from the pier and begin the slow process of negotiating its way out the channel to the open sea. It was a painstaking process. The ship had to turn around, get its bow pointed out. And turning the *King of the Seas* around in the channel at Isla Paradiso was like parking an elephant in a broom closet—an improbable proposition on the face of it, one that had to be approached with finesse. The ship, like some willful pachyderm, often seemed to move of its own stubborn accord. And its response time was anything but lightninglike.

The channel was just shy of a half mile wide near the pier, more than enough leeway for the typical cruise ship. But the *King of the Seas* was more than a quarter mile long, so turning around near the pier presented no shortage of risks. The channel widened as it approached the sea, so the standard procedure was to back out from the pier and then wait until the channel offered a bit more room before getting the ship's bow pointed out. Even then it was touchy and time consuming.

Captain Palmano was anxious to get going. And the frat boys weren't cooperating. One of them had lurched to the side of the pier and was now on his hands and knees, retching into the water. A couple of his buddies sat down on the gangway to watch him.

"Imbeciles," Captain Palmano muttered.

He grabbed the bridge-wing phone, called the security checkpoint on Deck Six, and told the officers to go out on the pier and drag the drunks aboard if that's what it took. The ship could wait no longer.

As Captain Palmano hung up he was joined on the bridge wing by the ship's first officer, Enzo Perlini. The two had served together for nearly a decade and soon Perlini would be leaving the *King of the Seas* to captain one of the cruise line's other ships. Palmano had brought the younger Perlini along, almost like a son, and while he was proud of his protégé, he was sad to see him go.

Palmano nodded out to sea.

"How does it look out there?"

"Good as can be. The tide is falling. The wind about fifteen knots. But the sea, it is reasonably flat. No storms anywhere to be seen," Perlini said. "There is just one thing."

"What is that?"

"Another ship has approached. A cruise ship."

"One of ours?"

Perlini shook his head, no.

Now that was curious, Palmano thought. Isla Paradiso was a private port, the exclusive domain of the *King of the Seas* and the ships owned by its cruise line. Other ships typically kept well offshore, avoiding the hazards of the Windward Passage as it met the Isla Paradiso promontory. They usually pointed more to the east and put in at Cap-Haïtien or Labadie.

"What ship is this?" Palmano asked.

"We are not certain," Perlini said. "It is still about ten miles to the northwest. And we have not been able to make positive identification."

"Did you radio it?"

"Yes, twice already," Perlini said. "But so far it has not answered our calls."

67

It was full-on dark and the *Boukman* had been motoring along on its auxiliary tank for almost forty-five minutes when Mommie Leena called from the bow.

"Gade!" she shouted. "Genyen! Genyen!"

She was pointing dead ahead. We had approached the ship from its stern and, without the benefit of seeing its full profile, were bearing down on it before Mommie Leena cried out.

I ran to join her at the bow. The ship was still a good mile away, but I could make out the pattern of lights on its decks. A cruise ship for sure. But was it the *Royal Star*? Still too far away to tell.

I strained to see it better. Whatever it was, it seemed to be sitting at idle. We were closing the gap between it and us at a pretty good rate. A few minutes and we'd be on it.

So what now?

As much as I'd hoped that we'd find the *Royal Star*, my plan, such as it was, had hinged on coming across another ship first. And then calling for help.

I didn't have a backup plan. But if this was indeed the *Royal Star* there wasn't much time for strategizing.

"When in doubt, sail straight at 'em, boys."

Who was it said that? Horatio Hornblower? Jack Aubrey?

Not that it mattered. They both had cannons and plenty of crew to back up their boldness. As for me . . .

The engines coughed, coughed again. I looked at Girard, who had taken over at the helm. He backed off the throttle. The engines purred along for a moment, then sputtered and conked out altogether. So much for running a full hour on the auxiliary tank.

Already the *Boukman* was falling off to starboard and Girard reacted quickly, letting out the mainsheet while Celeste unfurled the jib, making sure the *Boukman* didn't lose all of its forward momentum.

Mommie Leena and I stepped away from the bow as the head sail billowed out and caught the wind. Celeste shouted something and the men, women, and children cleared off the deck and went back down below.

The ship lay straight in the teeth of the wind. It would take at least two tacks, maybe three, before we could reach it. For better or worse that bought some time.

I returned to the cockpit. Celeste stood by Girard at the helm.

"Is that the ship?" she asked.

"Can't tell."

Celeste had already taken the *Boukman*'s emergency kit from the console. And now she reached into it, pulled out a flare gun.

"Hold off on that until we know for sure," I told her.

If it was the *Royal Star*, then the last thing I wanted was to draw attention to us.

We ran five minutes to the southeast, then Girard called out the command, the boom swung around, the jib collapsed then refilled, and we began our tack to the northeast.

In that moment, two things happened: I made out the name *Royal Star* on the ship's transom. And then its lights went out.

68

FRIDAY, 9:00 P.M.

Glenroy didn't know why he hadn't thought to extinguish the ship's running lights before then. Too much on his mind, too many balls in the air.

The previous several hours had consumed every bit of his attention and energy. Extracting the last bit of moisture from the big container in the engine room. Dividing the white powder, the Mother of Satan, into five plastic bags. Distributing the plastic bags to key points throughout the ship.

And all the while, making sure the *Royal Star* remained on course, its loopy route tightening and tightening, the ship closing ever inward on its prey.

It had been exasperating. With the bridge closed off to him, Glenroy had to rely on cameras in the engine control room to scan the waters ahead. He didn't fully trust them. So he had regularly been forced to stop what he was doing, dash up to Deck Four, and eyeball things for himself.

While he was up there, he had checked in on the waiters, the passengers, and the crew. Rigging up Jebailey had done the job. Things were quiet, under control. Yes, the pregnant woman was causing a commotion. The baby could be popping out at any moment.

Fine, let it happen, thought Glenroy. Add one more to the body count.

He wondered what the final number might be. Two hundred and fourteen aboard the *Royal Star*. They'd all die. That was a given. That alone would outnumber the deaths aboard the SuperFerry in the Philippines, until then the deadliest terrorist attack at sea. More than eight thousand passengers and crew aboard the *King of the Seas*. It was inevitable that some would escape. But the timing couldn't be any more ideal. Hundreds would still be in the dining rooms. They'd be climbing each other's backs trying to get out. Hundreds more in the bars, discos, and entertainment lounges. Sheer pandemonium.

Glenroy imagined the explosions, the fiery inferno as the *Royal Star* ignited, a blazing torpedo striking the *King of the Seas* directly abeam. Given such chaos, such utter destruction, the crew of the *King of the Seas* would not be able to launch the lifeboats. People would hurl themselves off the ship. They would drown, they would burn, they would get sucked down in the death spiral of the two ships.

How many would die? Three thousand? Four thousand?

Oh, glorious day. It could easily double the deaths from 9/11. Jihad in the Caribbean. The world would never be the same.

Just after sunset, Glenroy had spotted the notable promontory at Isla Paradiso and, looming large against the beach, the glittering mountainous mass that was the *King of the Seas*.

That's when Glenroy had taken the *Royal Star* off autopilot and let it idle well offshore. The officers on the bridge of the *King of the Seas* had probably sighted the *Royal Star*. They might have even tried to raise it on the radio. But since the *Royal Star* was still at a substantial distance and posed no obvious hindrance to their navigation, they likely hadn't given it more than a passing thought.

Indeed, the officers aboard the *King of the Seas* gave scant thought to any other ships. Theirs was the biggest, most expensive ship afloat and they acted accordingly. Glenroy remembered Captain Luca Palmano from the months he had worked aboard the *King of the Seas*. Arrogant, just like all the Italian officers Glenroy had ever known. Far haughtier than the Norwegians or the Swedes. But all of them holier-than-thou when it came to how they treated the grunts on the lower decks, especially the black grunts.

Soon they would get their comeuppance. Soon the Day of Doom would be at hand.

Glenroy knew the exact coordinates of the channel at Isla Paradiso, where the mouth of the channel met the waters of the Windward Passage, where the *King of the Seas* would be at its most vulnerable. He'd had the numbers memorized for weeks. And he had plugged them into the GPS in the engine control room, watching as the screen flashed up the distance—9.2 miles.

From idle to top cruising speed, the *Royal Star* could reach its target in well under thirty minutes. And as Glenroy flipped off the running lights, he knew it would buy him even more time, allow him to get even closer without raising alarm. Except for the lights in the engine control room, he doused all the other lights, too, leaving on the auxiliary system, just enough to bathe the ship's interior in a soft amber glow.

Viewed from a distance, the *Royal Star* was dark, dark as could be. By the time the *King of the Seas* finally saw it coming, it would be too late to do anything about it. Caught broadside in the channel, the lumbering brick of a ship could not possibly escape.

69

We readied for our third tack, the *Royal Star* about three hundred yards off starboard.

I'd hatched a plan. Not much of a plan really. More like a total shot in the dark. If nothing else, it would inspire my epitaph: "He took what life dealt him and he improvised. Too bad it didn't work."

The *Boukman*'s dinghy was equipped with a claw anchor, a galvanized Lewmar four-pounder. Its line was far too thin for my purposes, so I rerigged it with thicker line taken off one of the boat's bigger anchors. I tied a series of overhand knots at two-foot intervals along the line.

I rummaged around in the lockers and came up with a big can of pine tar. You usually find it on wooden boats, not on fiberglass vessels like the *Boukman*. Mixed with linseed oil and mineral spirits, it makes a preservative known as "boat soup." On its own, pine tar can patch a hole, fill a seam, or help fix a split stave. And since the *Boukman* frequently encountered leaky old wooden boats fleeing Haiti, Girard and Celeste made sure they always had the sticky resin on hand in case they needed to come to the rescue.

I scooped out several gobs of the stuff, rubbed it into the anchor line. When I was done my hands were black and gummy, but I could have held on to a pass rocketed by Dan Marino in his prime.

Everyone except Girard and Celeste had gone below. If the waiters were patrolling the decks, they wouldn't hesitate to open fire. I'd wanted Celeste to go below, too. But she wouldn't hear it.

"If Girard is here, then I am here," she said.

Two hundred fifty yards. The wind holding steady. Yes, this tack would take us there.

Girard had offered me the shotgun. But there would be no way for me to carry it. And several of the men had volunteered to come with me. While I appreciated their selflessness—indeed, their gesture damn near brought me to tears—I turned them down. No use making this any worse than it already was. I'd go it alone.

I'd argued briefly with Celeste and Girard. They didn't like the idea of me boarding the *Royal Star* by myself. They preferred that we make a run to shore. But sailing into the wind, that could take at least another hour. Time I couldn't afford to waste.

So we had settled on a compromise. Once I'd boarded the *Royal Star*—a giant if—they would head for the nearest port, Isla Paradiso. Even this far out, we could see a ship moored there, big as any ship I'd ever seen. They'd get out the word about the hijacking, even if it meant jeopardizing the success of their own mission.

"We've come too far not to commit," Celeste said. "A chance we'll have to take."

"You'll get more fuel, set out again?"

"No, we cannot risk that. We'll leave as soon as we have found help."

"All the way to Florida on wind and prayers? No way . . ."

Two hundred yards.

Now I had the chart out and was going over it with Celeste and Girard. By our best calculations, Duncan Town lay about 180 miles back to the west. It's the only settlement on Ragged Island, part of the Jumento Cays, the croissant-shaped chain of islands that descends about a hundred miles south of Great Exuma in the Bahamas.

"Bad shoals to the east," I said. "You'll have to sail past Duncan Town, then hook back and approach from the west. Look for the radio tower by the pink house. Point for that."

Celeste nodded. She folded the map, put it back in the console. I saw a notepad and a pen inside it. I grabbed them, began writing:

Hello my friend,
These people saved my life. Do whatever you can to help them.
   I'll be in touch as soon as I can. Still polishing that helmet of
   yours?
Cheers, Zack Chasteen.

Then I folded the paper in half and wrote a name on the outside: Brindley Sawyer.

Only about seventy-five people live in Duncan Town. But I knew one of them.

Five years earlier, fresh out of federal prison and anxious to restore some degree of honor to my name, I had landed in a world of hurt on Harbour Island, up by Eleuthera. Brindley Sawyer was one of several people who had helped me out of that jam. Back then, he was a rookie policeman who spent most of his time listening to the radio and keeping his helmet bright and shiny. I used to give him a hard time about it.

A couple of years ago Brindley had married a pretty girl from Duncan Town. I'd gone over for the wedding. And now he just happened to be the recently appointed police commissioner for the Jumento Cays. The first-ever police commissioner actually.

Duncan Town lies only about fifty miles across the Old Bahama Channel from the Cuban port of entry at Vita Bay. More and more cruisers were using it as a jumping-off point on their way to Cuba. Their numbers would increase as the U.S. moved closer to its long overdue détente with Castroland. And, as is the nature of things in Baja Florida, more and more developers were eyeing the uninhabited cays as potential sites for resorts and marinas.

The Bahamiam Royal Police, in an uncharacteristic display of forward thinking, figured they would get ahead of the crime wave that would surely follow. And Brindley was their one-man force in Duncan Town.

A hundred yards.

I said, "Let's get this party started."

Celeste gave me a funny look.

"What?"

"Aw, nothing. Just a line I once heard someone say."

Not even twenty-four hours earlier. Seemed so much longer.

I gave Celeste a hug. I think it surprised her, but she recovered quickly and hugged me back. A nice, un-nunlike hug.

Girard offered a hand and I shook it.

"Thanks. Let's meet again over a bowl of fish water."

"And room!"

"Yes, by all means, room."

I picked up the claw anchor and the length of line. On my way out of the cockpit, I saw Mommie Leena watching me from the hatchway. Behind her, the men, women, and children watched me, too.

Mommia Leena reached out a hand and I took it in mine.

"*Alle avec deis,*" she said.

Celeste said, "She tells you, 'Go with god.'"

"That the Vodoun god? Or the Catholic god?"

Celeste smiled.

"Does it matter?"

"Not to me it doesn't," I said. "Any gods want to come along, I welcome them for the ride."

I made my way to the bow.

Fifty yards. The *Boukman* slowing down now. The ship's hull stealing our wind. The jib beginning to luff.

I didn't know why the *Royal Star* was just sitting there, idling. But it was a gift. And I'd take it.

Still, I was attempting to board the *Royal Star* from the worst possible position. Along both sides of the ship, beginning about a third of the way forward, Deck Four was open. Here at the stern, Deck Four was enclosed. That's where the dining room was. Deck Five, the location of the Galaxy Lounge, was enclosed, too. The upside—we were out of the wind here. Plus, I hoped that boarding the ship at the stern presented less chance of being spotted.

But where to plant my improvised grappling hook?

The closest open deck from this vantage point was Deck Six, its white railing almost a hundred feet above us. No way could I hurl the anchor that far.

And then I spotted it. Welded into the hull, a series of ladder rungs descended from Deck Six to the top of the marina hatch. The lowest rung sat about fifty feet above the water. That's what I'd be aiming for.

Thirty yards.

Girard cut the wheel hard to port. The boat came around, in irons, pointing at the *Royal Star*'s transom, both the jib and the mainsail flapping now. The ship's engines, even at idle, were causing a slow boil on the water. But nothing so violent that it would throw us off.

Twenty yards.

Celeste grabbed a jib sheet and pulled the head sail over to port. Girard pushed on the boom, letting the mainsail swing to starboard. Backwinding us, putting on the brakes.

Ten yards. Inching closer and closer.

I leaned over the bowsprit, gave out a foot or two of line. I eyed the lowest rung, let the anchor swing back and forth, getting a little momentum.

I let it fly . . . up, up, up.

The anchor clanged off the hull, well short of the rung, and dropped into the water.

I reeled it in, tried again.

This time I hit the rung, but the anchor's prong didn't catch. Back into the water again.

As I hauled in the anchor, a vagrant gust of wind caught the jib. It turned the *Boukman*'s bow, began pushing us away from the ship.

I ran from the bow, headed down the starboard deck.

Last shot. Sudden death overtime. This could be the ball game.

I let loose the line. Adrenaline added loft to my shot. The anchor sailed up past the lowest rung and caught the third rung from the bottom. Worked for me.

As the stern of the *Boukman* swung around, I headed for the transom, keeping the line tight. Celeste and Girard were shouting back and forth, trying desperately to dump wind from the sails, trying to keep the trimaran from getting knocked back even more. But it wasn't working.

I grabbed a knot in the line with both hands and leaped from the transom.

I'd imagined a graceful arc that would send me swinging toward the *Royal Star*. Just call me Zack the ape-man, Tarzan of the tropics. But there was too much line out. It dumped me in the water. The line went slack. For one awful moment I thought the anchor had slipped loose.

But I yanked hard, got a tight line in return. I pulled myself toward the ship. And hand over hand I began making my way up the line.

70

Two of the assistant security officers had gone out on the pier to retrieve the drunken frat brothers. No small effort on their part. The puker had passed out and two of his buddies, inspired by the chunklicious display, had lost their lunches and fed the fish, too.

But they were now safely aboard, all passengers accounted for, the gangway raised.

As the thrusters began edging the *King of the Seas* away from the pier, Captain Palmano left the starboard bridge wing and stepped inside the bridge. He bummed a cigarette from Perlini. He was trying to quit. Anywhere else, he stuck to it. But nicotine was such a pervasive part of the bridge culture that he found it hard not to take part in the communion.

The bridge was cool and dark and smoky. Not unlike a cocktail lounge, Palmano thought. He took a long drag and exhaled slowly, enjoying the way the smoke transformed into green vapor as it wafted toward the console and caught the light from the bank of luminous screens and gauges.

It would take the better part of an hour for the ship to reach the end of the channel and get its bow pointed out. Palmano would bum more cigarettes before the maneuver was complete. Most of the bridge officers had switched to Dianas, the mild Italian brand originally marketed to women. Perlini still smoked MS unfiltereds. Yes, Palmano was going to miss Perlini.

When he had finished the cigarette, Palmano left the bridge and stepped out to the portside bridge wing. It offered a better view of the pilot boats and the open water at the end of the channel. Perlini joined him.

Palmano said, "So where is this ship you mentioned?"

Perlini pointed.

"It's out . . ."

He stopped, not finding it.

Perlini checked the radar on the bridge wing console. The ship was definitely showing up on the screen, still about ten miles offshore.

Perlini said, "Perhaps they are having electrical problems."

"Get on the radio," Palmano said. "Try raising it again."

71

FRIDAY, 9:20 P.M.

Glenroy studied the bank of monitors in the engine control room. The *King of the Seas*, big as it was and lit up like Manhattan, presented a pretty picture even at this distance.

No, it wouldn't be a problem steering from down here. A target that giant, no way he could miss.

Glenroy watched as the *King of the Seas* gave the first barely perceptible hint that it was moving away from the pier.

As anxious as he was to make his move, Glenroy kept the *Royal Star* at idle. Still, he could begin readying the engines so that when the time was right the ship would leap into action.

He reached for the throttle, powered up a notch . . .

72

I was hanging from the line, halfway up the transom to the lowest rung in the ladder. Catching my wind, arms and shoulders aching like hell. This brilliant little enterprise was taking a lot longer than I'd predicted.

I took some comfort in the fact that despite all the clanging of the mis-thrown anchor, no one had come snooping around.

Yet.

What if one of the waiters spotted me and opened fire? What then? I'd have no choice but to drop back into the sea. I doubted I'd be able to hold out very long this time around.

I looked out, trying to spot the *Boukman*. But no longer could I pick out its sails as it tacked toward shore. Swallowed by the night.

I sucked in air, tried to will the breath to my shoulders, hoping maybe that would release the tension, ease the pain. Wasn't working.

Then . . . the hull shuddered. Engines revved. Like the ship was preparing to move. I didn't want to be dangling from the stern when that happened.

I reached for the next knot, got a grip—thank you, pine tar—inched upward. Then did it again.

I looked up, saw the lowest rung in the ladder. Maybe ten knots away.

I could do this. Had to do this.

Up two knots. Then a thirty-second breather. Up two more knots. Then a full minute to recover. Then only a single knot before I had to take a break.

Getting old. It truly sucked.

The last ten feet were an absolute act of will.

The very last knot. Up, up. One hand on the rung. Then the other. I planted my feet against the hull and pulled myself up until I was standing on the bottom rung.

I freed the anchor. My lucky anchor. I couldn't quite bear to part with it. I stuck the line between my teeth, held the anchor in one hand, gripped the rungs with the other, and climbed up.

I reached the railing, slipped under it and onto Deck Six. I made a tight hank of the line, tying it off with the bitter end, and held on to it, the anchor slung over a shoulder as I moved forward along the deck. As a weapon, thoroughly medieval, but it would have to do the job.

Once again I tried to recall the ship's layout, get my bearings, make sense of all the stairwells and corridors.

Barbara was one deck below in the Galaxy Lounge. That's where I needed to go. But I couldn't just bull my way in.

How to do it? Think, Chasteen, think.

The two women who had sneaked out of the lounge, the ones I'd encountered outside the main dining room, the ones I scared the bejesus out of. How had they gotten there?

The older one saying, "*Stairs in the kitchen. They lead up to the lounge, behind the stage.*"

The galley was on Deck Four. Somehow I had to get down there, locate the stairs, and head back up to the lounge.

But what stairwells led down to the galley? And which ones would be guarded?

I was on Deck Six and . . .

Only then did I recall the lifeboats. The lifeboats that held the emergency signaling devices. Where were they? Right here on Deck Six. Where I had been heading with Carl Parks and Captain Falk when Pango and the big guy in the blue jumpsuit waylaid us in the stairwell.

Change of plan. Head for the lifeboats first, set off a signal, call in the cavalry. Then go find Barbara.

It was dark on the deck, the only illumination coming from a few scattered low-wattage lights inside. Eerie. Like a ghost ship.

I slowed as I approached a set of glass doors leading to a foyer. No one in sight.

I continued on, briefly startled by the whoosh of the doors opening automatically as I moved past them. Just ahead, I could see three lifeboats. Each rested in a cradle that hung from two davits.

Then I froze. A figure had moved from the shadows and stepped to the farthest lifeboat. A man. Not one of the waiters.

I moved closer. I watched as the man picked up a suitcase and heaved it into the lifeboat. A Halliburton.

"Diamond," I whispered. "Is that you?"

73

He whipped around, a hand already up, pointing a pistol at me.

"Chasteen," he said. "Thought you were dead."

"O ye of little faith." I nodded at the lifeboat. "Going somewhere?"

He waved the gun.

"Back off," he said. "And whatever that is you're holding, put it down."

I don't know much about pistols, but I've read that unless you are very, very good you can only count on them at extremely close range. I didn't think Diamond was very good, but he was only about ten feet away. And I'm not exactly a small target. I lay the anchor on the deck.

"What the hell are you up to, Diamond?"

"I'm going to get help. I promise."

"You can get help right now. All you have to do is reach into that lifeboat, find the emergency bag. It will send out a distress signal. Then we can do something to help the people inside."

"You're of your mind, Chasteen. There's a half-dozen guys with guns in there. You think the two of us can go up against all of them?"

"Don't love the odds, but it's the only bet on the table."

"They're armed to the teeth, Chasteen. And the guy in charge, Glenroy . . ."

"Big black dude? The one in the jumpsuit?"

Diamond nodded.

"He's crazy. He's got the ship wired to blow up."

"How do you know that?"

"Saw it with my own eyes, standing in the bridge. We were watching him on the monitors, in the engine room or someplace, mixing chemicals in a big jug. There's already been one explosion. In the galley. We all heard it."

"Who's we?"

"This Korean kid, I don't know his name. He's the computer guy. Was. He's dead. Todora shot him. The housekeeper. She's dead, too. Glenroy threw her right off the side of the fucking ship. I shot him, but . . ."

"You shot the black dude?"

"Only hit him in the hand. Then I got out of there," Diamond said. "I've been hiding, waiting until it got dark enough for me to lower one of the lifeboats and get away."

"Look, Diamond, do the right thing. Reach into the lifeboat, find the emergency bag, activate the distress signal."

"No," he said. "You're trying to trick me."

"Then let me do it."

I took a step toward him. He stuck out the gun.

"Stop right there. I'll shoot. I swear to God I'll shoot."

A pair of chains secured the lifeboat in its cradle. Keeping the pistol trained on me, Diamond unfastened the chains, let them fall to the deck.

"What's in the suitcase, Diamond?"

"Business papers."

"You got a nice way with euphemisms."

Diamond gave the lifeboat a push. The davit arms folded out and the cradle extended over the railing. The cables that lowered the lifeboat were operated from a control box at the end of a flexible gooseneck conduit attached to the side of the vessel.

Diamond grabbed the control box, pressed a button. The whirring of a motor, cables moving over pulleys, easing the lifeboat down. When the lifeboat was even with the rail, Diamond pressed another button. The cables stopped.

"Impressive," I said. "You operate that thing like a real cruise ship professional."

"I'm a smart guy," he said. "Unlike some people I know."

"You don't know me, Diamond. Because if you knew me, you wouldn't get on that lifeboat. If you knew me, you'd know that I will hunt you down and make you pay. And believe me, when I'm done with you, it's going to wind up costing a whole lot more than what you're taking away in that suitcase."

"Good-bye, Chasteen."

Diamond kept the pistol on me as he backed onto the boat. He pressed the down button. At the same time, he saw what was on the floor of the boat. And suddenly, he didn't want to be there anymore,

But the way some lifeboats work these days, they have computers. And when the down button is pushed and the computers recognize there's weight in the boat—even if it's only one person—they don't mess around. The computers signal the motor, the motor spins the cables, and the lifeboat drops. And because the computers think it's an emergency, the lifeboat drops fast.

Just how fast came as a big surprise to Ronald Diamond. I could tell that by the look on his face, the lifeboat dropping, him grabbing a cable and struggling to keep his balance.

I stepped to the rail. I leaned out and watched the lifeboat hit the water a hundred feet below. The impact tossed Diamond around in the boat. It tossed around the other bodies, too. The engine-room crew, the security officer and his assistant, the three officers shot on the main deck, the watch command, First Officer Swenson and Captain Falk. Sixteen bodies in all, getting just a tad ripe now.

Diamond made it to his feet, but there was no place he could stand without stepping on a dead person.

He looked up at me. He opened his mouth. He might have yelled something. Or maybe the words just wouldn't come out.

I gave him a big friendly wave.

Bon voyage, you lousy bastard.

74

When I'd been on this same deck the night before—when I'd discovered those bodies for myself—there was something different about the lifeboats.

Tarps. That was it. The lifeboats had been covered by blue tarps. Now the tarps were removed and lying on the deck.

Had Diamond done that before I got here? Or someone else?

I climbed into the closest lifeboat, remembered Hurku Linblom telling me where to find the emergency kit with the flares and the distress signal: *It's in an orange bag under the bow.*

The bow compartment was open. I rummaged around inside. A case of bottled water. A first aid box. Some terry-cloth towels. But no orange bag.

I opened other compartments. Nothing there either.

I searched the other two lifeboats. Nothing.

Had Linblom been mistaken about the emergency kits? Or had someone come along and removed them?

Damn, damn, double damn. So much for calling in the cavalry.

But no time to brood over it. I picked up the anchor, slung it over my shoulder. Had to keep moving. I went through the automatic doors, found a stairwell, and headed down.

The galley still smelled like a burn zone. Whatever awful thing had happened here, I didn't want to be anywhere near if it happened again.

The place was so torn up I hardly recognized it from when I'd walked through the night before. I stayed clear of the gaping hole in the wall, the night wind rushing in. I climbed over prep tables, past pots and pans and broken dishes.

At the rear of the galley, I found a stairway, the door to it blown off its hinges. Only way to go was up.

Two flights and then a door. I opened it. A narrow hallway. Directly across from me another door. I stepped across the hall, eased open the door, and found myself backstage, behind the curtains at the Galaxy Lounge.

I stood there, listening. Soft voices, muffled conversation.

A man's saying: "Don't push, don't push. It's not time yet."

I parted the curtains, just enough to peek through. The lights were dim but I saw all I needed to see.

Saw women on the stage floor, some of them sleeping, others sitting in small groups. Men beyond them in the lounge, sitting on chairs and sofas. One waiter standing at the back of the lounge, near the door to the atrium. A second waiter sitting near the stage. Saw Sam Jebailey sitting in the middle of the stage, trussed up with a deadly looking package taped around his torso.

And I saw Barbara.

She was at the far end of the stage, a blanket over her, legs bent, sitting up on her elbows. Eyes closed, face strained, breathing like they taught us in Lamaze class. Her hair was matted, her cheeks flushed. A few hours earlier, I thought I'd never see her again. Never had she looked more beautiful to me.

A man with gray hair and wire-rimmed glasses knelt beside her. Dr. Louttit. And behind Barbara, offering comfort and support, sat the same woman I'd encountered in the dining room, the one who had told me about the staircase leading from the galley to the lounge.

Barbara let out a moan. She pounded a fist on the stage.

It was killing me to stand back and watch. I wanted to burst through the curtains and be by her side.

Dr. Louttit checked his watch.

"About six minutes apart," he said. "You've still got a little ways to go. Just relax. Breathe."

I parted the curtains just a little more so I could get a better look. And that's when the woman sitting behind Barbara spotted me.

Her eyes went wide.

I put a finger to my lips. Then I mouthed: "I'll. Be. Back."

Yeah, Schwarzenegger owned the words, but I wasn't feeling particularly original.

The woman understood. She nodded.

I stepped away from the curtain and out the door.

75

The elevator to the marina sat at the far aft end of the galley and that had spared it from damage by the explosion.

I got on and took it down. I gripped the anchor, ready to use it if I needed to. The doors opened. I took a cautious step out. No one in sight. I slung the anchor over a shoulder and hurried across the cavernous room, heading for the boat bay.

I needed to get everything ready—the tender, the skiffs, the Jet Skis, whatever would take people away from the ship. I was trying to visualize how it would play out, how I could make it happen.

Maybe I would create a diversion in the atrium, distract the waiters long enough so the passengers could get out of the lounge and down to the marina. That still left the crew to worry about. Where were they being held? Probably somewhere in the same general vicinity. Maybe someplace where they could be locked up. There were only five waiters. Four if you took away the one we had beaten up on Deck Two. And I was pretty sure that we had decommissioned him, at least for the short term.

But what about the big guy? Glenroy, that's what Diamond had called him, the one running the show. Where was he? On the bridge? Someone had steered the *Royal Star* to its present location. Was Glenroy capable of that? Or were some of the ship's officers still alive and maybe Glenroy was forcing them to take the ship where he wanted to go?

I flashed on Diamond standing in the lifeboat with all those bodies. Seemed like a lot of them were wearing officers' whites. More than just the three I'd seen gunned down on the main deck. And what was it that

Diamond had said about being on the bridge, when he'd watched Glenroy on the monitors mixing explosives? Who else was there with him?

This Korean kid, the computer guy . . . Todora, she's dead, too.

No mention of any officers on the bridge. Meaning, I couldn't count on them for help. I had to operate under the assumption they'd all been killed.

So. The waiters and Glenroy. Me versus them.

Plus they were holding a trump card—Sam Jebailey, sitting on the stage, with who knows what-all strapped to his body. The neutralizing factor. If anyone made a move, they'd blow up the whole shebang.

How to deal with that?

One step at a time, Chasteen. And first, make sure you have an exit plan.

I rounded a tall stack of pallets. The boat bay lay just ahead. I wasn't sure how I would open its gate, but I'd find a way. Had to.

Turned out not to be an issue.

The gate was wide open. One of the Boston Whalers had been dragged out on its skids, away from the other vessels. I stood there looking at it. Lined up by its fuel well—nine Halliburtons. My, my, my . . .

"Hey there, buddy."

I turned around.

Carl Parks. Holding a rifle. Pointed at me.

76

Parks said, "Thought you were dead."

"Why, if it isn't Little Sir Echo."

A blank look from Parks.

I said, "Ron Diamond told me the exact same thing, not more than ten minutes ago."

"Diamond? Where's he?"

"Floating in a lifeboat. With a bunch of bodies. And one Halliburton."

Parks thought about it. A smile crossed his face. The smile became a laugh.

"He can have that suitcase. It's all his. He deserves it," Parks said. He looked at the anchor I was holding. "What's with that?"

"In case I need it."

"Best put it down," he said. "Real slowlike."

I rested the anchor by my feet.

"Now step away from it," Parks said.

I stepped away.

Parks had a towel wrapped around an upper arm, blood seeping through. I could tell it was hurting him.

"Caught one in the shoulder right after you hauled ass," he said. "Things went to hell after that. Ran out of ammo. Had to leave those poor fuckers up there to fend for themselves."

"They didn't fend too well. They're all up in the lounge now, being held at gunpoint. My wife's up there. She's getting ready to have our baby."

"Hunh," said Parks. "Hell of a thing, isn't it?"

He still had the rifle pointed at me. I looked around, saw the provisions master's body lying by his desk.

"I got down here, must have been right after they killed that poor son of a bitch," Parks said. "Plenty of places to hide, all these boxes and pallets and shit. So I just hunkered down and bided my time."

I looked at the boat, at the Halliburtons.

"All things come to he who waits," Parks said. "That fat little maître d', he came along and left his rifle where I could grab it. Then he came back down here with the keys to the boat bay and unlocked it. By the looks of it, he must have been planning his own getaway. Then there was this explosion came from up above somewhere . . ."

"The galley," I said. "Diamond said they've got explosives aboard, plan to blow the whole ship."

"Then it would behoove me to shit and git. Which is where you come in." He nodded at the Whaler. "A man with a bum arm can't launch that boat. Tried already. A big strong guy like you though . . ."

He waved the rifle at the Whaler.

"Get to work, Chasteen."

I didn't move.

Parks said, "Guess maybe all this is coming as a big surprise, huh?"

"Not really. Had my doubts about you all along."

"Do tell."

"For starters, you talked too much. I've met more than my share of Feds, believe me. And as a rule, they're a pretty tight-lipped bunch. Just the bare facts, little more. They don't talk out of school," I said. "But you rolled it all out, gave me the full la-dee-da. Details about Jebailey. Details about Diamond. Details about bulk-cash smuggling and ICE opening a fake bank on St. Kitts. Like you were trying hard to convince me that you were who you said you were. Trying a little too hard."

"Plenty of details about you, too, Chasteen."

"Yeah. And that's what had me on the fence about you, Parks. Because you knew so much about me. More than anyone just casually snooping around could ever possibly know."

Parks grinned.

"Hell, Chasteen, I might be a crook, but I still do the homework," he said. "I asked Jebailey to give me a list of all the guests who would be on board. I checked out everyone. But you were by far the most interesting. So I checked you out some more. Know what I thought at first?"

"What?"

"I thought you might be in on it, too. Thought you might have signed on with Jebailey to move a little money. Thought you might have bought yourself a Halliburton or two. It fits your profile. A convicted smuggler. A friend of Freddie Arzghanian. A man with any number of offshore bank accounts."

"You've got it wrong. The conviction was overturned. Freddie Arzghanian's no friend of mine. And as far as offshore accounts go, I've only got one. And it's legal."

"Still," Parks said. "You're no choir boy, Chasteen."

I didn't say anything.

Parks said, "If it makes you feel any better, you were only half wrong about me. I used to work for ICE. We parted ways a few years back."

"Their idea or yours?"

"Let's just say it was mutually beneficial and leave it at that."

"Well, as long as we're sharing, you want to know the other thing that gave you away, Parks?"

"Sure, tell me."

"Up there in the cabin, when we were figuring out what to do, you cared more about the money than the people. You were even willing to give me some of it for helping you out. It just didn't ring right with me. I'm no fan of the Feds. But they've got a code and they stick to it, most of them. A real ICE agent, he would have taken care of the people first, worried about the money later."

"So sue me," Parks said. "Now, if you don't mind, I've got a boat to catch."

He waved the gun at the Whaler again.

I didn't move.

"In case you're contemplating making a move on me, Chasteen, this SAR I'm holding has seven rounds left in it. I can have every single one of those rounds in you, in a very tight upper-torso pattern, before you get halfway to me."

"That would leave you high and dry."

"No, not really," Parks said. "I figure even with one arm I can drag out a Jet Ski, get away on that. Might not be able to take all nine of those Halliburtons. And that would sadden me, it really would. But I can strap on four or five of them for sure. Call it eight or ten million dollars."

"Not a bad return on your investment."

"Hell of a return, considering."

"Considering what?"

"Considering I didn't invest a dime."

"Thought you said the buy-in with Jebailey was two million dollars."

"Yeah, it was," Parks said. "But, see, I know this Panamanian crew. Best paperhangers in the business. They owed me. They owed me big time. They owed me at least two million dollars."

"Of counterfeit money."

"Bingo," Parks said. "I didn't think Jebailey would pay it close attention. And I'd have two million dollars, less his commission, in an offshore account. But then, that's why Jebailey, he's one of the best in the business, too. He sniffed out that the Halliburton I gave him was filled with funny money."

"So why'd he even bring it on board?"

"Maybe he didn't figure it out until after we'd already set sail. Maybe even then he thought he might try to slip it past the bank in St. Kitts," Parks said. "Or maybe not. Still, counterfeit money is worth something. Especially primo counterfeit like this stuff. It would go for a dime on the dollar easy. Worth a couple hundred grand. You damn sure wouldn't throw it away."

I said, "So Jebailey, he culled that one suitcase from the rest."

"And that's why Diamond found it," Parks said, "but not the others."

"Poor Diamond."

"Yeah, my heart bleeds," Parks said. "Now, if you don't mind . . ."

Again with the gun.

I walked over to the Whaler, put both hands on the transom, and pushed it on its skids all the way out of the boat bay. I went to the bow and pushed on it so the stern would be facing out. I stepped over to the wall and pressed the button that raised the marina hatch. As it creaked open, I found the Whaler's bowline and pulled it out of the boat. I checked the ignition. The keys were in it.

The *Royal Star* wasn't moving, so only a small bit of water flowed into the marina this time. Most of it pooled under the Whaler, just enough to help me launch it. I pushed on the bow. The Whaler slid out the hatch and floated behind the ship. I fed out about twenty feet of line. There was a cleat near the hatch. I tied off the bow line on it.

"Nicely done," Parks said.

I stepped between him and the boat.

"You're not getting on it," I said. "Not until after you help me out. You do that, you go your way, I go mine."

"Help you out?"

"You and me, we had a deal," I said. "Up there in the cabin. You said if I helped you get the money, then you'd help me. I've done my part. It's your turn. We shook on it."

"We shook on it? Goddam, Chasteen, you're telling me I'm supposed to give a shit about a handshake?"

"Yeah, that's what I'm telling you," I said. "And I'll tell you the same thing I told Ron Diamond. If you don't help me out, when all this is over, I will hunt you down. I will find you. And I will bring you pain."

"Diamond didn't pay you any attention either, did he?"

"No, you're right, he didn't. And he's already regretting it. Before this is all over, trust me, he'll regret it even more. But you, you're different, Parks."

"Yeah? How?"

"Diamond, I'm not so sure there was ever much good about him. But you, time was, I bet you were a pretty good man. A man of his word."

Parks started to say something, stopped. He glanced away. And when he looked back at me, there was something different in his eyes.

"You don't know me," he said.

"I know enough. I know you had ideals once. Some pretty lofty ones even. Else you wouldn't have signed on with the Feds in the first place. Where did you start out? DEA back in the eighties?"

"Nineteen-eighty-four. With SLED."

"South Carolina Law Enforcement Division."

Parks nodded.

"Then DEA? Then ICE?"

"Couple of years in between with ATF."

"Heckuva résumé."

Parks shrugged.

"What'd you put in, about twenty years?"

"Twenty-two."

"OK, I'm guessing that for at least sixteen of those twenty-two years you were as rock-solid as they come. Rose through the ranks. Commendations galore. A credit to the corps and all that. But then something turned. Could have been wife trouble. Could have been kid trouble. Could have been you didn't get a promotion you thought you deserved. Could have been all that. All bundled up and eating at you. So you slipped a little. You took something you shouldn't have taken. You benefited way above your pay grade. But, hey, you rationalized it. Told yourself that everyone did it. And besides, hard as you worked, you were owed it. So you took. You took and you didn't get caught. But things kept eating at you. So you slipped a little more. You started taking a lot. After a while you were no better than the bad guys. And then you slipped so much that the only choice you left yourself was to burn the bridges and go your own way."

Parks was quiet for a while. All we heard was the low rumble of the ship's engines at idle, waves lapping across the marina hatch.

Then Parks raised the gun.

"Step away from the boat, Chasteen."

I did what he said.

Parks pulled himself onto the bow of the Whaler. He stepped to the console. He turned the key, then hit a button on the throttle. The outboard engine lowered into the water. When it was down, Parks turned the key all the way. The engine turned over, then stopped. Parks pushed the choke, tried again. The engine turned over, caught. He let it idle.

Then he hopped out of the boat. He walked up to me, looked me straight in the eye.

"For the record, out of my twenty-two years all but the last one was rock-solid, rock-solid to the core. You got that?"

I nodded.

He said, "I shoulda got out before I did, but you do what you know how to do and you keep doing it. Sooner or later it starts limiting your options. Starts making you regret. Starts making you do things to wash away that regret. Yeah, Chasteen, I slipped. But no worse than some." He took a deep breath. "My first wife, she left me. Because I was always working, doing undercover, never home. She got the kids. Haven't seen them in a long time now. My second wife, she left me, too. No kids. But the same deal. After a while . . ." He paused. "After a while, I just said fuck it."

"Happens."

"There's not much difference between the good guys and the bad guys, Chasteen."

"I know that," I said. "And I know you still lean mostly to the good."

"I'm not looking for redemption."

"Not offering it."

"I might have slipped . . ."

"We all do."

"But I'm a man of my word."

He stuck out a hand. I shook it.

"You're signing up for a shitstorm," I said.

"Yeah, but when it's over, I've got a boat in the water, the engine's running, and I'm out of here," Parks said. "Now let's go do this goddam thing."

77

Unlike other cruise ship captains of his acquaintance, men who spent their days off as far from the water as possible, Captain Palmano enjoyed getting out on his boat. He kept a Donzi 38 ZX dry-docked in Coconut Grove, right behind Scotty's Landing. Twin Merc 525s. On a flat-water day it could hit seventy mph easy.

Palmano loved the Donzi. Loved it because it was everything the *King of the Seas* was not. The ultimate go-fast boat. Point it in the right direction. Hit the throttle. And you were there. Governor's Cut to Bimini in just over an hour.

It was at times like this, when the *King of the Seas* was plodding away from port, going nowhere fast, that Palmano conjured up the Donzi. Such speed. The wind stinging his face, going so fast he had to wear specially made boater's goggles, so fast it almost took the curl out of his hair.

The *King of the Seas*, it was so damn slow. Half an hour away from the pier and they were just now nearing the end of the channel, approaching the spot where the ship could begin to turn around. And that would take at least another half hour.

Palmano was on the bridge, standing to one side of the console, letting Perlini run the show. The chief pilot of Isla Paradiso, a tall Haitian by the name of Genereau, stood alongside Perlini, radioing back and forth with the two pilot boats. As soon as Genereau gave the all clear, Perlini would issue the order to the helmsman and the *King of the Seas* would finally begin to point its bow toward open water.

Palmano drummed his fingers on the bridge console. This whole thing was taking so long.

Perlini noticed the captain's impatience.

"Porco del Mare," Perlini said.

Palmano smiled, nodded.

"*Sì, certo,*" he said. "Porco del Mare."

The private nickname the Italian officers had given the ship.

Porco del Mare. Pig of the Sea.

78

Glenroy kept his attention glued on the monitor, the one showing the *King of the Seas*. The fatigue he'd felt earlier had vanished. He felt newly energized, more alive than ever. A result, no doubt, of the *salat* he had offered just a few minutes earlier. His final *salat* before entering Paradise.

Kneeling on the floor of the engine control room, he had given praise to Allah, asked for strength and guidance. A quick prayer, just the basics, over in no time.

He had settled into the chief engineer's chair. Here, in this very spot, he would meet his fate, join the ranks of the most illustrious martyrs. Nothing could stop him now.

The *King of the Seas*, lighting up the monitor . . .

The change in its course was barely perceptible, but Glenroy picked it up. The ship had stopped and, ever so slowly, its bow was inching toward the sea.

Glenroy reached for the console . . .

79

Not much had changed in the Galaxy Lounge. The two waiters held the same posts, one at the door, one by the stage. The passengers were all pretty much the same as when I'd stepped away a few minutes earlier. Exhausted, listless. Long hours of despair taking their toll. Sam Jebailey sat rigid on the stage. Too scared to even breathe.

Barbara looked relaxed. As relaxed as she could be anyway, given the circumstances. Her eyes were closed. She was resting. In between contractions, I guessed.

The woman sitting beside her stroked Barbara's hair. She spotted me peeking between the curtains. She leaned down, whispered in Barbara's ear. Barbara opened her eyes. The woman gently rolled Barbara's head in the direction of the curtains.

And then Barbara saw me. We connected. It was everything I could do not to run out there and hold her.

Barbara tried to sit up, but the woman whispered something else and Barbara eased back down, never taking her eyes off me.

I gave her the thumbs-up. She smiled, blinked her eyes. She put a hand on her stomach, smiled again.

I pulled back from the curtains, let Parks have a look.

While he was doing that I scoped out the lounge for cameras on the walls. I found two of them, one near the door, one near the stage. But there weren't any behind the curtains where we were. The cameras in the marina had been destroyed. I'd seen to that. And the explosion had knocked out the ones in the galley. Lots of blind spots on the *Royal Star*. So whoever might be monitoring things, there was a pretty good chance they hadn't spotted us. Yet.

Parks pulled back from the curtains.

He said, "You didn't tell me about the bomb on Jebailey."

"Wanted it to be a surprise."

"I hate surprises."

"Life's full of 'em."

"Kiss my ass, Chasteen."

"Know anything about bombs?"

Parks shrugged.

"A couple of training sessions. But nothing beyond the classroom."

"What's that one look like to you?"

Parks peeked through the curtains again.

"Looks like the standard-issue suicide-bomber package. Only it's got a remote detonator. Any idea who's controlling it?"

"No," I said. "What kind of explosive?"

Parks looked some more.

"Hard to tell from here. Sticks of something, can't tell what because of all that duct tape. Not C-4. Maybe trinitrotoluene. TNT."

"Dynamite?"

Parks shook his head.

"No, TNT and dynamite are two totally different things. Dynamite is a mixture of nitroglycerin and an absorbent material of some kind. TNT is a specific chemical compound. Either way, both are easy enough to come by. Too easy."

"Diamond said something about seeing the guy in charge, Glenroy, mixing chemicals down in the engine room."

Parks thought about it.

He said, "That would be something else altogether. Not what we're looking at here. Diamond say what kind of chemicals?"

I shook my head no. Parks thought about it some more.

Then he said, "Fuck."

"That bad, huh?"

"TATP," he said. "Triacetone triperoxide. The baddest of the bad. Made from stuff that's probably just lying around the ship—industrial-strength hydrogen peroxide, acetone, hydrochloric acid. Mother of Satan they call it. Volatile as hell."

"That explosion in the galley."

"Yeah, that would explain it," Parks said. He looked out through the curtains again. "But that's not what they've got on Jebailey. The wires, the switching devices. That's all part of the detonator, runs from the walkie-talkie stuck on Jebailey's chest. The remote detonator, it's just another walkie-talkie. You use that kind of rig with TNT or dynamite. Not with TATP. With TATP you don't need a detonator. That stuff, it's the detonator and the explosive all in one."

"So," I said.

"So," Parks said.

"Now's the part when one of us is supposed to say: 'OK, here's what we're gonna do.'"

"I'm waiting," Parks said.

"We could find the guy with the other walkie-talkie, take him out," I said.

"You know where to look?"

"Not a clue," I said.

That's when the ship lurched forward. It happened so abruptly that I tumbled into Parks. In the lounge, gasps and cries—passengers reacting to the sudden motion. The *Royal Star* was moving. And it was moving somewhere with purpose.

"Whatever we're doing," I said, "we better do it fast."

80

In the end, it was the woman sitting beside Barbara who got things rolling. While Parks and I were fiddle-farting around, plotting our best plan of attack, I heard the woman say: "Taking a leak here, boss."

Right out of *Cool Hand Luke*. When Paul Newman heads for the bushes, getting ready to escape the chain gang. It didn't turn out so good for him. Still . . .

The woman said it loud. Meant for me to hear.

I peeked out through the curtain. The woman was standing up. As soon as she had made sure that I was watching, she started walking across the stage. She stopped at the far end, where several ice buckets were lined up.

The waiter nearest the stage trailed her the whole way, watching her every move.

"Don't you dare watch me, you little creep," she said.

The waiter turned away.

The woman looked directly at me. She hiked up her skirt and sat down on the ice bucket. She flashed three fingers at her side. She mouthed: "On three."

She waited for me to confirm that I understood. I gripped the anchor.

"Get ready, Parks."

"Ready for what?"

"I'm not sure. Just get ready."

He moved beside me, looked out through the curtain.

"I can't just start shooting," he said. "Too many people."

"Just do what you have to do."

The woman was still waiting. I gave her a nod.

She flashed a finger.

"One," I said.

Barbara was sitting up now, looking at me. Dr. Louttit had spotted me, too.

The woman flashed another finger.

"Two," I said.

The second waiter was stepping into the doorway, looking into the atrium, not paying any attention to what was going on in the lounge.

She flashed a third finger.

"Go!"

We burst through the curtains yelling, Parks and I. It scared hell out of everyone. As the waiter by the stage whipped around, the woman grabbed the ice bucket and slung it at him, its contents splattering all over him, the bucket catching him square across the nose. He reeled backward.

I crossed the stage in three bounds, leaped off and swung the anchor. It cracked against the waiter in the jaw. He dropped his rifle and went down. He didn't move.

Parks took a position on the steps leading up to the stage. The waiter in the doorway turned around, leveled his rifle.

I saw Parks moving off the steps, past chairs and sofas, trying to get a better angle, not wanting to shoot through the male passengers who were getting to their feet, just now beginning to absorb what was going on.

Parks shouted, "Down! Everybody down!"

Some men flattened on the floor. Parks still didn't have a clear shot.

The waiter in the doorway moved his rifle, from left to right, threatening, jabbing it at the crowd.

"Zack!"

Barbara opened her arms to me. I ran to her, expecting the waiter to start shooting. I pulled Barbara to me, wrapped myself around her.

I saw Parks move behind a sofa, waving male passengers out of the line of fire.

I held Barbara close, braced for the shots.

I locked on Sam Jebailey, sitting frozen, not ten yards away, eyes shut, ready for the worst. No way any of us could brace for that.

Waited.

But nothing happened.

I looked up, saw the waiter throwing down his rifle, running out the door.

Parks took aim. But the waiter had already disappeared into the atrium. I could hear him yelling for the other waiters.

I looked at Jebailey.

"Help me," he said. "Please help me."

"Just hold tight," I said.

Parks moved from behind the sofa, began making his way up the aisle toward the atrium. Men fell in behind him. One of them had grabbed the rifle from the waiter I'd clobbered with the anchor. I saw Kane Kinsey and some other men breaking apart tables, ready to use the legs as clubs.

"Oh, Zack," Barbara said. "I thought I'd lost you."

I covered her mouth with mine. I kissed her hard. I hugged her tight.

"How's Critter?"

"Critter's going to be just fine," she said.

I put my hand on her stomach. I looked at Dr. Louttit.

"Soon?"

"Real soon," he said. "I'd say within the hour."

"I need you to get her out of here," I told him. "I need everyone out of here."

Barbara said, "Zack, how did you . . ."

"Later. We'll talk about it later."

A commotion now on the stage. Some of the women crying out, not sure where to go, what to do. Others calling for their husbands.

Parks crouched by the doorway, aiming into the atrium. The men took positions behind him, ready to charge. More yelling coming from somewhere. Not the waiters. The sound of banging on walls and doors. A real ruckus. The crew?

And then Parks, charging into the atrium, the men falling behind him, yelling, letting out a mighty roar.

Gunfire . . .

Pop-pop. Just two shots.

Then more yelling. An even louder uproar from the atrium.

Seconds later, Kane Kinsey appeared in the doorway.

"We got 'em!" he yelled into us.

And then he was gone.

The woman who had slung the ice bucket at the waiter returned to Barbara's side.

"Nice work," I told her.

"You, too."

I nodded to the curtains.

"You remember your way out of here?"

"Bet your ass I do."

"Stairway to the galley. Don't be alarmed by what you see down there. Just head to the back, to the elevator. Take it down to the marina."

"Got it." She turned to Barbara. She held out her hand. Resting in the palm—Barbara's wedding ring, the ring that had belonged to my mother. "Here ya go, honey."

"Oh, Marie," Barbara said. "Thank you, thank you, thank you."

Barbara started to put it on, hesitated.

"Don't worry, I wiped it clean already," Marie said. She touched an emerald brooch hanging around her neck. "You ask me, a little piss just gives it extra sparkle."

Barbara looked at me.

"You don't want to know," she said.

Marie was already marshaling the women off the stage.

"Get moving, girls," she said. "Follow me."

I helped Barbara to her feet. Dr. Louttit took her arm, started to lead her away.

"Zack," she said. "What about you?"

"Go," I told her. "I'll catch up."

81

Glenroy watched it on the monitors—the two men storming into the Galaxy Lounge, the big man hitting Tony, knocking him to the floor. Marcos, throwing down his empty rifle, running away. The other waiters joining him, fleeing the atrium.

Then the man with the rifle firing. The male passengers swarming around him. The waiters freezing on the stairway, giving themselves up.

And now the crew members in the casino, heaving a blackjack table through a window, breaking their way out.

Some of the passengers busting in a door, freeing the crew in the library.

It was everything Glenroy could do not to grab his rifle and run up to Deck Five. He had a full clip left in the SAR. He might not be able to stop everyone, but he could take out a few, maybe halt the mass exodus for a few minutes longer.

No, he had to hold tight, stay right here in the engine control room. The *Royal Star* was approaching top speed and Glenroy would have to steer it manually the rest of the way. He checked the GPS—9.5 miles from the *King of the Seas* and closing. Less than twenty-nine minutes. He could not let this setback distract him from the target. He had to focus on the greater goal. So what if the passengers and crew managed to escape the *Royal Star*? It was of minor consequence in the broader scope of things. There were more than eight thousand people aboard the *King of the Seas*.

And they would have no opportunity for escape until the ship was already in the throes of death.

And now the monitors were showing the lounge emptying of people. Just two remained—Sam Jebailey and the tall man, the one who had put up a fight at the bon voyage party, the one who the waiters had fired at as he jumped overboard. How had he gotten back on the ship? How? Who was this guy?

The tall man was kneeling on the stage, inspecting the makeshift vest that Glenroy had strapped onto Jebailey. Glenroy was proud of his little creation. It had served its purpose. It had kept the passengers at bay. It had bought Glenroy some time.

This next part would be most interesting, Glenroy thought. Fun to watch.

The walkie-talkie sat on the console in front of him. He looked at it, allowed himself a smile.

82

o you have any experience with bombs? Have you ever done this before? Do you have any earthly idea what you're doing?"

"No. No. And no," I said.

"Then go find someone else," Jebailey said. "There has to be someone
else."

"It's just you and me, pal. Enough with the bitching or it'll be just you."

It shut him up.

The lounge was empty now. After escaping from the casino and the library, the crew had sprung into action. Some had helped escort passengers
down to the marina. They would launch the tender and set off in it. Others had gone up to Deck Six to lower the lifeboats. They were a well-oiled
bunch. The evacuation was proceeding with speed and efficiency.

As for the waiters, they'd been roughed up, but the mob of male passengers had stopped short of doing them in altogether. The waiter I clobbered had regained consciousness. And all five of them had been hauled
away to depart the ship in one of the lifeboats.

Still no sign of the guy in the blue jumpsuit, Glenroy. He had the other
walkie-talkie, the detonator. A few members of the senior crew—the
purser, the cruise director—had briefly entertained the notion of finding
him, of heading for the bridge and trying to regain control of the ship.
But none of them knew the pass code. And no one was particularly zealous
about sacrificing any more lives to the cause. Besides, the device taped to
Jebailey could go off at any moment. Who knew what kind of hell it
might unleash?

So the order of business had become: Get off the ship with all due haste. Call in the troops. And let them handle it.

Help might already be on the way. The *Boukman* couldn't possibly have tacked its way to shore yet, but it could have encountered another boat and raised the alarm.

I was anxious to get down to the marina, to be with Barbara. But I couldn't let Jebailey just dangle in the wind. I kept looking over my shoulder, hoping Carl Parks might come strolling in. As little as he professed to know about bombs, it was volumes more than I knew. But I hadn't seen him since he had led the charge into the atrium.

I knelt in front of Jebailey, studying the contraption that had been fastened to him. I kept asking myself: Why hasn't it gone off yet?

The optimum time for detonating it would have been when Parks and I stormed into the lounge. The blast could have put an end to us, easy. Surely Glenroy had been watching on the ship's monitors. Why hadn't he done it then?

I looked at the red cylinders, duct tape wrapped around their middle portions. Dynamite, TNT, whatever it was. The metal contacts, the wires connecting them. More wires leading to the walkie-talkie in the middle of Jebailey's chest.

Was it just a matter of yanking off the wires? Would that defuse the thing? Or would that set it off? A better question: Did I have the balls to try it?

"Please," Jebailey said. "If you don't mind . . ."

"What is it?"

"My nose," he said. "It itches."

"What? You want me to scratch it?"

"Yes, please. I'm afraid to raise my hand."

Nose scratcher to a billionaire. A money-smuggling billionaire. Ah, at last I'd found my true calling.

I stood.

"Where on your nose?"

"Near the tip."

I scratched.

"Farther down."

I scratched farther down.

"Little to the right."

I scratched to the right.

"Yes, there."

I scratched there.

I was looking down on the cylinders now. I hadn't seen them from this angle. I didn't know what a stick of dynamite or TNT looked like. But what I was looking at, I'd seen somewhere before.

"Thanks," Jebailey said.

I just couldn't place it. The ends of the cylinders were covered with red paper that had been drawn together, given a little twist and tucked back inside the cylinder, gave it a kind of puckered-up look.

"OK," Jebailey said. "That's good."

Like a Roman candle. Only it wasn't a Roman candle. It was a . . .

"Enough," Jebailey said. "You can stop now. Please stop."

"Sorry."

I knelt in front of Jebailey again. I looked at the cylinders, all twelve of them. In making the contraption, Glenroy had gone to great lengths to cover a precise portion of each cylinder with duct tape. An inch from the bottom, an inch from the top. About three widths of the tape. He could have gotten by with a single wrapping. That would have easily held each cylinder in place and connected it to the adjacent cylinder. Or he could have wrapped the entire cylinder. But no. He had meticulously gone about covering up a specific section of each cylinder. Why?

On one of the cylinders, a corner of the tape had peeled up. I reached out and took hold of it.

Jebailey said, "What are you doing?"

"Just taking a little peek," I said. "Keep still."

I peeled back the tape, just enough to reveal the letter "D." I peeled some more, got a "Y." Then an "N."

Would a stick of dynamite actually have the word "DYNAMITE" printed on it? Maybe. Life does, after all, imitate "Roadrunner" cartoons.

But I had a pretty good idea where this was going now.

I peeled a little more and got "-," a hyphen. That was followed by an "O," another hyphen, then an "F" and an "L."

Vanna, I'll buy a vowel please.

"A."

Yes, yes, yes. All those emergency kits missing from the lifeboats? Glenroy hadn't taken them to get rid of the signaling devices.

I ripped off the rest of the tape.

"Dyn-o-flare," I said. "A Boater's Best Friend."

"Huh?"

"You've never seen the commercials? Pretty girl in a boat. Boat breaks down. She whips out her handy-dandy Dyn-o-flare. Shoots it off.

Handsome guy comes to the rescue. Girl smiles at the camera and says, 'Dyn-o-flare. A boater's best friend.' You've never seen that?"

Jebailey just looked at me.

"You really need to spend more time watching the Outdoor Channel," I said. "You ask me the whole thing's kinda phallic. The girl. The stick. The guy."

"So that's not . . . ?"

"Not a bomb. A fake bomb. And a pretty good one, I might add," I said. "Dyn-o-flares. Damn. I keep those on my boats. I knew I'd seen them somewhere."

I unwrapped the rest of the duct tape, yanked off the flares. I helped Jebailey to his feet.

"Let's get the hell out of here," I said.

83

With the ship moving and the hatch open, water was shin-deep in the marina by the time Jebailey and I got there.

The tender was launched and ready to go. But there was no sign of the Whaler or Carl Parks. Fair enough. He'd manned-up when I'd needed him. And now he was gone. With a boatload of Halliburtons.

The tender was jam-packed with passengers and crew. Some of the crew were busy launching the second Whaler so more people could get on it. I got a couple of them to help me wrap the provisions master's body in a tarp and load it on the boat. I owed him that at least.

The ship's wake tossed the tender around and the passengers with it. They'd made room in the stern for Barbara to stretch out. Marie and Dr. Louttit were at her side. Barbara looked to be in pain, in the middle of another contraction.

I ran to the side of the tender. I had to yell to be heard over the roar of the ship's engines, the thrashing of the sea.

"Barbara!"

She opened her eyes, saw me. She held out a hand.

Behind me, the dockmaster, a deeply tanned guy with sun-bleached hair, was facing off with an older woman. Her long silver hair was pulled back in a loose bun. She was crying, refusing to climb aboard the tender.

I said, "What's the problem?"

"Says her husband's still on board somewhere," the dockmaster said. "Says she won't leave the ship until we find him. I sent some guys down to look already, but . . ." He shook his head. "Have to get the tender out of here. Can't take the pounding much longer."

I turned to the woman.

"Who's your husband?"

"Linblom," she said. "Hurku Linblom. We must find him, please . . ."

The dockmaster said, "We checked all the cabins down on Deck Two. Nothing."

"I'll go back down, give it another look. I'll find him," I told the woman. "But right now, you have to get off the ship."

She gave in. She thanked me. She took the dockmaster's hand and let him help her onto the tender. It was bouncing around like crazy. The dockmaster reached into a pocket, pulled out a card key, and handed it to me.

He said, "This'll get you in the cabins down there."

I stuffed it away.

I looked around. Where was Jebailey? I hadn't kept an eye on him after we reached the marina. Now I spotted him in the storage area, struggling to drag a pair of big boxes our way. Computers. The provisions master hadn't tossed all of them overboard. A couple dozen were still stacked atop a pallet.

I ran to get him.

"What the hell are you doing?"

"The computers," he said. "We have to . . ."

"Screw the computers."

I grabbed him, pulled him away. He fought to get loose.

"No! Please . . ."

I hooked an elbow under his neck and hauled him to the tender and shoveled him on board. The dockmaster got on behind him.

The second Whaler was loaded now. It was pulling away. Beyond it, I spotted two of the lifeboats bobbing on the waves.

I was the last one left in the marina.

"I can't hang around to wait for you. Too risky," the dockmaster said. He pointed to the boat bay. "Jet Skis. You'll have to use one of them. Keys are in 'em."

I looked at Barbara. Again, she reached out for me. She started to say something, then stopped, her face contorting in pain.

"I'll be there!" I shouted. "I promise. I'll be there!"

I kept watching her as the tender pulled away and disappeared into the night.

Then I ran off to find Hurku Linblom.

84

I ran straight to the cabin where we'd been held the first night, jammed the card key in the door, and pushed it open. No one inside. I yelled anyway.

"Linblom! Linblom, where are you?"

I looked in the closet, looked in the head. Nothing.

I went up and down the hall, checking all the other cabins. No sign of him.

The ship was surging now, moving faster, much faster, than it had at any time since we'd left port. And this close to the engine room, the turbines were louder than ever.

Linblom hadn't been in good shape when I'd last seen him. He was on medication. And he'd mentioned something about his heart, about recovering from surgery. For all I knew, his ticker had finally conked out on him.

But why would he have left the cabin?

I went back there. I stood in the doorway. I looked the cabin up and down.

"Linblom! Linblom, can you hear me?"

Ridiculous. Of course he couldn't hear me. He wasn't in there. He was dead. I'd tried to find him. But it was time to call off the hunt. I had to get off the ship.

I turned to leave. And that's when I heard it—a tap-tap-tapping. Metal against metal. Then something pounding. On the ceiling.

I looked above the bed, the hole up there, where we'd removed the ceiling tiles. I stepped across the cabin, hopped on the bed, stuck my head in the hole. It was dark. I couldn't see a thing. I squeezed my eyes tight, opened them.

"Linblom?"

A voice, weak, barely a whisper.

"Here, over here."

I could just barely see him. Maybe ten feet away in the narrow crawl space.

"Are you OK?"

"Stuck," he said. "I'm stuck."

I tried to squeeze up through the hole to reach him. Too big for it.

"Hold on," I said.

I dropped down onto the bed. I stood on it, ripping out more of the ceiling tiles. I tried again. This time I made it up, got my shoulders and chest through. I grabbed some sort of conduit, pulled myself up a little farther.

The new holes cast more light into the crawl space. I could see Linblom better now. It looked like he had somehow wedged himself under an AC duct.

But what was he doing up here?

I reached for him.

"Grab my hand."

I felt his fingertips brush against mine. He was struggling. I squeezed farther into the hole. But I could only go so far. Eighteen inches of crawl space. Is that what Linblom had said? And I was filling every bit of it.

I leaned, I stretched. I grabbed a finger, then another, grabbed his hand, got a good grip. I pulled. He groaned.

"You OK?"

"Yes," he said. "Again."

I pulled, gained an inch or two, grabbed his wrist. Pulled again, got his elbow. Pulled again, and he was out from under the duct and crawling toward me. I backed out of the hole, helping him down, onto the bed.

Linblom didn't give me time to ask him why he'd gone up into the crawl space.

He said, "We have to stop him!"

"Stop who?"

"Him, the one in the engine room. He's going to blow it up!"

"Yeah, blow up the *Royal Star*. That's why we need to get off. Now."

"No, he wants to blow up both of them."

"Both of them?"

"Yes, this ship. And the other one."

"What other one?"

"I am not certain," Linblom said. "But I think it is the *King of the Seas.*"

85

We left the cabin, Linblom explaining things as we headed for the stairs. He seemed to be OK, moving along fairly well.

After the shooting broke out on Deck Two, he heard Pango and the waiters in the hall, heard them rounding up the male passengers and taking them away, going through all the cabins to make sure they had gotten everyone. Linblom hid in the crawl space and he had stayed up there the whole time, except for a few brief minutes when he'd returned to the cabin to retrieve his medicine. Then he'd gone back up to the crawl space and fallen asleep.

"The pills," he said, "they make me drowsy. But when I woke up, I was feeling better, much better."

And so he decided to explore. Having designed the ship, Linblom knew how the crawl space connected to other passageways where he could move about undetected. Eventually he found himself just above the engine control room. He saw Glenroy mixing the chemicals.

"He was being very, very careful," Linblom said. "So I knew whatever he was making was very, very dangerous."

The explosion in the galley sent so much smoke into the ceiling passageways that Linblom had to stay put until it cleared. He could see the monitors in the engine control room and follow some of what was going on around the ship. Not an hour earlier, he had watched as Glenroy punched in a new course. And he had seen the outline of another ship light up on the monitor.

"Do you have any idea where we are?" he asked.

"Just a few miles off the northwest coast of Haiti."

"Isla Paradiso. Always the last stop on the itinerary for the *King of the Seas.*"

He told me about the ship. He knew all its stats, right down to its tonnage.

"He's going to blow it up," Linblom said.

And judging by the speed at which the *Royal Star* was moving, it could happen very soon.

Limblom said we had no chance of directly confronting Glenroy and trying to wrest away control of the ship. He kept his rifle close at hand.

"And there are long catwalks leading to the control room," he said. "You cannot approach it without being seen."

"Can we get back up in the crawl space, above the engine control room?" I was thinking maybe we could drop down on him from there.

"Me, yes. You, no. And it is doubtful that I alone could do much to stop him. Besides, that will take too long. It is a very long way to crawl," he said. "We must go to the bridge."

86

How good it felt to know that he was now all alone on the ship. Nothing to get in his way, no one who could possibly stop him from carrying out his mission.

Glenroy had watched the man rip the fuses off Jebailey. A brave man. A man to be reckoned with. A man, Glenroy was relieved to know, who had fled the ship with all the others.

The exterior cameras had shown the boats leaving the *Royal Star*, each of them loaded to the max. And since then, the other cameras—the ones that were still working anyway—had shown no signs of anyone. The boats were far behind now. Nothing they could do. Nothing anyone could do.

Glenroy looked at the course monitor, the *King of the Seas* glowing bright at its center. Less than five miles away. Fifteen minutes and counting . . .

87

Leaving Deck Two I grabbed a steel bar, one of the discarded weapons left behind by the male passengers, and I carried it with me as we headed for the bridge. Whenever I passed a camera, I gave it a good whack. I probably decommissioned a dozen of them on the way up to Deck Six. Not quite as good as poking Glenroy in the eye with a sharp stick, but for the time being, the next best thing.

Linblom seemed to think we had at least a slim chance of gaining entry to the bridge.

"The main door, that is impossible," he said. "But the bridge wing doors, they are vulnerable."

"What do you mean vulnerable?"

"I mean, maybe with that bar you can make something break."

We headed onto the promenade deck and up the steps to the starboard bridge wing. The sight ahead of us stopped me dead in my tracks. Linblom had told me how big the *King of the Seas* was—the biggest cruise ship in the world—but I was unprepared for just how big that really was. We were still a few miles away from it. Yet it was as if I could reach out and grab it. The fact that we were seeing it broadside made it look even more immense.

And the *Royal Star* was aimed directly at its midsection.

Linblom stepped to the bridge wing door, put his hand on the window, tapped it.

"Ah, we may be in luck," he said. "My specifications called for triple-insulated Plexiglas. But Jebailey cut some corners here and there. This is only double-insulated. I suggest you strike it directly in the middle."

And so I struck. And struck again. I struck that window every possible way there was to strike it. Using the steel bar like a hammer, like a battering ram. Three minutes of bashing it and I got nowhere.

I looked off our bow. The *King of the Seas* kept getting bigger.

88

It was Captain Palmano who spotted it first. He had just bummed another cigarette from Perlini, his third one, and was lighting it when he happened to glance at the primary radar panel. A green blip on the screen, vectoring in on them.

"Perlini!"

Palmano pointed at the radar.

All attention on the bridge had been directed to the pilot boats and the maneuvers close at hand. Now every eye was on the green blip.

And in that moment of stunned silence came an instant and profound understanding—something was going bad, bad wrong.

Palmano looked out the bridge window, tried to locate the ship. Couldn't see a thing.

He shot another glance at the radar. It gave the distance—3.2 miles. Closing at twenty plus knots. But no gadget on the console could tell Palmano what he didn't already know: If the other ship kept coming, collision was imminent. The *King of the Seas* couldn't get out of its way. The best Palmano could hope for was to lessen the blow.

Palmano shouted: "Full on the stern thrusters!"

Had to make the *King of the Seas* turn faster, avoid getting hit broadside, let the other ship strike the bow.

The dozen men on the bridge leaped into action.

"Get that fucking ship on the radio!" Palmano yelled. "Tell them to avert course at once!"

He ran out to the portside bridge wing. The line of sight was better here.

And yet he still had to strain before he found the oncoming ship—a black shadow above the water, heading straight at them.

89

I studied the keypad by the bridge-wing door.

"You have no idea what the code is?"

"No," Linblom said. "That is determined by the captain. And it is shared only with those officers who have access to the bridge."

Linblom was pacing now, anxious. Another minute, maybe two, and we would have to head for the marina, abandon ship. Even then, we'd be cutting it close, maybe too close.

It was a typical alphanumeric keypad. Buttons numbering one through nine, zero at the end. A-B-C on two, W-X-Y on nine, the rest in between.

"One thing I know," Linblom said. "It is an eight-sequence code. Enter four numbers. It beeps. Enter the last four numbers. It slides open."

"Well that certainly makes it easier," I said.

As if I could even begin to imagine what sort of security code a stoic Norwegian cruise ship captain might devise. A pet's name? A son, a daughter? His favorite character from a play by Ibsen?

Oh captain, my captain. Where are you when we need you, Captain Falk? Floating in a boat with Ron Diamond, that's where.

Falk. Four letters.

"What was Falk's first name?"

"Thorvald," Linblom said. "Thorvald Falk."

Thorvald. Eight letters. Could I really be that lucky?

I stepped closer to the keypad, started punching. 8-4-6-7. Beep. 8-2-5-3. The door didn't open.

So much for Thorvald.

Linblom said, "Everyone called him Thor."

Thor Falk. Eight letters.

I punched again. 8-4-6-7. Beep. 3-2-5-5.

Same lousy result.

Get inside the guy's head, Zack. Numbers, letters, what would he pick? I might as well just close my eyes and start punching at random. I'd been around Falk for how long? All of three minutes? Wasn't like we were intimate. OK, beyond the fact that I'd watched him die.

Him lying there in the hallway, life seeping away. Me telling him I'd head for the lifeboats first, and then to the bridge. He'd nodded . . .

Yes, the bridge. Get to the bridge. And . . .

And what? He was slipping away, convulsing, struggling to speak . . .

Oslo.

Oslo?

Four letters. Capital of Norway. The ship's officers were all Norwegian. Easy for them to remember. But just four letters. I needed eight. Even if Oslo was the first part, what was the rest of it?

Linblom put a hand on my shoulder.

"Zack, really, we must go."

"Just give me a second."

Eight letters. Oslo-Oslo? What the hell, worth a try.

6-7-5-6. Beep. 6-7-5-6.

The door didn't open.

"Zack, really. We've done everything. It's time."

Oslo. The last word from Falk's lips. Why would he say it if it didn't mean something?

Wipe the slate clean, Zack. Go at it from a different direction. Forget matching letters to numbers on the keypad.

O-S-L-O.

O. The what? Fifteenth letter in the alphabet. S. Nineteenth. L. Twelfth. O. Fifteenth.

15-19-12-15.

That wouldn't work.

Or would it?

I punched.

1-5-1-9. Beep. 1-2-1-5.

The bridge door slid open.

90

The alarm was sounding now, echoing in every quarter of the ship.

Above it, Captain Palmano's voice boomed over the PA: "All passengers proceed immediately to their assigned lifeboat stations. Repeat. Proceed immediately to assigned lifeboat stations."

In the disco, the deejay squelched the volume on Donna Summer and "Hot Stuff." Three hundred gyrating bodies instantly froze, then just as instantly began a mad rush for the door.

On an aft deck, a tractor salesman from Little Rock snatched a last piece of pizza as he hustled his family away from the late-night buffet. His daughter grabbed a cupcake.

And in their cabins, five frat brothers from Georgia Tech performed a symphony of syncopated snores. Out for the count. They didn't hear a thing.

91

Once we were inside the bridge, Linblom headed straight for the helm.

"You ever steer one of these things before?"

"On occasion. But only for a minute or two, far out at sea, when a captain was entertaining guests on the bridge and let everyone have a go," Linblom said. "But I am familiar with the instruments. I know what is what."

He studied the console. I looked out the bridge window. The *King of the Seas* filled the horizon. Eight thousand people. A floating city. And this ship could soon destroy it.

The bridge was dark, so dark that it took me a moment to see the body on the floor. A young man. Asian. The computer guy. Shot in the face.

Between him and me—two laundry bags, like the one the housekeeper had carried when she forced me to empty my safe. The bags had spilled open. Cash, watches, jewelry littered the floor of the bridge.

Linblom was still studying the console. He punched a button.

I said, "What's that?"

"Engine control room override. See?" He pointed at a label on the button. It was clearly marked. "It makes it so the ship can only be steered from up here."

"Meaning, Glenroy ain't got game," I said. "What next? Throw it in reverse?"

Linblom shook his head.

"Can't do that. It is like slamming your car into reverse when you are going ninety on the highway. If the shift is too abrupt it will destroy the engines."

"To hell with the engines, Linblom. Just stop this goddam thing."

"Can't stop it."

"What do you mean you can't stop it?"

"At this speed, the ship has so much momentum that it will continue forward and . . ."

"Run smack-dab into the *King of the Seas*."

"Correct," he said. "So we must first turn the ship."

"So turn it already."

Linblom reached for the joystick. He pushed it hard to port.

A bell rang. It rang loud. It kept ringing. Few things strike terror like a bell ringing loud.

"What's that?"

"I don't know," Linblom said. "I think maybe . . ."

"You think what?"

"I think maybe it is an alarm . . ."

"No shit."

"An alarm that tells me we are going too fast to attempt such a turn."

He let off the joystick. The alarm stopped.

Linblom stared at the console, unsure what to do next.

I saw a black lever that looked like it might be the throttle. I pulled back on it . . .

There is a reaction time on a cruise ship that is much like a brontosauraus eyeing some fleshy green plant and thinking: *Mmm. Food. Mouth. Open.* It can take a while.

Finally, the ship began to slow. But it was still heading straight for the *King of the Seas*.

"Yes, yes. Very good," Linblom said.

He grabbed the joystick, pushed hard to port again.

Long brontosaurus seconds passed.

We waited, we waited.

And the ship began to turn.

92

First, Glenroy heard it—the high whine of the engines backing off to a less insistent roar. And then he felt it—momentum tailing off, the ship slowing down.

He reached for the throttle. It was engaged, full forward.

What was going on?

And then a sharp shift to port. The ship was turning.

Glenroy grabbed the joystick, pushed it to starboard. The ship kept turning.

A red light flashed on the console. The engine control room override, activated from the bridge. No way to counter it.

Only then did he look at the bank of monitors. Several of the screens were empty, their feeds interrupted. But the bridge cameras showed two people standing at the helm.

One was an old man, slight and frail. Glenroy had never seen him before.

The other man he recognized all too well.

Glenroy grabbed his gun.

93

Linblom was still holding the joystick, banking the ship to port as hard as it could go. Our bow no longer pointed directly amidship the *King of the Seas* but was tracing an arc toward its stern.

I pulled back on the throttle, slowing us down even more. But Linblom was right. There was no stopping the *Royal Star*. Ships are built to take full advantage of their momentum. And the sleek design of the *Royal Star*—Linblom's design—was enabling its forward glide.

We were within a few hundred yards of the *King of the Seas* now. It didn't seem possible that we could miss the giant ship, but we might just graze it, deliver a glancing blow. Still, that could be all it took to unleash whatever awfulness Glenroy had rigged below.

A broad beam of light shot out from the *King of the Seas*, sweeping over our deck, illuminating the bridge. So bright it was blinding. Linblom and I both had to shield our eyes from the glare.

A loudspeaker blared: "Desist at once! Repeat. Desist at once!"

"What the hell do they think we're doing?" I yelled: "We're desisting, goddammit! We're desisting our asses off! How 'bout desisting with that goddam light."

As if they could hear . . .

Linblom leaned into the joystick, straining to get every inch of turn out of *Royal Star*.

And it was working. Our bow was pointing off the *King of the Seas's* stern now. We were going to miss it. Just barely, but . . .

"Our stern," Linblom said. "We cannot let it swing around and hit the other ship."

Hadn't considered that. Shit.

Linblom pushed the joystick to starboard, straightening our course, starting to bring our stern around.

We could see past the *King of the Seas* now. Ahead of us, maybe a quarter mile—five red lights, arranged vertically on a tall pole, flashing in sequence top to bottom. It announced in no uncertain terms: Stay away.

"The breakwater," Linblom said.

I pulled all the way back on the throttle. The engines wound down. But still the *Royal Star* continued forward.

Even in the dark, I could pick out a long line of chop—whitecaps over rocks below. The breakwater extended a full mile out to sea. There'd be no dodging it.

I looked at Linblom. He looked at me.

I grabbed the laundry bags.

Time to go.

94

We were heading down the steps from the bridge when, from the far aft deck, doors opened and Glenroy ran out.

We stopped. He stopped. He raised his rifle . . .

We turned and headed back toward the bridge.

The sound of gunshots . . .

Bullets chewed into the deck, well behind us.

I had Linblom by the arm, hurrying him along. We could return to the bridge, close the door, and there'd be no way that Glenroy could get to us. But when the *Royal Star* rammed into the breakwater . . . that would be all she wrote.

I wasn't too keen about jumping off the ship again. Would if I had to. But Linblom. I doubted he would survive such a fall.

I wasn't coming up with much in the way of alternatives. Then Linblom pointed to the bow.

"The LRAD," he said.

It took me a second to figure out what he was talking about. Long Range Acoustical Device. The sonic cannon. The latest thing for repelling pirates at sea.

It was mounted on the deck just ahead of us. I hadn't paid it much attention until now, mainly because it was draped in a black cover and I couldn't really tell what it was.

Now Linblom was pulling off the cover, shouting: "Grab the handles, turn it around."

The whole thing was as tall as me, a broad metal base with a swivel platform topped by what looked like a satellite dish, the kind you stick on your roof so you can pick up all the channels. Two handles protruded from each side. I grabbed the handles and turned the dish so it was pointing back toward the steps, where Glenroy would soon appear.

"What do I do?"

"Just aim it," Lindblom said. "I'll take care of the rest."

Just aim it? How do you aim a satellite dish? I did my best to zero in on the steps.

Linblom squatted by the base of the LRAD, flipping switches, turning dials. A pair of safety headphones dangled from a cord. He put them on.

At first the sound was almost imperceptible—a high whine, like some far-off whistle. Then it grew and grew. Not loud, but piercing. As if that whistle had become a sonic knife.

Glenroy. At the top of the steps.

The heart of the dish was pointed right at him. It stopped him cold. He staggered, dropped to his knees, hands going for the side of his head.

Later I learned that a trained, professional LRAD operator always wears safety headphones and never fires the damn thing when there's the slightest chance of striking an object that might cause the sonic burst to bounce back at the person who fired it. An object, say, like the hull of a ship.

The sound was way beyond deafening. It penetrated every cell of my body, reverberated in my skull. It was as if a pair of tiny, vicious wolverines had gotten trapped inside my head and were trying to gnaw their way out through my ears.

I held on to the handles, kept the dish pointed at Glenroy. He collapsed on the deck and lay still.

Things happened in a blur after that. I saw Linblom taking off the headphones, saw him moving his lips. I couldn't hear him.

I said, "What?"

I couldn't hear me either.

I'd never been deaf before. It throws everything off, let me tell you. Especially when it comes out of the blue. It takes a while to sink in. Most of my brain was still taking care of business, making me move away from the LRAD, telling me I had to hurry and get off the ship. But one small part of it was on strike and that part was short-circuiting and raising Cain.

Hey, I'm running here, my feet are pounding the deck. But where's the sound? What's up with that? And Linblom keeps moving his lips. Why can't I hear what he's saying?

Yeah, it can throw you off.

I remember standing over Glenroy, looking down at him. Blood was trickling out one of his ears. I touched his neck, felt a pulse.

I knelt, got my arms under him, tried to lift him up. Big guy. It wasn't working. I put him down. Maybe I could somehow sling him over a shoulder. Had to figure out a way.

But then Linblom was pulling on me, his goddam lips moving again and he was pointing off the bow. I looked. We were almost at the breakwater.

Had to make a choice. I could burn time we didn't have trying to get Glenroy off the ship. Or leave him lying there.

You'd think a choice like that would be easy. It wasn't. It troubled me.

It troubles me still.

95

The deck crew kept the big lights trained on the ship as it swept past, missing the stern by less than thirty feet.

It still hadn't answered the radio calls. But Captain Palmano could now see the name on its hull, *Royal Star.*

The billionaire's ship. What did he call it? The most exclusive cruise ship in the world. Well, it was on an exclusive course for the breakwater now.

All Palmano could do was watch.

A cry from the bridge: "In the channel!"

More lights shone out to sea, picking up a tender heading in. Behind it—lifeboats, a skiff.

Palmano returned his attention to the *Royal Star.* He saw two men at the marina hatch, boarding a Jet Ski, saw it speeding away from the ship.

And as the lights swept along the length of the *Royal Star,* Palmano saw a solitary figure, a man, pulling himself to his feet on the foredeck. The man stood at the rail for a moment, gazing out at the *King of the Seas* as the two ships moved farther apart.

Then the man turned away and walked to the end of the bow. The crash into the breakwater was imminent now, just seconds away.

The man threw back his head, raised his arms to the sky . . .

96

We were a hundred yards from the *Royal Star* when the ship crashed into the breakwater. I didn't hear the explosion. Didn't need to. The shock wave from the blast slammed us from behind, spun the Jet Ski around, and gave us a full-on view of the fiery spectacle.

A two-stage detonation. First the bow. A long beat. And then the rest of the ship consumed in horrible conflagration, fingers of fire reaching out in all directions. For one awful moment it seemed as if the blaze might grab us. The heat slapped our faces. The sky lit up, day for night. And as flaming chunks of this and that rained down around us, hissing as they hit the sea, I gathered my senses enough to power up and speed us away.

I'd lashed the laundry bags to the Jet Ski with their drawstrings. And Linblom locked his arms around my waist as we skittered across the water.

Ahead of us, I spotted the tender just as it tucked behind the *King of the Seas*, sheltered from the blast. It took another five minutes for me to make it all the way around the monstrous vessel. By then the tender was bobbing in the lee of the ship, a few yards from its boarding platform.

My head was clearing now. The gnawing wolverines had been replaced by giant cotton balls that gummed up my earways. I could hear, sort of. But it was just a white noise, reverb from the explosion, dissonant sounds that did not wholly connect with my brain.

Passengers filled the decks of the ship, throngs of people on every level. Some had already boarded lifeboats that had been dispatched toward shore. Others were waiting to board. Bright beams radiated from the ship, swooping across the sky and the water, like klieg lights on Oscar night, bathing the scene in an unsettling aura of urgency and festivity.

I pointed the Jet Ski at the tender, pulled up alongside, and cut the engine as we bumped against it.

I left Linblom to take care of himself—I was still a little peeved that he'd hogged the safety headphones—and hopped up to the hatchway. My view was blocked by a throng of men and women, their attention on the floor just beyond them.

I pushed through the crowd. Dr. Louttit stood with his back to me and I could see him handing something to Barbara, something slippery and squirming. A tiny human thing swathed in all its baby goo, umbilical still attached, and kicking up a storm.

I moved past the doctor, fell to my knees beside Barbara. She saw me but, in truth, she was far more interested in the child she now cradled against her.

A girl.

A beautiful girl. Slick black hair. Rosy skin. Her little face wrinkling as she opened her mouth.

I heard it loud and clear: my daughter's cry.

SAFE HARBOR

97

There was plenty of room aboard the *King of the Seas*, mainly because most of its passengers chose not to get back on, opting instead to fly home from Port-Au-Prince. The ship spent two more days in the harbor at Isla Paradiso, days during which the passengers and crew of the *Royal Star* were lavished with every indulgence the *King of the Seas* had to offer—food, drink, spa treatments—and questioned exhaustively by men and women representing an assortment of acronymic U.S. government agencies.

I didn't tell anyone but Barbara about being rescued by the *Boukman*. Doing so would have initiated a search for the boat—the last thing I wanted to happen. I could only guess that having seen the *Royal Star* go up in flames, Girard and Celeste had decided, wisely, that there was little they could do and turned the *Boukman* westward. I'd checked with the bridge officers of the *King of the Seas* and none of them reported having seen a trimaran that matched the *Boukman*'s description.

I told the authorities a vague and not-all-that-convincing story about jumping off the *Royal Star*, then grabbing a lifeline the provisions master tossed to me just before he was gunned down by one of the waiters. I told them I had hung on to it for hours, thrashing about in the ship's wake before finally managing to pull myself aboard. And then I'd hidden out for a few more hours before finding Carl Parks and joining forces with him to overcome the waiters.

I shunned interviews by the media horde that had descended upon Isla Paradiso from all over the world. Instead, I let the spotlight shine on

Hurku Linblom. The reporters fell in love with the story line: Frail seventy-two-year-old ship designer thwarts hijackers and prevents deadly collision with the world's largest cruise ship. *People* magazine rushed out a special edition featuring Linblom on the cover with Kane Kinsey, Kinsey shirtless and his arm still in a sling. The issue carried Kinsey's exclusive first-person account of the ordeal. And a Showtime movie was said to be already in the works, in which Kinsey would play himself.

Sam Jebailey basked in his share of glory, not seeing fit to mention that the bomb that was strapped to him for all those hours wasn't really a bomb. He boasted that the *Royal Star* "would rise like a phoenix from the flames" and that he would build an even grander ship, financed by the insurance payout from Lloyd's of London.

After endless interrogation, the waiters were still steadfastly maintaining that they had never planned to blow up either ship and were in it only for the money. Within twenty-four hours of the explosion, Reuters reported that the chief hijacker, Glenroy Patterson, aka Inshallah Shaheed, had been linked to a radical, Trinidad-based sect known as Islaam Karibe. The sect's leader had so far escaped capture but authorities in Miami had arrested a Trinidadian national they suspected of having funneled money to finance the operation and other arrests were forthcoming.

Yet another headline-grabbing story emerged on the second day when Ron Diamond was found floating in a lifeboat in the Windward Passage. Suffering from exposure, to the elements and to his seventeen lifeless boatmates, Diamond was reported by CNN to have been "incoherent and physically drained by the experience." But after being medevaced to the infirmary aboard the *King of the Seas* he granted a bedside interview to the *Los Angeles Times* in which he told the reporter of having "shot and mortally wounded the mastermind of the hijacking" before escaping in the lifeboat to seek help.

By then, all the stories had taken on such lives of their own that even had I wanted to, there was little I could say that would set the record straight.

That was OK. I had other matters, much more important matters, deserving of my attention.

98

"She's got your nose," Barbara said.

"Not the nose I've got now."

"No, your nose before it was ever broken."

"I've broken my nose at least a half-dozen times. You've never known me without a mangled nose."

"OK, then. Your nose as I imagine it might once have been."

"My nose was never that dainty, but I'll claim that part of her anyway," I said. "She's got your eyes."

"You think so?"

"Definitely," I said. "Just look at the way she's staring at me—complete and utter adoration."

"And you think that's how I look at you?"

"Well isn't it?"

Before Barbara could answer, our little girl let out a yelp, began to fuss and fidget.

"I think she's hungry," Barbara said. "She wants to eat all the time."

"Takes after her father," I said.

I got up from the bed so Barbara could feed her. But I couldn't take my eyes off the two of them. My wife, our child. With all due respect to Ringling Bros. and Barnum & Bailey, this was the greatest show on earth.

Despite her early arrival, she'd been pronounced perfectly healthy by Dr. Louttit. She'd weighed in at five pounds, two ounces. A tad on the small size, but definitely a keeper. And I'd been enjoying the one-on-one time in our swell digs.

Much to the chagrin of Sam Jebailey, who had wanted them for him-self, we'd been given the best accommodations on the ship—the King's Quarters, a three-thousand-square-foot, two-level suite located just under the ship's bridge with a spectacular forward window, at least forty feet wide. The *King of the Seas* was heading home now and we were taking in a sweeping, panoramic view of the Gulf Stream as the ship plowed toward the distant, twinkling cityscape of Miami, awakening to a brilliant Octo-ber morning.

"So we've got to decide," Barbara said.

"A name, you mean."

"Yes, a name."

"What's the hurry? We won't have to fill out a birth certificate until af-ter we get back to Florida. We can wait a while yet."

"No we can't," said Barbara. "Kerry will be arriving any moment. And I want her to have a name by then."

Kerry was Kerry Sanders, the Miami-based correspondent for NBC, and an old friend of Barbara's. In less than thirty minutes, *The Today Show* would broadcast his live report from the *King of the Seas* featuring the "baby born on a boat," a happy ending to three days of round-the-clock coverage of an otherwise grim event.

We were in our stateroom and *The Today Show* crew was already setting up gear outside in the main salon. Despite the early hour, a small crowd had gathered to witness our daughter's television debut—Hurku Linblom and his wife, Kane Kinsey and his girlfriend, Penelope. Marie Lutey had arrived on the arm of Dr. Louttit. The two had become something of a couple over the previous few days.

"Well," I said, "I'm already on the record about my number one choice."

"So, you're sticking with Shula?"

"The man means a lot to me. Any objection?"

"No, to tell you the truth, the name's grown on me. I think it can work for a girl," Barbara said. "But I would like to offer a slight modification."

"And what would that be?"

"I'd like to name her after someone who means a lot to me, too."

"And who would that be?"

"She's sitting out there in the salon. Marie Lutey. I couldn't have made it through this without her. She was my rock when you weren't there."

"Fair enough," I said. "But . . ."

"But what?"

"Shula Lutey Chasteen? Not a name that rolls off the lips."

"And not what I was thinking," Barbara said.

"Shula Marie Chasteen?"

"Has a nice ring to it, don't you think?"

"Shula Marie Chasteen," I said. "I like it."

"Rather poetic, don't you think?"

"I believe we have a winner."

"Yes, we do," Barbara said. "We truly do."

99

The Today Show crew had just cleared out of our suite when there came a knock on the door. Barbara and Shula had already headed back to the master stateroom for another feeding session.

I opened the door to find a man and a woman, both wearing dark shapeless suits. The man had on a tie with a white button-down oxford. The woman wore her collar open. Otherwise they might have been in uniform, right down to their black laceups. I've never much cared for suits on women. I'm not saying it can't work. But this particular suit on this particular woman did nothing to change my opinion.

"I'm Agent Sullivan," the woman said. She nodded at the man. "This is Agent Delafonse. We're with Immigration and Customs Enforcement."

"The ICE man and woman cometh," I said.

It got nothing out of them. Maybe they were sick of literary allusions. Maybe they'd never read Eugene O'Neill. Or maybe they were just two Feds in dark suits there to do a job.

Sullivan said, "Mind if we come in?"

"Please, by all means," I said. Wasn't like I hadn't been expecting them.

We sat in the salon. Sullivan got right to business. Delafonse's job was to sit there and give me his hard-ass stare, as if to say, "We've already made up our minds about you, pal, and there's nothing you can say to change things."

Sullivan said, "What's your relationship with Carl Parks?"

"Platonic," I said.

"I'd appreciate a straight answer," Sullivan said.

"We don't have a relationship," I said. "Never saw him before I got on the *Royal Star*. Haven't seen him since."

Sullivan and her partner exchanged a look.

She said, "Were you and Parks planning to rendezvous at some point?"

"OK, I'll 'fess up. Parks wanted to take our relationship beyond platonic. Only I wouldn't put out. So Parks dumped me."

"We don't have time for this, Chasteen."

"Oh, really? What do you have time for then? A Bloody Mary? Things are getting a little dull. A drink might liven it up."

"What do you know about Carl Parks?"

"Only what he told me."

"And that is?"

"Used to work for you guys. Now he doesn't."

"So now the two of you work together?"

"Ooh, smooth. You almost tricked me," I said. "I told you. Never saw him before, don't plan on seeing him again."

"You probably *won't* be seeing him again."

I waited.

Sullivan said, "A boat belonging to the *Royal Star*—a seventeen-foot Boston Whaler—was found yesterday afternoon washed ashore in the village of Giton, about twenty miles east of Isla Paradiso. Is that the boat Parks left in?"

"He left in a Whaler, yes."

"The boat was carrying cargo. You have any idea what that cargo might have been, Chasteen?"

"Toys for tots?"

Delafonse said, "Asshole."

I said, "Careful, there's a child in the next room."

"Fuck you."

"Good thing I'm a tolerant parent."

"Else?"

"Else I'd be feeding you my daughter's dirty diaper."

Delafonse made a move for me. Sullivan held him back. It was a half-hearted move. It didn't take much holding back.

Sullivan said, "We think maybe you double-crossed Parks."

"Double-crossed? How so?"

"We found some Halliburton suitcases on board the Whaler. Know what was in them?"

I shook my head, no.

Sullivan said, "Computer parts."

I didn't say anything. I tried hard not to register any reaction to what Sullivan had just said, but I don't know that I succeeded. She had surprised me. Surprised the hell out of me.

"How many Halliburtons exactly?"

"Five," Sullivan said.

Four less than Parks had left with.

"Hard drives and mother boards and all kinds of worthless circuitry. All just stuck inside those suitcases."

So maybe Parks had opened the four suitcases, seen the junk inside them, said to hell with it, and abandoned the boat and everything in it. Maybe he'd fallen off the boat and drowned. Maybe, maybe, maybe.

Sullivan said, "We're thinking you stuck all those computer parts in there, Chasteen."

"Why would I do that?"

"So you could take what was supposed to be in the suitcases."

"That being?"

"Money," Sullivan said. "We've been watching Parks. We know he's made some forays into the bulk cash smuggling trade. We just don't know who he's been partnering with."

"And you think maybe it's me?"

"That's right," Sullivan said.

"And that I double-crossed him?"

"Right again."

"And that I have the money."

"What money is that, Chasteen?"

"Ooh, there you go again, trying to trick me."

I stood. I gestured to the door.

"Agent Cellophane. Agent Dental Floss. Thanks so much for dropping by."

Sullivan said, "We aren't finished yet."

I said, "Oh, but you are."

100

The visit by Sullivan and Delafonse had put me into a sociable mood. So I made some calls of my own.

The first was a phone call. The *King of the Seas* was within a few miles of Miami now, close enough for cell service. I borrowed a phone from our steward. It took some doing—phone connections in the Bahamas are iffy, to say the least—but I finally got through to Ragged Island.

"Chief Inspector Brindley Sawyer's office," a man's voice said.

"Is this the chief's secretary?"

"No, this is Chief Inspector Brindley Sawyer. How may I help you?"

"Love that title," I said. "You don't have a secretary, do you?"

He didn't say anything.

"Bet you don't even have a real office, huh? Bet you're sitting in your house, in your underwear, talking on the phone, maybe eating a bowl of chicken souse."

"Zack, that you?"

"Am I right?"

"Sheep's foot souse," Brindley said. "Dorice made it last night. She's right here. She says hi."

"Tell her she's too good for you."

"I tell her that every day."

"How's the crime business?"

"Been real slow. Until day before yesterday."

"Get some visitors?"

"I did," he said. "You're putting me in a hard spot, Zack."

"They aren't criminals, Brindley."

He didn't say anything.

"They still there?"

"Uh-huh," Brindley said. "I showed them a little cove where they could put in on the west side. Folks won't pay them too much mind there. But they don't have any gas. And they're running out of food. I can give them a little something, but it's not like we have a lot extra to go around on Ragged Island. I start rounding up some major provisions and folks will get suspicious."

"Thought you were the chief inspector."

"That'd make them double suspicious," Brindley said.

"I need a coupla days," I said.

"I'll do what I can do," he said. "Saw your baby on the TV."

"Cute thing, isn't she?"

"Uh-huh. Don't look a bit like you."

101

My second social call was to Sam Jebailey's suite. It was a whole lot smaller than the King's Quarters. I tried not to gloat.

I could tell Jebailey wasn't overjoyed to see me. But he was nothing if not gracious.

"Again, my deepest personal thanks for all that you did," Jebailey said as he showed me in. "I am forever in your debt."

"You got that right," I said.

He looked at me.

I said, "Just finished a nice little chat with two suits from Homeland Security."

I thought I'd toss around the name of the umbrella agency. It had a lot more oomph than ICE.

Jebailey flinched just the tiniest bit, but he recovered with a smile.

"Yes, I spoke briefly with them myself," he said. "It is a great relief to know that our government is putting all its resources toward making sure such a terrible thing never happens again."

"Cut the crap, Jebailey. Did they accuse you of being in cahoots with Carl Parks?"

"Cahoots?"

"Yes, as in conspiring with him and Ron Diamond and a few other people to smuggle cash into St. Kitts? Bulk cash smuggling, I think they call it. To the tune of twenty million dollars?"

Jebailey's face lost its color. His jaw tightened. He didn't speak.

"No, they didn't ask you about that, did they? Because they don't know.

I figure that's because they've got such a hard-on about Carl Parks, their former colleague, that they can't see the forest for the trees. And they've got their heads so far up their asses that they think I'm somehow involved in all this."

"Please, all this what?" he said. "I don't know of what you speak."

"The innocent routine is wearing thin, Sammy boy. Matter of fact, it's starting to piss me off. And if I get pissed off then I might just have to schedule another talk with Agents Sullivan and Delafonse, tell them what I do know. Not my style really. The way I see it, the government should do its work. I should do mine. And seldom, if ever, the twain shall meet. But like I say, you're starting to piss me off."

Jebailey sat back on the sofa. He studied me for a long moment.

Finally he asked, "How much do you want?"

"Oh, please, don't insult me. This isn't a shakedown," I said. "Well, it's kind of a shakedown. But it's not money that I want."

"What is it then?"

"I'm curious, that's all. I just want to know how you did it. Or rather, how you planned on doing it. Before everything went south on you."

Jebailey crossed one leg over the other, jiggled his ankle. He didn't say anything.

"OK, how about I start telling it like I see it and you just jump in whenever you feel like it," I said. "Those computers. All that talk about reaching out and enriching young minds, that was all just smoke and mirrors to make you look good, wasn't it?"

Jebailey shook his head.

"No, actually. I bought those computers with every intention of giving them to the schoolchildren, just like I said. Really. But . . ."

"But what?"

"I got scared. Simple as that," Jebailey said. "I had never done anything on such a scale as this. The night before the *Royal Star* was to set sail, I began to reconsider. I thought maybe it was not such a good idea to leave the ship carrying those Halliburton suitcases. And while I had reached out to certain people in St. Kitts, people of power . . ."

"Reached out, meaning bribed?"

Jebailey shrugged.

"In such cases, you can never be sure that you have reached out to all the people who need to be touched," he said. "And then there was the money brought by Carl Parks."

"Counterfeit money."

"Yes, that. It was very good counterfeit money. An excellent job. But that's what concerned me. Because by then I had also learned about Parks's background . . ."

"With ICE."

"Yes. And I thought perhaps it was all part of a trap on their part. You know, make Parks look like an agent gone bad so it would give him more credibility in a deal like this."

I thought about it. I was pretty sure neither Parks nor ICE was capable of pulling off such an elaborate ploy. No, Parks was in it for himself. And that was that.

"Go on," I said.

"That's it, really. I got scared. I had some of my people take out the guts of the computers and put them in the Halliburtons."

"All except one. The one with the counterfeit money."

"Yes, that one I kept separate," Jebailey said. "I did not know what to do with it. I didn't want to deposit two million dollars in counterfeit money in the St. Kitts bank. If it were to be discovered, then it would not be good for my own credibility."

"So the money, just eighteen million dollars of it now . . ."

"Into the computers. About two hundred fifty thousand dollars in each one. I believe seventy-two computers in all."

"Which explains why you wanted to drag them along with you when we were trying to get off the ship."

"I am a businessman," he said. "But sadly, they are gone. All gone."

"Cry me a river," I said.

102

My third and final social call was to Ron Diamond. They had moved him out of the infirmary and into a cabin. All the suites were taken, so they had stuck him in an inside room. No window, no nothing. A pair of twin beds. Bottom of the heap.

He looked like hell. Face blistered from the sun. Lips cracked. Worn and spent. My grandfather had a saying: "Fellah looks like he's had all the shit slung out of him." That was Diamond. And he looked even worse when he saw it was me.

He backed away from the door, put up his hands to protect himself.

"Please," he said. "Don't . . ."

"Relax, Diamond. I'm not here to hurt you."

"You aren't?"

"No, I'm not going to lay a finger on you," I said. "Still, what I told you that night on the deck? I meant every word of it. I'm going to bring you pain. More pain than you have ever imagined. Pain that will be with you for the rest of your miserable life."

He kept backing away, sat down on his bed. The closet door was open, a Halliburton sitting inside. He saw me looking at it.

He said, "You want money?"

"What's with guys like you, Diamond? Always thinking it's just a matter of money?"

"How much do you want? Just tell me."

I shrugged.

"OK, I'll play. How much you got?"

"A million?"

"How about two million?"

"Sure, two million. No problem. You can have it all."

"That's how much is in the suitcase?"

"Yes, two million dollars."

"And it belongs to you?"

"Yes, yes it does."

"OK, then . . ."

I still had the cell phone I'd borrowed from the steward. I pulled it out, punched some numbers.

Diamond said, "Who are you calling?"

"Just hold your horses." Then I spoke into the phone: "Yes, Miami, please. U.S. Secret Service Office."

I grabbed pen and paper from the desk, wrote down a number. There's a way to enter a number in the phone while you're talking to someone, save paper, but I don't know how to do that. I clicked off the phone.

I said, "You know what the Secret Service is in charge of, Diamond?"

"Protecting the president."

"Whoa, you are *such* a good citizen. I'm proud of you. Know what else they're in charge of?"

He shook his head.

"Counterfeit money," I said. "Know what you got in that suitcase?"

"It's not counterfeit. I know it's not. It's real."

"You sure of that? Did you personally pack that suitcase? Could it possibly have been confused for one of the many other overpriced, fancy-ass aluminum suitcases that were on the *Royal Star*?"

"No, I mean I don't . . ."

"Let's call in the experts, let them have a look."

I started punching numbers.

"No!" Diamond shouted. "Don't . . ."

I clicked off the phone.

"Wise move," I said.

"I've got more money," Diamond said. "Real money. I can get you that. Two million, three million. Whatever you want."

"No, no, no. Repeat after me, Diamond. It's not . . ." I waited. "Come on, repeat after me. It's not . . ."

"It's not . . ."

"About."

"About."

"The fucking money! You got that, Diamond?"

He nodded. He was all the way back on his bed now, against the wall.

"Now hold that thought, OK? Because I want to share something else with you," I said. "I was the last person to leave the bridge of the *Royal Star*. You know what I took with me?"

"Those laundry bags?"

"Besides them, idiot stick."

"No, what?"

"A small stack of DVDs," I said. "Know what was on them?"

He shook his head, no.

"The feed from the ship's security cameras. Dozens of cameras, all over the ship," I said. "Might take a while, but I'm pretty sure if you and me sit down and watch those DVDs we're going to find some fine performances by you. You on the bridge trying to barter for your life. You on the deck, pointing that pistol at me."

I was lying my butt off. But he had no way of being sure.

"So like I say, Diamond, I'm going to bring you pain. And you know what you're going to do?"

"No, tell me. Just tell me. I'll do it."

"You're going to take it like a man, Diamond. I'm going to dish it, and you're going to shut up and take it. And you aren't going to say a thing about it. Because if you do, then I'll dish it out again. I'll dish it out with calls to the Secret Service and DVDs and whatever it takes. And it's never going to end. I'm always going to be watching you and if you start pulling crap I don't approve of, then I'll bring you down. We clear?"

"Sounds like blackmail."

"Wrong. It's not *like* blackmail. It's exactly blackmail. This is going to hang over your sorry ass the rest of your living days. You got that?"

He swallowed. He nodded.

"What do you want me to do?"

So I stood there and told him.

103

Boggy was there to meet us when the *King of the Seas* pulled into the Port of Miami. He scarcely spoke to Barbara or me, and quickly laid claim to Shula. He held her in his outstretched arms, looking her up and down. For her part, Shula considered Boggy with a level and unblinking gaze.

He turned away from us, speaking to her in words only the two of them could hear.

"Yo, Boggy," I said. "Don't start laying that Taino mumbo-jumbo on her already. She's barely three days old."

"Oh, let him be, Zack. He's as excited to finally meet her as we are."

We watched as Boggy continued whispering to Shula. Then he cupped an ear and put it close to her mouth, as if she were talking to him. This went on for a few minutes as Barbara and I waited for the porters to bring our bags.

Barbara said, "I'm glad Boggy is going with you."

"Me, too. I wouldn't do it without him," I said. "You sure you're OK with me going?"

"Yes, of course, without a doubt," she said.

"You're not just saying that?"

"No, I'm not just saying that. I don't like that you have to do it. Still, you absolutely have to do it," she said. "Besides, it will give Shula and me a little extra bonding time."

"I'm jealous," I said.

"You should be."

We watched Boggy and Shula some more. He had taken her to the edge of the broad concrete pier and appeared to be pointing out various things to her: the sun, the water, a seagull in the sky, fish feeding around the pilings.

"He's naming the world," Barbara said.

"Doing what?"

"A Taino tradition. He told me about it a few weeks ago. When a child is born in the Taino culture, the shaman immediately comes and holds the child, telling it the names of all the things it sees. That way the child will be confident in the world and walk tall among all people and things."

"Mmmmm," I said. "Only one problem with that."

"What?"

"We aren't Taino."

"Oh, Zack, really. What harm can it do?"

"No harm I guess, but if she starts talking Taino then he's going to be the only one who can understand her."

"You ask me, the two of them are already speaking a language all their own."

Boggy had once again cupped his ear close to Shula's mouth. He was nodding. He whispered something else to her as he walked back our way.

He passed Shula back to Barbara and said, "We will soon have her naming ceremony. In three, maybe four months."

"We've named her," I said. "Shula Marie Chasteen. It's plenty of name already."

"No, Zachary, this is her Taino name. Her secret name."

"My daughter has a secret Taino name?"

"Why yes, of course, Zachary," Boggy said. "What do you think she was just telling me?"

104

Ronald Diamond's private helicopter picked us up about two hours later. It delivered us to George Town, Great Exuma, by 1:00 P.M. By 1:30 P.M. we were on the *Ace of Diamonds* and pulling out of Elizabeth Bay, heading south, with a crew of seven—a captain, a first mate, three deckhands, an engine master, and a chef. By 2:30 P.M., after Boggy and I had fairly well acquainted ourselves with the yacht and its capabilities, we presented ourselves at the helm.

The captain was a stocky guy of about thirty. He wore the same uniform as the rest of the crew. White calypso pants, blue deck shoes, scoop-necked T-shirt with thick blue horizontal stripes, a blue scarf tied in a knot around his neck, and a jaunty burgundy beret. I kept expecting him to break out with a rousing rendition of "The Gondolier Song."

I told him he needed to step away from the helm. We'd be taking charge of things the rest of the way.

"Excuse me?"

"Stand down," I said.

Before he could protest, I directed his attention to the stern, where the rest of the crew was preparing to launch the yacht's "dinghy," a thirty-seven-foot Grady White.

"That will get you back to George Town," I said. "I'll tell you the same thing I told them. You don't want to be on this yacht over the next thirty-six hours or so. We will be engaged in an illegal activity. If we are intercepted, this yacht will be impounded and you will go to jail."

"Mr. Diamond knows about this?"

"He does."

"He OK'd it?"

"Oh, yes. He embraced the opportunity."

"And he OK'd it for you to release his captain and crew?"

"No, he did not. I didn't tell him I was going to do that," I said. "But trust me, you don't want to be on this yacht."

The captain turned and looked at the rest of the crew. The Grady White was idling and they were ready to go.

"Are we going to get fired for this?" the captain asked me.

"No," I said. "In fact, I will personally guarantee that as long as Ronald Diamond has money in the bank that you will have employment. Although, for the life of me, I don't see why you would want to work for anyone who makes you dress up like that."

"He's got a lot of money," the captain said.

"Then I guess you've got job security."

He gave me a little salute.

"Good travels," he said.

105

It was just after dark when we reached Ragged Island and came upon the *Boukman* in its quiet little cove. It took us a while to find it. Brindley had sent them to a good spot. The cove was removed from sight of the main channel, rimmed with thick mangroves. Even knowing the boat was there, we still had a devil of a time locating it.

The *Ace of Diamonds* drew too much water for me to pull all the way in, so we anchored about a quarter mile off the cove. The yacht also came with a twenty-one-foot skiff, and Boggy and I took it into the *Boukman*.

The night was hot and still and most everyone was trying to keep cool on the deck.

I had already told Boggy how Mommie Leena and the other Haitians were firmly convinced that I was some character named Azacka, one of their Voudon spirits.

"Have you ever heard of such nonsense?"

"Why yes, Zachary, I have. And it is not nonsense. It is not nonsense at all. Spirits are always walking right beside us on this earth."

Boggy's gaze suddenly shifted to a point just behind my shoulder. His eyes went wide. I looked. He laughed.

"That was the spirit Gotchya," he said.

"Taino humor," I said. "It's so very highbrow."

After dispensing with greetings and introducing everyone to Boggy, I asked Celeste: "Anyone hungry?"

"Starving," she said. "Nothing but fish water and hard biscuits since last we saw you."

"Well, pile aboard," I said. "And tell everyone to bring their belongings with them now. That way we won't have to come back for them later."

No one had very much in the way of belongings. Plastic bags filled with a change of clothes, that was about it. It took three trips in the Mako for me to get everyone aboard the *Ace of Diamonds.*

While the *Ace of Diamonds* wasn't my kind of boat, not by a long shot, it was everything that its owner had boasted it to be. Diamond had spared no expense in outfitting his yacht—165 feet of pleasure. And for these folks it was the equivalent of a visit to Disney World, Six Flags, and Sea World all in one.

At first, the men, women, and children held back, afraid to roam around the yacht, as if they feared they'd get in trouble.

"Tell them that if they don't start having some fun then Azacka is going to get seriously mad," I told Celeste.

To get everyone in the spirit of things, I stood up and did my butt-wiggling dance. It worked.

Before long, the party was cranking. Kids were splashing in the hot tub. Music was blaring from the speakers. The plasma TV in the main salon was showing *Pirates of the Caribbean.* Some of the women took turns taking bubble baths in the bathroom of the master salon. Some of the men tried their hand at billiards in the rec room. We found good cigars and we smoked them.

Mommie Leena and a few other men and women took over the galley. The yacht had been provisioned for Diamond's upcoming trip to St. Bart's so the larder was filled with all sorts of delectables. We broke out stinky cheeses, aged prosciutto, and a two-pound loaf of foie gras. We ate steaks and ribs and chickens. I popped a few bottles of Veuve Clicquot Brut and we passed them around. There was Belgian chocolate and Italian ice cream for dessert.

At some point, Celeste came to me and said, "I need to make a few calls."

I showed her to a phone. I listened as she connected with her people at Haiti Liberte Internacional.

"Where should I tell them to be, Zack? And what time?"

I told her what they needed to know.

Then we went back to the party. We turned up the music even louder. I uncorked some vintage cognac. Most of the men and some of the women took a little sip. Girard took some big sips. He started dancing with a mop. I danced with Mommie Leena. I danced with Celeste. I cut in on Girard and danced with the mop. It was that kind of an evening. We all needed it.

Around midnight we got a call on the radio. Brindley checking in.

"Why don't you and Dorice come out and join us," I said. "Kick up your heels."

"Like to, but it might be a bad career move for a chief inspector to party with illegals. Especially if a Royal Navy patrol boat decides to pay a surprise visit."

"That ever happen?"

"Oh, every other month or so. One was here last week, so I don't think you have to worry. Besides, if I stay here I can keep an eye out for them, give you a heads-up."

"I owe you big time," I said. "How you feel about steaks and champagne?"

"Feel pretty good if it's you buying."

"More like appropriating than buying. Makes it taste even better," I said. "I'll put together a cooler for you, leave it stuck up in the mangroves. You can come by and pick it up in the morning. We'll be gone."

"That's called graft," Brindley said.

"Fine, you take the high road."

"Ain't but one road."

"My kind of cop," I said.

106

We all threw in together to clean up the yacht when the party started winding down. Celeste and Girard bid tearful farewells to everyone. I motored them back to the *Boukman* on the skiff.

They were both a little tipsy, ready to call it a night. They expressed their gratitude. I told them it didn't even begin to pay off my debt to them. We said our good-byes.

As they were hopping off the skiff, I said, "You still have those computers?"

"Yes," Celeste said. "But I am afraid you were right. They are no good. Already they begin to rust."

"Thought I might tinker with them a little bit," I said.

"Now? It is so late . . ."

"Do not put off today what you can do whenever the heck you want to do it," I said. "You got tools I can use?"

Celeste opened a drawer on the console.

"In there, along with a flashlight," she said, stifling a yawn. "Sorry, Zack, but we really must call it a night. Again, much thanks. Go with God."

She and Girard headed into the main salon, shut the hatch behind them.

The computers were lined up on the deck under a sheet of canvas. Four of them. I pulled out the flashlight and a toolbox and got to work on the one closest to me.

It only took a couple of minutes to remove the back panel on the computer's workstation. And there it was, pretty as could be, a stack of bills about the size of a shoe box. Two hundred fifty thousand dollars. Plus or minus. Another ten minutes, I was all done.

I found a nylon bag and stuffed the money in it. Then I slipped off the *Boukman* and motored away.

107

All hands aboard the *Ace of Diamonds* were a bit bleary-eyed come morning. Still, we cast off just after dawn and by early afternoon we had reached the open waters between the Bahamas and Florida.

As big-ass yachts go, the *Ace of Diamonds* was surprisingly trim and tight. She cut nicely through the water and offered smooth passage to the forty-two guests lounging in her quarters, even when we hit an afternoon squall line. By nightfall, as we closed in on Coronado Inlet, the squall line had collided with thunderstorms swirling along the land mass of Florida and morphed into a stalled low-pressure system that stretched all the way from Fernandina Beach south to Stuart.

Coronado Inlet is one of the narrowest inlets along Florida's east coast. Jetties jut out along each side. The south jetty is shorter. It's a favorite spot for fishermen and the nearby stretch of beach is a popular surf break. The north jetty extends out for about a half mile, a bony finger of concrete bulwarked by huge hunks of rock. Given the relentless nature of coastal erosion, the U.S. Army Corps of Engineers must come along every couple of years and dredge the inlet. Even then, a few good storms can create shoals where shoals aren't expected, or marked on charts, and a ship can easily run aground.

Under the best conditions, Coronado Inlet is a tricky stretch of water. With the wind and the rain from the low-pressure system, the seas had kicked up into eight-to-ten-foot rollers that splashed against our bow. A real mess.

And just the kind of weather I was hoping for. Bring it on. I could only pray it might hold for a few more hours. If it got even uglier, all the better.

The inlet bumped us around a bit, but the *Ace of Diamonds* sliced through it in fine form. A half hour later we were floating in the channel behind my place in LaDonna. The dock lights were on and I could see a few people moving about in the boathouse.

As Boggy and I shuttled the first boatload of people ashore, the rain still coming down hard, I saw Barbara waiting for us under the tin roof of the boathouse. She was holding Shula.

"How's my little girl?" I said, stepping onto the dock. I'd brought the black nylon bag with me from the *Ace of Diamonds*. I set it down so I could hold Shula.

"I think she missed her daddy," Barbara said.

"Amazing," I said.

"That she misses her daddy?"

"No, that she's changed so much in less than two days. A blink of the eyes and she's a whole new person."

"Much more to come," said Barbara. "Stay tuned."

"Wouldn't miss it," I said.

Barbara eyed the nylon bag.

"What's in that?"

"Goodies."

"Goodies I need to know about?"

"Later," I said.

A dozen or so people were standing at the other end of the boathouse. One of them, a small black man wearing a long green raincoat, split away and approached us. As he got closer, I saw the clerical collar peeking out from under his raincoat.

He introduced himself as Father Jean-Luis Lescoart, with Haiti Liberte Internacional.

"The vans are ready. Eight of them. They are in your driveway," he said. "This is an enormous risk that you take. HLI thanks you. I thank you."

"What will happen after you get them down to Miami?" I asked him.

"They will be taken care of. We are a large community in South Florida," he said. "The men and women will find work. The children will go to school. It might not be easy for them. Not at first anyway. But it will be much easier than what they left behind. They will assimilate. They will become Americans."

"Great country," I said.

"Yes," he said. "It can be."

As Father Lescoart stepped away and began leading people to the vans, Barbara told me she needed to put Shula to bed.

"Will you be long?" she asked.

"Another few hours," I told her.

"Be careful."

"I've got an extra reason to now."

"We'll be waiting for you," Barbara said.

My office is in the boathouse. I stepped into it, closing the door behind me. I pulled up a sisal rug to reveal the concrete floor and the small strongbox that is anchored in it. I opened the strongbox. I took three bundles of cash from the bag, stuck it in the strongbox, locked it, and put the rug back on top. One bundle of cash was left in the nylon bag.

I sat at my desk and watched Boggy shuttle people from the *Ace of Diamonds*. Mommie Leena was in the last boat to arrive. As she and Boggy headed into the boathouse, I opened the office door and waved them in to join me.

I closed the door behind them. I handed the nylon bag to Mommie Leena. She looked inside it, said something to Boggy.

"She wants to know what it contains," Boggy said.

"Tell her there's somewhere in the neighborhood of two hundred fifty thousand dollars in that bag. Enough for every man, woman, and child who just got off the boat to have about five thousand. Tell her I'm trusting her to see to it that it is divided equally among them. Tell her that Father Lescoart can help her start bank accounts for everyone if she chooses to split it up that way."

Boggy spoke to her. Most people, if you told them they had just been handed a quarter million dollars, they might whoop and holler, show a little excitement. Not Mommie Leena. She absorbed the news with little more than a nod, didn't even bother to look in the bag and check it out for herself.

She spoke to Boggy. He said, "Mommie Leena says she had a dream last night and this dream told her to expect such a gift."

I said, "Tell Mommie Leena that her Voudon powers are very strong. I'm impressed. It has been a pleasure for me to meet her."

Boggy told her this. Mommie Leena shrugged: It's nothing. Then she stepped closer to me. She looked me up and down. She said something.

Boggy said, "Mommie Leena says she has changed her mind about you. She is now convinced that you are not Azacka after all."

"Oh, yeah, why's that?"

"She says Azacka is a greedy spirit and that he would never be so stupid as to give away so much money."

"Tell her that if she wants to honor the spirit of Azacka then she can always give the money back."

Boggy spoke to her. Mommie Leena threw back her head and laughed. Then she said something else. This time, Boggy laughed.

"What did she say?"

"It is nothing," Boggy said. "Hard to translate."

"Try," I said.

"More or less, Zachary, Mommie Leena says you can blow it out your ass."

108

It was after midnight and the vans were long gone when I called the Customs and Border Patrol office in Daytona Beach. It's open around the clock. An officer answered and I gave her all the necessary stats. I told her I was a U.S. citizen who had just captained a vessel, the *Ace of Diamonds*, from George Town, Exuma, to my home in LaDonna.

"Do you have anything to declare?" she asked.

"No."

"Fruits or vegetables?"

"No."

"Currency in excess of ten thousand dollars?"

"No."

I listened to her tap the information into her computer.

I said, "Officer, sorry, but I forgot to mention one thing."

"What is that, sir?"

"I'm signed up with the Local Boater Option program."

"Oh, very good, sir. That makes it much easier. We can do all this over the phone. What's your LBO number?"

I gave it to her.

The Local Boater Option program exists for owners of noncommercial boats who travel frequently between Florida and the Bahamas. You register with the customs office and they give you a thorough checkout to make sure you are an upstanding citizen. If cleared, you are given a number and can typically avoid a customs and immigration inspection upon your return from foreign waters. All you have to do is notify the customs office immediately upon your arrival home. For the record and despite any evidence to the contrary, I am an upstanding citizen. In my own mind, anyway.

The officer said, "Did you have a nice time in the Bahamas, Mr. Chasteen?"

"Had a great time," I said. "Such a great time that I'm heading back over tonight."

"Tonight, sir?"

"Yep, soon as I get off the phone."

"Lucky you. You're good to go, sir," the officer said. "Have a safe trip."

109

Boggy stood beside me at the helm of the *Ace of Diamonds* as we entered Coronado Inlet and pointed toward the Atlantic. No sign of other boats, so we wouldn't be putting anyone else in danger.

The storm had intensified, just as I had hoped. No one in their right mind should be going out the inlet in this kind of weather.

"Appreciate you coming along," I told Boggy.

"Like I had a choice," he said. "No one would believe that you had set out for the Bahamas all by yourself in a boat this size."

"Nice boat," I said.

"I liked the hot tub," Boggy said.

"Helluva sound system, too."

The waves were bigger than any I'd ever seen in Coronado Inlet. We would ride up the face of one and take on water over the transom as we rode it down. Then the waves got even bigger. The wheel spun from side to side. I could no longer do much to steer the *Ace of Diamonds*. Not that I was trying all that hard.

The north jetty was within fifty yards of us now, the ocean crashing against its jagged rocks, the surge drawing us in. I'd never wrecked a boat on purpose before. I doubt few people have. And a boat like this, what was it worth? Three or four million? Maybe even more.

Pain, awful pain. That's what Ron Diamond would feel. And if he ever presented me with another opportunity, he'd feel it again.

I had a brief moment of regret as we drew nearer to the jetty. Not for Diamond, but for the boat. It was almost as if the *Ace of Diamonds* could sense her fate. She nosed out, away from the rocks, fighting it, fighting it . . .

The U.S. Coast Guard Station/Minorca Beach is less than a mile inside the inlet. We'd passed it on our way out.

A giant breaker rolled over the bow, bringing us broadside to the jetty. I heard the awful sound of rock chewing into the hull, the boat shuddering. I grabbed the radio.

"Mayday! Mayday!" I said.

110

We spent a long time at the Coast Guard station. Lots of questions, lots of paperwork. Lots of sitting around. I answered the questions, took care of paperwork. Boggy slept.

I knew the chief duty officer, Lieutenant Osborne. We'd gone fishing a time or two. That didn't stop him from giving me a thorough dressing down.

"What were you thinking, Zack? Do I need to run a breathalyzer on you?"

"No, I'm sober. Probably more sober than I've ever been."

"Then what the hell? You're an experienced captain, Zack. You know these waters like your own backyard," Osborne said. "Not like you to make a mistake like that."

I hung my head. I tried to look contrite. I'm not real good at it.

"You're right," I said. "Making a mistake like that, it's not like me at all."

Osborne stepped into his office and I sat around some more. It gave me plenty of opportunity to think over what I still had to do to bring this whole thing to an end.

I'd be calling Bill Cuthill as soon as I got home. He's my banker in Bermuda, a trustee and a signatory on my account. I'd ask him to contact Haiti Liberte Internacional and handle the particulars of the transfer— seven hundred fifty thousand dollars. From an anonymous donor. To use however they saw fit. I didn't think there would be any problems.

It would drain my account considerably. Yes, I could replenish it with the money in my strongbox. But doing it would be dicey. Smuggling cash is no business for amateurs.

I'd figure a way. I always had.

I knew one thing—I damn sure wouldn't be sticking it on a cruise ship.